D0893495

BEYOND *These* HILLS

Center Point
Large Print

Also by Sandra Robbins and available from
Center Point Large Print:

Angel of the Cove
Mountain Homecoming

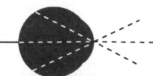

BEYOND
These
HILLS

SANDRA
ROBBINS

CENTER POINT LARGE PRINT
THORNDIKE, MAINE

This Center Point Large Print edition is published
in the year 2014 by arrangement with
Harvest House Publishers.

Copyright © 2013 by Sandra Robbins.

All Scripture quotations are taken from
the King James Version of the Bible.

The text of this Large Print edition is unabridged.
In other aspects, this book may vary
from the original edition.
Printed in the United States of America
on permanent paper.
Set in 16-point Times New Roman type.

ISBN: 978-1-61173-958-9

Library of Congress Cataloging-in-Publication Data

Robbins, Sandra (Sandra S.)
 Beyond these hills / Sandra Robbins. —
  Center Point Large Print edition.
 pages ; cm
 ISBN 978-1-61173-958-9 (library binding : alk. paper)
 1. Mountain life—Fiction.
  2. Great Smoky Mountains (N.C. and Tenn.)—Fiction.
  3. Tennessee—History—20th century—Fiction.
  4. Large type books. I. Title.
 PS3618.O315245B49 2013b
 813′.6—dc23
                                                    2013027860

Chapter 1

Cades Cove, Tennessee
June, 1935

The needle on the pickup truck's speedometer eased to thirty miles an hour. Laurel Jackson bit back a smile and glanced at her father. With his right hand on the steering wheel and his left elbow hanging out the open window, he reminded her of a little boy absorbed in the wonder of a new toy.

The wind ruffled his dark, silver-streaked hair, and a smile pulled at the corner of his mouth as the truck bounced along. His eyes held a faraway look that told her he was enjoying every minute of the drive along the new road that twisted through Cades Cove.

If truth be told, though, the truck with its dented fenders wasn't all that new. He'd bought it a few months ago from Warren Hubbard, who'd cleaned out a few ditches in Cades Cove trying to bring the little Ford to a stop. Rumor had it he kept yelling *Whoa!* instead of pressing the brake. The good-natured ribbing of his neighbors had finally convinced Mr. Hubbard that he had no business behind the wheel of a truck.

Laurel's father didn't have that problem. He took to driving like their old hound dog Buster took to trailing a raccoon. Neither gave up until they'd finished what they'd started. Mama often said she didn't know which one's stubborn ways vexed her more—Poppa's or Buster's. Of course her eyes always twinkled when she said it.

The truck was another matter entirely. Mama saw no earthly reason why they needed that contraption on their farm when they had a perfectly good wagon and buggy. To her, it was another reminder of how life in Cades Cove was changing. Laurel could imagine what her mother would say if she could see Poppa now as the speedometer inched up to thirty-five. *Land's sakes, Matthew. If you don't keep both hands on the wheel, you're gonna end up killing us all.*

But Mama wasn't with them today to tell Poppa they weren't in a race, and he was taking advantage of her absence to test the limits of the truck. At this rate they'd make it to Gatlinburg earlier than expected. When she was a little girl, the ride in their wagon over to the mountain village that had become a favorite of tourists had seemed to take forever. Now, it took them less than half the time to get there.

She glanced at her father again and arched an eyebrow. "You'd better be glad Mama stayed home."

Her father chuckled. "Do you think she'd say I was driving too fast?"

Laurel tilted her head to one side and tried to narrow her eyes into a thoughtful pose. "I'm sure she wouldn't hesitate to let you know exactly how she felt."

A big smile creased her father's face, and he nodded. "You're right about that. Your mother may run a successful business from a valley in the middle of the Smoky Mountains, but she'd just as soon pass up all the modern conveniences the money she makes could provide her. Sometimes I think she'd be happier if we were still living in that one-room cabin we had when we first married."

Laurel laughed and nodded. "I know. But I imagine she'll be just as happy today to have us out of the way. She can unload her latest pottery from the kiln and get the lodge cleaned and ready for the tourists we have coming Monday."

Her father's right hand loosened on the steering wheel, and his left one pulled the brim of his hat lower on his forehead. "It looks like business is going to be good this year. We already have reservations for most of the summer, and our guests sure do like to take home some of her pieces from Mountain Laurel Pottery."

Laurel frowned. There would be guests this summer, but what about next year and the year after that? A hot breeze blew through the open window, and she pulled a handkerchief from her pocket. She mopped at the perspiration on her forehead before she swiveled in her seat to face her father. "Having the lodge and the pottery business is kind of like a mixed blessing, isn't it?"

He frowned but didn't take his eyes off the road. "How do you mean?"

Laurel's gaze swept over the mountains that ringed the valley where she'd lived all her life. Her love for the mist-covered hills in the distance swelled up in her, and she swallowed the lump that formed in her throat. "Well, I was just thinking that we get paid well by the folks who stay at our lodge while they fish and hike the mountain trails, and Mama makes a lot of money selling them her pottery. But is the money worth what we've lost?" She clasped her hands in her lap. "I miss the quiet life we had in the Cove when I was a little girl."

Her father's forehead wrinkled. "So do I, darling, but you're all grown up now, and those days are long gone. Change has been happening for a long time, but our way of life officially ended twelve years ago with the plan for the Smokies to become a national park. Now most of the mountain land's been bought up by the government, and there's a park superintendent in place over at Gatlinburg. I guess we have to accept the fact that the park is a reality."

A tremor ran through Laurel's body. She clutched her fists tighter until her fingernails cut into her palms. "No matter what we're doing or talking about, it always comes back to one question, doesn't it?"

Her father glanced at her. "What's that?"

"How long can we keep the government from taking our land?"

"Well, they don't have it yet." The lines in her father's face deepened, and the muscle in his jaw twitched. "At the moment, all the land that borders our farm has been bought and is part of the Great Smoky Mountains National Park. There aren't many of us holding on in the Cove, but we're not giving up without a fight. I have a meeting with our lawyer in Gatlinburg today to see how our court case is going. You can get your mama's pottery delivered to Mr. Bryan's store, can't you?"

"I didn't know you had a meeting with the lawyer. Don't worry about the pottery. Willie and I can take care of that."

A smile cracked her father's moments-ago stony features at the mention of her younger brother, who was riding in the truck's bed. "You make sure that boy helps you. He has a habit of disappearing every time I have a job for him. I sure wish he'd grow up and start taking on some responsibility around the farm."

Laurel laughed. "Willie's only twelve, Poppa. When he's as old as Charlie or me, he'll settle down."

Her father shook his head. "I don't know about that. He's always gonna be your mother's baby."

Before she could respond, the truck hit a bump

in the road and a yell from behind pierced her ears. Laughing, she turned and looked through the back window. Willie's face stared back at her. "Do it again, Pa," he yelled. "That was fun."

Her father frowned, grabbed the steering wheel with both hands, and leaned over to call out the window. "Be still, Willie, before you fall out and land on your head."

Willie stood up, grabbed the side of the open window, and leaned around the truck door to peer into the cab. "Won't this thing go any faster?"

Her father's foot eased up, and he frowned. "We're going fast enough. Sit down, Willie."

The wind whipped Willie's dark hair in his eyes. He was grinning. "Jacob's pa has a truck that'll go fifty on a smooth stretch," he yelled. "See what ours will do."

The veins in her father's neck stood out, and the speedometer needle dropped to twenty. "If you don't sit down and stay put, I'm gonna stop and make you sit up here between your sister and me."

"I'm just saying you ought to open this thing up and see what she'll do."

The muscle in her father's jaw twitched again, and Laurel put her hand over her mouth to keep from laughing out loud. How many times had she seen her no-nonsense father and her fun-loving brother locked in a battle of wills? Her father took a deep breath and shook his head.

"Willie, for the last time . . ."

Willie leaned closer to the window, glanced at Laurel, and winked. "Okay. I'll sit, but I still think we could go a little faster. Jacob's gonna get to Gatlinburg way before we do."

The truck slowed to a crawl. "Willie . . ."

A big grin covered Willie's mouth. "Okay, okay. I'm just trying to help. I know Mr. Bryan is waitin' for these crates of Mama's pottery. I'd hate to get there after he'd closed the store."

"He's not going to close the store. Now for the last time, do as I say."

"Okay, okay. I'm sittin'."

Willie pushed away from the window and slid down into the bed of the truck. Her father straightened in the seat and shook his head. "I don't know what I'm going to do with that boy. He's gonna put me in my grave before I'm ready."

Laurel laughed, leaned over, and kissed her father's cheek. "How many times have I heard you say that? I think you love sparring with him. He reminds you of Mama."

For the first time today, a deep laugh rumbled in her father's throat. "That it does. That woman has kept me on my toes for twenty years now." He glanced over his shoulder through the back glass toward Willie, who now sat hunkered down in the bed of the truck. "But I doubt if I'll make it with that boy. He tests my patience every day."

Laurel smiled as she reached up and retied the

bow at the end of the long braid that hung over her shoulder and down the front of her dress. "I doubt that will happen. You have more patience than anybody I know. There aren't many in our valley who've been able to stand up to the government and keep them from taking their land. Just you and Grandpa Martin and a few more. Everybody else has given up and sold out."

There it was again. The ever-present shadow that hung over their lives. Cove residents were selling out and leaving. How long could they hang on?

"Seems like we're losing all our friends, doesn't it?" Her father shook his head and pointed straight ahead. "Like Pete and Laura Ferguson. We're almost to their farm. I think I'll stop for a minute. I promised Pete I'd keep an eye on the place after they moved, and I haven't gotten over here in a few weeks."

Ever since Laurel could remember there had been a bond between her father and the older Pete Ferguson. Each had always been there to lend a hand to the other, but now the Fergusons were gone. Their land sold to the United States government and their farm officially a part of the Great Smoky Mountains National Park.

She glanced at her father's face, and she almost gasped aloud at the sorrow she saw. The court case he and Grandpa Martin had waged over the past year had taken its toll on him. He was only a few months away from turning fifty years old, and Grandpa would soon be sixty-five. They didn't need the worry they'd lived under for the last twelve years. Why couldn't the government just give up and allow them to remain on their farms in the mountain valley that had been their family's home for generations? That was her prayer every night, but so far God hadn't seen fit to answer.

Her father steered the truck onto the dirt path that ran to the Ferguson cabin. The wildflowers Mrs. Ferguson had always loved waved in the breeze beside the road as they rounded the corner and pulled to a stop in the yard.

Laurel's eyes grew wide, and she stared, unbelieving, through the windshield to the spot where the Ferguson cabin had stood as long as she could remember. Her father groaned and climbed from the truck. For a moment he stood beside the vehicle's open door, his hand resting on the handle. He shook his head as if he couldn't believe what he saw. Then he closed the door and took a few steps forward.

Laurel reached for the leather bag that sat on the floorboard near her feet, unsnapped the top flap, and pulled out her Brownie box camera before jumping from the truck. She hurried to stand beside her father, who stood transfixed as he stared straight ahead. Willie, his face pale, climbed from the back of the truck and stopped next to their father. No one spoke for a moment.

Willie pulled his gaze away and stared up at their father. "Where's the house, Pa?"

Their father took a deep breath. "I guess the park service tore it down, son."

A sob caught in Laurel's throat as they stared at the barren spot of land that had once been the site of a cabin, barn, and all the outbuildings needed to keep a farm productive. "But why would they do that, Poppa?"

Her father took a deep breath. "Because this land is now a part of the park, and they want it to return to its wild state."

Willie inched closer to their father. "Are they gonna tear our house down too?"

Her father's eyes darkened. "Not if I can help it." He let his gaze wander over the place he had known so well before he took a deep breath and turned back to the truck. "Let's get out of here. I shouldn't have stopped today."

Laurel raised the camera and stared down into the viewfinder. "Let me get a picture of this before we go."

Her father gritted his teeth. "Take as many as you want. Somebody's got to record the death of a community."

None of them spoke as she snapped picture after picture of the empty spot that gave no hint a family had once been devoted to this piece of land. After she'd finished, the three of them returned to the truck and climbed in. When her father turned the truck and headed back to the road, Laurel glanced over her shoulder at the spot where the house had stood. She had always looked forward to visiting this home, but she didn't know if she would be able to return. Too many of her friends were gone, scattered to the winds in different directions. The holdouts who still remained in the Cove lived each day with the threat that they too would soon be forced from the only homes they'd ever known. If her family had to leave, they would be like all the rest. They would go wherever they could find a home, and the ties forged by generations in the close society of their remote mountain valley would vanish forever.

Andrew Brady set his empty glass on the soda fountain counter and crossed his arms on its slick white surface. The young man who'd served him faced him behind the counter and smiled. "Can I get you somethin' else, mister?"

Andrew shook his head. "No thanks. That cold drink helped to cool me down some. I didn't expect it to be so hot in Gatlinburg. I thought it would be cooler here in the mountains."

The young man grinned and reached up to scratch under the white hat he wore. "Most folks think that, but our days can be a bit warm in the summertime." He glanced at several customers at the other end of the counter and, apparently satisfied they didn't need any help at the moment, turned his attention back to Andrew. "Where you from?"

Andrew smiled. "Virginia. Up near Washington."

The young man smiled and extended his hand. "Welcome to Gatlinburg. My name is Wayne Johnson. My uncle owns this drugstore, and I work for him."

Andrew grasped his hand and shook it. "Andrew Brady."

"How long you been here, Andrew?"

"I arrived Thursday."

Wayne picked up a cloth and began to wipe the counter. He glanced up at Andrew. "You enjoying your vacation?"

Andrew shook his head. "I'm not in Gatlinburg on vacation. I'm here on business."

Wayne shrugged. "I figured you for a tourist. Guess I was wrong. They come from all over now that the park's opening up. I hear that we had about forty thousand people visit Gatlinburg last year. That's a far cry from what it was like when I was a boy. We were just a wide spot in a dirt road back in those days. But I expect it's only gonna get better."

Andrew glanced around the drugstore with its well-stocked shelves and the soda fountain against the side wall. "It looks like this business is doing okay." He shook his head and chuckled. "I don't know what I expected, but I wouldn't have thought there'd be so many shops here. Mountain crafts are for sale everywhere, and the whole town is lit up with electric lights. It looks like the park has put this town on the map."

Wayne propped his hands on the counter and smiled. "I guess folks in the outside world thought we were just a bunch of ignorant hillbillies up here, but we been doing fine all these years. We've even had electricity since back in the twenties when Mr. Elijah Reagan harnessed the power on the Roaring Fork for his furniture factory. He supplied to everybody else too, but now they say we're gonna have cheap electricity when TVA gets all their dams built."

Andrew nodded. "I guess it's a new day for the people in the mountains."

"It sure is, and we're enjoying every bit of it." He picked up Andrew's dirty glass and held it up. "You sure you don't want a refill?"

Andrew shook his head. "No, I'd better be going. I have some things to do before I head out to Cades Cove tomorrow."

Wayne cocked an eyebrow. "Only one reason I can think why you might be going out there. You must be joining up at the Civilian Conservation Corps."

Andrew pulled some coins from his pocket to pay for his soda and laid them on the counter. "No, I'm not with the CCC. Just intend to visit with them a while."

Wayne shrugged. "There're a lot of CCC camps all over the mountains, and those boys are doing a good job. You can see part of it when you drive into the Cove. They built the new road there. It sure makes gettin' in and out of there easier than it did in years past. I reckon Roosevelt did a good thing when he put that program in his New Deal."

"Yeah, it's giving a lot of young men a chance for employment." Andrew smiled, picked up the hat that rested on the stool beside him, and set it on his head. "Thanks for the soda."

Wayne studied Andrew for a moment. "You never did tell me exactly what your job is. What brought you to Gatlinburg from Washington?"

"I work with the Park Service. I'm here on a special assignment."

Wayne's eyes narrowed, and his gaze raked Andrew. "Special assignment, huh? Sounds important, and you look mighty young."

Andrew's face grew warm, and his pulse quickened. Even a soda jerk could figure out that a guy who looked like he'd barely been out of college for a year couldn't have gotten this job on his own. But with his father being a United States congressman and a supporter of President Roosevelt's New Deal, it hadn't been hard for his father to arrange this appointment.

The worst part for him, though, had been his father's command that Andrew had better not embarrass him on the job. He swallowed the nausea rising in his throat and tried to smile.

"I guess I'm just lucky they thought I was qualified."

"Well, congratulations. Come in for another soda the next time you're in town."

"That I will." Andrew turned and headed for the exit.

When he stepped outside the drugstore, he stopped and stared at the newly paved road that wound through the town. Before long that stretch of highway would wind and climb its way up the mountainsides all the way to Newfound Gap that divided the states of Tennessee and North Carolina. He'd heard that spot mentioned several times as the ideal location for the dedication of the park, but the event was still some years away. His assignment here would be one of the factors that determined when it would take place.

Andrew took a deep breath of fresh mountain air and turned in the direction where he'd parked his car. Several tourists brushed past him, but it was the approach of a young man and woman who caught his attention. Obviously honeymooners, if the glow of happiness on their faces was any indication. Ignoring everybody they passed, they stared into each other's eyes and smiled as if they had a secret no one else knew.

Andrew shook his head in sympathy as they walked past him and wondered how long it would take them to face up to the reality of what being married really meant. He'd seen how his friends had changed after marriage when they had to start worrying about taking care of a family. He'd decided a long time ago it wasn't for him. He had too many things he wanted to do in life, and getting married ranked way below the bottom of his list. Convincing his father of the decision, though, was another matter. The congressman had already picked out the woman for his son's wife. "The perfect choice," his father often said, "to be by your side as you rise in politics."

Andrew sighed and shook his head. Sometimes there was no reasoning with his father. He wished he could make him . . .

His gaze drifted across the street, and the frown on his face dissolved at the sight of a young woman standing at the back of a pickup truck. Her fisted hands rested on her hips, and she glared at the back of a young boy running down the street.

"Willie," she yelled. "Come back here. We're not through unloading yet."

The boy scampered away without looking over his shoulder. She shook her head and stamped her foot. Irritation radiated from her stiff body, and his skin warmed as if she'd touched him.

As if some unknown force had suddenly inhabited his body, he eased off the sidewalk and moved across the street until he stood next to her. "Excuse me, ma'am. Is there anything I can do to help?"

She whirled toward him, and the long braid of black hair hanging over her right shoulder thumped against her chest. Sultry dark eyes shaded by long lashes stared up at him, and a small gasp escaped her lips. "Oh, you startled me."

His chest constricted, and he inhaled to relieve the tightness. His gaze drifted to the long braid that reached nearly to her waist. He had a momentary desire to reach out and touch it. With a shake of his head, he curled his fingers into his palms and cleared his throat.

"I'm sorry. I heard you calling out to that boy, and I thought maybe I could help."

Only then did her shoulders relax, and she smiled. Relief surged through his body, and his legs trembled. What was happening to him? A few minutes ago he was mentally reaffirming his commitment to bachelorhood, and now his mind wondered why he'd ever had such a ridiculous thought. All he could do was stare at the beautiful creature facing him.

She glanced in the direction the boy had disappeared and sighed. "That was my brother. He was supposed to help me move these crates into the store, but he ran off to find his friend." She smiled again and held out her hand. "My name is Laurel."

His hand engulfed hers, and a wobbly smile pulled at his lips. "I'm Andrew. I'd be glad to take these inside for you, Laurel."

"Oh, no. If you could just get one end, I'll hold the other."

He studied the containers for a moment before he shook his head. "I think I can manage. If you'll just open the door, I'll have them inside in no time."

She hesitated as if trying to decide, then nodded. "Okay. But be careful. These crates are filled with pottery. My mother will have a fit if one piece gets broken."

He took a deep breath, leaned over the tailgate of the truck, and grabbed the largest crate with *Mountain Laurel Pottery* stamped on the top. Hoisting the container in his hands, he headed toward the store and the front door that she held open.

As they entered the building, a tall man with a pencil stuck behind his ear hurried from the back of the room. "Afternoon, Laurel. I wondered when you were going to get here."

She smiled, and Andrew's heart thumped harder. "We didn't leave home as early as we'd planned." Her smile changed to a scowl. "Willie was supposed to help me, but he ran off." And just as quickly, her expression changed again to a dazzling smile. "Andrew was good enough to help me get the crates in."

Mr. Bryan helped Andrew ease the crate to the floor and glanced up at him. "Any more in the truck?"

Andrew nodded. "One more, but it's smaller. I don't need any help getting it inside."

"Then I'll leave you two. I'm unboxing some supplies in the back." Mr. Bryan turned to Laurel. "If anybody comes in, holler at me, Laurel."

"I will."

A need to distance himself from this woman who had his heart turning somersaults swept over Andrew, and he hurried out the door. Within minutes he was back with the second container, but he almost dropped it at the sight of Laurel kneeling on the floor beside the first one. She opened the top, reached inside, and pulled out one of the most beautiful clay pots he'd ever laid eyes on. Swirls of orange and black streaked the smoky surface of the piece. She held it up to the light, and her eyes sparkled as she turned it slowly in her hands and inspected it.

He set the second crate down and swallowed. "Did you make it?"

She laughed and shook her head. The braid swayed again, and he stood transfixed. "No, my mother is the potter. I help her sometimes, but I didn't inherit her gift. This is one of her pit-fired pieces."

She set the pot down and pulled another one out. She smiled and rubbed her hand over the surface. Her touch on the pottery sent a warm rush through his veins.

"Exquisite." The word escaped his mouth before he realized it.

She cocked her head to one side and bit her lip. "Exquisite?" she murmured. She glanced up at him, and her long eyelashes fluttered. "I've searched for the right word for a long time to describe my mother's work. I think you've just given it to me. They are exquisite."

He swallowed and backed away. "Is there anything else I can do for you?"

She shook her head. "No, thank you. You've been a great help."

"I'm glad I could be of service." He searched his mind for something else to say, something to prolong his time with her, but his mind was blank. He took a deep breath. "I need to go. It was nice meeting you, Laurel."

She smiled. "You too, Andrew. Goodbye, and thanks again."

"Goodbye." He slowly backed toward the door.

Outside in the fresh air he took a deep breath and pulled his hat off. He raked his sleeve across his perspiring brow and shook his head. What had just happened? He'd felt like he was back in high school and trying to impress the most popular girl in his class.

He closed his eyes for a moment, and the image of her holding the pottery in her hands returned. He clamped his teeth down on his bottom lip and shook his head. She'd misunderstood. It wasn't the pottery he was describing when the word had slipped from his mouth.

Exquisite? The word didn't do her justice.

And she had a beautiful name too. Laurel. He straightened, and his eyes widened. He hadn't even asked her last name.

He whirled to go back inside the store but stopped before he had taken two steps. His father's face and the words he'd spoken when Andrew left home flashed in his mind. *Remember who you are and why you're there. Don't do anything foolish. People in Washington are watching.* He exhaled and rubbed his hand across his eyes.

For a moment inside the store he'd been distracted. He was the son of Congressman Richard Brady, and his father had big plans for his only living son.

He glanced once more at the pickup truck that still sat in front of the store and pictured how Laurel had looked standing there. When he'd grasped her hand, he'd had the strange feeling that he'd known her all his life. How could a mountain girl he'd just met have such a strange effect on him?

He pulled his hat on, whirled, and strode in the opposite direction. Halfway down the block he stopped, turned slowly, and wrinkled his brow as he stared back at the truck. The words painted on the containers flashed in his mind, and he smiled.

It shouldn't be too hard to find out her last name. For now he would just call her Mountain Laurel. His skin warmed at the thought. A perfect name for a beautiful mountain girl.

He jammed his hands in his pockets and whistled a jaunty tune as he sauntered down the street.

Chapter 2

Laurel set the last piece of pottery on the shelf and stepped back to survey the display. She propped her hands on her hips and tilted her head to the side as her gaze drifted over the pieces her mother had sent.

There had been a lot of spaces left in the section of the store that Mr. Bryan rented to Mountain Laurel Pottery. That only meant one thing. The tourists who came to Gatlinburg liked her mother's work and were willing to pay the price to take a piece of mountain-made pottery home with them.

The bell over the door jingled to signal someone had entered, and her father stepped into the store. He smiled when he spotted her, but the troubled look she'd seen in his eyes earlier at the Ferguson farm hadn't disappeared.

He stopped beside her, put his arm around her shoulders, and studied the pottery on the shelves. "Thanks for taking care of this."

She looped her arm around his waist and moved closer to him. "I enjoyed doing it. A lot of the pieces we brought two weeks ago have sold. Mama is going to be happy."

Her father nodded, then glanced around. "Where's Willie?"

Laurel tensed and moved out of her father's embrace. "Uh, off with Jacob, I think."

"Did he say when he'd be back?"

"No, but we can probably find them down by the Little Pigeon River when we get ready to leave."

"I guess so."

Laurel breathed a sigh of relief. At least he hadn't asked her how long Willie had been gone. The last thing she wanted was to get Willie in trouble, but she wouldn't lie if her father asked her about it. Luckily, he hadn't said anything yet. In fact, he seemed rather distracted. She glanced back at him and frowned.

"Poppa, how did it go at the lawyer's office?"

He took a deep breath and shook his head. "Nothing to concern yourself about, darling. I'll go settle up with Mr. Bryan so we can start home. I don't want to be too late. Your mother will want to have an early supper so she'll have plenty of time tonight to go over her Sunday school lesson for tomorrow morning."

"I know." Laurel sighed and reached down to put the top back on the open crate at her feet. "I hope she has somebody in her class tomorrow. The Whitsons moved out of the Cove this week, so that's two more children gone."

Her father nodded but didn't say anything as he headed to the back of the store where Mr. Bryan was helping a customer. Something had happened to cause her father to be so distracted. The lawyer must not have had good news to share.

Frowning, she carried the empty container outside and loaded it into the back of the truck. This had certainly been a day of confusing emotions. The sorrow she'd felt at the Ferguson farm and her anger at Willie for abandoning her outside the store had been forgotten in the thrill that had swept through her when she turned to see a handsome young man standing beside her.

She leaned against the truck's side for a moment and glanced up and down the street. There was no sign of him now. With all the tourists in town he was probably at one of the hotels. With his wife. Her body stiffened, and she pressed her hands to her suddenly hot cheeks.

Had he been wearing a wedding ring? Her eyes narrowed, and her forehead wrinkled into a frown. She didn't remember seeing one, but maybe she hadn't noticed. But some men saw no reason to wear a ring. Her father didn't wear his because he was afraid it would get hung on a piece of farm equipment and injure his finger. But Andrew was no farmer. She'd known that when his soft fingers curled around hers. They felt nothing like the work-roughened hands of a farmer. He must have a good job if he could afford to vacation in the Smokies.

She gritted her teeth and pounded her doubled fists against the side of her legs. What difference did it make what kind of job he had? She doubted she would ever see Andrew whatever-his-name-was again.

"Is something wrong?" Laurel jerked to attention at the sound of her father's voice. He stepped up beside her and shoved the other crate into the back of the truck.

"No, just waiting for you." She grabbed the tailgate and slammed it into place. Her father reached out and locked both ends. "It didn't take you long to settle up with Mr. Bryan," she said.

He nodded and smiled. "Your mama is gonna be happy with her sales." He glanced around and took a deep breath. "Still no sign of Willie, huh? Let's drive down and see if he and Jacob are at their usual place on the Little Pigeon."

Laurel walked to the truck's passenger side and opened the door. Her hand tightened on the handle, and she gazed down at the running board for a moment before she reached up and stroked the braid that hung down her chest. Her breath had caught in her throat when Andrew's gaze traveled the length of her plaited hair. But it was his dark-eyed stare that locked on her when he set the second container down that had made her heart almost explode in her chest.

No man had ever looked at her like that, and for a moment she feared her voice had deserted her. With few people left in the Cove, she'd had little experience talking with young men. Her shoulders sagged. What if he thought she was a silly mountain girl who didn't have a rational thought in her head?

She closed her eyes for a moment and shook her head. She wasn't silly, but these confusing thoughts were. Her reaction to meeting Andrew could be because with nearly all her friends gone from the Cove she'd been lonely for a while. It was something she'd have to talk to her mother about.

"What are you waiting for, Laurel?" Her father, his hands on the steering wheel, leaned across the seat and stared at her.

"N-nothing."

She heaved a sigh and stepped onto the running board. Time to go home. Back to the place she loved so much. But how long would her family be able to stay before the government forced them to sell their land? That's what she needed to be thinking about, not some chance meeting she'd had at Mr. Bryan's store.

In all truth, it had been a confusing day. One she wasn't likely to forget. Before she slipped into her seat, she shot one last quick gaze up and down the street. Andrew was nowhere in sight.

• • •

Andrew pulled his car to a stop in front of the Mountain View Hotel and stared at the building. It had originally been built to house lumbermen coming to the area. In recent years it had been enlarged to accommodate the growing tourist trade, but until the new headquarters was completed the Park Service's main office would be located here as well.

He'd been disappointed on his arrival to find that Superintendent Ross Eakin was out of the office for a few days, but he'd spent the time becoming familiar with the area. Hiking the trails in the area had introduced him to the wonders of nature in the Smokies, and it thrilled him that he was going to have a small part in its development.

He climbed from the car and ambled into the hotel lobby. Several men, more tourists no doubt, sat on plush sofas and chairs in the center of the room. They lowered their newspapers as he passed by and nodded. He returned the greeting and headed for the desk at the other side of the room.

A young man wearing a white shirt with a black tie looked up from the desk as Andrew approached. "May I help you?"

"I'm a guest here. Andrew Brady, room 10. Are there any messages for me?"

"I'll check, sir." He turned toward the pigeon-holed wall behind the desk, reached into the one numbered *10,* and pulled out an envelope. "This was left for you earlier, sir."

"Thanks." Andrew turned and sauntered to the side of the room. He stopped in front of one of the windows with a view of the surrounding mountains and ripped the envelope open.

Dear Mr. Brady,

I'm sorry I was out of town when you arrived in Gatlinburg. However, I returned today as planned and am pleased to accept your invitation to supper tonight. I will meet you in the dining room of the Mountain View Hotel at 6:00 p.m.

Sincerely,
J. Ross Eakin, Superintendent
Great Smoky Mountains National Park

Thank goodness. He'd finally returned. Andrew glanced at his watch. Four o'clock. He had some time before dinner to write his father a letter and then read over the information about the CCC camps he'd brought with him. He headed toward the hallway where his room was located but veered back toward the desk before he left the lobby.

The same young man glanced up as he approached. "Is there something else I can help you with, sir?"

Andrew cleared his throat before he spoke. "Do you know where I can find the studio of Mountain Laurel Pottery?"

The clerk's forehead wrinkled, and he rested his fist on the counter. His index finger tapped on its surface. "Mountain Laurel Pottery?" he said. After a moment he shook his head. "It's probably one of the local artists, but there're so many. I'm new in Gatlinburg and haven't learned all of them yet. I can ask the manager though."

Andrew shook his head. "That won't be necessary. It's not important. I'm leaving in the morning and won't have time to visit it anyway."

He turned and hurried toward the hallway that led to his room. Once inside he slammed the door behind him and raked his hand through his hair. Why in the world had he asked the clerk that? A chance meeting, that's all it was. He'd unloaded some boxes, chatted a few minutes, and then left. Nothing else had happened. Nothing.

He sat down on the edge of the bed, propped his elbows on his knees, and bent forward. He grasped both sides of his head and groaned. Who was he kidding? If it was really nothing, his heart wouldn't pound like it was hitting an anvil every time he thought of the girl with the long black braid.

He would give himself a week or so to attend to his mission in Cades Cove, and then he was going to find Mountain Laurel Pottery and the girl he couldn't get out of his mind. Surely someone in one of the shops in town could tell him where the studio was located. Maybe once he'd seen her again, he could put her out of his thoughts and move on with his work here.

Smiling, he lay back on the bed and stared up at the ceiling. It sounded like a good plan. Get acquainted with the Cove, find the studio, and convince himself how silly his instant infatuation had been.

Matthew glanced in the rearview mirror of the truck as he turned into the yard of the cabin he and Rani had lived in when they first married. He couldn't see Willie, who had settled down in the back of the truck when they'd left Gatlinburg. Perhaps he sensed something was troubling his father because he'd been quiet all the way home. Even Laurel seemed lost in thought, and he wondered what she was thinking.

He pulled the truck to a stop in front of the cabin that now housed Rani's studio. The minute the truck stopped Rani stepped onto the front porch, propped her hands on her hips, and smiled. His gaze raked over her, and his heart pumped just as it did every time he looked at his beautiful wife. They might have been married for twenty years, but to him she was still the young girl he'd first encountered at the mountain laurel bush when he'd returned to the Cove.

He heard Willie scramble from the back of the truck. "Hey, Mama," he yelled. "Where's Charlie?"

"At the barn. He said for you to come help him with the milking when you got back."

Willie waved to them and dashed off toward the barn in the distance. Matthew smiled at his wife and turned to Laurel. "I'll get the crates out of the back and take them inside for your mother. You can drive the truck on up to the house."

Her eyes grew wide, and she cast a quick glance at her mother. "You're going to let me drive the truck in front of Mama?"

He reached over, chucked her under the chin, and winked. "It's about time she learned I've been teaching you to drive. But try not to hit a tree on the way to the house."

Laurel's face turned crimson, and she swatted at his hand. "Oh, Poppa, quit teasing. You make it sound like the house is miles away instead of a few hundred feet. I think I can handle this."

"I know you can, darling."

Matthew planted a swift kiss on his daughter's cheek and climbed from the truck. Within minutes he'd pulled the crates from the back and stepped back as she slid into the driver's seat and headed toward their house.

He turned toward Rani, whose surprised gaze followed the retreating truck. She faced him as he walked up the porch steps, stopped beside her, and set the containers down. "Is there something you haven't told me?"

He laughed and nodded. "I've been teaching Laurel to drive, and she's really good. When are you going to learn?"

She moved closer to him and wrapped her arms around his waist. Her dark eyes stared up at him. "Why would I want to drive when I have you to do that for me?"

His arms circled her waist, and he pulled her closer. "That's what I'm here for, to take care of your every need."

She smiled and tilted her head to one side. "And you always have." Her arms tightened around him. "Have I told you today how much I love you?"

He closed his eyes and breathed in the scent of her. She smelled of wet clay and paint, and it stirred his senses. "I think so, but I never get tired of hearing you say it." His lips brushed hers, and he sighed. "Some nights I still dream that I'm back in the railroad camps and I'm beating some poor soul senseless. I wake up drenched in sweat with my heart pounding, and then I hear you breathing. I reach out and touch your cheek just to make sure you're beside me, and only then can I relax. I still don't know what I ever did to deserve you, Rani."

She reached up and traced her finger down the side of his face. "I knew how special you were the first day at the mountain laurel bush."

"And I'd never seen a more beautiful woman in my life. I couldn't believe it when you finally married me."

She pulled out of his arms and reached down to pick up one of the crates. "Our life has been good here, Matthew. But for how much longer? Did you see the lawyer?"

He picked up the other container and headed inside the cabin. Rani followed behind. When they were inside, he set the crate down and faced her. "I saw him, but it wasn't good news."

Rani clenched her fists and took a step toward him. "What do you mean? We've already won our lawsuit."

"The suit that Simon and I brought saying the government had no right to our land was only upheld in our local court."

Rani nodded. "I know that."

"The state appealed it to the Tennessee Supreme Court, and they've overthrown the decision."

She sucked in her breath and frowned. "So what do we do now?"

Matthew blinked and glanced at her. "Now?"

Rani narrowed her eyes. "Surely we're not going to roll over and play dead just because the government wants to take our land. This is *our* land. You were born here, and so were our children. I was born in the cabin where my parents live. We can't just throw up our hands and give up." She clenched her fists at her side and took a step closer. "There must be something else we can do."

"There's one more thing. The problem is I don't think it's going to do anything but buy us a little more time here." He rubbed his hand across his eyes and exhaled. "Mr. Smith wants us to file a countersuit saying that our land is worth more than what the government has offered. It'll be tied up in court for a while. If they win that, we'll file another suit."

Rani nodded. "I think that's a good idea. Did you tell him to go ahead?"

"I did. But all the way home I've wondered if I did the right thing."

"Why would you think you'd made a mistake?"

His shoulders drooped, and he raked his hand through his hair. "We can keep them tied up in court for years, but in the end it's not going to do any good. They're going to win, and we will have to sell our land. The park is a reality, and the government's not going to let a few farms remain in the middle of it."

Rani's face turned crimson. "What are they going to do? Pick us up and move us out by force?"

Matthew tilted his head to one side and flashed one of the exasperated looks that he reserved for his wife. "Rani, I don't think it's going to come to that. But we have to be realistic. Your father is sixty-five years old, and he's not in good health. I'm afraid the stress of prolonging a lawsuit will take its toll on him. Do you want that?"

Her dark eyes filled with tears, and she studied him for a moment before she responded. "I can't stand the thought of our court case harming him—or you either. If something happened to you because of this . . . I . . . I don't know what I'd do."

He gathered her into his arms again. "Don't worry. I won't let it come to that. We'll have to pray that God will show us what to do." Matthew rubbed his hands down his wife's back and sighed. "He knows what's in the future, but it sure is hard waiting for it to happen. We'll just have to hold on to our faith."

She was quiet for a moment, then she pulled back to stare into his eyes. "Ten years ago the park supporters assured us that the people in Cades Cove would be allowed to keep their farms and we could live within the park. Were we foolish to believe them?"

Matthew sighed. "It looks like we were."

Her arms wrapped around his neck, and she smiled. "Do you remember how we thanked God on our wedding day for the blessings He was already sending our way?"

He smiled. "I do."

"Then I guess we'll just have to continue to do that. No matter what happens, He's going to take care of us."

He pulled her close again, and his lips brushed hers. "You always help me see what's important in life. Thank you for that."

She laughed and kissed his cheek. "I thought you did that for me. Now why don't we go round up our children and get ready for supper?"

He smiled and released her. "That's the best idea I've heard all day long."

Hand in hand they exited the small cabin and headed toward the house in the distance. As they passed the mountain laurel bush his father had planted, Matthew pulled Rani to a stop and gazed into the distance. The setting sun's rays cast a warm glow over the house he'd built for his family. To its left some distance away stood the lodge he and Simon had constructed.

He circled her shoulder with his arm. "Do you remember the first day we stood here? I told you I had a dream to build a lodge for tourists who wanted to come to Cades Cove to hike and fish and just enjoy the beauty of the mountains."

She snuggled closer. "I do. That was the day you kissed me for the first time."

He smiled at the memory. "I know. All I ever wanted was to come back to the Cove and live among people I knew. Then I met you, and I wanted you more than anything else I'd ever dreamed of." He glanced down at her. "God gave us what we wanted, but it may be time for us to pass on this beautiful place to other generations."

"I think that sometimes too, but then I push the thought out of my head," she whispered.

Matthew sighed and hugged her closer. "I guess time will tell."

They gazed out for a few more moments before they trudged toward the house they'd shared for years. Matthew tried to shake the thought from his head, but something told him that the way of life he'd known for decades was slipping through his fingers. Trying to be brave for Rani and his children was beginning to wear on him. If the government did take their land, he didn't know whether or not he could survive somewhere else. And would he be a failure to his family if he let their home slip through his fingers—just as Pete and Laura had?

That question kept him awake many nights, and he doubted if tonight would be any different. In the meantime, he wanted to enjoy every moment with his family here in the place that had sheltered them for years.

Andrew chewed the last bite of his roast beef and studied the man sitting across the table from him: J. Ross Eakin, the man who'd been chosen to be the first superintendent of Great Smoky Mountains National Park. With his short, stocky build, round face, and bushy eyebrows, Superintendent Eakin looked like he would be more comfortable hiking through the mountains instead of having the responsibility of shaping a wilderness for others to enjoy. But in the hour since Andrew had first sat down with him in the Mountain View Hotel's dining room, he had discovered that a sharp mind resided behind the man's quiet façade.

Superintendent Eakin glanced up at him. "I'm sorry I wasn't here to welcome you when you arrived. I've been at several of the work sites in the park for the last few days and couldn't get back until this afternoon."

"I understand, sir. I took advantage of the time to hike some of the trails around here and introduce myself to the area."

"Good. I've been a lot of places, but I must say I've never seen anything to equal the beauty of the Smokies."

Andrew nodded. "I agree. But I wanted to ask you about something. What's the story of the buildings on the property next to the hotel? The first time I went down the footpath that runs from the hotel to it, I was amazed to find a school and a clinic and all kinds of other buildings."

Superintendent Eakin smiled. "That's a settlement school. It was founded as a literacy project in 1912 by Pi Beta Phi Fraternity for Women. The organization started Gatlinburg's first school there, but they also wanted to make an economic impact on the mountain people. For years they've been helping the people get their crafts to markets outside the mountains, and they started Gatlinburg's first hospital too. Their nurses have done a great service to the people in this area. Now doctors and dentists come from Knoxville regularly to help them out. That group has been a real blessing to these mountains."

Andrew shook his head in amazement. "I knew from all the activity I saw over there it had to be something important. And you say there's a hospital there too?"

Superintendent Eakin laughed. "Well, I'm sure the Jennie Nichol Health Center isn't as well-equipped as the hospitals in Washington, but it serves its purpose here in the mountains."

Andrew dropped his gaze to his plate and laid his fork down. "There's so much history in this area, and I can't wait to learn more about life here. But I know you'd rather be home tonight after returning from your trip than having dinner with me and orienting me to my new surroundings. I do appreciate your meeting with me before I head out to Cades Cove."

Superintendent Eakin wiped his mouth on his napkin and cocked his head to one side. "No problem. I thought it important that we get together. Everything's arranged for your assignment here. You're to stay at the CCC camp in the Cove. Lieutenant Gray, the superintendent there, will help you with any needs you have."

Andrew smiled and nodded. "Thank you. I'm

sure I'll make it fine. From what I've heard around town, the men at the camp are doing a great job."

"They are." Superintendent Eakin pushed his plate away and leaned back in his chair. "They've been working on constructing hiking trails, especially the one up to Gregory's Bald, and they've also cleared and built some fire control roads. Fires are one of the things that we have to be very watchful for. Even though the land has been bought from the lumber companies, they're still logging in certain areas. That, along with the increased tourist traffic, makes fires more likely to occur."

"We're fortunate to have the CCC workforce to help with the park construction."

The superintendent nodded. "That's right. But I didn't meet with you to talk about park construction. I'm more concerned right now with the assignment you've been given. Do you think you can handle it?"

Even though the room was warm, a slight chill rippled down Andrew's spine at the unexpected question. His eyes grew wide, and his throat constricted. "That sounds like you may have some doubts about my abilities. Is that right?"

Mr. Eakin studied Andrew's face for a moment as his fingers tapped on the white tablecloth. "Let me be honest with you, Andrew. Right now the government has bought up nearly all the land

44

needed for the park with the exception of the holdouts in Cades Cove. When we requested a new negotiator to come here and convince the Cove residents to sell their land, I never dreamed it would be somebody just out of college. You're young, and rumor is you got this job because your congressman father pushed for you to have it."

"But, sir . . ."

Superintendent Eakin held up his hand to stop him. "I want you to understand that this project is important to me. We've accepted the challenge of taking on an 816-square-mile wilderness in Tennessee and North Carolina to preserve it for generations to come. I can't afford to let anything endanger what has taken us years to get approved. Now I'll ask you again. Can you handle this job?"

Andrew's face burned with embarrassment, and he balled his hands into fists to keep Mr. Eakin from seeing how they shook. After a moment he cleared his throat. "I understand how you could be concerned about me. You're right. I'm young. I graduated from Virginia Military Institute a year ago and went to work with the National Park Service. And you're also right in thinking my father pushed for me to get this assignment. He did." Andrew swallowed before he continued. "He thinks if I can convince the Cove people to sell when others couldn't, it will give me the experience I need to convince voters to elect me when I run for public office. That's what he wants."

"I see." Mr. Eakin sighed and glanced down at the tabletop. His fingers curled into his palms. Disappointment flashed across his face.

Andrew leaned closer. "But that's not what I want. You're wrong if you judge me on my age and my father's influence. From the minute I heard about this assignment, I wanted it with all my heart. I've come to the Smokies prepared to do whatever I have to do to be successful. I know I'll make mistakes from time to time. If I do, I won't make excuses or hide behind my father's influence. But the fact is, I didn't come here to fail."

A slight smile pulled at Mr. Eakin's mouth. "And how can you be certain you won't?"

Andrew took a deep breath. "I may have grown up in an affluent home, but please don't judge me on that alone. I graduated from VMI. If you know anything about the school, then you know life there is tough. The deprivations students endure are designed to instill pride, discipline, and confidence. I've come here with the belief that I can succeed where others haven't, and I don't intend to fail. My father's actions tend to focus on pleasing voters. That's not my reason for coming here."

"Why did you want this job, Andrew?"

He took a deep breath and stared at Mr. Eakin. "My parents brought me to the Smokies on vacation when I was a boy. My brother and I loved the mountain streams and the scenery. But one day while we were here, my father took us out to one of the Little River Lumber camps. I have never forgotten how barren those hillsides looked stripped of their timber. When I heard about the park, I knew I wanted to be part of preserving this beautiful wilderness. If we don't it's going to vanish, and future generations won't get the chance to see what I did."

Superintendent Eakin stared at him without speaking for what seemed like an eternity before he extended his hand. "You haven't completely convinced me yet, but I hope you'll be successful."

His words disappointed Andrew. But who could blame him? The only thing the people working for the Park Service knew about him was that he was the son of a congressman who'd pushed for his son to have this assignment.

Andrew squared his shoulders and grasped Superintendent Eakin's hand. "I'll work hard, sir. Before I leave here, I hope you'll be able to call me a member of the team with more conviction in your voice."

A look of surprise flashed on the man's face, but before he could reply a waiter appeared with a pot of coffee. They remained silent as he poured the steaming liquid in their cups. When he walked away, Mr. Eakin picked up a small pitcher and poured some cream in his cup. As he stirred, he glanced up. "I hope so too, Andrew." He stared into his coffee cup a moment before he continued. "Have you thought about how you'll approach the people still living in the Cove?"

"I want to get to know them first. I know this is difficult for them. They don't want to give up their homes. Some of those families have lived on the same land for generations."

Mr. Eakin sighed. "And they're good people. Two of the leaders in the community are some of the finest men you'll ever meet. Simon Martin's family goes back for generations. He's still preaching at the church where he started in 1891. His wife is a legendary midwife in the Cove, and his son-in-law, Matthew Jackson, owns a lodge that attracts tourists from all over the country. Salt of the earth, as my mother used to say, but they can't win against the United States government. They know that, but they can't bring themselves to give up."

"How do you suggest I approach them, sir?"

"Go to see them. Get to know them, and try to help them understand it's only a matter of time before the courts are going to force them to move. They're law-abiding folks, so they'll be civil to you even if they disagree with you. My friendship with them has taught me a lot about how to treat other people. But the end for them is coming, and they're going to need friends on the other side of this situation when it does. Help them to accept the inevitable, Andrew." His eyes lit up with a sudden thought. "Since you're going to the Cove tomorrow, why don't you head out there early and stop at Simon's church for their service?"

Go to church? That wasn't how he usually spent his Sunday mornings, but it would give him the opportunity to meet the Martins and the Jacksons. "Thanks for the suggestion. I'll do everything I can to help ease the remaining families through the transition."

Superintendent Eakin smiled. "Good. That's all any of us can do."

They finished their dessert and coffee in silence, and thirty minutes later Andrew was back in his room and ready to crawl in bed. He lay down, put his hands behind his head, and stared up at the ceiling.

It had been an interesting but troubling day. His father's influence might have opened doors to get him this job, but now he was on his own. He had to find a way to convince the remaining holdouts they were fighting a losing battle. In Washington he'd convinced himself he'd finish this job in no time, but now that he was here, he wasn't so sure.

From what he was learning the people in the Cove saw the government as an enemy who wanted to destroy their way of life, and he was the messenger who had to convince them their way of life was over. Doubt flooded his mind. Maybe Superintendent Eakin was right. Maybe he was too young to take on such an important job. He shook the thought from his head and tried to concentrate on the people of the Cove.

Martin and Jackson. The names repeated over and over in his mind. They must have a deep love for their land if they were willing to fight in the courts to stay on it. He couldn't blame them.

Tomorrow he'd go to their church and introduce himself to them. He was sure after they got to know him they would come to see their fight was futile. After all, he'd been one of the star debaters at VMI, and a few mountain farmers shouldn't be difficult opponents for him. With any luck he'd have all the Cove land bought up and be on his way back to Washington by the end of the summer. That was the last thought that ran through his head just before he nodded off to sleep.

Chapter 3

When Laurel was a little girl, Sunday mornings had been her favorite time of the week. Now they served as a reminder that nearly all of her friends were gone from the Cove. No longer could she look forward to talking to Celia Butler or Mary Ann Long at church. Their families had moved months ago. With the congregation decreasing every week, she wondered how many people would even be at Sunday services this morning.

Her father and mother had been quiet ever since they left home. Laurel wondered if they were still thinking about his visit to the lawyer yesterday. Even Willie had behaved himself today. Maybe that was because their seventeen-year-old brother, Charlie, was keeping him company in the back of the truck.

"I hope Mama doesn't go to a lot of trouble cooking dinner for us today. She hasn't been feeling well lately. I tried to get them to come to our house instead, but she wouldn't hear of it," Rani was saying.

Laurel's mother's voice pulled her from her thoughts. Her grandmother was sick? She tried to twist in her seat to face her mother, but with the two of them wedged into the front seat of the truck with her father she only succeeded in bumping shoulders.

"What's the matter with Nana?" she asked.

Her mother's eyebrows arched. "She says it's nothing, but I think she's wearing herself out taking care of Granny. Granny needs help getting out of bed by herself, and she needs somebody to hold onto when she walks. Mama lifts and pulls on her all the time. I've tried to tell her she needs to take care of herself, but she is determined Granny isn't going to want for anything."

"Can you blame her?" Laurel's father said. "Granny is a second mother to Anna and Simon both."

51

Her mother sighed. "I know. I guess it's hard for me to believe my parents are in their sixties and Granny is going to turn ninety-one next week." Her mother laughed. "But maybe I'm just thinking about how old I'm getting."

Her father grinned, leaned over, and gave her a peck on the cheek. "Well, you're the best looking forty-year-old I've ever seen." He winked in Laurel's direction. "You know she was just a child when I married her."

A flush covered her mother's face as she swatted at her father's arm. "I was not. Now behave yourself. What will your daughter think?"

He shrugged. "I can't see that I'm any different than I have been all her life." He darted another glance at Laurel. "I just hope when she gets married, Laurel finds a man who loves her like I love her mother."

Laurel smiled and nodded. "I do too. But I don't think I'll have to worry about getting married. There aren't any boys my age left in the Cove. And I sure don't want to marry Nate Hopkins."

Her parents both laughed at the mention of the eighty-year-old widower who lived on the far side of the Cove from them. He'd made no secret of the fact that the government would have to pick him up and carry him out of the Cove if they wanted his land, and he let everybody know he kept his shotgun close by just in case they tried.

Her mother shook her head. "No, I don't think

that's a good match. But there is somebody I haven't heard you mention lately. You know Josie is coming for a visit next week. She hasn't seen Jimmy since he signed up with the CCC camp. I'm sure he'll be at our house a lot too while she's here."

Laurel's eyes widened and she wagged a finger at her mother. "Josie may have been your best friend all your life, but you two need to quit trying to get Jimmy and me together. I love him like a brother, and he thinks of me as a sister too."

Her mother arched an eyebrow. "I don't know about that. Josie says his letters are just full of talk about how he's enjoyed seeing you since he's been at the CCC camp in the Cove."

"I've enjoyed having Jimmy visit with us when he could get away from the camp, but she's wrong if she thinks there's anything between us. I hope the two of you won't try to promote anything while she's here. Concentrate on having a good time with your best friend."

"Oh, I expect we'll have a great time," her mother said. "I haven't seen Josie in a year. Since she started managing that hotel in Tremont, she's been so busy she can't get away. She probably couldn't have come next week if it weren't for her parents living with them now. Mr. and Mrs. Davis are going to take over for a few days so she can visit us. They think she needs the rest."

Laurel's father exhaled. "I sure did hate to see

Cecil and Pearl sell out and move away, but I know they're a big help to Josie. From what you tell me Ted's job with the Little River Lumber Company keeps him busy."

"Yeah, he's worked his way up into a good position with them." Her mother chuckled. "I remember how angry I was with him when he left the Cove to work for them. I thought he was being disloyal to his friends by working for a company that was clear-cutting their way across the Smokies."

Her father sighed. "We don't have to worry about that anymore. One good thing about the park being established is that they've bought up the lumber companies' land, and there won't be any logging in these hills ever again. They're about to close down and leave, but our time here is short too."

Laurel leaned forward and glanced past her mother to her father. "I wish every conversation we have didn't come back to the same thing—that we have to move away. I don't want to leave this valley. This is all I've ever known."

Her father's mouth quirked in a sad smile. "We all feel the same way, darling. Your mother can continue her pottery business anywhere, but I have no idea what I can do outside these hills. There's no way I can re-create the farm I have in the Cove, and with the country suffering with the depression, there aren't any jobs to be had. But I worry about Simon more. I'm afraid leaving his home will be too much for him to bear."

Laurel clasped her hands in her lap and stared out the truck window. The mountains looked so beautiful today. The thick mists drifted over the peaks, and the sun sparkled on the green slopes. There couldn't be a more beautiful place in the world.

"Mama," she whispered, "the clouds on the mountains remind me of our special Bible verse. You know, the one from Psalms that Grandpa taught you when you were a little girl."

Her mother reached over and covered Laurel's clutched fist with her hand. " 'He looketh on the earth, and it trembleth: he toucheth the hills, and they smoke,' " she said. "He put us here to see the beauty of His creation, Laurel. No matter where we go, we'll always carry this beauty in our hearts."

"I know." Laurel squeezed her mother's hand.

No one spoke again until they pulled into the yard of the church. Grandpa's buggy and two trucks sat parked at the side of the building. It looked like the crowd would be smaller today than she'd thought.

"I don't see the truck that the CCC camp boys ride in when they come to church. I guess Jimmy won't be here today," Laurel said.

Her mother nodded. "I was hoping he could go to Mama's for dinner with us. She always enjoys his company so much."

Her father pulled the truck to a stop, and Laurel stepped out. Willie jumped from the back and took off running toward the church, but Charlie waited beside her as their parents joined them. Her mother reached up and tried to smooth Charlie's cowlick into place, but it popped back up.

He frowned and recoiled from her. "Mama, don't do that. I'm not a baby anymore."

She smiled and straightened the collar of his shirt. "It pleases me to take care of you, son."

Charlie scowled at her, and glanced over his shoulder. "Mama, not so loud. What if somebody hears you?"

Their father cocked an eyebrow at Charlie. "Don't sass your mother, young man." He took a deep breath and let his gaze drift over all of them. "Now, everyone, let's go inside."

As they walked toward the front door, Charlie trailed behind Laurel and their parents. She glanced back once at her brother. Something akin to anger shadowed his dark eyes, and the surly expression on his face told her he was in one of his defiant moods. She didn't understand his frequent shifts in attitude, and she knew it worried her parents.

She turned her attention back to her mother just as she glanced up at her father, flashed him a smile, and slipped her hand through the crook of his arm. The look that passed between them made her forget her concern for Charlie. She'd seen that same look in her grandparents' eyes, and it made her wish for something she doubted she would ever have.

Someday she wanted a man to look at her with love lighting his face. She wanted to love and be loved so fiercely that she could hardly breathe unless he was with her. Was it too much to hope for? Somewhere there had to be a man God had chosen especially for her.

But how would he find her? There were no prospects at the present time, and she had no intention of marrying Jimmy Ferguson just because their mothers wanted it. If God did have someone for her, she sure wished He'd hurry up and let her know about it.

Andrew pulled his car to a stop between two trucks that sat in the yard of the church. A sign in front of the building identified Simon Martin as the pastor, so he had to be in the right place. From the looks of the few wagons and buggies also in the yard he knew there couldn't be many people in attendance today.

He sat still for a moment as he tried to decide what to do. His father had no time for church, and Andrew hadn't felt comfortable when he'd attended chapel services at school. But he wasn't here to find God. He was here on another mission—to get to know the families he had to persuade to sell their land. The sooner that was done, the sooner the Park Service could finish up their work.

He stepped from his car and walked around the church to the front steps. He listened, hoping for some sound from inside. If he heard singing, he could tell himself services had already started. That would be a good excuse to put off meeting the Martins and Jacksons. No sound reached his ears.

Andrew put his foot on the first step but hesitated. A chill rippled up his spine, and his skin prickled. For the first time fear at what lay before him surged through his body. Others had tried to reason with these mountain people and had failed. What made him think he was any different?

He took a step backward and whirled to leave but his legs threatened to collapse at the sight of the young woman facing him. His chest tightened, and he gasped. The sun sparkled on the black hair that hung down her chest in the long braid he'd thought about ever since yesterday. Her dark eyes were wide with surprise, and her mouth gaped open as if she couldn't believe what she saw.

"Andrew?"

"Laurel." His tongue felt paralyzed. No other words came to mind.

She frowned and tilted her head to one side. "What are you doing here?"

He pulled his hat off and held it in front of him with both hands. "I . . . I c-came to church."

She shook her head. "No, I mean what brings you to *our* church. Are you visiting someone in the Cove?"

He searched his mind for a reply, but his heart was thumping so hard he couldn't think straight. "I'm on my way to the CCC camp."

His skin warmed at the smile she directed at him. "Oh, I see. Some of the men from the camp come to services every once in a while. They're not here today, but we're glad to have you. I had come outside after Sunday school to get a drink of water at the well and was on my way back inside. I'll be glad to show you in and introduce you to my family."

His fingers curled around the brim of his hat. "Thank you, Laurel. I'd like that."

She moved past him, and his pulse pounded at the scent of lavender. Without speaking he followed her up the steps and into the church. He hung his hat on a rack just inside the door and followed her into the small sanctuary. One glance at the congregation told him he'd been right about attendance today. There couldn't be more than twenty people sitting in the pews. Two men stood in deep conversation about halfway down the aisle, and Laurel led him toward them.

The white-haired older man smiled as they approached. The younger of the two glanced from

Laurel to Andrew, a wary expression on his face. They stopped in front of them, and Laurel smiled. "We have a visitor today. This is Andrew . . ." Suddenly she turned to him, an embarrassed grin on her lips. "I'm sorry. I don't know your last name."

He swallowed before he spoke. "It's Brady."

She turned back to the men. "Andrew Brady. He's on his way to the CCC camp." She pointed first to the white-headed man. "This is my grandfather, Simon Martin. He's the preacher here." Then she motioned toward the other man, "And this is my father, Matthew Jackson."

Her father? Her grandfather? Andrew opened his mouth, but all he could do was gasp. He took a deep breath. "Then your name is Laurel Jackson?"

Her forehead wrinkled, and she nodded. "That's right." Her frown dissolved into a smile, and she laughed. "Oh, of course. I never told you my last name either." She glanced back at her father. "I met Andrew yesterday at Mr. Bryan's store, but we only exchanged first names."

Her grandfather smiled and reached out to shake hands. "Welcome to our church, Andrew. We're always glad to have men from the CCC camp worship with us."

Andrew's face grew warm as he shook the pastor's hand. "Thank you, sir."

Laurel's father stretched out his hand. "I'm

Matthew Jackson. Laurel didn't tell me she met anybody yesterday."

Andrew swallowed before he spoke. "I helped her get some crates out of the back of a truck and inside a store." He turned back to Laurel. "Afterward I wondered what your name was, but I remembered the name stamped on the crates. Mountain Laurel Pottery."

Mr. Jackson nodded. "That's my wife's pottery. She sells some of it at Mr. Bryan's store."

"I must say it's some of the most beautiful work I've ever seen. I promised myself I'd look up the studio before I left the mountains. I had no idea I'd find out about it today."

Laurel laughed and pointed to a woman who was entering the sanctuary from a room at the front of the church. "That's my mother coming in now. She's the potter. You'll have to tell her. I believe you described her work as exquisite."

Andrew's face flushed and he looked down at his feet. "Did I?"

From the front of the church an organ began to play a quiet tune, and Reverend Martin smiled. "That's my wife at the organ. She's giving me a signal that it's time for services. Why don't you take a seat, Andrew? I'd better get things underway."

"Thank you, sir. I will."

He stepped toward the pew on his left, but Laurel shook her head. "Don't sit back here by yourself. Come up front and sit with my family and me."

Her father and mother stood beside a pew at the front of the church, and her father motioned for Laurel to come. Two young boys had already slid into the pew and were staring over their shoulders at him. He shook his head. "I don't want to intrude."

She laughed, and the sound stirred his blood like nothing ever had before. "You aren't intruding. We'd love to have you sit with us."

He hesitated only a moment. "All right."

"Then follow me."

Andrew didn't look to the right or left at the congregation as he walked behind Laurel to the pew. She scooted in next to one of the boys, and he followed right behind. A few seconds later he found himself seated with Laurel on his left side and her mother on his right. He turned toward her mother. "Mrs. Jackson, my name is Andrew Brady. Laurel insisted I sit with your family."

"We're glad to have you visiting with us today. My husband tells me you're on your way to join the CCC camp."

Andrew's heart dropped to the pit of his stomach. Had he misled Laurel's family when he'd been introduced? He certainly hadn't meant to, but as he thought back over their conversation, he saw how they had gotten the wrong idea.

"Actually I'm on my way out there . . ."

"Everyone take out your hymnals and turn to number fourteen." Reverend Martin's loud voice drowned out the rest of his explanation to Mrs. Jackson. He'd have to set them all straight after services.

Laurel opened a hymnal and held it out for him to share. He took hold of one side of the book and looked down at the words. He'd never heard this song about standing on the stormy banks of what he supposed was a river. The few worshippers sang the song with so much enthusiasm that by the third verse he was singing right along with them.

When they'd finished singing, Laurel's arm brushed against his. His body gave an involuntary jerk, and he darted a glance at Mrs. Jackson to see if she had noticed. She didn't look his way, and he breathed a sigh of relief.

He started to ease down on the pew, but someone in the congregation called out another number. Before Laurel could find the page, her grandmother had played an introduction and the voices were raised again in song.

By the time they'd sung the fourth song, he was really enjoying himself and was sorry when Reverend Martin asked them to be seated. As they settled onto the pews, Reverend Martin stepped behind the pulpit. "Let us pray."

Andrew bowed his head as the pastor began to pray. "Lord, we come today thanking You for this beautiful day in our valley. We see the sun on our mountains, the wildflowers blooming after the long winter, and the greenery of the trees that dot the mountainsides and the forests in this paradise where You've placed us. We pray that You'll make us ever mindful of how You've provided for us and those before us in this remote region. We know we face dark days ahead, Father, but we know You're with us. Help us to remember Your blessings that have made life so good here and help us not to dwell on our problems. We know You've told us You'll be with us anywhere we go. Now be with us as we look to Your Word today for the guidance we need in our lives. Amen."

Several muffled *amens* rose across the church, but Andrew didn't look around to identify where they'd come from. The sentiments in Reverend Martin's prayer were those of everybody gathered here. For the first time it hit him how devastating it would be to be uprooted from the only home one had ever known and move somewhere else. And he was the messenger that the end was coming. Would the people hate him when they discovered his reason for being here? He glanced at Laurel, and she smiled. Would she when she knew why he was really in Cades Cove?

He pushed the thought from his mind and tried to concentrate on Reverend Martin's sermon, but he found it impossible. All he could think about was the young woman beside him and how right it felt to be sitting in church with her on this beautiful Sunday morning. From time to time he caught a few words of the pastor's sermon, and he picked out words and phrases like *thirty pieces of silver, Judas,* and *betrayal.*

Andrew might not have gone to church much in his life, but he'd heard the story of Judas in chapel at school. He remembered how Judas, one of Jesus's disciples, had betrayed Him for money. The similarity to his situation didn't go unnoticed. The thought of his true purpose—to gain the land of the very people who had welcomed him and asked him to sit with them in church— troubled him. Would they equate him to Judas when they found out his reason for being in the Cove?

The longer the sermon lasted the more Andrew squirmed in his seat. The air became stuffy and perspiration ran down his face. He put his finger inside the collar of his shirt and pulled it away from his neck where it kept sticking to the skin. It seemed strange that no one else in the church appeared to be suffering from the heat like he was. He wished the preacher would quit so he could get out of there.

After what seemed an eternity the congregation was dismissed. His hope of escaping to the aisle and exiting the church was delayed, however, when he found himself trapped in the pew between Laurel and her mother. He felt a tug on his sleeve, and he looked around at Laurel.

"I want you to meet my grandmother," she said.

The pastor's wife stood in the pew in front of them. She smiled, and he was struck by the sincere friendliness that sparkled in her blue eyes. "Hello, Mr. Brady. I'm Anna Martin. We're so glad you came to our church today."

At that moment her husband joined her and stuck out his hand. "Let me echo my wife's words. I hope you'll come again, Andrew."

Out of the corner of his eye, Andrew saw that Mrs. Jackson had moved out into the aisle. On the other side Laurel was turned away talking to an older woman. He inched toward the end of the pew in hopes of escaping, but the Martins stepped around the end of their pew and blocked his exit.

"I'll make a point to return to your church. I enjoyed the service."

Mrs. Martin smiled. "I know you enjoyed the hymns. I could hear you singing even over the music from the organ. I love to hear a man sing with such spirit. It made me happy to be in the Lord's house today."

He hesitated before responding. No one had ever complimented his singing before. In fact most of his friends at school had made fun of his off-key voice every time he tried to sing. But he sensed that Mrs. Martin had indeed meant what she said, and it made him smile.

"Thank you, Mrs. Martin. I'm glad you noticed how much I enjoyed singing with the congregation. Maybe it was the way you played the hymns. How long have you played the organ at this church?"

Her husband put his arm around her waist, and she patted his hand. "I began playing when I first came to this valley in 1894, and I've played ever since."

Andrew glanced back at Laurel, but she was still in deep conversation with the woman. "I suppose I should be going now." He held out his hand. "It was good meeting you. You have a wonderful family."

Reverend Martin grasped his hand. "No need for you to rush off. We're having our daughter's family for dinner today, and we'd like for you to join us."

Andrew shook his head. "Oh, I couldn't do that. I'll come some other time when you've invited me."

Mrs. Martin laughed. "But we've invited you today. I always cook enough extra for special guests. Besides, we want you to come. You need to meet Granny, our ninety-one-year-old second mother. When someone new enters her valley, she thinks she has to question them and find out everything about them."

Andrew's shoulders slumped, and he shook his head. "Reverend Martin, Mrs. Martin, the truth is you may not want to have me in your home when you find out why I'm really in the Cove."

Reverend Martin frowned and glanced at his wife. "But I thought Laurel said you were joining the CCC camp."

Andrew swallowed the bile in his throat. He really liked these people and he didn't want them to hate him. He especially didn't want Laurel to hate him, but they probably would after he revealed his real purpose to them. He took a deep breath.

"Laurel misunderstood me. I told her I was on my way to the CCC camp. That's true because I'm going to stay there while I'm in Cades Cove. But the truth is that I work for the National Park Service in Washington. I'm on special assignment here."

The pastor's eyes darkened, and he frowned. "What kind of special assignment?"

"I'm here to convince the holdouts in the Cove to end their court cases and sell their land to the government so the park can be completed. Your family was one of the first I intended to see."

Neither of them spoke for a moment, and then Reverend Martin nodded. "Was that your reason for coming to church here today?"

Andrew found it difficult to meet the preacher's steady gaze. "Yes, sir. I only wanted to get to know you. I didn't realize I'd already had my first introduction with Laurel yesterday. She's a very nice young woman. I'd like to get to know her and all of you much better, but I'll understand if you don't want that. No matter what my reasons for coming today were, though, I really enjoyed the service. Now I'd better leave, but I will be by your house to talk to you about selling."

Reverend Martin shook his head. "No need to do that. You can talk to Matthew and me after dinner today. No time like the present to get started."

Andrew's mouth gaped open. "You mean you still want me to come?"

Mrs. Martin laughed. "Of course we do. Just because we stand on different sides of an issue doesn't mean we can't be friends. I have lots of food cooked, and I know for a fact that government employees get hungry just like anybody else. We'd be honored to have you share a meal with us."

Moisture flooded Andrew's eyes, and he blinked. He cleared his throat and nodded. "No, it's I who would be honored to come to your home." He grasped both their stretched-out hands. "Thank you for being so kind to me."

They squeezed his hands and smiled. Laurel turned at that moment, and a small frown furrowed her brow as she stared at the three of them. "What's going on?"

Andrew released them, and Mrs. Martin waved her hand in dismissal. "Nothing. We invited Andrew to come for dinner. We're going on home, but tell your father to make sure Andrew finds his way there."

"I'll tell him." She watched her grandparents exit the church before she turned back to him. A big smile lit her face. "Who would have thought yesterday when we met we'd be having Sunday dinner together? If you're ready to go, I'll show you which truck you need to follow."

"Okay."

He stepped back to allow her to precede him up the aisle. As she brushed past him, he closed his eyes for a moment as a tingle of pleasure raced up his arm. Taking a deep breath, he followed her up the aisle.

What was it about this young woman that made her seem so different from every other one he'd ever met? He couldn't dismiss the attraction he felt to her, but it sure wasn't going to lead anywhere. Something told him that Laurel wouldn't be as understanding of his mission as her grandparents were, and that made him sadder than anything ever had before.

Chapter 4

Matthew had just reached his truck in the churchyard when he heard Simon call out to him. Simon and Anna walked toward him, her two hands grasping her husband's arm in support.

Matthew's heart constricted at the stoop of Simon's shoulders and the shuffle of his feet. The man he loved like a father looked fragile today. He'd talked to Simon about slowing down and getting someone else to come preach from time to time, but it did no good. As long as Simon had breath, he would continue to minister to those around him. Every day he prayed to be more like Simon. He wasn't sure he would ever succeed in reaching that goal, though. The man was one of a kind.

He waited for them to stop beside them. They exchanged quick glances, and Matthew sensed something troubled them. "You look upset. Has something happened?"

Simon looked over his shoulder as if to see if anybody could overhear them before he spoke. Satisfied they were alone, he leaned close to Matthew. "I thought I should warn you. We invited Andrew Brady to our house for dinner."

"That was neighborly of you. I'm sure he could use a good home-cooked meal."

"That's not what has me worried. Laurel didn't understand what he meant when he said he was on his way to the CCC camp. He's only staying out there. He really works for the Park Service, and he's here to try and convince us to sell our land to the government."

"What?" Matthew's voice exploded in a rush. "And you still invited him to dinner?"

Anna reached out and patted Matthew's arm. "Now calm down, Matthew. Andrew is not the enemy. He's been honest with us about his job here. Just because he works for the government doesn't mean we can't be friends with him. You know we've had Superintendent Eakin to eat at our house several times."

He stared at her for a moment before he grinned. "No matter how old I get, you still have the power to make me feel like the little boy I was when I first met you. You helped me learn to love and to accept people when I came back to the Cove over twenty years ago, and you're still doing it." He sighed and rubbed the back of his neck. "I guess it's not his fault he's got a job that he's gonna fail at."

Simon laughed. "That's the way to look at it." His smile disappeared, and he stepped closer. "But I want to warn you. I watched him and Laurel while I was preaching. They sure did exchange glances a lot."

Matthew's eyes grew large. "You don't think she's interested in him, do you? She only met him yesterday."

"I know, but what worries me most is that she thinks he's with the CCC. How's she going to react when she finds out the truth?"

Matthew propped his foot on the running board of the truck and pushed his hat back on his head. "If I know my daughter, and I think I do, she won't take the news very well. She hasn't recovered from seeing what the Park Service did to Pete and Laura's home."

Simon nodded. "I can understand that. After all they're Jimmy's father's parents."

Anna nudged Simon with her elbow. "We need to get home so I can get dinner on the table. We'll see you there."

Matthew shook his head in bewilderment as the two headed toward their buggy at the side of the yard. No matter how much he tried to convince them to get an automobile, he doubted they ever would. They'd traveled all their lives by buggy, and they didn't see any need to change.

A gentle laugh alerted Matthew that his daughter was near. He watched as she appeared around the side of the church with Andrew Brady beside her. When she saw him, she smiled, and Matthew narrowed his eyes. Laurel's face beamed, and her eyes danced. She reminded him of another girl, one he'd first encountered at the mountain laurel bush over twenty years ago.

When had Laurel grown up? It seemed like only yesterday he was picking her up and swinging her onto his shoulders. Now she walked beside a young man, and he'd never seen her so animated. He wondered how she would feel when she found out the truth about her new friend. He took a deep breath and brushed his hand across his eyes.

Laurel stopped beside him. "Poppa, Andrew is going to follow us to Nana's house."

He nodded. "Fine. Since your mother is riding with us, I'm sure I'll be going slow enough that he'll have no trouble keeping up."

Rani walked around the church in time to hear his last words. "What's that you're saying?"

"Nothing to concern yourself with, my dear. Just waiting for all the family to get here. Where are those boys?"

As if in answer to his question, a loud whoop echoed across the churchyard and Willie ran around the side of the church, his brother chasing him. "Willie, I'm going to thump you good when I catch you."

Willie squealed and ducked behind their mother's back. "You have to catch me first!"

Charlie dived toward Willie, but his mother grabbed him by the arms. "What's wrong?"

Charlie snarled at his brother, who was sticking out his tongue. "He chucked a rock at me. It hit me on the leg."

Matthew grabbed Willie by the arm and hoisted him into the back of the truck, then jerked his head in Charlie's direction. "Get in the truck, Charlie. And you two settle down. Try to remember this is Sunday and act like you've been to church."

Rani suppressed a giggle and shrugged in Andrew's direction. "I'm sorry about that, Andrew."

Andrew smiled and shook his head. "I like to see boys having a good time together. It reminds me of how I used to aggravate my older brother."

"Then you'll feel right at home around our family." Laurel's words were laced with laughter.

Matthew's body stiffened as he studied his daughter's face. There was a glow about her he'd never seen before. It reminded him of how Rani had looked at him when they were young and just getting to know each other. His teeth clenched and the muscle in his jaw flexed. Laurel hadn't been around any young men in a while. It was only natural she would be excited to have male company, but if she had any romantic notions rolling around in her young head he had to put a stop to them right away.

He turned to Andrew. "Simon tells me we misunderstood why you're here. You aren't with the CCC group. You really work for the Park Service, and you've been sent to persuade us to sell our land."

Andrew blinked and his mouth dropped open. He cast a quick glance at Laurel, whose stunned look made Matthew's heart lurch. Andrew took a deep breath. "Yes, sir, that's right. I didn't mean to mislead you."

Laurel took a step back from Andrew. She frowned and shook her head. "You're here to persuade us to give in to the government?"

Andrew nodded. "Yes. I didn't mean to give the

wrong impression, Laurel. I just wanted to get to know all of you first."

"I see." Her lips trembled, and she closed her eyes as she placed her hand on her forehead. "It's getting hot out here. Poppa, isn't it time we were going?"

Matthew tried to think of something to say that would ease the tension that crackled in the air, but nothing came to mind. Laurel whirled and headed to the passenger door of the truck, her mother right behind her.

Andrew, his lips pursed and his eyes narrowed, stared after her. When she climbed into the truck, he turned to Matthew. "Mr. Jackson, I can understand how you must feel about the government right now. Promises you were given when the park was in the planning stage weren't honored. I'm sorry about that."

Matthew nodded. "Back when the promoters of the park brought prospective donors here to show them the land, I let them stay in my lodge. We were assured our homes wouldn't be touched. Once the final bill was passed to create the park, that promise was forgotten."

"I know, sir, and I'm sorry. But now we have to deal with the present. That's why I'm here, to help the last of the people in the Cove do that."

Matthew snorted. "I don't think we'll ever be able to deal with it."

Andrew glanced toward the truck, where

Laurel's straight back was visible through the window between the cab and the bed. "I'm glad I came to church today and met all of you. I want you to know I didn't come to Cades Cove to cause any problems, especially in your family. I liked Laurel when I met her yesterday. When I saw her today, I hoped we might be friends. That doesn't seem too likely now. Maybe I shouldn't go to the Martins for dinner. Will you make my apologies to Mrs. Martin and to your wife?" He swallowed. "And to Laurel?"

Matthew opened his mouth to tell Andrew he agreed it would be better for him to go on to the CCC camp instead of coming to Simon and Anna's home, but the way Andrew's glance darted to the truck window where Laurel was visible stopped him.

The day he had ridden into Cades Cove over twenty years ago popped into his mind. It had been a June day then, and he had returned with the fear that the son of one of the most notorious men who had ever lived in the valley wouldn't be welcomed. Simon, Anna, and Rani had helped him to face the problems he'd encountered. They'd been his friends even when he hadn't deserved them. Now another young man had arrived in the Cove, and he faced an even greater chance of being despised. What would God have him do about this unhappy-looking boy standing in front of him?

The answer rang clear in his mind. He took a deep breath and shook his head. "If you give up that easy when a young woman gets upset with you, what are you going to do when an angry farmer threatens to blow your head off if you don't get off his porch?"

Andrew's face paled. "Well, I guess I never thought . . ."

Matthew laughed and slapped Andrew on the shoulder. "Well, son, you'd better start thinking or you're gonna have a mighty tough time in the Cove. Now you get in your car and follow me all the way to Simon's house. Today we won't talk business. It'll just be a time for us all to get acquainted. There's time for you to worry about your job this coming week."

Andrew grinned and glanced toward Laurel once more before he stuck out his hand. "Thank you, Mr. Jackson. I'd like to get to know your family better."

Matthew shook his hand. "Then let's go."

He watched as Andrew hurried back to his car and climbed in before he got into the truck. Rani studied his profile as he started the engine. "Well?" she said, her eyebrows raised.

Matthew faced her. "Well, what?"

"Did you tell that boy not to come to Mama's house for dinner?"

Matthew frowned. "Now why would I do that? Just because we disagree on what the government's trying to do to us is no reason not to be neighborly. Lots of folks with strange ideas have stayed at our lodge, and we treated them like they were friends."

"But this is different, Matthew. He's a . . ."

Matthew held up his hand to stop his wife. "He's a boy who's come here not knowing how folks are going to treat him. But he's come anyway. I remember another boy who came to the Cove wanting folks to give him a chance. I guess it's time for me to return the favor. He's got a hard road to hoe if he's going to try and persuade the folks still here that they have to leave."

Rani's eyes glistened with moisture and a smile pulled at her lips. She squeezed his arm. "You're a good man, Matthew Jackson."

He covered her hand with his. "It's because I had a good teacher."

"Hey, Poppa, are we gonna sit here all day, or are we going to Grandpa's for dinner?"

Matthew grimaced at Willie's loud voice and turned to see his nose pressed against the rear window of the truck. Matthew sighed and put the truck in gear. "Sit down, Willie, before you fall out."

"Well, I was just wond'rin' if you was asleep or somethin'."

"Sit down, Willie."

"Okay, don't get mad. I'm just asking."

Matthew's face grew hot and then hotter at the

sound of Rani and Laurel's giggles. "Willie . . ."

"I'm sittin'."

Matthew took a deep breath. "All right, everyone. If you're all ready, we'll go to Simon and Anna's now."

As the truck pulled out of the churchyard, Matthew cast a glance at his wife and daughter beside him and then to his two sons in the back of the truck. Laurel's obvious unhappiness over her discovery about Andrew troubled him. He needed to think of something to take her mind off the young man who'd appeared in their valley.

Then there was Willie. He had no idea how he was ever going to tame that boy, but even more of a concern was Charlie. The older he got, the more sullen he became. He never knew what Charlie was thinking. There was something in Charlie's eyes that frightened Matthew. It was a look he remembered from his childhood—the cravings and wanderlust in his father's eyes that had led to his destruction as well as that of Matthew's mother and brother.

The fear he'd harbored for several years rushed through him, and he gripped the steering wheel tighter. He'd vowed he would be a better father than his abusive, drunkard father had been, and he'd tried. But there were some things born in a person you couldn't fight. Rani wasn't aware of his concern about Charlie, and he hoped he would never have to tell her.

• • •

Andrew pulled his car to a stop behind the Jacksons' truck in the yard of a log cabin. He studied the sturdy structure with a chimney at one end that reached from the ground to far above the wood-shingled roof. A black two-door Chevrolet coupe sat underneath a tree at one end of the front porch where Simon Martin sat in a rocking chair. He rose to his feet as they pulled into the yard, walked to the edge of the steps, and smiled.

"Get out and come on in," he called out.

The two boys jumped from the back of the Jacksons' truck and raced toward the porch. The younger one said something Andrew couldn't hear. Their grandfather answered and pointed to the corner of the house. Both boys whooped and dashed around the house.

Andrew inhaled a deep breath, opened the car door, and stepped out. His stomach churned as he walked toward the front porch. Now that the family knew about him he couldn't believe they still had insisted he come. This just didn't seem right. He couldn't imagine his father extending an invitation like this to one of his opponents on an important matter before Congress. In fact, he'd do everything in his power to find the person's weak spot and use it against him. Was that what Reverend Martin had in mind?

Laurel and her mother stopped to give the

reverend a hug. "Where did Charlie and Willie run off to?" Laurel asked.

Reverend Martin laughed. "They asked where Noah was. I told them he was checking on Molly's new litter of puppies at the barn, and they took off to find him."

Mr. Jackson turned to follow his sons. "I'd better go down there too. I promised Willie we would get one of the puppies. I'll go see if he's picked out the one he wants when they're weaned."

Mrs. Jackson shook her head and laughed. "That Willie. He's been so excited over the expected puppies and Noah's visit. All he and Charlie have talked about is getting him to take them for one more ride in his car before he leaves this afternoon."

"Maybe he will."

Laurel had already disappeared inside the house. Her mother followed. Andrew swallowed his disappointment when Laurel didn't even look back at him. Reverend Martin stood at the top of the porch steps, his hand resting on one of the posts. When Andrew reached the top of the steps, the old reverend held out his hand. "Welcome to our home, Andrew."

Surprised again, Andrew grasped his hand and shook it. "Thank you, Reverend Martin."

The pastor's dark eyes twinkled as he laughed. "None of that Reverend Martin stuff. I'm Simon to my friends, and I sure hope you're going to be my friend."

Friends? That was totally unexpected. He had hoped he would make friends in Cades Cove, but the reality was that he probably wasn't going to be welcomed by many of the residents. Maybe this invitation was a pretense to put him at ease. Simon Martin and Matthew Jackson didn't want him to succeed, and he was sure they would do every-thing they could to keep their neighbors from selling their land.

He arched an eyebrow. "Why would you want to be friends with me?"

Simon laughed again. "Because you seem like a nice young man."

"But that doesn't make sense. I'm here on a mission that you oppose."

Simon's eyes narrowed and his hand squeezed Andrew's shoulder. "Andrew, when I was a young man, God called me to the ministry. I've tried to serve Him ever since. That calling has put me in opposition to a lot of the things that go against the teachings of the Bible. I've come in contact with people who have let sin take over their lives to the point where they're almost destroyed, but I've always let them know I hate the sin in their lives, not them. Now you've come here on a mission I don't support. It's your job, and I respect that. I don't like your job. I don't want you to succeed, but that doesn't mean I don't like you. I was honest when I said I wanted to be your friend. We all do. You may not understand that now, but maybe in time you will."

Andrew shook his head in amazement. "That's quite an amazing statement, sir. I'll think about what you've said." In an effort to change the subject, Andrew pointed to the car beside the house. "Nice looking car. Is it yours?"

Simon threw back his head and laughed. "Heavens, no. You won't catch me driving one of those things. I'd probably run over somebody. It belongs to Noah Campbell, our adopted son. Noah came to live with us when he was just a boy. He's a preacher over at Pigeon Forge now, but he's been visiting us for the last week. He's going home this afternoon."

Before Andrew could respond, a raspy voice called out from inside the cabin. "Simon, I hear we got comp'ny. You gonna bring him inside so's I can meet him or not?"

Simon laughed, walked to the front door, and held it open for Andrew to enter. "Come on inside and meet another member of our family."

As Andrew entered the house, he inhaled the most delectable smells he had encountered in a long time. His stomach growled at the scents drifting into the room. He'd overslept and skipped breakfast this morning, and his stomach was reminding him of it. His face grew warm and he glanced at Simon. "Something sure smells good."

Simon nodded, walked across the room to a chair where an elderly woman sat, and put his hand on her shoulder. "Anna sets the best table in all the Cove, and we have this lady here to thank. She taught Anna everything she knows about cooking and about a lot of other things. Andrew, this is Granny Lawson."

Andrew's gaze raked the woman as he eased across the floor and came to a stop in front of her. Even seated and with her shoulders stooped, Andrew could see that she had once been a tall woman. Her white hair was pulled back in a bun at the back of her head, and her eyes sparkled behind the lenses of her wire-rimmed glasses. She held out a wrinkled hand and Andrew grasped it.

"Hello, Mrs. Lawson. I'm happy to meet you."

A cackle burst from her lips. "Land's sakes, boy, I ain't been called Miz Lawson since the preacher hitched me and my husband 'bout seventy years ago. Ev'rybody in these parts just calls me Granny, and that's what you need to do too."

Andrew smiled and nodded. "All right, Granny. I'm still happy to meet you."

She shifted in her chair and tilted her head to stare up at him better. "Laurel tells me you're the latest one the gover'ment done sent here to make us give up our homes."

His face warmed, and he glanced at Simon. The preacher shrugged. "I wouldn't quite put it that way, but I have come to talk with the people in the Cove about their options."

Granny's eyes grew wide, and she pushed her glasses up on her nose. "Options? We ain't got no options, son. The gover'ment says we cain't live in the middle of no park and that we have to move. Now that may sound easy to do to folks up in Washington who ain't never had to face losing their home, but I'm here to tell you it's a hard, hard thing for somebody who done lived as long as me in this here valley."

Her voice trembled on the last words, and Andrew's heart pricked. Simon motioned to a chair beside Granny, and Andrew eased into it. "How long have you lived in Cades Cove, Granny?"

"Why, I was born here. I'm gonna be ninety-one years old this week, and I remember about eighty-eight of those years in the Cove. It was always like a big fam'ly a-livin' together in this valley. We knew each other, and we took care of ev'rybody. I was a midwife here 'til I got too old to handle the job. That's when Anna took over for me. She asked me once how many babies I'd delivered, but I lost count years ago of how many I brung into the world in these mountain cabins."

"A midwife? That must have been interesting work."

A laugh rumbled in Granny's throat. "I guess you could call it that. Sometimes it got real inter'stin' when a baby decided to be stubborn.

But I reckon ev'ry cabin in the Cove had one of my babies a-livin' in it at one time or another." A sigh rippled from her lips. "Now they's all gone. Just scattered like leaves in the wind."

Andrew glanced up at Simon. He was standing behind Granny's chair, his hand on her shoulder. She reached up and squeezed his fingers, and Simon's Adam's apple bobbed. A twinge of sorrow for the plight of these people flowed through Andrew. What would they do when they left their homes? They would be strangers in new communities without the support of friends they'd known all their lives. Outside their remote valley the only thing greeting them was a depression where jobs were scarce and many families struggled every day to put food on the table. Even with the small amount of money the government would pay them for their farms—and Andrew knew they wouldn't get nearly what the farms were worth—it would be a hostile new world for them.

"I'm sorry, Granny." There were no other words he could think of to reply.

Matthew Jackson walked into the room from the back of the house at that moment. He walked over to Granny's chair, leaned down, and kissed her on the cheek. "Hello, Granny. How are you feeling today?"

She reached up and patted his cheek. "Just fine, Matthew. Noah and me had us a church service right here at home whilst all of you was gone. I shore am glad that boy came to visit. It ain't been the same since he left to go off to school. Now he's got his own church. Married and gonna be a daddy soon. My, my, who would've thought how things would turn out?"

Simon and Matthew both laughed. "I think you were the one who always told him to follow the plan God had for his life. He's done just that," Matthew said. He reached down and grasped one of Granny's arms. "Anna says it's time to eat. Simon and I will help you to the table. Andrew, follow us."

The two men lifted Granny to her feet and guided her carefully to the door that Andrew assumed led to the kitchen. He watched the three as they inched along and thought about how evident it was that this family loved each other. It was in every look they gave, in every word they spoke, in every movement of their bodies. He'd never encountered that closeness before.

To his father, Sunday was just another workday. To the public Congressman Brady extoled the virtues of family values, but in private it was an entirely different matter. Their family had ceased to be many years ago on the banks of the Potomac River.

Tears threatened to flood his eyes, but he blinked them back. He couldn't think about that time now. He had other concerns to address. He'd been sent here to talk the Cove residents into selling their land, but at the moment that didn't seem as important as something else.

He wanted Laurel to understand he wasn't some monster who had descended on the Cove to trick everyone into leaving. For some reason he felt drawn to her, and he wanted to know her better. But from the way she'd acted since finding out why he was really in the Cove, he didn't know if she would want to be his friend or not.

In an effort to put the troubling thought out of his mind, he shook his head and followed Simon, Matthew, and Granny into the kitchen. Maybe she would talk to him during dinner. He certainly hoped so.

Chapter 5

Laurel fidgeted in her chair and tried to avoid the probing stare that Andrew seemed to direct at her every few minutes. She should never have sat across from him, but by the time she'd had a chance to find an empty chair at the table it was the only spot left. Throughout the meal she'd tried to steer most of her conversation to Noah and her father, but she couldn't help glancing at Andrew from time to time. With dessert almost over, she'd be able to escape his brooding eyes soon.

Ever since she'd encountered him yesterday in front of Mr. Bryan's store she hadn't been able to get him out of her mind. But she would never have dreamed he would show up at their church this morning. Now he sat at her grandparents' table having a meal with the people she loved most in the world, and they all seemed to be enjoying his company—especially Granny. She had kept him entertained during the meal with stories about her early days in the Cove and how she'd prayed God would send her a helper. Then Anna had arrived, and they'd been family ever since.

Granny might be enjoying his company, but Laurel couldn't help feeling she'd been betrayed. Why hadn't he told her when he first arrived at church his real reason for being in the Cove? The answer to that question seemed obvious to her. Since he'd been quick to tell her grandparents who he worked for, he must consider her just a simple mountain girl who had no business meddling in matters better left to the heads of the family.

If he thought that, he could think again. The question of whether or not they would sell their land affected her because it meant the loss of the only home she'd ever known. Just the thought of having to leave the Cove frightened her, and she glared at Andrew. He glanced at her at that moment, and he cocked one eyebrow. As his gaze drifted over her face, her pulse raced. Her fingers shook, and the fork she held slipped from her fingers and clattered against the plate.

All conversation at the table stopped momentarily, and her cheeks warmed. She jerked her hands to her lap and clasped them together as she stared down at her plate.

"Laurel, are you all right?" her mother asked.

She took a deep breath and directed a wobbly smile at her mother as she pushed to her feet. "My fork slipped out of my grasp." She picked up her plate and glanced around. "Can I take anybody else's plate?"

"I'm through, Laurel." Andrew's deep voice rumbled from across the table.

Her grandmother pushed to her feet and began to gather up the plates of those sitting near her. "Simon, take the men in the front room while Rani and Laurel help me clean up the kitchen. Then we'll join you."

From his seat at the head of the table her grandfather stood slowly. "All right. Matthew and I'll help Granny back to the front room."

He started around the table toward Granny, but she frowned and waved her hands at him. "No need for that, Simon. I think I'll take a nap. Andrew and Laurel can help me to my bedroom. Then I think Laurel ought to show Andrew around the farm."

Laurel gasped and stared at Granny, who returned her startled expression with a sweet smile. "B-but I need to help clean up the kitchen."

Granny chuckled and shook her head. "Your mama and grandmama can do that just fine without you. Besides, it's a beautiful day and I'll just bet you done brought that there camera with you to take some pi'tures. Am I right?"

"Y-yes, Granny, but . . ."

"Andrew's new to these here mountains. Show him around. He might be able to see something you need to photograph that you missed."

Laurel looked toward her mother, but she and Nana were already pouring water from the kettle into the dishpan. Her father and grandfather exchanged quick glances before they turned and headed for the front room.

She turned to Noah, her last hope. "Why don't you . . ."

Noah was already shaking his head. He pushed his chair back and pulled his lanky legs out from underneath the table. He glanced across the table at Andrew. "I wish I had time to take you on a tour of the farm, Andrew, but I'm going to have to head back to Pigeon Forge before long, and I promised Charlie and Willie I'd take them for a ride in my car before I leave."

Laurel tilted her head to one side and pulled her lips into a pout. "Please don't leave so early. I've hardly gotten to see you this week."

Noah laughed, put his finger under her chin, and tilted her face up. "I know you'd like to wrap me around your little finger like you did when you were a little girl, but that sad face won't work anymore. Geraldine is at her folks' house, and

I'm right eager to see her." He glanced across the table at Andrew. "We're expecting our first baby in a few months, and we didn't think she needed to travel right now. She sure did want to come, though. She loves the Cove almost as much as I do."

"After seeing how beautiful it is here, I can understand that. And congratulations on the baby, Noah." Andrew smiled, but it didn't blot out the hurt look in his eyes. Laurel's heart gave a lurch. She hadn't fooled him one bit. He knew she didn't want to spend time with him.

She straightened her shoulders and stared into his eyes. "It looks like the task of showing you the farm where my mother grew up has fallen to me, Andrew. I hope you're not too disappointed."

He gave a slight shake of his head. "On the contrary, I couldn't be more pleased."

A slight tremor ran up her arm at the intensity of the look he directed at her. Taking a deep breath, she walked around the table until she stood opposite Granny. "If you'll grasp her arm, I'll take the other. We should be able to get her to her feet."

"Land's sakes," Granny grumbled. "You'd think a body couldn't get herself out of a chair. I'll have you know, young lady, that I been a-takin' care of myself for a lot of years, and I can still do it."

Laurel laughed and gave Granny a quick hug. "I know you can, Granny. It's just that we love you so much we want to help you all we can."

Granny waved her hand in dismissal. "Now there you go a-tryin' to butter me up like you been doin' ev'rybody in this family all your life. Just help me to my bed, then you two young people get outside and enjoy this purty day God done give us."

A few minutes later, with Granny safely settled in her bed, Laurel and Andrew stepped out the cabin's front door. Laurel walked over to the wooden railing of the porch, wrapped her fingers around the top, and leaned against it. Andrew stood next to her with his hands in his pockets.

Laurel gazed at the mountains that ringed their valley and winced. Ever since she could remember she'd thanked God every day for letting her live in such a beautiful place. Now most days she prayed God would keep her family here. Her fingers tightened around the railing.

"Why didn't you tell me you worked for the government?" She didn't look at him, but she heard his sharp intake of breath.

"I didn't mean to mislead you, Laurel. I was so shocked when I saw you at the church, I couldn't think straight. When you asked me what I was doing there, the first thing that popped out of my mouth was that I was on my to the CCC camp. That's true. I realize now I should have told you more at the time, but it seemed I was inside being introduced to everybody before I knew what was happening. Then to find out you're Matthew

Jackson's daughter was too much for me to take in."

She jerked her head around and glared at him. "But you had no problem telling my grandfather."

"Because he and your grandmother invited me to dinner. I didn't want to come under false pretenses. I wouldn't do that to your family." He covered her hand with his and swallowed. "Please don't be angry with me, Laurel. Ever since I met you yesterday, I've been kicking myself because I didn't get your last name. I was going to find Mountain Laurel Pottery so I could find out more about you. Then there you were at the church, and I was stunned."

She told herself she should pull her hand away, but that wasn't what she wanted. She stared at him without moving. "You wanted to find me? Why?"

"I don't really know why. It's just that in the few minutes we spent together you touched me in some way. Maybe it's because I'm away from home and I want to make friends so I won't be lonely. I'd really like to be your friend, Laurel. What do you say?"

Her breath hitched in her throat, and she shook her head. "How can we be friends? You're here to take away everything my family has worked for and the only life we know."

His hand tightened on hers. "I'm only the messenger, Laurel. Your father and grandfather are intelligent men. They know they're only prolonging the inevitable. Sooner or later the government is going to get all the land in the Cove."

She clenched her teeth and jerked her hand away from his. "You're wrong if you believe that, Andrew. If you've come here thinking we're just some simple mountain folks you can smooth talk and get us to sign our X on a bill of sale, then you need to check with your superiors. I'm sure they can tell you not to underestimate the Martins and the Jacksons."

"I know that, Laurel. I have the highest respect for your family. I would never do anything to hurt any of you."

She tossed her head, and her braid thumped against her chest. "Does that include me, Andrew?"

A hissed breath escaped his lips. "Especially you, Laurel. I told you I want to be friends with you."

She narrowed her eyes and studied him for a moment before she shook her head. "I don't think that's going to be possible, Andrew. Now if you'll excuse me, I'm going to look at Molly's puppies. Alone. I think it would be a good idea for you to let Grandpa show you around the farm later. While you're looking, you can be calculating how much money it's going to take to steal the home he and Nana have lived in for forty years."

He reached out a hand to her, but she backed away. "Please, Laurel, I don't want you to think that badly of me."

Her chin trembled, and she struggled to blink back the tears filling her eyes. "I'm afraid I already do."

She brushed past him and ran down the steps. All she wanted was to get away from those eyes that made her heart leap in her chest and the hand that had sent tingles up her arm when he touched hers.

She had met Andrew less than twenty-four hours ago, but it seemed like he was someone she'd known all her life. Her lips might spout the words that she didn't want to be friends, but her heart knew the truth—she wanted it more than she'd ever wanted anything in her life.

"Laurel, please come back." His voice called out to her as she ran toward the barn. She pressed her hands to her ears and didn't look back.

It didn't matter that she wanted to run back so badly that her heart was pounding like a drum in her chest. She would not be friends with a man who wanted to destroy the only way of life she'd ever known.

Later that afternoon Andrew stopped his car at the entrance to the Cades Cove CCC camp. His right hand lightly gripped the steering wheel and his elbow rested on the open window as he gazed at the U-shaped camp nestled on the hillside in the distance.

Even from this far away he could tell this camp followed the standard that had been set for all CCC camps across the country to contain twenty-four wooden buildings. He could pick out the one that housed the headquarters because it was larger and had a flagpole in front. The others would be the administrative buildings and enrollee and officers' barracks as well as the mess hall, hospital, garage, and schoolhouse. Each one sported a cleared space in front for assemblies and sports activities.

There was little movement around the camp this afternoon. Not surprising, being it was Sunday. The men would be out tomorrow when the sun came up and would disperse across the Cove in forty- to fifty-man work crews, tackling projects intended to provide future tourists with a better wilderness experience.

As he thought of the plans the Park Service had for this area of the new park, he was reminded of Laurel and his conversation with her earlier. His hand tightened on the steering wheel. She hadn't returned to the house after she'd told him she didn't want to be friends and he'd spent the remainder of his time talking with Matthew and Simon. It felt strange to address two older men by their first names, but they'd insisted.

He sighed and put the car in gear. There was no

need to think about Laurel now. He had a big job ahead of him in the next few months, and he would run into her again. Maybe their next meeting would be more pleasant.

The flag on the pole in front of the administration building waved in the breeze as if it welcomed him to the camp. He drove straight toward it, pulling to a stop in front and surveying the rolling landscape around him. Whoever had picked out this spot had chosen one with a spectacular view of the surrounding mountains. A small creek—Tater Branch if he remembered correctly—bubbled along at the far edge of the camp. Metal piping, probably having something to do with the camp water supply, ran along the banks.

He stepped out of the car and turned toward the headquarters building. A sign nailed to the wall beside the front door proclaimed this the home of CCC Camp Number 1214. Mountain wildflowers bloomed in circular beds outlined with stones on either side of the entrance. Evidently the young men who lived in the camp weren't content to only enhance the beauty of the wilderness; they wanted it in the place that would be their home for the duration of their assignment here.

He headed toward the front door but stopped when it opened. Two men who looked to be in their early twenties stepped out onto the porch. The taller of the two nodded to Andrew. "Good afternoon. Can we help you with anything?"

"I'm Andrew Brady with the Park Service. I'm here to see Lieutenant Gray."

The young man pointed inside. "We just saw him go into his office. You'll see it inside. His name's on the door."

"Thanks."

The two hopped off the porch and Andrew watched them head to one of the long barracks before he walked into the building. Just as he entered a man stepped out of one of the offices and stopped to stare at him. He held some long rolls of paper in his hands.

His eyebrows arched. "Mr. Brady?"

Andrew nodded and approached with his hand extended. "Yes. I assume you're Lieutenant Gray, the superintendent."

The man shifted the papers and grasped Andrew's hand. "I am. I've been expecting you all afternoon. I thought you'd be here earlier."

"I would have been, but I stopped to go to church. Then the pastor and his wife asked me to go home with them for dinner."

Lieutenant Gray's lips pulled into a big smile. "That sounds like Simon and Anna Martin. I've had a few meals in their home too. They're some of the finest people I've ever known."

"They were very kind to me. Their daughter and her family were there too. I never would have believed that on my first day here I'd be eating with the two men who've waged court battles against the government. But they didn't let that stand in the way of being very hospitable to me."

"They're good people." Lieutenant Gray stepped back toward his office. "Let me put these maps on my desk and then I'll take you over to the officers' barracks where you'll be staying while you're here."

"Thanks. I'd appreciate that."

A few minutes later Lieutenant Gray was ushering Andrew into a small room in the officers' barracks. He glanced at his watch. "You'll have time to get settled before supper—that's at five thirty. The men have free time until lights-out at ten. Reveille is at six in the morning and breakfast forty-five minutes later. If you need anything while you're here, let me know and I'll get it for you. Do you have any questions?"

Andrew shook his head. "No, not right now."

"Then I'll leave you to get settled and I'll see you in the mess hall for supper. You'll eat at the officers' table."

Andrew set his bag on the small cot where he'd sleep and turned back to Lieutenant Gray. "Thank you for putting me up while I'm in the Cove."

Lieutenant Gray shrugged. "No problem. See you later."

With that the man turned and strode into the hallway. Andrew stood in the middle of the sparsely furnished room where he would be living for the next few months and looked around. Not like home, but it would meet his needs. A cot, a desk with a chair, a small table next to the bed, and a foot locker completed the list of furnishings. On the bright side there was a small closet where he could hang his pants and shirts. The best thing about the place, though, was that the camp had electricity, and the room was well lit with two lamps and an overhead light.

He turned back to his bag and opened it. The framed picture lay on top of his packed clothes, and he pulled it out. He stared at the woman in the photograph and frowned. Lucy had given him the picture after dinner on his last night at home, and he'd promised her it would have a place of honor in his room. Now that he was here in the Cove, he wasn't so sure he should have done that.

Lucy really was a beautiful woman and a very rich one, with family who had helpful contacts in the political world, as his father was constantly reminding him. She and both their families fully expected him to propose. The perfect wife for him, they all said. A woman who could be a great asset in building her husband's political career.

If his father had his way, Andrew would not only marry Lucy, he would use every one of her contacts to help him climb the ladder of elected office all the way to Washington. There was only one thing wrong with his father's plan. It wasn't what Andrew wanted.

Andrew closed his eyes and shook his head. Why couldn't he make his father understand that? He'd told him over and over, but his protests did no good. Maybe he hadn't been able to make his father understand how he felt because he hadn't figured out yet what he did want in life. He was twenty-four years old with a degree in engineering from Virginia Military Institute, and he was drifting through life without a clue where he was going.

He'd hoped his summer in Cades Cove would give him some time to think and figure out his future. He'd been in the Cove for less than a day, and he already had more questions than he'd had when he arrived. Already his expectations of the people living here had been shattered. The Martins and the Jacksons were nothing like his family. They didn't have the wealth his father had accumulated, and the Martins' cabin couldn't begin to compare with the large home his family owned in the rolling Virginia countryside. Yet they had something his family didn't. They were happy and content with what they had. And their love for each other was evident in every word they spoke and every look they gave each other.

Now he'd come to take their way of life away from them and send them into an unknown world outside their mountain valley. The thought squeezed the breath out of him. How could he do that to them? How could he hurt Laurel?

He glanced down at the picture he held of the woman who was about to become his fiancée. His hands trembled. The ridiculous thought popped into his head that he wished the face smiling at him was a dark-haired beauty with a long braid and flashing brown eyes.

His hand tightened on the frame, and he closed his eyes. "Mountain Laurel," he whispered.

There might be a lot of things he was unsure of in his life, but one thing he was certain about. He had to know her better. No matter what she said, he intended to do just that. He didn't know how, but he would figure out a way.

The afternoon quiet made Laurel sleepy, and she nodded in the rocker on the front porch of her grandparents' cabin. Noah had left, her father and grandfather had taken her brothers and driven over to the site of Cecil Davis's cabin to see if it had been torn down by the Park Service, and her mother and grandmother were in the kitchen discussing a dress pattern. She and Granny had sat beside each other for the last thirty minutes without speaking.

Laurel took a deep breath and straightened in her chair. "Are you okay, Granny?"

"I'm fine, child. I just been a-sittin' here soakin' up my mountains. It's one of my fav'rite things to do."

Laurel chuckled. "I know."

Granny rocked a few times before she spoke

again. "It shore has been a beautiful Sunday in the Cove."

Laurel nodded. "It has. Everything is so green, and the air smells so good. It gives me a happy feeling."

Granny's eyebrow arched and she directed a somber stare at Laurel. "Are you sure you feel good? I thought you seemed kinda down and out after Andrew left."

"I don't know what you mean, Granny. I didn't care one way or another when he left." Laurel's fingers curled into her fists, and she clasped them in her lap.

"Well, you coulda fooled me. My eyesight may not be as good as it used to be, but you looked right disappointed when you come back from seeing the puppies and found out he'd already left. I figured you was upset 'cause you didn't get to tell him goodbye."

Laurel sniffed and shook her head. "Why would I be upset? Andrew Brady means nothing to me."

"Well, that may be so, but I could tell he was right taken with you. He must've asked me a hundred questions 'bout you during dinner."

"A hundred? Now, Granny, I think you're exaggerating."

Granny laughed. "Well, maybe a bit, but he did talk about you a lot. And he shore looked at you plenty of times." She reached over and grasped Laurel's hand. "There's nothing wrong with that, darlin'. You're a pretty young woman, and he's a good-looking man. It's natural that you'd want to be friends."

Laurel shook her head. "He said he wants to be friends with me, but I can't do that, Granny. He's here to take our land and our homes. If he has his way, I'm scared of what will happen to us. I have to think of him as my enemy."

Granny sighed and squeezed her hand. "He's not our enemy, darlin'."

"But Granny, he works for the government and they want to take our homes from us."

Granny rocked a few more times and stared toward the mountains in the distance. "I been a-readin' my Bible all my life and trying to be more like Jesus. And I gotta confess, I done had a time trying to figure out what He'd want me to do about this mess we find ourselves in. Sometimes I get so mad at the government I can't stand it. Then I think about how so many died to give us the freedom we have in this land, and I feel guilty. I've had a hard time figuring out which is the right way to feel, but I think I know now."

"What is it, Granny?"

"I read in the Bible where Peter was a-talkin' about honoring your government leaders, even the bad ones, even when you disagreed with them. He said that no matter what is done to us, believers were to be honorable."

Laurel leaned back in her chair and narrowed

her eyes as she twisted the end of her braid between her fingers. "I think Poppa and Grandpa have been honorable, a lot more than I would have been in their places."

"They have been," Granny said. "That's because they know it's the right thing to do. The Bible says even when we have disputes with the government we are to treat those in charge with respect. We can dislike what they're doing without hatin' 'em."

Laurel gripped the arms of her chair, her body rigid, and faced Granny. "But what if we suffer because they're wrong?"

"Suffer? Child, we don't know what suff'rin' is compared to the early Christians who were killed for their beliefs. Fact is, we've had it mighty good for a lot of years in this here valley. Now we have us a disagreement with the government, and we don't know what's a-gonna happen." A sigh rippled from her mouth. "And I'm a-feared I may not like the outcome. But I cain't let that influence me. All I can do is what God would have me do —be more like Christ and show Him in my actions. That's what all of us need to do."

Laurel thought about what Granny had said for a few minutes before she responded. "That's what Poppa and Grandpa have done, isn't it? I've wondered how they could be so kind to the government people that keep showing up here. They've always been respectful to them—just like they were with Andrew today. I've seen the strain it's put on Poppa at times, and I wondered why he kept being so nice. Now I understand."

"Your pa is a fine man, Laurel. I knowed he was gonna be when he was a little boy and tryin' so hard to be the man of his family after his pa died. This argument with the government's been hard on him, maybe more so than anybody else in the Cove. Because deep down he knows we won't win." She paused and stared back at her mountains. "So we keep tryin' to hang on to what's ours, but we don't take it out on people like Andrew. Just try and remember Andrew didn't make this here problem anymore than we did. We just happen to have dif'rent notions about the outcome. But no matter what happens when this thing is settled, I want folks to say we acted like Christ in ev'rything we did."

Laurel scooted out of her chair and eased onto the floor at Granny's feet. She leaned forward and laid her head in Granny's lap like she'd done so often when she was a little girl. The soft stroke of Granny's fingers on her hair filled her with a longing for childhood days when she thought her family could make everything in her world right.

No matter how much she wished, though, she wasn't a child anymore. She was a woman with three strong women in her life. Maybe someday she would be like her grandmother, mother, and Granny. She hoped so.

"Thank you, Granny. You've given me a lot to think about."

Maybe it was possible for her and Andrew to be friends. There was something about the young man from Virginia that fascinated her. At least she'd thought so before she knew who he really was. Now she knew why he had come to the Cove and her emotions were tangled in a heated battle. Her head told her to keep her distance from the young man whose brooding eyes made her pulse race, but her heart still whispered that her first impression had been right.

Chapter 6

On Monday morning Andrew whistled a familiar tune as he drove toward the farm he'd chosen for his first visit. A map of Cades Cove with the locations of the farms still to be purchased lay in his briefcase. He'd studied it so much he knew exactly where every holdout lived. This morning's visit would be to the Ezra Nash farm. The Nash family had farmed their land for generations and Ezra had been outspoken with other agents who'd tried to talk with him. Andrew hoped today would be different.

He pulled into the yard of the neat cabin and looked around. It sat at the end of a road off the main loop. The view of the mountains from the yard was one of the most magnificent he'd seen since arriving in the Cove. He stepped out of the car and took note of the outbuildings. A barn and what he supposed to be a henhouse and a smokehouse sat to the rear of the cabin. A long open-sided shed in the field next to the house looked like it contained beehives. He'd heard that some of the best honey in the mountains came from Cades Cove, and he made a note to get some before he went back home.

Andrew climbed the steps to the front porch and peered through the screen door. The front door stood open with a cast iron doorstop pressing it against the inside wall. Andrew knocked and called out. "Hello, anybody home?"

Footsteps sounded from the back of the cabin and a woman appeared behind the screen. She wiped her hands on her apron and stared at him. "Can I help you?"

"Mrs. Nash?"

"Yes."

"I'm Andrew Brady with the Park Service. I need to talk to your husband. Is he home?"

Her eyes narrowed and she glanced over her shoulder. "Ezra, somebody from the Park Service here to see you."

A tall man wearing overalls appeared next to her. "I'm Ezra Nash. You wantin' to see me?"

Andrew smiled. "Yes sir. I'm Andrew Brady, and . . ."

"You that feller wanting to git my land?"

Andrew cleared his throat. "Well, I wouldn't put it quite that way. I'm here to talk to you about selling."

Ezra's face hardened into angry lines. "My land ain't for sale. Not today. Not any time in the future. Now get off my porch 'fore I throw you off."

Perspiration popped out on Andrew's forehead. "There's no need for threats, Mr. Nash. If you'll just listen to what I have to say . . ."

The man's hand pushed on the screen. "Ain't no threat. It's a promise. Now git off my porch."

Andrew backed toward the steps. "All right, if that's the way you want it. But I'll be back."

"Don't bother coming back. I ain't changin' my mind."

Andrew retreated down the steps and to his car. As he drove out of the yard, he glanced back. Ezra Nash, his body rigid and his hands clenched into fists, stood on the porch glaring at him.

A shaky breath trickled out of Andrew's body. They'd told him the people who hadn't sold their land would be difficult to deal with, but he'd been sure he could handle them. Now he wasn't so sure. Over the next few days he had visits planned to Thomas Bennett's and Joseph Prince's farms. He hoped they'd be different. For now he thought he'd better head back to the CCC camp and reevaluate his approach to the good folks of Cades Cove.

● ● ●

By Wednesday, Andrew was ready to throw up his hands in surrender and slink into Washington like a defeated general returning from war. What was he thinking when he took this job?

From five hundred miles away in the nation's capital this job appeared to be just a matter of tying up a few loose ends. For a smart college boy who'd been one of the best at getting his point across on the school debate team these mountain folks would be easy pickings. He had figured it might take him a month—six weeks at the most— to get the signatures of the twenty-four remaining families on the bills of sale.

Now he was here, and it was nothing like what he'd thought. His visits on Tuesday with Thomas Bennett and Joseph Prince had ended as badly as had the one at the Nash farm on Monday.

Now it was a new day, and he was on his way to Nate Hopkins's farm. He knew the elderly man was a widower with no family left. He had to realize that selling his land and settling some-where else where he could be close to neighbors would be the best thing for him.

Andrew pulled to a stop at the small cabin where Nate lived and looked around. The front porch sagged, and the roof looked like it needed repairing. The fields surrounding the cabin hadn't been planted this year. All appearances pointed to the fact that Nate could no longer keep up with the work required to run this farm.

Andrew made it about halfway to the front porch before the door opened and a wiry little man with stooped shoulders stepped outside. A few strands of white hair framed his bald head and his mouth was barely visible behind his bushy white beard. Andrew's eyes widened, not at the man's appearance but at what he held.

Nate's finger curled around the trigger of a shotgun that he had pointed straight at Andrew's head. "Get off my land, government man!" he shouted.

Andrew took a step back. "Please put the gun down, Mr. Hopkins. I just want to talk with you."

"I don't have time to talk to nobody a-wantin' to steal my land. Now git!"

Andrew held out a hand and shook his head. "Now, Mr. Hopkins, I know you're not the kind of person who would murder a man in cold blood. Please put the gun down and let me talk to you."

The man's forehead wrinkled, and he nodded. "You're right. I'm not gonna kill you. Couldn't live with myself if I took a man's life." His eyes shifted to Andrew's car, and he aimed the gun at the front tires. "But I shore don't mind killin' your car. I reckon this old gun could do a lot of damage to a good-lookin' car like that."

"Please, Mr. Hopkins, don't do that."

He raised the gun and took aim. "I reckon you got 'bout thirty seconds to git in that there contraption and hightail it outta here. And I'm a-countin'. One, two, three . . ."

Andrew ran to the car, cranked the engine, and roared out of the yard. As he pulled onto the road, he heard Nate Hopkins's voice once more. "And don't come back."

Seething at how he'd let the elderly Mr. Hopkins make him run like a frightened rabbit, he sped along the Cove road on his way back to the CCC camp. He needed to talk to somebody about how to approach these stubborn people. But who? Most of the men were out on work crews, and the ones left behind had jobs to complete at the camp. Even Lieutenant Gray was away from his office today.

At that moment a familiar cabin came into sight, and the answer popped into his head. Simon Martin was the man to give him advice. He knew everybody in the Cove better than anyone else did. Granted, he didn't want to see Andrew successful in making his friends sell their land, but at least he could explain what it took to get them to have a conversation with him.

He slowed the car and turned into the yard of Simon and Anna's cabin. A voice from the front porch greeted him as he climbed out of the vehicle. "Well, if it ain't our visitor from Washington. Good to see you, Andrew. Come up on the porch and keep an old lady comp'ny."

He laughed, climbed the steps, and sat down in

the rocker next to Granny. "Thanks, Granny. You're the first Cove resident I've seen today that's had a kind word for me." He leaned over the arm of the chair and frowned. "You don't have a shotgun hidden anywhere, do you?"

Granny threw back her head and laughed. "Land's sakes, no, boy. But in my day I could shoot as straight as any man in the Cove."

He shook his head and leaned back in his chair. "I don't doubt that for a minute." He glanced over his shoulder at the door to the cabin. "I stopped by to see Simon. Is he here?"

"No. On Wednesday he and Anna visit folks. 'Course now they don't have as many visits to make. When Anna was deliverin' babies, they had somewhere to go all the time. Now all the young women are gone from the Cove and there ain't no babies bein' born here anymore." Granny's shoulders drooped, and she wiped at her eyes. "It shore ain't like it used to be around here."

Andrew wanted to say something to break the veil of sadness that had descended over Granny, but his mind was a blank. He suddenly remembered how careful all the family had been on Sunday as they helped Granny move about the cabin. Yet today with Simon and Anna gone she sat on the front porch alone.

"Granny, how did you get out here on the porch?"

"Simon and Anna helped me out here before they left."

He stiffened in surprise. "How would you get up from the chair if you needed to go inside?"

Her lips curled up in a playful grin. "I guess I would ask Laurel to help me since she's staying with me this afternoon."

His eyebrows arched, and he grabbed the arms of the rocker. "Laurel's here?" He jerked his head around and stared at the cabin door. "Where is she?"

"She's in the kitchen. Her mama sent over two quarts of the grape juice she made last year. Laurel's inside gettin' me a glass of it. Why don't you go tell her you're here? I bet you're mighty thirsty after driving over our dusty roads and could use a cool drink yourself."

Andrew pushed to his feet and glanced at the door and back at Granny. "I-I don't know, Granny. Maybe I'd better leave. Laurel made it clear on Sunday that she doesn't want to have anything to do with me."

Granny rocked back and forth a few times as she stared at Andrew. "I see. And how do you feel about that?"

His eyes grew large, and he swallowed. "I told her I'd like for us to be friends, but I don't think I want to hear her tell me again she's not interested in that."

Granny nodded. "I kin understand why that might put you off a bit. That girl can be mighty fierce in what she says sometimes. Takes after her mama in that way. But you ain't afeared of a little girl like her, are you? I 'spect you can stand your own ground right good."

He started to tell Granny he thought it better to leave things the way they were, but his tongue refused to cooperate. As he stared at Granny, he remembered how his knees had grown weak when he saw Laurel in Gatlinburg. Then how he'd enjoyed sitting next to her in church. He liked her, and she'd led him to believe she liked him too . . . until she'd found out about his job.

Well, he wasn't about to let her have the last word on this issue. For the last two days he'd had doors slammed in his face, had curses hurled at him, and had faced a shotgun-wielding mountain man. Surely he could dredge up enough courage to have a conversation with Laurel.

He clenched his fists at his side. "I think I can do that, Granny." Without saying another word, he marched into the house and stopped at the kitchen door. Laurel had her back to him and was pouring grape juice from a pitcher into a glass. He took a deep breath and opened his mouth to speak to her, and the words rushed from his throat in a booming voice. "Laurel, I'd like to talk to you."

She squealed a high-pitched scream and jumped. The pitcher slipped from her hand and left a swath of purple down her white dress before it crashed to the floor and shattered. Grape juice ran in rivulets across Anna's kitchen floor.

Andrew stared in shock at the scene before him.

A stunned Laurel, her arms spread to her sides, stared at her stained dress and the grape juice that had now run under the kitchen table before she looked up at him. Her mouth moved, but no words came out. Then a slow change began to emerge on her face.

Her eyes narrowed, and her eyebrows pulled down across her nose. Her jaw turned rigid, and her teeth clenched. "Andrew Brady," she snarled, "what do you mean scaring me like that?"

He wished he could run from the wrath evident on her face, but his feet felt rooted to the spot. "I . . . I didn't mean to scare you, Laurel. My voice came out louder than I meant."

She took a step toward him and her foot slipped in the juice on the floor. With a gasp she grabbed for the back of a chair at the table and caught herself. She straightened, looked at her dress again, and then glared at Andrew. "Look at my dress. It's ruined. I'll never get this stain out."

A dish towel lay on the kitchen table. Andrew grabbed it and took a step toward her. "Here. Let me help you wipe it off your dress."

She recoiled as he neared her, then reached out and jerked the towel from his hands. "You've done quite enough to help me today." She swiped the towel down the front of her dress, but the juice had already seeped through the material. She glanced up at him, her lips trembling. "This was my favorite dress. I don't guess I'll be wearing it anymore."

Andrew's heart plummeted to the pit of his stomach. "Laurel, please forgive me. All I wanted was to talk to you. I didn't mean to scare you." He raked his hand through his hair. "Oh, I feel awful. What can I do to make it up to you?"

She glanced down at the juice on the floor. "Well, to start with you can help me clean up this floor."

"Of course. But you sit down and let me do it." He unbuttoned his shirt cuffs and rolled his sleeves up to his elbows.

"No, I'll help."

He shook his head. "I'll feel better if you'll just let me clean this mess up by myself." He pulled a chair out of the puddle of juice on the floor and set it against the wall. "Now sit down here, and I'll have this cleaned up in no time at all."

She eyed the purple pools of juice on the floor and then glanced at the wall where it had spattered. "Are you sure you can do it?"

"Of course I can. I've cleaned up worse. Now do like I said and sit down."

She glanced at the floor again before she eased into the chair. "Well, okay, if you're sure."

Andrew put his hands on his hips and glanced at the kettle on the stove. "I see there's some hot water. Where can I find a pan to pour some in?"

"In the bottom of the dry sink. Just open the door underneath and pull one out."

"The what?"

"The dry sink."

"I don't know what that is. Where is it?"

"It's right there beside you." With a sigh Laurel pushed herself up from the chair, sidestepped the juice by the table, and walked over to the dry sink. She opened the door underneath and pulled out a pan. "Here's one you can use."

Andrew took it and nodded. "Thanks. Now you sit down and let me take care of this." He set the pan on the table and poured some water from the kettle in it. Then he glanced back at the dry sink and frowned. "I don't see any soap. Where does your grandmother keep it?"

"Look on the shelf above the sink."

He let his gaze drift over the items on the shelf and shook his head. "There isn't any here."

Laurel got up and came over to where he stood. She pushed up on her tiptoes and pulled a box of soap powder from behind a can of coffee. "Here it is."

"Thanks, I didn't see it."

Laurel headed back to the chair, but before she could sit down Andrew stopped her. "Where can I find some cloths to use?"

She turned and stared at him for a moment before her lips twitched and pulled into a big grin. "Andrew, there's no need for me to sit down if

I'm going to have to keep getting up to help you help me."

"No, now you sit back down . . ." He stopped babbling as his gaze drifted over her face. The anger was gone now and had been replaced by a smile, and his heart thumped in his chest. He walked over to where she stood and stopped in front of her. "I'm really sorry I scared you, Laurel. All I wanted was to talk to you about what you said Sunday."

Her long lashes fluttered and his skin warmed. She tilted her head to one side. "I've wanted to talk to you too."

"You have?"

She nodded. "I'm afraid I behaved rather badly. You asked me to be your friend, and I refused when I really wanted to say yes. Can you forgive me?"

"There's nothing to forgive, Laurel. I understand why you wouldn't like me. But please believe me when I say I don't want to hurt your family in any way. I've been sent here to do a job. Please try to like me in spite of it."

Her dark eyes sparkled. "But I do like you, Andrew. That's what I wanted to tell you, and I'd like to get to know you better while you're in the Cove."

His heart pounded so that he thought his chest might burst. "Do you really mean that?"

"Yes."

"I want that too." He reached for her hand, and she threaded her fingers through his. His head was spinning from her nearness and the sweet smell of lavender mixed with grape juice. "I think about you all the time, Laurel," he whispered.

Her eyes grew large. "Really?"

"Yes, I've never . . ."

"Laurel!" Granny's shout from the front porch shattered the moment between them.

She pulled her hand away and hurried to the kitchen door. "Yes, Granny?"

"What's keeping you two so long?"

"I spilled the grape juice. We're cleaning it up. We'll be out in a few minutes."

"No hurry," Granny hollered. "I just wondered what was a-goin' on."

Laurel turned back to him and smiled. "I think we better get this mess cleaned up before my grandparents get back. And I think it'll get done faster if we work together."

Andrew grinned. "Whatever you say, ma'am. I'm just glad to be here with you."

Her cheeks flushed, and she lowered her gaze to the floor. "I'm glad you're here."

Andrew took a deep breath and poured some more water in the pan. "Let's get Anna's kitchen back to normal."

She laughed, and the sound sent a thrill through him like he'd never felt before. Everything he'd endured in the last two days was worth the reward of being with Laurel at this moment. Later he would try and figure out his new emotions, but for now he just wanted to enjoy being with her.

With the kitchen cleaned up Laurel and Andrew sat on the front porch with Granny. Laurel drank the last drop of grape juice from her glass and set it down beside her chair. "I'm glad Mama sent two quarts of juice today. We wouldn't have had any otherwise."

Granny chuckled and handed Laurel her glass. "I shore would have liked to see Laurel's face when that pitcher hit the floor."

Andrew shook his head. "Oh, no, Granny. Like you said earlier, Laurel can be fierce at times, but I expect she'd never been as mad as she was then."

Laurel sat up straight in her chair and stared at him. "Fierce? Granny said I was fierce?"

Andrew held up his hands as if to ward off her blows and laughed. "Oh, Granny, I've done it now. We're about to see how fierce she can really be."

Granny chuckled and nodded. "Yeah, like I said, she shore does take after her mama. That girl's tongue could make the bark on a tree curl up."

Laurel sank back in her chair and laughed. "I've heard you say that before, but I never thought I was that much like her."

Granny reached over and patted her arm. "As

far as I'm concerned, the best compliment I could ever give you is to say you're like Rani. I've loved that girl since the day I brought her into this here world. And your pa too." She stared past Laurel to Andrew. "You know I was the midwife in the Cove until I turned my work over to Anna. Between the two of us, there ain't no tellin' how many babies we delivered."

"That's really something, Granny," he said. "And I agree with you. I only met Mrs. Jackson Sunday, but I could tell she's a wonderful person." He stared back at Laurel. "And I think her daughter is too."

Laurel's heart skipped a beat and she sucked in her breath. She heard Granny chuckle, but she didn't turn to face her. At the moment she was enjoying staring into Andrew's dark eyes that appeared to be devouring her. A tingle of pleasure skipped up her arm, and she wondered why she had thought she could stay away from this man. There was some quality within him that pulled her to him.

Before she could find an answer to her puzzled emotions, a horse pulling a buggy trotted into the yard. Her grandparents were back from their visits. Instead of heading around the house toward the barn, her grandfather pulled the horse to a stop, climbed from the buggy, and tied the horse to a tree at the edge of the yard. He walked around to the other side of the buggy and helped her grandmother step down before they headed toward the porch.

"Afternoon, Andrew," her grandfather called out.

She and Andrew rose as her grandparents ascended the steps to the porch. Andrew stuck his hand out. "Hello, Simon. Anna. I stopped by to visit." He glanced at Anna. "You may have wished I hadn't when you see your kitchen."

Anna's eyebrows arched as she looked from him to Laurel. Her eyes fastened on the purple stain that covered the front of Laurel's dress from above the waist to the hem. "What happened to your dress?"

Laurel laughed and waved her hand in dismissal. "We had a little mishap with the grape juice, but thanks to Andrew your kitchen is back the way you like it."

Her grandmother's brow wrinkled. "Good. I think."

Andrew shuffled from one foot to another. "I'm really sorry about Laurel's dress. I hope the stain will come out."

Anna narrowed her eyes and studied the purple on the white dress. "We'll see." Then she glanced at Granny. "Did you make it all right while we were gone?"

"Just fine. I don't know when I've enjoyed anything like vis'tin' with these young folks. Reminds me of when you came to the Cove and how you and Simon kept me laughin' all the time."

Laurel glanced at Andrew, detecting a flush on his cheeks. She hoped Granny hadn't embarrassed him. She cleared her throat and directed her attention to her grandfather. "I think Andrew really came to see you, Grandpa. He's had a rough time this week with some of our neighbors, especially Nate Hopkins."

Her grandfather laughed and glanced at his wife. "That doesn't surprise me a bit. But I don't think you need to worry. He really wouldn't shoot you, although he might threaten to."

"He didn't threaten me, sir. It was my car."

"I see. I'll talk to him about that. I don't want him to accidentally hurt you or himself."

Andrew nodded. "I don't either. But no one will even talk to me, Simon. I hope you know I'm not here to hurt anyone or try to steal their land from them. They do need to hear what I have to say, though, even if they don't like the message."

Her grandfather furrowed his brow and nodded. He didn't speak for a long moment. Finally he took a deep breath. "How about if I arrange a community meeting of all the remaining families? We can have it at the church, and you can address everybody at one time."

Relief shone on Andrew's face. "I would really appreciate that."

Simon held up a hand and cocked his head to one side. "I will tell you as well as my friends that this will be an orderly meeting. There will be no arguing, no name-calling, and no guns. Anyone can say what's on their mind as long as it's done in a peaceful manner."

"I would agree to that." He stuck out his hand. "I don't know how to thank you."

Her grandfather grasped his hand. "You do understand I will not support you at this meeting, but I will see to it that you get your chance to address everybody."

"I understand, and I still thank you."

The rocking chair creaked, and Granny scooted to the edge of the seat. "Now that we have that settled, how 'bout somebody a-helpin' an old woman back in the house? I 'spect I'd like to take a little nap before I help Anna cook supper."

Nana bit down on her lip, but it didn't stop the smile from escaping as she and Grandpa helped Granny to her feet. "Don't sleep too long. You know I can't cook without you sitting at the table giving me instructions."

A little groan rippled from Granny's mouth as she stood. "You make me sound like a smart aleck, missy. Don't you forget who taught you how to cook."

"How can I? You never quit reminding me." Both of them burst out laughing, and Nana gave Granny a quick hug. "And you were the best teacher any girl could ever have."

Seeing them together and the easy manner in which they joked with each other touched Laurel's heart. She was glad Andrew had gotten to see the love her family had for each other. Maybe it would help him understand how they needed to stay together in this valley where their roots went back for generations. The thought of facing the unknown in the world outside the mountains that sheltered their valley filled her with more fear than she'd ever known in her life.

As her grandparents moved toward the door with Granny, she glanced at the sky and was startled to see that the sun had begun to sink into the west. "Oh, I didn't realize how late it was getting. I need to get home."

Before she could take a step, Andrew was at her side. "How far do you live from here?"

"About a mile and a half."

"Did you walk here this afternoon?"

She laughed. "Of course I did. I've always walked everywhere I went in the Cove."

Andrew glanced past her to her grandfather who had now reached the front door. "Simon, I'd like to ask your permission to take Laurel home in my car."

All three stopped and looked back over their shoulders. Laurel's grandparents exchanged quick glances. "Well, Andrew, I don't . . ." Simon began.

Andrew took a step nearer them. "I promise I'll take her right home and deliver her to her front door safely. It's the least I can do after ruining her dress."

Granny sighed and elbowed Simon in the ribs. "Oh, go on, Simon. The boy just wants to make amends for ruinin' Laurel's dress. Besides, it's gettin' late, and Matthew will be worried. I wouldn't doubt them meetin' him on the road on his way over to see what's keepin' her."

Anna gave a slight nod of her head, and Simon exhaled. "All right. But no stopping along the way. Take her straight home and nowhere else. Understand?"

"Yes, sir. I understand. You can trust me." He turned back to Laurel. "Are you ready to go?"

She nodded and hoped he couldn't see the excitement in her eyes. When she'd left home earlier, she wouldn't have dreamed she'd be returning in Andrew's car. She dashed over to her grandfather and gave him a kiss on the cheek. Then she kissed Nana and turned to Granny. "Thank you, Granny," she whispered in her ear before she kissed her cheek.

Granny winked at her before the three of them disappeared inside the house. With her heart pounding in her chest, Laurel turned back to Andrew. "I'm ready to go."

He smiled, made a sweeping bow toward the car, and extended his arm toward her. "Your ride awaits, madam. May I escort you down the steps?"

She laughed and looped her arm through his. Together they descended the stairs and walked to the car. When they were settled inside, she swiveled in her seat to face him. "This is a very nice car. Is it new?"

He nodded and cranked the engine. "My father bought it for me right before I left home." He wrapped his fingers around the steering wheel and stared at them for a moment before he looked back at her. "You're the first person to ride in it with me."

The pulse in her neck felt as if it would burst through her skin. She clasped her hands in her lap and directed a shaky smile at him. "I'm glad."

"So am I," he whispered before he eased out on the clutch and drove into the road.

Chapter 7

The trip to Laurel's home was over far too quickly for Andrew's liking. They'd spoken little on their way here. He could hardly speak because his chest squeezed so tight every time he glanced at her that he could barely breathe. He doubted she felt the same way, but a little smile had pulled at her lips the entire way here.

He pulled off the road where she directed and drove past a small log cabin with a sign that identified this place as the home of Mountain Laurel Pottery. He chuckled and pointed to the cabin. "So that's your mother's studio."

"Yes. My father built this cabin when he moved back to the Cove, and this is where they lived after they married. In fact I was born in that cabin." She pointed to a large house that sat perhaps five hundred feet down the road from the cabin. "That's where we live now. Poppa built it when I was about five. Our lodge is to the left of our house and nearer to the creek at the back of the farm."

He studied the large white house as he drove toward it. This was no cabin. It was a large, two-story white house that one might see in neighborhoods in any American city. He pulled to a stop in front of the house. "So this is where the Jackson family lives."

"Yes, this is our home."

The emphasis she put on the word *home* wasn't lost on him. He realized she wanted him to know how important this place was to her. "It's beautiful. I can see why you love it." He turned in his seat to face her. "I've really been unhappy about how we parted on Sunday. I'm glad I stopped by your grandparents' home today."

"I am too."

"When I left you at the store in Gatlinburg, I realized I hadn't asked your last name, but I remembered the name of your mother's studio. I asked the clerk at the hotel if he knew where it was, but he didn't."

Her eyebrows arched. "You did?"

He nodded. "I felt sure I could find you again,

but I didn't expect it to be at church the next day."

She tilted her head to one side. "Why did you want to find me?"

"I don't know. I just knew I had to."

She swallowed. "I'm glad you did."

He wanted to reach out and caress her braid, but he willed his fingers to be still. "I'd like to see you again, Laurel. Do you think your folks would object if I came over after supper one night to visit?"

"I don't think so. They seemed to like you fine last Sunday."

"They were being nice to me because I was a stranger in the Cove. This is different. They may not want me to come again if they think I'm interested in their daughter."

"A-are you interested in me?"

"Yes. I am." The words came out in a rush. "I definitely am."

"Then I'd say the decision is up to me, not my parents, whether you can come again or not. After all, I'm eighteen years old, and this is 1935. Things have changed in the world. I don't need my parents' permission to make friends with someone."

"Laurel, I would never dishonor you by asking you to go behind your parents' backs on anything. I'll only come back if your father gives me his permission. Do you think he's here so I could speak to him?"

She smiled. "He's here and now's your chance. I see him coming around the side of the house."

Andrew jumped out of the car and ran around to open Laurel's door. She laughed and stepped out beside him just as her father stopped, facing them. His eyes held a questioning look.

"Laurel, I was just about to start over to Simon's to see what was keeping you."

"Grandpa and Nana were a little late getting back, and Andrew offered to drive me home."

Andrew swallowed and glanced at her before speaking. "I asked Simon's permission to bring her home, Matthew, and he said I could."

"I see." Her father's gaze drifted down to her dress, and he frowned. "What happened to your dress?"

Laurel slid her hand down the purple stain and chuckled. "I spilled the grape juice Mama sent to Granny."

Andrew took a half step closer to her father. "It was my fault. I startled Laurel, and she dropped the pitcher. But we got the kitchen cleaned up."

Her father's eyebrows arched. "Did you now?" He glanced at Laurel. "Anything else happen while you were gone?"

"No." Then her eyes lit up. "Oh, yes. Grandpa is going to arrange a meeting of all the residents so Andrew can talk to them and explain the government's point of view."

Her father's eyebrows arched. "Oh, he is?"

Andrew nodded. "Yes, and I really appreciate it. I hope you'll come to the meeting."

"I'll be there. If anybody's going to talk about taking my farm, you can depend on me being there."

"Good. I'm glad to hear that." He took a deep breath and glanced back at Laurel before he spoke again. "Matthew, there's something else I'd like to ask."

"What's that?"

Andrew straightened his shoulders. "I wanted to ask your permission to come back and visit with Laurel. I really do like your daughter, and I want to get to know her better. If we were in a town like Knoxville or Asheville, I'd ask her out to supper and take her to a movie, but I can't do that here. So I would like to come to your home and spend some time getting to know her."

Her father's brow wrinkled, and he pushed the straw hat he wore back on his head. "Andrew, you seem like a nice young man, but you and Laurel come from two different worlds. She's lived an isolated life here in the Cove and doesn't know much about the ways of people outside these mountains. I'm not sure being friends with you would be in her best interests."

"I understand how you feel," Andrew said. "But please know I respect your daughter, and I would never do anything to hurt her. I just want to get to know her better."

Andrew's legs trembled from the stare Matthew directed at him. After a moment he turned to his daughter. "How do you feel, Laurel? Do you want this?"

She nodded. "Yes, Poppa. I do."

Her father sighed and shook his head. "Then very well, but be careful. I'd hate to see either one of you hurt."

Andrew stuck out his hand. "Thank you, sir. I appreciate it."

Laurel smiled at her father. "Thank you, Poppa."

He gave a snort of disgust. "Don't go thanking me for something that may be the worst decision I ever made." He glanced at the house. "Now I'll go on in and see if your mama needs any help with supper. You say your goodbyes to Andrew and then come on in."

Neither Andrew nor Laurel spoke until he had entered the house. Then Andrew wiped his sleeve across his forehead. "Well, that didn't go too badly. Can I come back to see you tomorrow night?"

She nodded. "I'd like that."

He walked back and opened the driver's side door of the car. Before he got in, he hesitated and stared at her over the roof of the car. His gaze raked the braid that hung over her shoulder. His Adam's apple twitched, and another bead of perspiration trickled down the side of his face.

"I really am sorry about your dress, Laurel."

He smiled, climbed into the car, and slowly

drove away from the house. He glanced in the rearview mirror and saw her still standing where he'd left her. His stomach clenched when she reached up and stroked her braid. That sight would probably keep him awake tonight—that and the anticipation of seeing her again tomorrow.

He didn't understand these strange feelings Laurel evoked in him, but he did know one thing for sure. Something important had happened in his life the day he saw Laurel standing behind that pickup truck in Gatlinburg.

Matthew heard the loud voices before he reached the kitchen. Rani and Charlie were again engaged in one of their difference-of-opinion discussions, as Rani called them. Matthew groaned and rubbed his hands over his eyes. He'd had a busy day getting ready for the guests at the lodge, and he was hungry. All he wanted was to eat supper, take a nap in his favorite chair afterward, and wake up in time to go to bed. Instead he'd probably be playing referee between his wife and son for the remainder of the evening.

"We're not going to discuss this any further, Charlie." His wife's stern voice drifted through the kitchen door.

"But I want to talk about it." Matthew's ears pricked up at the anger in his son's voice.

"I've told you it's out of the question, and I don't want to discuss it." Rani's voice grew louder.

"I'm not a child anymore, Mama. I'm seventeen, and I should be able to make my own decisions. You know I want this, and I'm going to do it whether you like it or not."

"You most certainly are not. You're not of age yet, and you'd have to have your parents' signature. We're not about to sign anything for you right now."

"But that's not fair. It's like you're holding me a prisoner. When I'm eighteen I'll do it anyway."

"We'll face that when the time comes, but for now you're still living here. And as long as you do, you'll follow the rules your father and I have set."

"Well, I won't be here much longer if you continue to treat me like a child."

Matthew's heart dropped to the pit of his stomach. Rani and Charlie's arguments in the past had been heated, but they had never progressed to this point. Matthew stepped into the kitchen. "What's going on in here?"

Charlie and Rani faced each other in the middle of the room. Rani held a wooden spoon that she pointed like a weapon at Charlie's angry face. She dropped her arm to her side when she saw Matthew.

"Charlie and I are having a difference of opinion."

Matthew nodded. "I think all of our neighbors within a mile probably know that. What's this about?"

Charlie glared at him, and Rani shook her head. "It's nothing for you to worry about, Matthew. Charlie thinks I'm trying to keep him from growing up."

Matthew turned to his son. "And what do you want to do that your mother doesn't approve of ?"

Charlie darted a glance at his mother and lifted his chin. A defiant look flashed across his face. "I want to join the navy."

Matthew didn't know what he expected his son to say, but it definitely wasn't that. "The navy? Where did this come from? I haven't heard a word about that."

Rani sank down in one of the kitchen chairs and tossed the spoon onto the table. "You've had enough to worry about with our court case and trying to hold on to our land. I thought Charlie would get over wanting this, but he hasn't."

Matthew frowned and shook his head. "But why the navy?"

Charlie gritted his teeth and clenched his fists at his side. "Because I've always liked reading about ships, and I want to get out of this valley and see the world. The navy is my ticket to do that. I'm tired of feeling like I'm stuck in the middle of nowhere and missing out on what's going on outside these hills."

"But this is your home. Your mother and I worked hard to make this farm a success so we could leave it to our children. That's why I'm fighting to keep it—because I want you to have part of it."

Charlie shook his head. "Well, I don't want it. I hate this farm, and I hate living in the Cove. If you had any sense, you'd sell and get out of here before they come and force you out. You can't fight them forever, Poppa. Give up and take their money. Then we can put this farm and everything else in this valley out of our lives."

Rani jumped to her feet, grabbed both of Charlie's arms, and gave him a hard shake. "How dare you speak to your father like that? He loves you more than you'll ever know, and he's worked hard to give you what his father never gave him—love, a home, an inheritance. For you to speak to him like that breaks his heart, and it does mine too. You owe him an apology."

A crushing pain seized Matthew's chest, and he grabbed the back of one of the table chairs to steady himself. He gritted his teeth and took a deep breath. Rani and Charlie stood nose to nose a few steps away, but neither noticed his discomfort.

Charlie jerked free of his mother. "Well, I think both of you owe me an apology. You're making me stay in a place where I'm miserable and you won't let me make my own decisions about what's best for my life. But you can't do that forever." He pointed a finger in his mother's face. "I'll show you."

With that he turned and ran from the kitchen.

Rani rushed to the kitchen door. "Charlie!" The only answer was the slam of the front door.

The pain in Matthew's chest eased and he wiped at the perspiration on his brow. Rani sank down at the table, propped her elbows on the table, and covered her eyes with her hands. "I'm sorry you walked in on that. I've been trying to spare you this problem. I thought it would be one more of Charlie's whims that would pass with time, but it doesn't seem to go away." She reached over and covered his hand with hers. "And I'm really sorry he said he hates it here and doesn't want the farm. He didn't mean that."

Tears glistened in Rani's eyes, and Matthew squeezed her hand. "Yes, he did, Rani. I've always known this day would come. He's just like my father. I was struck speechless by how much he looked like him standing there arguing with you. For a moment I felt like that little boy again, listening to my father scream at my mother about how he hated living here, how we had ruined his life by tying him down, and how he was going to leave us so he could go see what was going on in the rest of the world."

A tear trickled down her cheek. "Matthew, I'm so sorry Charlie said those things."

He shook his head. "I couldn't change my father, and I can't change my son." He reached over and wiped the tear from her face. "Don't cry, Rani. I love you more today than I did the day we married. I just wanted us to raise a family and be happy on this little piece of land God gave us. Now we're going to lose it, but that seems like nothing in the face of losing our children."

Her eyes grew wide. "Matthew, we're not going to lose our children."

He sighed. "I think we already have, Rani. Charlie is stubborn. He won't give up any more than my pa ever would. We'll wake up one morning and Charlie will be gone just like my pa did so many times. It's not the navy he wants. He wants to get out and show the world he's a man. I hope he doesn't end up dead on some tavern floor like my father did."

Rani closed her eyes as fresh tears streamed down her face. "Oh, don't say that. I can't stand to think something like that."

"I know. Neither can I." He took a deep breath. "And then there's Laurel."

Rani's eyes popped open. "Laurel? What are you talking about?"

She listened without speaking while he told her of Laurel's afternoon. "Andrew seems like a nice young man, but he's different from Laurel. I'm afraid he'll hurt her. She's never known anything but life here, and he's lived very differently from her. He's only here for a short time, and I don't want her to get too attached to him. I just don't know how her sweet spirit can deal with a broken heart."

Rani got up from her chair and knelt beside Matthew. She reached up and smoothed his silver-streaked hair away from his face. "You're such a good man, Matthew, and I love you with all my heart. I don't know what the future holds for us, but I do know one thing. God won't abandon us. He's got good things coming our way. We just have to trust Him and see what He has planned for us."

Matthew nodded, leaned down, and kissed his wife. The pain in his chest had subsided, but it had been replaced by a nagging fear in the pit of his stomach. At that moment it became clear to him that life as they had known it in the Cove had come to an end. Soon his family would be scattered to the winds. He didn't know if he could bear it or not.

Charlie didn't appear for supper and Rani made excuses for him to Laurel and Willie. Matthew tried to enter into the conversation around the supper table, but he found his mind straying at times to the days when he and Rani were young and excited about the life they were building together. Then the thought would return that everything they'd accomplished had turned to sand and was trickling through his fingers.

Later when he lay beside Rani in bed, he listened to her steady breathing and thanked God for the strength her presence gave him. He kept an ear peeled for Charlie to come home, but he hadn't returned by the time Matthew drifted off to sleep.

At breakfast Rani informed him that Charlie's bed hadn't been slept in and some of his clothes were missing. Matthew nodded and continued to chew the mouthful of eggs that tasted as if they'd turned to dust in his mouth.

All day he hoped to see Charlie with a contrite look on his face walk back down the road to their house and act as if nothing had happened. But Charlie didn't come home. By supper time they had all arrived at the same conclusion. Charlie was gone and wasn't coming back.

Chapter 8

The house had been like a tomb all day long. Nobody spoke as they went about their chores. Every once in a while Laurel caught a glimmer of tears in her mother's eyes, and her heart pricked for the pain she had to be feeling.

How could Charlie hurt their parents so? And what about her and Willie? Did he care so little for them that he could leave without telling them goodbye?

Now with supper over she and her parents sat in the parlor, and the thick silence that covered the room threatened to crawl into her body and squeeze the life from her. She glanced at her parents and blinked back tears.

Her father sat in his favorite chair, his Bible open in front of him. Laurel was sure he hadn't turned a page since he'd first opened the book. Her mother sat across from him in another chair. She'd been mending the same sock for the last twenty minutes. Willie had slunk off to his room soon after supper, and she had no idea what he was up to. He seemed to be taking Charlie's departure harder than anyone else in the family.

Just when she thought she could bear the silence no longer, the roar of a car engine broke the silence. She jumped to her feet and ran to the open front door. Her heart pounded at the sight of Andrew's car approaching the house. She didn't move until the car had stopped and Andrew had climbed the steps to the front porch.

He smiled at her, and for the first time she noticed a dimple in his cheek. It winked at her, and her chest tightened. A sweet smell tickled her nose, a result of the pomade that gave a damp look to his slicked-back dark hair. She let her gaze travel to his broad shoulders and down his arms to the rolled-up sleeves below his elbows. His fingers flexed, a hint that he was as nervous about his visit as she was.

His gaze raked over her before he swallowed and spoke. "Hello, Laurel. I hope this is a good time for a visit."

She pushed the screen door open and smiled at

him. "Good evening, Andrew. Come on inside. Mama and Poppa are right here."

Her parents rose from their chairs as he entered the room, and Andrew stepped over to shake her father's hand. "Good evening, sir." He turned to her mother. "Good evening, Mrs. Jackson. It's good to see you again."

Her mother smiled. "Welcome to our home, Andrew." She motioned toward the sofa. "Have a seat."

He glanced around for Laurel, and with a smile she eased down on the sofa and patted the cushion next to her. "Yes, have a seat, Andrew."

He waited for her parents to be reseated before he dropped down beside her and cast a nervous glance in her direction. She almost laughed when he swallowed and his Adam's apple bobbed. He certainly didn't look like a confident government employee tonight. He looked more like a scared schoolboy. His gaze drifted around the room, and his eyes widened in surprise. "I really like your house. We have electricity at the CCC camp, but I didn't realize the homes in the Cove did."

Her father nodded. "I put in a Delco battery system when we opened the lodge. I thought that would make our guest rooms more comfortable. Of course we have tents for those who really want to rough it."

"I see." Andrew started to say something else, but he stopped and pointed toward a framed picture of a mountain covered with fall foliage. "That's a beautiful photograph."

"It's Mount Guyot, the second highest peak in the park. Laurel made that picture a few years ago," her father said.

Andrew stared at her, his eyes wide. "You made it?"

Her face grew warm, and she ducked her head. "Yes, one afternoon at sunset. It's one of my favorite photographs."

He stood up and walked over to study it more carefully. When he turned, he smiled and shook his head in disbelief. "It's absolutely amazing, Laurel. It looks so professional. Do you have more?"

She waved her hand in dismissal. "Lots of them. It's my hobby."

"It's more than a hobby," her mother said. "I've tried to get her to sell some of her photographs to our tourists, but I haven't been able to convince her."

Laurel shook her head. "I'm really not good enough for that."

"You know what your father and I think. You should . . . Well, never mind what we think." Her mother picked up her mending and then appeared to have second thoughts. She dropped the sock into her lap and straightened in her chair. "Have you had supper, Andrew? I can get you something to eat if you'd like."

He shook his head and returned to the sofa. "No, ma'am. Thank you. I ate with the men at the CCC camp."

"Maybe you'll want something later. Laurel made some delicious tea cakes earlier today. It's one of Granny's recipes."

He glanced at Laurel. "That sounds good. Maybe she'll let me have one later."

Her father closed his Bible and set it on the table next to his chair. "She might even let you have a glass of grape juice too."

Andrew's face turned red, and Laurel darted an angry glare at her father. She started to scold him, but the teasing glint in his eyes made her laugh instead. "Poppa, Andrew's not used to your joshing. You'll have him running back to the camp if you don't watch out."

Her father laughed. "I couldn't resist. It appears he's not yet over ruining your dress yesterday."

Andrew's shoulders relaxed, and he smiled. "I don't think I'll ever forget that awful experience. I was sure Laurel was going to pick up a pan and whack me on the head."

She arched an eyebrow. "I thought about it, but you were too remorseful for me to stay angry with you for long."

"I'm glad."

They sat in silence for a long minute before her father cleared his throat. "How was your day today, Andrew? Did anybody threaten you with a shotgun?"

Andrew laughed and shook his head. "Not today. I visited with Will Connor over on the far side of the Cove. He signed the paper to sell, so he'll be leaving in the next few weeks. And I talked with Bruce Jenkins. I think he's about ready to sell."

Her father exhaled, and Laurel winced at the momentary look of sorrow that flashed on his face. "So another one's given in. I should have expected it, though. Will's wife isn't well, and he wants to be nearer a doctor. Bruce's children have all left home, and he and his wife want to go over to Townsend to live near one of them." He sighed. "So the list of holdouts is getting shorter."

"Yes, sir. That leaves twenty-two families, but I hear Wayne Henderson is thinking about leaving."

A frown puckered her father's forehead. "If he sells, that will leave the core group who has been the most outspoken about selling. You'll have a hard time with all of us."

Andrew met her father's steady gaze. "I know that, sir."

No one spoke for a moment, and then her mother coughed. "How are things going for you over at the CCC camp, Andrew? Are they taking care of you?"

He leaned back on the sofa and smiled. "Yes, ma'am. Everybody has been very nice. The food's good, the people are nice, and the camp has a beautiful setting."

"Yes, it does," she said. "Have you met many people there?"

"A few. Mostly the people in charge, like Lieutenant Gray."

Her mother nodded. "He's a nice man. I also know a young man who's stationed at the camp. Have you met Jimmy Ferguson, by any chance?"

"The name's not familiar, but I haven't met many of the men."

Her mother smiled at Laurel. "Jimmy is the son of my best friend, and he's a special friend of Laurel's."

Andrew's face paled, and he turned a wide-eyed stare at Laurel. "A special friend?"

Laurel shook her head. "More like an older brother. We've been friends all our lives."

Her mother stood. "Josie, his mother, is coming tomorrow to spend a week with us. We haven't been together in quite a while so I'm looking forward to having her here. Jimmy will be here for the weekend too."

"Is that so?" Andrew muttered.

Laurel glared at her mother, who had pasted a sweet smile on her face. She might as well have said that she and Jimmy were engaged. Why did she do that? Before Laurel could speak, her father rose to his feet.

"Rani, I have some paperwork to do for the

lodge and I could use your help. Why don't we let Laurel and Andrew visit in here?" He grabbed his wife's arm and steered her toward the kitchen door. "It's good to see you, Andrew. Come again."

Andrew rose from his seat. "Thank you, Mr. Jackson. And you too, Mrs. Jackson."

When they had disappeared into the other room, Andrew sat back down and turned to her. "Is there something wrong? Your parents were friendly enough, but I sensed something when I came in."

She clasped her hands in her lap and wiggled her nose in an effort to keep the tears in her eyes from spilling down her cheeks. "It has nothing to do with you, Andrew. We've had something happen that has upset our family."

He scooted closer to her and took one of her hands in his. "I'm sorry, Laurel. Is there anything I can do to help?"

"I don't think anybody can help with this." She looked up into his face. "My brother Charlie has run away from home."

"What?" His mouth gaped open as if he couldn't believe what she'd just said. "When?"

"Sometime last night. Mama discovered him missing this morning when she went to wake him up. Mama and Poppa are both frantic, but they're trying to act as if nothing has happened. But I can tell."

He squeezed her hand. "Oh, Laurel. I'm so sorry. Did your father go look for him today?"

"No. He has no idea which way to go. Charlie's been telling Mama he wants to join the navy. If he tries that, he'll have to go to Sevierville. But he could have gone to Townsend and caught a train to anywhere."

"He can't join the military. He's not old enough. He'd have to have his parents' permission."

"Unless he lied about his age."

"Do you think he'd do that?"

She shrugged. "I don't know. Charlie's always had a hard time sticking to the truth. It's nearly driven Poppa crazy at times. If there's one thing Poppa expects from his family, it's honesty. He can't abide someone who lies, and neither can I."

"Maybe he'll see that being away from home isn't as exciting as it seems, and he'll come back."

"I hope so."

Laurel glanced down at his hand covering hers. His thumb rubbed back and forth across her knuckles. A warm rush spread through her body. She swallowed hard and straightened her back. "I wanted to explain about Jimmy Ferguson. Mama made it sound like there's something between us. That's not true, Andrew. Jimmy and I've known each other all our lives. Mama and Josie would like for it to be more, but it's not."

"I'm glad. I know we've only known each other for a few days, but I can't stand to think about you being interested in another man."

Her heart raced at the way his eyes bored into

hers. "And what about you? Is there a woman in your life?"

He released her hand and sighed. "Yes, there is."

When she'd asked the question, she hadn't expected that answer. She struggled to keep the shock from showing on her face, but she could see it reflected in the expression on his. She pushed to her feet and walked to the fireplace. She heard the sofa squeak as he rose to his feet, but she didn't turn around.

He walked over and stood behind her so close that she could feel his breath on her neck. "The minute I laid eyes on you I knew I had to know you better. You're in my thoughts all the time, and that's never happened to me before. I don't know what's going to happen between us, Laurel. Maybe nothing and then maybe something special. But you said a few minutes ago that you can't stand liars. So we can't begin any kind of relationship unless we're honest with each other. That's why I need to tell you about Lucy."

She straightened her shoulders and took a deep breath. "Her name is Lucy? Are you in love with her?"

He put his hands on her shoulders and turned her to face him. "No, I'm not in love with her any more than you are with Jimmy. Come sit down on the sofa and let me tell you about her." She hesitated, and his fingers tightened on her shoulders. "Please."

"All right," she said, and allowed him to lead her back to the sofa.

When they were settled again, he turned to her. "You don't know much about me, Laurel, but you need to. My father is a congressman in Virginia, and I've grown up in the world of politics. My father decided when I was a young boy that I would also enter that world when I grew up. But he doesn't have his sights set on my being a congressman. He wants me to go all the way to the White House. He's had a plan for my life since the day I was born—the schools I would attend, the philanthropic endeavors that would later earn me public support, the jobs I would need to give me experience. A good resume and background is needed to run for public office, you know."

His last words held a sarcastic tone, and she frowned. "You sound like it's not what you want."

He shook his head. "It's not, but that doesn't matter. It's what my father wants, and I've always known the course of my life was set."

"I don't understand. If he wants you in politics, why are you here?"

Andrew chuckled. "Are you kidding? Roosevelt is trying to get the country out of the depression and back on its feet. And he wants to preserve this country's natural beauty and create places for families to visit. Right now the Great Smoky Mountains National Park is a big priority in Washington, but as you know there are a few people who are standing in the way of the park completion."

She swallowed. "The people who live in Cades Cove."

He nodded. "Yes. I'm here now because my father was able to get me a job in the Park Service and pull some strings to get me this assignment. Just think how good it will look in years to come for me to be known as the one who was able to persuade the holdouts in Cades Cove to sell their land when others couldn't."

She let out a shaky breath. "I must say you've given me quite an interesting look at your background, Andrew. But what does that have to do with a woman named Lucy?"

His shoulders sagged. "My father expects me to come back home in the fall and begin making plans for my campaign for a seat in the Virginia statehouse next year, the next step in the plan. Lucy is part of the plan too. Her father is a senator from Virginia, and he knows all the right people who can help me. My father and hers expect us to announce our engagement at Christmas."

Laurel's head whirled from all Andrew had said. She felt like she had the day Grandpa's mule had kicked her in the stomach. Somehow, though, the pain she was feeling now was even worse than that had been.

"Then I suppose I should congratulate you on your upcoming marriage."

He shook his head. "No. I told you all that is my father's plan. Since I graduated from college, I've come to realize that's not what I want."

"What do you want?"

"The truth is I don't know what I want." He raked his hand through his hair. "In fact it makes me sick to think about running for office, but I can't make my father understand. And I don't love Lucy. I've never kissed her or even held her hand. Lucy has been raised with the thought that her role in life is to be the woman behind the man. She wants to be the wife of a powerful politician, and my father wants her for my wife."

"Then what are you going to do about it?"

"That's what I've been trying to figure out for months." He stood up and walked back to the fireplace. He braced his hand on the mantel and stared down at the blackened bricks. "My father's reasons for wanting me to come to the Smokies weren't the same as mine. I came because I wanted to be a part of preserving this great wilderness for generations to come. And I thought while I was here I could figure out what I wanted to do with my life."

She rose and stood beside him. "And what about your father and Lucy?"

"I've got to find a way to make my father understand, and I have to put a stop to any notions Lucy might have about us." He stared at Laurel a moment and then put his hands on her shoulders.

"Right now all I know is that I'm here with you, and you make me happy when you smile at me. I want to know you better. I know I've run the risk of you telling me to get out of your house and never come back, but I hope you won't do that. I had to be honest with you."

For her own sake she needed to tell him to leave. There was no way a simple mountain girl like her could compete with a sophisticated woman who'd grown up in a senator's home. It would be painful not to see Andrew again, but a broken heart would be worse. As she debated what to do, the only answer she could give came to mind. "Thank you for being honest with me. I hope you'll keep coming to see me. I want to spend time with you and get to know you better."

His eyes widened in surprise. "Do you mean it?"

"Yes, I do."

His arm slipped behind her shoulders, and he drew her closer. "I've never felt so drawn to anyone in my life as I do to you."

Her gaze didn't waver from his. "Neither have I."

He lowered his head, and his lips sought hers. She pressed closer and welcomed his hesitant kiss. At her acceptance, his arms tightened, and the kiss deepened. She drew back and gently pressed her hands against his chest. "We don't need to move too fast, Andrew."

He swallowed and nodded. "You're right. I'm sorry."

She pulled out of his embrace and smiled. "Don't be sorry. Let's just save this for another time."

His eyes lit up, and he laughed. "You can count on that, Miss Jackson."

At that moment the grandfather clock in the corner chimed the hour, and he frowned. "I'd better be going. I need to be at camp before lights-out." He smiled at her. "Want to walk me to the door?"

She looped her arm through his and smiled. "I would be glad to." When they got to the door, he started to open the screen, but she stopped him. "Do you have plans for Saturday?"

"No. Why?"

"Poppa has a group of tourists coming to the lodge for the weekend. He's taking them on a hike up to Gregory's Bald. I'm planning on going with them to take some pictures. Would you like to go with us? It'll give you a chance to see one of the most beautiful spots in the Cove."

"I'd love to go. What time should I be here?"

"Come about eight and wear comfortable shoes. It's a long walk up there."

"I'll see you then." She followed him onto the porch and watched as he walked to his car. Before he got in, he looked back at her and smiled. "I enjoyed being with you, Laurel."

"I enjoyed it too."

She stood on the porch until the car's taillights

had disappeared into the night. Then she closed her eyes and let the sounds of the Cove seep into her. An owl's hoot drifted on the night, and in the distance a dog barked. Frogs croaked down at the pond near the barn. The sounds in a city couldn't be nearly as relaxing and peaceful as what she'd known all her life. How could she live somewhere else amid strangers with a different kind of life from hers?

She didn't think she could do it, but the reality remained that before long that was exactly what would happen.

Chapter 9

Andrew had never seen a day more perfect for a hike. The warm sun penetrated the hazy mists of the mountain peaks this morning to provide one of the most breathtaking sights he'd ever encountered. Every day he spent in the Smokies brought a new love for his surroundings and a fascination for the wonders of nature. The temperature hadn't reached its high yet, and he wore a jacket. No doubt it would wind up in his backpack as the day wore on.

He leaned against the side of Matthew's truck and waited for him and Laurel to bring the last of the hiking gear from the house. The screen door banged open, and Laurel emerged on the front porch. A camera dangled from a strap around her neck and six canteens hung from her shoulders. She smiled as she came down the steps.

He rushed to help her, and she slid three canteens down her arm. "Where do you want to put these?" he asked.

"We'll put them in the back of the truck for now. Poppa's coming with the lunches. Then we'll drive down to the lodge and pick up the guests."

As she dropped the remaining three canteens in the truck, the screen door opened again. Andrew glanced up to see a tall young man standing on the porch. His short blond hair and his lean body reminded Andrew of the men he saw every day at the CCC camp. Whistling a tune, the young man hopped down the steps, jogged over to Laurel, and draped an arm around her shoulders.

Andrew's eyes narrowed. The man's relaxed attitude toward Laurel infuriated Andrew. What did this guy mean by touching her in such a friendly way? He glowered at him, but the man didn't acknowledge his presence. "I wish you weren't going on this hike, Laurel," he said. "I don't get to see you much and then when I come to visit, you run off."

As if Laurel sensed Andrew's discomfort, she wiggled out of the man's grasp and swatted at his arm. "Quit trying to make me feel guilty, Jimmy. You had a chance to come with us, and you chose not to."

"Only because I hiked up there last weekend with some fellows from the camp, and I didn't want to make that climb again. I thought you and I would have some time today to be together."

"We will. At supper tonight. In the meantime you can spend the day entertaining our mothers."

He arched his eyebrows and groaned. "Oh, when those two get together I run and hide. They're like two jaybirds trying to see who can chatter the loudest."

Laurel laughed and turned to Andrew. "I suppose you've guessed that this is my friend Jimmy Ferguson. His mother arrived from Tremont yesterday morning, and Jimmy got here last night from the CCC camp." She pointed to Andrew. "Jimmy, this is Andrew Brady. He's staying at the camp while he's in the Cove."

So this man with the smug grin on his face was the one Laurel's mother had mentioned, her *special friend*. He would like to wipe that cocky grin off Jimmy's face to let him know that Laurel was off-limits to him.

Jimmy stuck out his hand. "I've seen you in the mess hall at the camp, but you're usually with the officers. It's good to meet you, Andrew. I understand you're here to finish stealing the land from the folks in the Cove."

The grin hadn't disappeared from Jimmy's face, but the tone of his words grated on Andrew's nerves. He crooked his mouth in what he hoped was a nonchalant smile, grasped Jimmy's hand, and squeezed as tight as he could. "Steal? I thought I was here to help them get the most for their land they could."

The pressure from Jimmy's grip increased. "I reckon I ain't heard of anybody gettin' what their land's worth. You must have been talkin' to the wrong people."

Andrew struggled to keep from wincing and forced his hand to respond. "Oh? And who are the right people I should talk to?"

Jimmy's mouth hardened. "My grandparents would be a good start. My pa's folks sold out, and there's not a trace left that they ever lived there. The money they got for their land wasn't near enough to pay them for all the work and sweat they put into that place. Then my ma's folks are another story. They didn't get much for their farm, but they put what they got in the bank. Next thing they know, the bank's failed and all the money is gone. Now they're living with my ma at the hotel she runs in Tremont."

Andrew's knuckles were turning white. It felt as if the bones in his fingers would crack any moment. "I'm sorry to hear that. In case you haven't heard, we're in a depression, and banks everywhere are failing. Perhaps your grandfather should have chosen a better place to put his money."

Tension crackled in the air, and they stepped

closer until they stood toe-to-toe. Jimmy gritted his teeth. "Are you saying my grandpa's not smart enough to handle his own affairs?"

"No, I'm saying . . ."

Laurel grabbed their interlocked hands and shook them. "Jimmy, Andrew, quit acting like two little boys engaged in a war of wills."

Andrew glanced at her and loosened his grip. Jimmy let go of Andrew's hand and frowned. He raked his hand through his hair and let out a long breath. "I'm sorry, Laurel. I guess I got carried away. I just get so mad when I think about what the government has done to the folks I love. Now they're going to do it to your family too."

She propped her hands on her hips and glared from one to the other. "We live with the threat every day, Jimmy, but none of what's happened here is Andrew's fault. He was young when all this started, and he doesn't know what we've lived with for the past few years." Before Andrew could feel relief at her defense of him, she turned on him and glared. "And Andrew, you shouldn't be so quick to pass judgment on Jimmy's grandfather. He thought the bank was stable, but he was wrong."

Andrew let his arm dangle to his side, and he flexed his fingers. He dropped his gaze to the ground and dug his toe in the dirt. "I'm sorry for losing my temper, Laurel." He looked back up at Jimmy. "And I didn't mean to sound like I was judging your grandfather. I'm really sorry that happened to him."

Jimmy exhaled and took a step back from Andrew. "I am too. It seems he's always had a tough way to go in life, but there's not a better man anywhere. My other grandfather had one of the best farms in the Cove. I had this dream that someday I'd come back and help him farm it. Now he and my grandmother are living in a little house that's rammed right up to their neighbor. It's a far cry from the open spaces they've always known. It's about to kill them."

Andrew's anger at Jimmy vanished, and his heart pricked at the thought of what his family had suffered. "I'm really sorry for what your family has faced. I wish I could change things, but it's gone too far now. The park is a reality, and everybody who's left in the Cove is going to have to come to grips with that." He glanced at Laurel. "Even your family."

She lifted her chin and narrowed her eyes. "We know that, Andrew. But we don't have to do it today. Now, why don't we forget this silly wrestling contest the two of you had and try to enjoy this beautiful day? I'm looking forward to the hike, and I don't want anything to ruin it."

"Neither do I," Andrew said.

Jimmy rammed his hands in his pockets, tilted his head to one side, and looked at Andrew.

"Have you done much hiking in the mountains?"

"Not much. Why?"

A wicked gleam flashed in Jimmy's eye, and he smiled. "I just wondered. Better take it easy, city boy. That climb's been known to lay a lot of folks low. I'd just hate to see it happen to you."

Andrew returned Jimmy's somber stare. "I just bet you would. But thanks for the warning anyway."

The screen door slammed and Matthew stepped onto the porch. The box he carried contained the lunches Rani had made for the hikers and two more canteens dangled from his shoulders. Jimmy dashed back up the steps to him. "You need any help, Matthew?"

He nodded. "I left the first aid kit in the kitchen. I'd appreciate it if you'd get it for me."

"Anything to help out." He glanced at Andrew over his shoulder before he disappeared into the house.

Matthew stopped beside the truck and set the box in the back. "I think we're about ready to go. When Jimmy gets back with the first aid kit we'll drive down and get the guests at the lodge. There are five going on the hike, so they can ride in the back of the truck to the trail. You two can ride up front with me. I hope you're ready for a long hike, Andrew."

"I am. Thanks for letting me come along today, Matthew. I'm looking forward to it."

"It's something you won't ever forget. You two go on and get in the truck."

Andrew followed Laurel to the front of the truck, opened the door, and stepped back for her to get in. Before she stepped on the running board, she looked up at him and smiled. "Don't worry about the climb. Jimmy was getting his last jab at you, and Poppa just wanted to make you feel comfortable about the climb. It's really not as bad as they're making it seem. We always take our time with the guests. You'll make it fine."

He smiled at her. "Thanks, Laurel. I'm glad you invited me." He leaned forward and spoke softly. "And just between the two of us, I'm glad Jimmy isn't coming along. I couldn't stand it if I had to share your attention with him today."

Her cheeks flushed, and she dropped her gaze before she climbed in the truck. He inhaled a breath of fresh mountain air and hopped in beside her. It was a beautiful day, and he intended to enjoy every minute of it with the woman next to him.

The group of hikers stood beside the truck that her father had parked at the entrance to the Gregory's Bald Trail. As he did every time he guided their guests up the mountain, Poppa was acquainting them with what to expect today. Laurel let her gaze drift over the three people from Knoxville—a man, his wife, and teenage son—and the two brothers from the Asheville area. The Morris brothers had hiked several mountain trails with them before, but this was the first time for the family from Knoxville. It was also Andrew's first time. It would be interesting to see how he fared today on the climb.

Her father's voice drifted to her ears, and she directed her attention back to him. "I thought I would give you some information about this mountain before we start out. A bald is a type of mountain whose peak is covered with wild grass instead of trees like the other peaks in the range. It occurs naturally and stands out in the midst of other forested peaks. Gregory's Bald is named after one of the early settlers in the Cove, Russell Gregory. During the last century the farmers in the Cove sent their cattle up this mountain to graze in the spring and summer when the fields were needed for planting. The summit has an elevation of just under five thousand feet, and we're going to climb three thousand of those feet today for five and a half miles from where we're standing now. Do you have any questions before we start?"

The woman from Knoxville raised her hand. "How long will it take us to reach the summit?"

Her father slid the hat he wore back on his head. "I'm not going to push you. If I was with an experienced group, I'd say about two hours, but today I expect to make it in about three and a half hours. I have rest stops scheduled, but if you need one before I call it, let me know. This is your trip, and I want you to enjoy it."

The woman nodded. "Thanks."

Her father glanced around. "Each of you has a canteen, and you're carrying your lunch in your backpack. We'll eat at the summit, which is covered at this time of year with blooming flame azaleas. You'll think it's the most beautiful dining room you've ever had. Any more questions? If not, I'll take the lead. My daughter will bring up the rear. Let us know if you need anything."

He stepped onto the trail, and the hikers fell into step behind him. Laurel smiled at Andrew. "Are you ready?"

He nodded. "I can't wait. Let's go."

An hour later they stopped for the first rest period. After checking with their guests to see if there were any problems, Laurel dropped down to sit next to Andrew on a large rock that jutted out from the ground.

"Are you making it okay?" she asked.

He took a drink from his canteen and nodded. "I'm fine. The climb hasn't been too hard, and the changing scenery along the trail is gorgeous. Sometimes there are trees all around, and then the trail cuts through wild grass that's almost knee-high. And the colors of the azaleas are amazing."

"Wait until you see them at the summit. You've never seen anything like it."

He didn't answer right away. Instead he took

another drink of water and swallowed. "I had a brother who died. My parents brought us to the Smokies when we were children. I've always remembered how beautiful it was, but my memories haven't done these mountains justice. Every day I see something else that makes me realize what a treasure this mountain range is, and I want to see it protected and preserved for future generations."

"I want that too, Andrew."

A pained look crossed his face. "But that comes with a price, Laurel. And your family and others like Jimmy's grandparents have to pay a big part of that price by leaving the only homes you've ever known. I truly am sorry about that."

She blinked back tears. "I am too."

He reached for her hand and threaded his fingers through hers. "Please don't hate me because of that."

"I don't."

"Can you accept me for who I am and not as an agent of the department that wants to take your home away from your family?"

"I try not to blame you for what we're facing, but sometimes it's hard to do." They stared at each other for a moment before she pulled free and sighed. "I think Poppa is ready to move on. We'd better join the group."

He didn't speak as they fell into line with the other hikers and continued their climb up the mountain. As the trail grew steeper, Laurel tried to concentrate on each step, but her thoughts kept returning to Andrew and her conflicting emotions.

No other man had ever excited her like Andrew did. Just one glance from him had the power to make her knees grow weak and her heart flutter like the wings of a butterfly about to take flight. From the minute he carried those crates into Mr. Bryan's store she had been helpless to resist his smile.

On the other hand, she'd never felt such a need to distance herself from anyone as she did with him. He might not have started the exodus from the Cove, but he had come to make sure it was completed. For that reason alone she couldn't let her emotions get the better of her good judgment. He might not be her enemy, but he had allied himself with them. Besides, he would be going back to Virginia when his work was completed, and she had no idea where her family would be then.

Maybe Mama was right. She needed to find someone like Jimmy who shared her background and family values. Andrew certainly didn't possess either of those characteristics, and yet she couldn't forget the thrill of their brief kiss. Her warring emotions were keeping her awake at night, and she didn't know which one to embrace.

When they stopped for a second rest an hour later, she kept her distance from Andrew. Instead she sat next to the woman from Knoxville and listened to her talk about her older son, who was a student at the University of Tennessee.

Laurel tried to listen, but she couldn't help glancing at Andrew from time to time. He'd stretched out beside the path and had his eyes closed. When her father called out it was time to go, Andrew fell into step beside him as they pushed for the summit. She wondered if Andrew, too, had concerns about their friendship.

She shook her head to rid it of her troubling thoughts. Today wasn't the time to think about this. They had guests to entertain, and if her family was forced to leave the Cove, she might never have another opportunity to photograph the blooming azaleas on Gregory's Bald.

She took a deep breath and forced herself to focus on the steep trail in front of her.

Only a few more steps and he'd be at the summit. Andrew pushed his aching body up the last incline and emerged into a large, grassy meadow that stretched across the top of the mountain. White, red, yellow, coral, and pink azalea bushes dotted the area in the biggest burst of color he'd ever seen. For a moment all he could do was stand still and breathe in the cool mountain air and absorb the vibrant landscape. He'd made it to the top, a feat he'd wondered earlier today if he would be able to accomplish.

Matthew walked to the middle of the meadow and stared toward the horizon. Andrew stumbled to a stop beside him and sucked in his breath at the sight of the rolling mountain range that seemed to go on forever.

"I've never seen anything as beautiful in my life."

Matthew flexed his right arm and winced before he answered. "I remember the first time I came up here. I was just a boy, but I was almost struck dumb by the sight. I didn't think I'd ever feel that way again, but it's the same every time I make that climb. I can't get enough of looking at God's creation."

A slight frown pulled at Andrew's brow as he gazed out across the mountain range. "I've never thought much about God, but seeing this makes me wonder if He really does exist after all."

Matthew turned and gave him a startled look. "He knows you exist. Why would you doubt that He does?"

Andrew shrugged. "I don't know. I've just never seen any evidence that makes me believe He's real."

Matthew stared at Andrew with unblinking eyes, then pointed into the distance. "Look around you, Andrew. We're standing on a high peak in the middle of the Smoky Mountains. In that direction you can see North Carolina." He turned and looked into the distance behind him. "Over there is Cades Cove. Do you think all of this just happened? I don't. I believe that God knew exactly what He was doing when He created the earth and man to enjoy it."

Andrew let his gaze drift over the mountains again. "It's beautiful, that's for sure. But that still doesn't prove to me that it was all created by something that I can't see."

"No, you can't see Him. No one can, but if you believe, you can feel Him. I know I do." He was silent for a moment before he spoke again. "I had a rough start in life. My father was a drunk and an abuser of his family. When I was nine, he was killed in a tavern brawl. Then when I was fifteen, my mother and brother died. For years I was so filled with hate and anger that all I wanted to do was strike out at everybody in my path. I left a lot of injured and maybe a few dead men behind as I roamed around the country."

Andrew's body stiffened. "I can't believe that."

Matthew closed his eyes and swallowed hard. "I wish it wasn't true, but it is. I thought if I could get back to the Cove I would be all right. The problem was that trouble followed me back here too. It took Simon to make me understand that even when I'd turned my back on God, God hadn't forgotten about me. When I finally gave up all the pride and hurt in my life and humbled myself to God, He made me a new creature. He'll do the same for anybody who accepts Him. He can give you the strength to face every problem that comes your way."

Andrew thought about Matthew's words for a moment. "That sounds good, Matthew, but there's a problem with what you're telling me. You're a smart man. You know you're going to have to leave the Cove sooner or later. If God takes care of your problems, why hasn't He worked out a way for you to stay?"

Matthew chuckled and shook his head. "God never promised He'd give us everything we want. But He did promise He would be with us when we were going through the tough times. I don't know what's going to happen in the future, but I do know one thing. God will take care of me and my family no matter where we are, and that gives me the peace and strength to face each day that I live."

Andrew had never heard anyone speak with such conviction before, and certainly not a man who spoke of having a dark past. A new respect for Matthew flowed through him, and he shook his head in amazement. "I've never known anyone like you, Matthew. I've had some things happen in my life that cause me to lose sleep at night. I wish I had a little of the peace you talk about."

"You can. All you have to do is ask Jesus to come into your heart. You'll be surprised how He can change your life. But He's given you the choice to decide which you want—a life filled with uncertainty or a life lived with faith in Him."

"I wouldn't know where to start to change my way of thinking."

"You have to start with the Bible. I have an extra one. Are you coming to church tomorrow?"

Andrew nodded. "Yes, Simon is going to make an announcement about the meeting for me to address the people who still haven't sold their farms."

"Then I'll mark some places for you to read and give you the Bible. It can change your life, Andrew."

"Thank you. I appreciate it."

"Just read it with an open mind and allow the truth in its pages to fill your heart."

Matthew turned and walked back to the group of hikers that had settled beside a large azalea bush to eat their lunches. Andrew watched for a moment before he ambled across the meadow to a small outcropping of rock and sat down.

He wrapped his arms around his knees as he sat staring across the rolling mountains in the distance. A click sounded beside him, and he glanced around to see Laurel. Her camera rested in her hands.

He grinned at her. "Did you just take my picture?"

She dropped down beside him. "I did. You looked like you were deep in thought, and I couldn't resist capturing the moment on film."

"I could tell from the picture I saw at your house that you really have a gift for photography. How long have you been interested in it?"

She shrugged. "Ever since I can remember. I even have my own dark room. It's just a small closet that Poppa converted for me, but it fits my needs just fine. But I've taken so many pictures lately that I've gotten behind with my developing."

"Why?"

A faraway look flickered in her eyes. "Because I may not be in the Cove much longer, and I want to have the memories from my years here. When I'm an old woman, I want to show my grand-children what my life was like growing up here."

"It's nice to have good memories." He reached down and, as was his habit when he was deep in thought, rubbed the burn scar on the inside of his left arm.

She glanced down. "What's that?"

His fingers stilled, and he stared at the wrinkled spot on his skin for a moment. "A bad memory from my childhood."

She scooted closer. "Want to tell me about it?"

The memory of the night when he was six years old flashed in his mind, and he rubbed his hands over his eyes as if he could erase the scene. He'd tried to do that for years, but he doubted he would ever forget the accident that had scarred his soul as well as his body.

He swallowed and nodded. "I was six years old,

and my parents were having a party. I was supposed to be in bed asleep, but I got up and slipped downstairs to see what was going on. There was a candelabra sitting on top of a table in the hallway. The wax had run down the sides of the candle, and I wanted to break some of it off to play with. I reached for one of the candles and the candelabra tipped over. A lit candle landed on my chest and ignited my pajamas. I was in flames before I knew it. I ran through the house screaming. I could hear my father yelling for me to stop, but I kept running. Then somebody fell on me and pinned me to the floor. We rolled and rolled until all the fire was out, but I'd been burned on my stomach and chest. I still have some scars from that fire."

"Who caught you?"

"It was one of the waiters my father had hired for the night. He didn't even know me, but he saved my life that night. He suffered some burns, too. I never saw him again after that night, but I've never forgotten him."

"It sounds like he was a real hero. It makes you wonder why some people react more quickly when there's danger than others do."

"I've often wondered if I could do something like that—put my own life in danger to help someone else."

She covered the scar with her fingers. "You could."

He frowned at her. "How do you know?"

"Because I believe you're a good person."

No one had ever told him before he was a good person. Not family, not friends, no one. Not until a girl who'd grown up in a world far removed from everything he'd known had said it. What was it about this place and these people that made him long for something more in his life than the hollow world of money, politics, and social standing?

He looked out across the mountains again. "I think I'm just beginning to understand how wonderful your life must have been here in Cades Cove, Laurel. I envy you that."

"Didn't you have a happy life growing up?"

He rubbed his hands across his eyes and sighed. "I did until my brother drowned when our family was on a boat trip on the Potomac when I was twelve. Winston was the life of our family, the best big brother any boy could have. He was supposed to follow our father in politics, not me. But after Winston's death, my father became obsessed with the idea that his remaining son would follow in his footsteps."

"What about your mother? Does she feel the same way as your father?"

He sighed. "My mother died six months after Winston." He turned to face her. "I can't figure out a way of telling my father how I feel. He's well respected in Washington, but I hardly know him. If I don't follow the plan he has for my life, he'll cut me off without a cent. I don't know if I can survive on my own. The more I think about it, the more confused I become."

Laurel put her hand on his arm. "I wish I could help you."

He took a deep breath. "I've never known anybody like you and your family. You make me question things in my life that I never have before."

She frowned. "I don't understand what you mean."

"When I stopped at your church last Sunday, I only did it because I wanted to meet Simon Martin and Matthew Jackson. I expected them to order me off the property, but they didn't. Instead they welcomed me and even fed me. That was a surprise."

She laughed. "I hope you'll tell your superiors in Washington that we're not quite the monsters we're made out to be."

"No, you're not. You have a wonderful family. I've thought a lot about your grandfather's sermon. Just now your father told me a little about his early life and how God changed him. My father has never had a conversation like that with me." He swiveled to face her. "How can your father be so at peace when I know he has to be worried about losing the farm, not to mention your brother taking off like he did?"

"I know it must be hard for someone who

doesn't believe in God to understand how we feel. It's how I've lived all my life and how I want to live until I die. I'm convinced it's the only true way to find happiness."

He clasped her hand in his, pushed himself to his feet, and pulled her up to stand beside him. "It's let me know there's something lacking in my life. Maybe while I'm in the Cove, I can find out what it is."

Her eyes sparkled. "I hope you can, Andrew. I really hope you can."

Chapter 10

Rani stopped at the bedroom door, leaned against it, and folded her arms across her chest. A soft snore drifted across the room, and she smiled at the sight of Matthew sleeping peacefully in his favorite chair. His head rested against the back of the chair and one hand lay on the open Bible in his lap.

Her chest tightened as her gaze traveled over the man she had pledged her love to twenty years ago. His hair might be streaked with silver, but to her he was still the dashing young man who'd ridden into the Cove to reclaim the land that had once been his family's. He had stood against those who would have denied him a peaceful life in the Cove and had won.

Now he fought another battle for their land. Deep in their hearts they knew they would eventually lose, but Matthew had vowed to her he would hold fast as long as he could. But with each passing day they approached the time when they could no longer keep the government at bay.

She tiptoed to the chair and leaned over to kiss his cheek. Before she could make contact with him, a grimace covered his face and he jerked in his sleep. His hand grabbed at his chest as a soft moan escaped his lips.

Rani gasped, her eyes wide, as his body twitched and his mouth opened as if offering a silent plea. His fingers curled and crumpled the page of the Bible in his grasp. Then, as quickly as it had appeared, the spasm seemed to pass and he relaxed again. Frightened, she shook his arm. "Matthew, wake up."

His eyes flew open and he straightened in the chair. He frowned, and his wild-eyed stare gave him a disoriented look. "Wh-what is it?"

She grabbed the sides of his face and turned him toward her. "Are you all right?"

He blinked and swallowed. "I'm fine, Rani. What's the matter?"

"You were moaning in your sleep." She placed her hand on his forehead and frowned. "Your head is wet with perspiration. Are you sure you feel okay?"

He glanced down at the Bible and frowned when

he saw the torn page. He smoothed it out with his hands then laid it on the table next to the chair. "I'm fine. Maybe I was having a bad dream."

Rani shook her head. "It looked like you were in pain. Maybe you were dreaming that you were hurt. Do you remember feeling anything?"

He shook his head and pushed to his feet. "I don't remember, but I'm sure that's what it was. It's nothing to worry about. I'm sorry it scared you."

Tears flooded her eyes, and she flattened her palms on his chest. "Are you sure you're all right?"

He laughed and wrapped his arms around her. "I'm fine, just a little tired from that climb today. Every time I go up that mountain I think it's gotten higher than the time before."

His words eased her mind some, and she draped her arms around his neck. "Do you think it might be because you're not as young as you used to be?"

He leaned forward and rubbed his nose against hers. "You may be younger than me, but I can still keep up with you. I'm not an old man yet."

His words held a soothing tone, but it was the flicker of worry in his eyes that concerned her. She caressed his cheek. "You can't fool me, Matthew Jackson. I know you're worried to death about Charlie. I am too. Where do you think he could be?"

Matthew exhaled and shook his head. "I don't know." He frowned and tightened his grip on her. "But we can't give in to our worry for him. All we can do is place him in God's hands."

"I know, but he's my baby, Matthew. Do you remember the night he was born?"

His Adam's apple bobbed, and he brushed away the tear that trickled from her eye. "I do. It snowed so much that night I was afraid I wouldn't get back with your mother. I was so scared that you'd have that baby without anyone here to help you."

"But you got Mama here in time, just like I knew you would. You've never let me down."

"I've tried not to, but I'm beginning to wonder if I have now."

She drew back in surprise. "Don't say things like that. I won't have it. You're my rock. I couldn't live without you."

His eyes darkened. "I've been thinking . . ." He hesitated a moment. "I've been thinking that if I'd been a better father to Charlie he wouldn't have run away. What did I do wrong?"

Her heart constricted at the sad look that flashed across his face. "Oh, Matthew, you didn't do anything wrong. Don't start thinking you failed him like your father failed you. No boy could have had a better father than Charlie had. I'm just sorry he didn't recognize it. Someday he'll realize it."

He pulled her close to him and nuzzled her ear with his lips. "You always know how to lift my spirit, Rani. I don't know what I did to deserve you, but I sure am thankful God gave you to me."

She smiled and kissed his cheek. "No, I'm the one who's thankful. God's blessed us, and we have to keep trusting that He'll take care of Charlie wherever he is."

"I know."

"We're going to be all right, Matthew, no matter what happens with the farm and with Charlie."

He didn't say anything for a moment, and then he gave her a light kiss on the lips. "I know."

A shiver ran down Rani's spine. Instead of reassuring her, his somber words frightened her. For the first time she sensed that their life in this place was coming to an end. Matthew already knew it, but he had never let her see it until now. And it really wasn't what she saw. It was in the tone of his voice that she recognized the sound of Matthew's resolve crumbling.

She glanced up at his face, and she almost gasped aloud. A defeated look darkened his eyes. She had seen it twenty years ago when he'd been haunted by the memories of his past. Now that look had returned, but it wasn't the past he feared. It was the future.

Rani grasped his shoulders and forced him to look at her. "Are you giving up on trying to save our farm?"

He closed his eyes for a moment and pinched the bridge of his nose with his thumb and index finger. "We can't win, Rani. I think it's time we faced the facts. The government is going to get our land."

"But Matthew, we can't quit now. We've come too far."

He cupped her chin with his hand. "We've just prolonged the inevitable. When this started, I wanted to save our farm for our children. Now Charlie's gone to who-knows-where. It probably won't be long before Laurel is married and settled somewhere, and that just leaves Willie. It'll be years before he's old enough to take on the responsibility of this place."

"But he'll have you to teach him until he's old enough," she insisted.

Matthew shook his head. "There's no time left, Rani. No matter what we tell ourselves, we're not going to win our court case."

She grasped the front of his shirt in her fists and stared up at him. "Are you saying we're going to lose our farm?"

"Yes."

"But . . . but I kept hoping . . ."

He pulled one of her hands free from his shirt, raised it to his lips, and kissed her fingers. "We have to face it. It's time to think about where we'll go when we leave here."

The tears now streamed down her face. She

wiped at them with a quivering hand. "Please don't talk like this. We don't have to decide anything right now."

"We can't put off talking about it much longer. I need to know my family has somewhere to go."

"But where would that be? I've never given a thought to living somewhere else."

Matthew sat back down in the chair and pulled Rani onto his lap. "You know John Cowden, don't you?"

"Of course I do. He's that woodcarver who sells his pieces in downtown Gatlinburg."

He nodded. "I've talked to him several times when I've been in town, and he says he's tired of selling on the streets. He and some of his friends have come up with an idea to start a Gatlinburg Arts and Crafts Community out on that loop road where he lives outside of town. Tourism is only going to increase in the mountains now that the park has opened. That road out there is a natural area to set up a craftsmen's community, a place where people can visit shops and buy the crafts we've made in these mountains for generations. He's talked to a lot of the others, and they're ready to join him."

"That sounds like a good idea, but what does it have to do with us?"

"I think we ought to buy a piece of land along that road and set up Mountain Laurel Pottery there. We can build the shop for you to work in and sell your pottery and we can have a house behind it for us to live in. If the Community grows—and John thinks someday that road will be filled with businesses—we'll have the opportunity to reach more buyers than we'd ever have working here in the Cove."

She tilted her head. "I don't know. I do well with the pieces I sell at Mr. Bryan's store."

He cocked an eyebrow and shook his head. "You have a few shelves over there. Out there on that loop road you could have a whole shop for your pottery and large workrooms to use. It won't be like living here in Cades Cove, but we'll all be together. And that's the important thing."

"It sounds like it would be perfect for me, but what about you? What would you do?" She reached up and stroked his cheek, and he closed his eyes at her touch.

Covering her hand with his, he pulled her fingers to his lips and kissed each one. "I'd help you in the shop, and I could still guide groups on trips through the mountains. Think about this, Rani. It may be the best place for us to go. We could build the house big enough for Simon, Anna, and Granny to live with us."

She laid her head on his shoulder and snuggled closer. "I never thought we'd be having this conversation. I suppose if it comes to our leaving here, living in an arts and crafts community would be the best place for us. We could still have an income. And like you said, we'd be together."

"I have to go to Gatlinburg to see our lawyer this week. I'll check into the land that's available for sale out there. Then we can talk about it more."

"Have you talked to Papa about this?"

"No, but I will. He knows the end is near in the Cove. This may be the best solution for all of us."

"All right, Matthew. You know I'll support whatever you decide." She closed her eyes and inhaled the scent of soap on his jaw. The familiar smell made her feel safe. "I love you, Matthew."

"I love you too, Rani. I promise I'll take care of you."

Andrew had intended to get to church early today in hopes of seeing Laurel before services began, but oversleeping had put an end to that plan. His mood grew darker when he walked into the church and spotted Laurel seated between her father and Jimmy. Scowling, he slid into the pew behind the Jackson family.

Matthew glanced over his shoulder as Andrew took his seat. "Good morning, Andrew."

He nodded in answer. "Matthew." Then he gritted his teeth as Jimmy turned to face him.

Jimmy's grin grew bigger as he took in the angry expression on Andrew's face. "Hello, city boy. I hear you made it to the top of Gregory's Bald without falling off the mountain. Congratulations."

Andrew arched his eyebrows. "Thanks, Ferguson. I hope you weren't disappointed."

"No, just surprised. I didn't think you could make that climb."

Laurel shot a warning glance at Jimmy and then to Andrew. "Hush, you two. Remember where you are."

Jimmy's eyes grew wide and he held up his hand in front of his mouth. "Oops, I'm sorry, darlin'. My mama taught me better than to act like that in church." His face drew into a sympathetic frown. "But maybe I'd better leave Andrew alone. He don't look too good. What's the matter, Brady? Did you get up on the wrong side of the bed?"

Laurel's lips twitched and she elbowed Jimmy in the ribs. "Jimmy, I'm warning you."

He glanced back at Andrew and winked. "Oh, don't pay no attention to me, Laurel. I just wanted to see if I could get a rise out of old Andrew. And I think I did." He reached over and chucked Laurel under the chin. "But this sweet young thing is right. I shouldn't be carrying on this way in church."

A giggle rattled in Laurel's throat and she swatted at Jimmy's hand. "Jimmy, you are a rascal. Now settle down."

"I'm settling." Jimmy folded his hands in his lap and turned to face the front just as Simon emerged from a door at the side of the pulpit.

Andrew seethed with such anger that he

couldn't concentrate on Simon's sermon. He kept his eyes on Jimmy and Laurel throughout the service. They stood too close when they shared a hymnal. Jimmy's shoulder kept brushing hers when they stood to pray. And he glanced at her way too many times while Simon was preaching. By the time the service was coming to an end, Andrew was about to explode. If the benediction didn't come soon, he was afraid he would pull Jimmy over the seat and punch him in the face.

The congregation sang the last verse of the closing hymn and Simon stepped down from the pulpit. His gaze drifted over the congregation, and an uneasy feeling ran through Andrew. Simon cleared his throat. "I want to remind all of you there will be an informational meeting here at the church Wednesday night at seven o'clock. Mr. Andrew Brady, a representative of the Park Service, will speak to us about the purchase of our land by the government." Andrew's heart lurched at the silence that met Simon's statement. No one stirred. After a moment he continued. "This is an important meeting. I hope you will all be here. Please pass the word on to your neighbors who don't attend this church. We all need to hear what Mr. Brady has to say. Now let us be dismissed."

Andrew bowed his head, but he didn't hear a word of the closing prayer. He was too busy wondering if he would be able to get safely back up the aisle without being attacked by a church member. When the prayer was over, Andrew opened his eyes and met Jimmy's hostile glare.

"I wish I could come to that meeting, but I won't be able to leave the camp." His mouth hardened into a straight line. "I guess it don't make no matter, though. My family's done lost all their land in the Cove."

Andrew started to respond, but he glanced at Laurel first. The anger that was evident on Jimmy's face flickered in her eyes. His shoulders sagged like the breath had left his body. The truth of his situation in the Cove hit him with the force of a lightning strike.

No matter how much he wanted it otherwise, he was the enemy. None of the people in the Cove could understand how much he wished they weren't facing what was ahead for them. Not even Laurel, the one person whose friendship he longed for more than any other.

But it was more than her friendship he wanted. He wanted her to look at him with laughter in her eyes like she had looked at Jimmy today. He wanted her to feel his pain at what his job demanded. And he wanted her to put her arms around him and tell him she would stand by his side.

Even as he began to see clearly the truth about his relationship with the residents of the Cove, another truth hit him. One that made him sadder than anything he'd ever known. The reason he wanted those things from Laurel was because he was in love with her. He'd never believed love could explode into one's life in a moment, but that's exactly what had happened the day he saw her standing at the back of a truck in Gatlinburg.

Love was supposed to bring happiness to your life, but he doubted if his would. There were too many obstacles in the path between him and Laurel. The Jackson and Martin families might not realize it yet, but their days in Cades Cove were numbered. And when they left, he would be one of those they'd hold responsible. No way would Laurel ever love a man who had cost her family so much.

He glanced back at Jimmy, who was still glaring at him. "I'm really sorry for your family's loss, Jimmy. I wish it could have been different." He took a deep breath and nodded to Laurel. "Good day, Laurel."

With that he turned and strode up the aisle and out the door. He was almost to his car when he heard her calling. "Andrew, Andrew, wait."

He paused at the car door and turned to face her. She walked toward him and his heart pounded. The blue dress with white polka dots hit her midway between her ankles and her knees and it swished about her legs from the sway of her hips. The braid was gone today, and her hair was tied at the back of her neck with a white ribbon. She'd never looked more beautiful.

"What do you want, Laurel?"

A small frown pulled at her eyebrows, and she held out a Bible. "Poppa wanted me to give you this. He said he'd marked a few passages for you to read."

He reached for the Bible and his fingers brushed against hers. "Tell him thank you for me. I'll keep an open mind while I read it."

A questioning look flashed across her face, and she tilted her head. "Is something wrong, Andrew?"

"No. Why?"

She narrowed her eyes. "I don't know. You seem like you're upset about something. I hope you didn't take exception to anything Jimmy said. He was just kidding you."

"No, I understand about Jimmy."

A tiny smile pulled at her lips. "Good. Well, Mama told me to ask you if you'd like to come home with us for dinner. Jimmy's mother went over to stay with Granny today so Nana could come to church—Granny was feeling poorly today. After Poppa takes us home, he's going to drive over to bring them to our house too."

"Where's Jimmy going?"

"He's going home with us. He'll have to go back to camp this afternoon."

Andrew shook his head. "Tell your mother I appreciate the invitation, but I can't come today."

She studied his face for a moment. "It's not because Jimmy is going to be there, is it?"

"I don't mind telling you I don't want to spend the afternoon trading insults with Jimmy, but that's not the main reason."

She frowned. "Then what is the reason?"

"It doesn't matter."

She stepped closer. "It may not matter to you, but it does to me. You're refusing an invitation to my home. Why?"

He raked his hand through his hair and gritted his teeth. "You know as well as I do, Laurel. Since the day I saw you, I've been tied up in knots. I think about you all the time, and I want to be with you more than anything I've ever wanted before. But I know it's not going to work."

"Andrew, I . . ."

He held up a hand. "You don't have to say anything. I sensed yesterday on the hike that you have reservations about a relationship between us, and I understand. You and your family are about to lose everything you've worked for, and I'm here to help take it away. Then there's my father and all the problems I have in my life. I think we've got too much working against us to pursue our friendship any further."

Her chin trembled. "It seems like you've thought about this quite a bit."

"I have, and if you're honest, you would probably say you have too. Jimmy and Lucy are complications as well. Your family has expectations for you and my father has them for me. I forget all about that when I see you and Jimmy together and you're laughing and joking. I want that with you, but I know it's not going to happen."

Tears filled her eyes. "But . . ."

"I have no idea how you feel about me, but I admit I'm attracted to you." Laurel started to say something, but he held up his hand to silence her. "I'm sure I'll get over it in time, and until then I think it's better for us to stay away from each other."

The only reaction he received from her was a blink of her eyes. She stared at him for a moment and then spoke. "Is that what you want?"

"Yes." He wished he could recall the word before it was out of his mouth, but he couldn't.

She nodded. "I think you're right. Maybe if things were different . . . but they're not."

"No, they aren't."

She raised her chin and straightened her shoulders before she took a step back. "Goodbye, Andrew."

He wanted to pull her into his arms and tell her they could overcome anything if they just worked at it. Instead he jerked the car door open. "Tell your father thanks for the Bible."

Before she could answer, he cranked the engine and roared out of the churchyard. He glanced in the rearview mirror and could see her watching as he drove away. He set his mouth in a grim line and looked away.

He'd done the right thing. There was no way a relationship with Laurel was going to work out. When the last of the Cove residents decided to sell he would be on his way back to Washington, and he had no idea where Laurel would go. It was better to nip their friendship in the bud. It might be harder later. He knew he was right, but that knowledge didn't make him happy.

Andrew didn't feel any better on Wednesday night when he went back to the church for the meeting Simon had arranged. When he arrived, he was surprised to see the yard filled with trucks, wagons, and a few buggies. The remaining Cove people had turned out to hear what the man from Washington had to say.

As he entered the church, he paused at the back and let his gaze drift over those in attendance. Some he knew because he'd already visited with them. Others he hadn't seen before. He recognized Nate Hopkins, the shotgun-wielding farmer, and hoped he'd left his gun at home tonight.

He walked down the aisle, and heads turned to follow his progress as he passed the pews. At the front Simon waited, his hand outstretched in welcome. They shook hands.

"It's good to see you tonight, Andrew. It looks like we have a good crowd."

Andrew nodded and looked around to get his first glimpse of the people's faces. Matthew sat next to Anna in the second row. His heart gave a small lurch when he realized Laurel wasn't in attendance. He couldn't resist asking Simon about her. "Is Laurel coming?"

"No, she and Rani are staying with Granny so Anna could come with me." He took a deep breath. "It looks like most of the folks are here. I'll introduce you and turn the meeting over to you."

"Thanks, Simon. I really appreciate your doing this."

Simon didn't say anything, just nodded and turned to the crowd. "Folks, thanks for coming out tonight. I know you've got lots going on with your crops, so it was even harder for you to come. But we have to make some decisions, hard decisions. One family's choice may not be another's, but it's got to be made. I think we need to listen to what this young man has to say so each of us can decide what we want to do. Please welcome Andrew Brady who works for the Park Service."

If Andrew had expected applause at his introduction, he would have been disappointed. Only silence greeted him as he rose to his feet. A nervous smile pulled at his mouth as he faced the people.

"Good evening. Thank you for coming. I don't

196

want to keep you long, so I'll get right to the point. You know as well as I do the history of the situation you find yourself in right now, but I'd like to review it for everyone if that's all right." He paused but no one said anything. "The idea for the park began in 1923 with some influential residents of Knoxville. They'd visited a national park in the west and thought the Smokies needed to be preserved too. There were two big obstacles to acquiring the land—mainly the lumber and pulp companies that were making a lot of money from stripping the land of its forests. The other one was the people who lived in the mountains."

Joseph Prince near the back stood up and shook his finger at Andrew. "Well, they got the land from the lumber companies, but they ain't got mine yet."

Andrew nodded. "That's right. And how did they get Little River's land and Champion Fiber's —who held out until the last? I'll tell you how. They brought condemnation suits against those companies. Whether you agree or not, under law the right to condemn property is given to states if that property is needed for something that will contribute to the greater good. In the end the state won, and Little River and Champion had to sell. The state's going to win here in the Cove too."

Joseph Prince shook his head. "Well, they better not condemn my land."

A loud chorus of agreement rang out across the

group. Andrew let his gaze drift over the men and women who'd come tonight. Their sun-bronzed skin told of long hours spent living and working the rich soil in the shadows of the mountains they loved. Their way of life was coming to an end, and they were frightened. They might appear angry, but underneath Andrew sensed a fear of the unknown. Where would they go? How could they exist in the outside world so different from their mountain valley?

Andrew took a deep breath. "I understand how terrible this is for all of you. Believe me, my heart goes out to you, but there is no way private citizens are going to be allowed to live inside a national park. If your land is condemned, you're going to have to hire a lawyer to represent you in court. Can you afford to waste money you may need to provide for your family when you move out of the Cove? Think about it. What is the best thing for you to do?"

No one spoke for a few moments, and then Ezra Nash rose to his feet. Andrew remembered him as the man who'd ordered him off his property. His dark eyes reminded Andrew of threatening storm clouds, and his fingers curled around the straw hat he held in front of him. "We been farmin' our land long as I can remember. What makes the government think they got the right to take what my family's worked for just so some folks can come look at our mountains?

Let 'em come as long as they leave me alone."

Andrew smiled. "I'm afraid they wouldn't leave you alone. We have no idea how many people will come into the park by the end of this century. We might be seeing thousands coming into Cades Cove every weekend just to camp and fish and hike. We can't have private property that's off-limits to visitors."

Ezra raised his hand that held the hat and shook it in Andrew's direction. "But it's our land! Ain't nobody got the right to take it away from me."

Nate Hopkins jumped to his feet. "I done told you what was a-gonna happen to anybody comin' to take my land away from me. I'll shoot the first man who tries it."

Before Andrew could reply, Matthew was on his feet. "Nate, that's not going to solve our problem. The only thing that will happen is that you'll end up in jail, and then they'll get your land anyway." He spread his hands in a helpless gesture. "We've talked about this and fought it for years. Now there's just a few of us left. I think we're going to have to face the fact that we're not going to win this fight."

Thomas Bennett jumped to his feet. "Matthew, how can you say that? You and Simon been the ones leadin' us in this here fight. If you give up, there ain't no hope for any of us."

Andrew spoke up before Matthew could reply. "What I'm telling you is that there is no hope left of saving your farms. Please believe me when I say I sympathize with you. All I'm trying to do tonight is let you know you can't win this fight. The government wants to end this standoff. They're giving you until the first of the year to sell or they will begin condemning your property. It will be taken from you." His voice quivered on the last words. He took a deep breath. "I'm sorry to be the messenger, but I've spoken the truth. Now it's up to you."

Simon stood and faced Andrew. "I've had the opportunity to speak with many of those who have sold out and left. It's hard to understand how prices the government pays vary so much from farm to farm. I have a question for you, and I believe you'll answer it truthfully. Do you agree with the way the land has been evaluated in the past?"

Andrew had dreaded this question, and now it had been asked. He stared at Simon and knew he could do nothing other than answer it truthfully. "As you know, the nation is in a depression, and land prices have been dropping since the 1920s. The average price paid per acre of farms in Cades Cove so far has been forty-one dollars and sixty-five cents. That price is arrived at by two or three government agents appraising the land, not the price the owner wants. Most land has sold at seventy-five percent of what the owner asked. Do I think that's fair? No, I don't. But those who argue otherwise say that value is a relative judgment. It makes it especially hard when the owner doesn't want to sell."

Simon nodded. "Thank you for your honesty, Andrew. Is there anything else you'd like to tell us?"

He shook his head. "I think we've covered it all. Think about what we've said tonight. I'll be dropping by your farms in the next few weeks to speak with you individually. If you're going to sell, it would be good to do it now. You'll be able to stay here until after the first of the year, and you can use the money you receive to be looking for a place somewhere else. Please believe that I want to help you any way I can."

"Thank you again," Simon said. "Now if you don't mind, we'd like some time to discuss this issue among ourselves."

Andrew realized he'd been dismissed from the meeting. He strode up the aisle and onto the front porch of the church. He stopped and sucked in his breath. That hadn't been as bad as he expected. He hoped he'd covered everything.

Matthew hadn't looked up at him as Andrew had passed where he sat. He wondered what he would tell Laurel when he got home. Andrew shook his head and headed to his car. It didn't make any difference what Matthew told Laurel. It wasn't going to change her feelings about him. The bad thing for him, though, was that he hadn't been able to change his feelings for her either.

Chapter 11

Two weeks after the meeting of the Cove holdouts Matthew, Rani, Laurel, and Willie arrived on a rainy afternoon at Simon and Anna's cabin. They had come for a family conference about their options for the future. The day outside was as gloomy as the atmosphere inside the house. Even Willie seemed subdued. Unable to play outside because of the weather, he ambled off to Noah's old bedroom, stretched out on the bed, and began to read some of the books Noah had read as a boy.

The rest of the family gathered around the kitchen table. One of Anna's blackberry cobblers sat in the middle of the table ready to be served, but food appeared to be the last thing on anyone's mind.

Finally, Matthew broke the silence when he took a deep breath and looked across the table at Simon. "Putting off what we need to talk about isn't going to make it any easier. We'd better get started, but Simon, I'd appreciate it if you would lead us in prayer first."

They all bowed their heads as Simon began to pray. "Dear Lord, You know how heavy our hearts are today. We come to You asking for guidance in the decision we're about to make." His voice cracked, and Matthew peered up from beneath his lashes to look at the man he'd thought of as a father since he was a child. Anna slipped her hand into Simon's, and they laced their fingers together.

After a moment he continued. "Oh, God, this valley has been our home ever since we can remember. And now we're being forced to leave the only life we've ever known. We fear what lies before us—where we'll go, what we'll do in a world outside this valley, how we'll live. But we know You will be with us. Touch us with Your divine knowledge and let us know what we should do. Do we continue our fight in the courts, or is it time to give in and leave our homes? We trust You, Father, and know You will be with us as we make the decision that will decide where we'll spend the rest of our days on this earth. Thank You for this wonderful family You've given us and keep us all close to You. Amen."

Matthew opened his eyes, leaned forward, and rested one arm on the table. He tapped his fingers on the white tablecloth and thought of Simon's words. "Ever since the meeting with Andrew two weeks ago I've been struggling with what we need to do. Rani and I have discussed it over and over. One day we think we know what we should do and the next we don't. All I do know is that time is running out. Our fight is coming to a close, and we're going to have to decide what to do."

Simon nodded. "I know. I feel the same way, Matthew. It's been difficult for me as I try to hang on and minister to those who haven't given up. But deep down, we all know we can't go on much longer. There are too few families left to fight the government. But if we leave, where will we go?"

"Rani and I have been talking about that, and we wanted to get your opinion. There's a group of mountain folks who are going to start a craftsmen community over at Gatlinburg out on the loop road off 321. We could buy a piece of land out there and build a shop for Mountain Laurel Pottery with a house behind it big enough for all of us to live in. I went to Gatlinburg a few weeks ago, and I looked at some land that would be perfect. If we buy it now, we can start building and have it ready by the time we get ready to move."

A frown pulled at Anna's forehead. "Have you discussed how you'll pay for it? It will be some time before we get paid for our land."

Matthew nodded. "I have a little saved up that we can use to get started. Then we'll settle up after the land's sold."

"We have some saved up too," Simon said. "Doc left his house in Maryville to Anna when he died, and we sold it. Between the two of us, maybe we'll have enough to pay for the land and begin building before we sell the land."

Granny stirred in her chair and looked at Simon. "Don't forgit 'bout my farm. If'n you sell your land, remember you got mine to sell too. I want that money going in on wherever you live."

Simon shook his head. "I know you gave Anna and me the deed to your property years ago, but we've always thought of it as yours. Any money that comes from the sale of that farm will be yours."

A sad smile pulled at her mouth, and her gaze drifted to those gathered around the table. "Then if it's mine, I want it a-goin' to build a place for all of you to live."

"A place for all of *us* to live, Granny," Simon corrected.

Anna reached over and covered Granny's hand with hers. "Of course you'll be with us wherever we go."

Granny's chin trembled as she stared into Anna's eyes. "You been more like a daughter to me than my own flesh and blood ever was, Anna," Granny said. She looked at Simon. "And you been the son I never had." Her gaze drifted to Matthew, Rani, and Laurel. "And you been my grandchildren. I love you all as much as if I'd given birth to this family, but I won't be a-goin' with you when you leave the Cove."

Everyone sat in shocked silence for a moment before Anna gave a nervous laugh. "Oh, Granny. Don't say that. Where one of us goes, we all go."

Granny shook her head. "Not this time, darling. I'll be stayin' behind."

Rani frowned and glanced at Matthew as if he could make Granny understand the situation they

205

found themselves in. When he shrugged, she sighed and faced Granny. "Think about what you're saying. You can't stay behind alone. You have to come with us."

"No, child, I don't. I'm ninety-one years old. I've lived all my life in this here valley, and I cain't see myself livin' nowhere else. I been a-talkin' to the Lord about this, and I've asked Him to take me on home with Him. There ain't no use in my tryin' to go nowhere else. My husband and daughter are both buried up there in the church cemetery, and I want to rest beside them in this part of the earth I love."

Simon got up and walked over to Granny's chair. He bent over her and put his arm around her shoulders. "Now, Granny, none of us know what God has planned for us. He may want you to keep on being the head of this family in the outside world. But I promise you if I'm still living when you pass away, I'll bring you back to the church cemetery."

She reached up and patted Simon's cheek. "You've always been a sweet boy, Simon, and I love you. But I don't think I'll be a-leavin' here."

Anna threw her arms around Granny and hugged her. "I can't stand to hear you talk like that, Granny."

Granny reached up and stroked Anna's hair. "Don't cry, darlin'. Things are a-gonna work out for all of us. When the time comes, remember you and Simon are to have the money for my land."

"We'll remember," Simon said.

Granny sighed and straightened in her chair. "Good. Now if I'm really the head of this fam'ly like Simon says, I'll tell you what I think. Matthew's got the right notion. I say build the house and shop over at Gatlinburg and move over there where you can all be together. Just don't forget to keep an eye on things in the Cove."

Simon shrugged and looked at Matthew. "Then I guess it's settled. Let's get on with plans to move to Gatlinburg."

"Okay, Simon. We'll head over next week to see about purchasing the property and getting a builder. Maybe we'll be ready to move by spring."

He glanced around the table at the faces of the people he loved. Simon had his arm around Anna, who wiped at the tears rolling down her cheeks. Laurel, who had remained quiet throughout the meeting, bit her trembling lip and looked like she was about to cry. Rani, his rock since the day he'd first seen her at the mountain laurel plant near his old cabin, returned his gaze without wavering. She had the look of a woman who could take on whatever the world threw at her and survive. He loved her more each day than he had the one before, and he couldn't imagine his life without her. He had no idea what lay ahead for his family, but he knew Rani would be by his side, encouraging and supporting him every step of the way.

A week later, Laurel sat on the front porch at her grandparents' home and stared at the mountains in the distance. She wiped the perspiration from her forehead and wondered how much cooler it was in those hills than in the valley this afternoon. She'd always enjoyed sitting on her grandparents' front porch and watching the mists swirl about the mountains, but today the haze appeared thicker than usual.

This had to be the hottest day of the summer. From the looks of things, that might change soon. The heat combined with the heavy vapor from the mountains had produced a thunderhead in the distance. They were in for a storm soon. Then the temperature would drop. She hadn't much more than finished the thought when the first breeze of the afternoon rustled the leaves on the trees.

"You gonna hold onto that there bean all day or are you gonna snap it?" Granny's voice cut into her thoughts, and she jumped.

She stared down at the green bean she held and then at Granny, whose wide grin made Laurel's face burn. She broke the bean into several pieces and dropped it into the pan in her lap. "I guess I was daydreaming."

"Seems like you been doin' that a lot lately. Land's sakes, girl, all afternoon you been quieter than a possum tryin' to fool folks into thinkin' he's dead. Is somethin' worryin' you?"

Laurel sighed and shook her head. Truth be told she had been a little at loose ends lately, but it was nothing a relief from the heat wouldn't fix. She picked up another green bean and snapped it. "I've had a lot on my mind lately. You know, with Charlie gone and all. I guess I got distracted from breaking these green beans for Nana." She glanced around. "Which reminds me, where did Willie go?"

"He's spent most of the afternoon out at the barn, but he's in the kitchen with Anna right now."

"Oh, good. I promised Mama I'd keep an eye on him while she and Poppa were gone to Gatlinburg. I don't know what Mama would do if something happened to him. She's grieving over Charlie enough, but then we all are." She sighed and picked up another bean.

Granny planted her cane on the porch beside her rocker and rested her hand on top of it. She regarded Laurel with a steady stare. "We're all upset over Charlie takin' off. He should've had more sense than to worry his family like he's done. But I git the feelin' that there's somethin' else worryin' you. Want to tell ole Granny what it is?"

Laurel smiled and shook her head. "What else would I have to be worried about?"

"Oh, I don't know. Maybe a certain young man

we ain't seen much of lately. How long has it been since Andrew come around?"

Laurel's face burned, and she busied herself with snapping another bean. "Oh, I don't know. A few weeks, I think."

"You *think?*"

The tone of Granny's voice told Laurel her nonchalant attitude hadn't fooled her. Laurel's hands stilled, and she sat back in her chair. "I haven't seen Andrew since he came to church when Jimmy was here. That was nearly three weeks ago."

"Did somethin' happen?"

Laurel blinked back the tears that filled her eyes at the thought of her last conversation with Andrew. "We decided it would be better if we didn't pursue a friendship." Laurel glanced at Granny, who sat silent. "At least that's what he said."

Granny's eyebrows arched. "And you didn't agree?"

"Well, yes, I did agree. That's the reason Andrew said we didn't need to see each other anymore. He knew I didn't want it."

Granny nodded. "Then I guess ev'rything worked out all right 'cause that's what you wanted too." Granny's eyes narrowed. "Is that what you wanted, Laurel?"

"Yes . . . yes, of course it is." She licked her lips. "At least I thought it was."

"You *thought* it was? What do you think now?"

Laurel set the pan of beans she'd been snapping aside, scooted onto the floor at Granny's feet, and laid her head in Granny's lap. A tear trickled from her eye. "I don't know, Granny. I've never been so confused in my life. We're about to lose our home. Our family's talking about building a pottery studio and a house outside of Gatlinburg. A part of me wants to blame Andrew because I'm going to have to leave the Cove."

Granny stroked her hair. "What does the other part of you say?"

Laurel swallowed and squeezed her eyes shut. "The other part of me wants to see him so badly I can't stand it. I liked being with him." She sat up and stared up at Granny. "He kissed me once, and I thought my heart would beat right out of my chest."

Granny laughed. "I reckon I remember that feelin'. Nothin' like it in the world. Sounds to me like you got your feelin's for Andrew all mixed up in your head. What you gonna do 'bout it?"

"Nothing. I think it's best to let it alone."

"But why? If you like the boy and he likes you, what's keepin' you from each other?"

"I don't know if I can ever forget that he helped put my family out of the Cove."

Granny frowned. "I thought we done had this conversation once 'bout showin' respect to the government. I guess I'll have to remind you."

"No. I remember, but it's hard to do."

211

Granny reached for Laurel's hand and stroked it. "None of us is happy 'bout what's a-comin'. We're all gonna be moved out of our valley, but we cain't change things. We got to trust the Lord to take care of us no matter where we go. I don't know what the Lord has planned for you. Maybe there's some nice young man outside this valley somewhere just a-waitin' for you to come along. Then maybe God sent Andrew here so you would have a strong man to lean on when you leave."

"It's hard to know what to do, Granny."

"It always is, child. All we can do is follow what we think God wants us to do." She put her fingers under Laurel's chin and tilted her face up. "But don't be afraid to have a little faith. Don't turn your back on something that could be wonderful just because you're scared. Trust God to take care of you."

Laurel smiled. "I will, Granny. But I think it's too late with Andrew. He sounded determined that he wouldn't be seeing me anymore."

"Then you ask God to show you what He wants from you, and things will turn out fine." She smiled. "Now why don't you take them green beans in the kitchen to your grandmother? She wanted to cook them for supper."

Laurel pushed to her feet. "All right. Then I think I'll go out to the barn and see how much Molly's puppies have grown. I won't be gone long."

Granny waved her hand in dismissal. "Take all the time you want. I'm a-gonna sit here and watch the storm roll in. Tell Anna I'm not ready to come inside yet."

"I'll tell her, Granny. And thanks for the talk. You always make me feel better." Laurel turned to leave but a gasp from Granny made her whirl around. Granny's mouth was drawn down at the corner and her hands clutched the arms of her chair. "Granny!" she cried. "Are you all right?"

Granny's face relaxed and her mouth pulled into a slight smile. "I'm fine, darlin'. Just had a pain. I've had a headache all day."

Laurel set the pan of beans down and placed her hands on Granny's forehead. "Do you have a fever?"

"No, child, I ain't got no fever." She waved a hand in Laurel's direction. "I have pains all the time. I reckon it ain't unusual for somebody ninety-one years old to have a few aches. Now take those beans to your grandmother so she can cook 'em."

Laurel tilted her head to one side and stared down at Granny. "Are you sure nothing's wrong?"

"I'm fine. Now scat and let me have some peace and quiet. I want to soak up my mountains for a while."

Laurel laughed and picked up the pan. "All right, then, if you're sure. I'll tell Nana to check on you in a little while."

As Laurel entered the house, she thought about the things Granny had said about her and Andrew. She didn't see how she and Andrew could ever have a serious relationship. There were too many obstacles in their way, but perhaps they could be friends.

Friends? She didn't know if she could stand to be called his friend when her heart wanted so much more. Granny was right. The only way she was going to solve this problem was to pray about it. Maybe then God would give her the answer.

The hot breeze blowing through the open car window fanned across Andrew and added to the bad mood he'd been in ever since he climbed out of bed this morning. He shouldn't be surprised that his attitude had only grown worse as the day progressed.

The last few weeks had been the worst of his life. The memory of Laurel wearing that polka-dotted dress had haunted him every minute of the day since then and produced a longing in him that could only be erased by seeing her again. But that wasn't going to happen. True to his word, he'd stayed away. Not because he wanted to, but because he knew it was best for both of them.

He should be happy today. Thomas Bennett had signed an agreement to sell this morning. The list he'd been given of farms to acquire had dwindled since he'd been in the Cove. Since the night of the meeting, the Nash and Prince families had given up their fight and were now making plans to leave the Cove. Ezra Hopkins was still holding out. As were Simon and Matthew.

Not a word had come from them, and he hadn't gone to see either of them. No doubt about it, the two families had become special to him since he arrived. Talking to them about leaving everything they'd ever known made him feel like the traitor Simon had preached about that first day he came to the Cove.

Did they think of him as a Judas? A man who pretended to like them to their face while all the time plotting to get their land away from them? He let out a ragged breath and shook his head. He hoped not, but he had to make sure. The only way to do that was to get up the courage to talk to them.

He'd start with Simon. His farm wasn't far down the road he was traveling now. If he was home, now would be as good a time as any to talk. Besides, he had a few questions about some things he'd read in the Bible Matthew gave him. He slowed the car as the cabin came into view. He pulled to a stop in the yard.

Granny sat on the porch in her rocking chair, and she waved as he got out of the car. "Land's sakes, Andrew, I been a-wond'rin' when you was gonna come back to see us. Come on up and set a spell with me."

He smiled as he climbed the steps to the porch and then dropped into the rocker beside her. He took off the hat he wore, pulled a handkerchief from his pocket, and wiped his forehead. "Thanks, Granny. It's good to see you."

"Good to see you too, boy. Where you been that you ain't come around in the last few weeks?"

He shrugged. "Oh, you know, busy. I've been talking to the folks about selling their land. I haven't had a chance to get by here."

She grinned at him. "Well, I'm glad you decided to stop today. You want a cool drink? Anna's in the kitchen, and she'll come if I holler for her."

He shook his head. "No, I'm fine, Granny. I wanted to talk to Simon. Is he here?"

"No, he's gone over to Gatlinburg with Matthew and Rani. We don't expect him home 'til later this afternoon. If'n you want to stay for supper, I know Anna would be mighty happy to have you, and you could talk to him then."

"I'd better not, but I appreciate the invitation. I've been meaning to get over here, though. I've been reading a Bible Matthew gave me, and I have some questions I'd like to ask Simon."

"What kind of questions?"

He thought for a moment. "I want to know how Christians, like all of you, have so much faith. I read a verse the other night that confused me. I wanted Simon to explain it."

"Which verse was that?"

"It was one where Jesus was talking to His disciples about faith. He said if they had faith the size of a mustard seed they could move a mountain." He pointed to the peaks in the distance. "Tell me how that's possible, Granny. Is Jesus saying that if I have faith in Him, I can look over at Clingman's Dome and move it somewhere else?"

Granny shook her head and chuckled. "No, that ain't what it means. The Bible can be hard to understand at times. That's why it takes so much studyin'. I been doin' that all my life. I know that verse, and He wasn't tellin' His disciples they could go out and move the mountains around. He was a-tellin' them that if they had faith even as small as a tiny mustard seed, they could do things that were almost impossible. As impossible as moving a mountain."

"Like what?"

"That depends on the person. Maybe help you forgive a person who's hurt you. Or stand up to someone who wants to run your life. Or move out of the only home you've ever known. Anything that looks like it's too difficult to do."

Her reference to moving out of a home wasn't lost on Andrew. He gazed at the mountains again. "But it's the faith that gives you that power?"

"It is. It's given me a lot of comfort all my life."

He swallowed and asked the question that he still had no idea how to answer for himself. "Do you think I might ever be able to have that kind of faith, Granny?"

She smiled. "If you put your trust in God and believe in Him, He'll give you the power and strength to face whatever comes your way, Andrew."

He stared into Granny's clouded eyes. "I've seen something in all of your lives since I've been in the Cove, and it makes me want it too. I'm trying to figure it all out."

She reached over and squeezed his arm. "All it takes is openin' your heart to Him. I hope you can do that."

"I do too. I'll come back and talk to Simon when he's home." He pulled his watch from his pocket and frowned. "I guess I ought to get on back to camp. Tell everybody I'm sorry I missed them." He put his hat on and started to push up, but he stopped. "By the way, how is the rest of the family doing?"

"Ev'rybody's doin' fine."

His eyebrows arched. "So Simon went with Matthew and Rani to Gatlinburg?"

"Yeah, they went yesterday." Neither of them spoke for a long moment. Then Granny chuckled and rocked back in her chair. "Boy, why don't you just come out and ask me what you want to know?"

The amused look on Granny's face made his face grow warm, and he cleared his throat. "I . . . I don't know what you're talking about."

"You don't, huh? Why ain't you asked about Laurel? You've skirted around mentionin' her name ever since you set down. Don't you want to know how she's doin'?"

His shoulders sagged, and he glanced down at the floor. "I do, Granny, but I know it doesn't matter to her." He paused for a moment and then looked back up at her. "How is she doing?"

Granny pursed her lips as if deep in thought before she answered. " 'Bout like you are, I'd say. She's quiet, don't say much. Looks like she'd cry if you crooked a finger at her. To tell the truth I'm right worried 'bout that girl."

Andrew sat up straight in his chair, his eyes wide. "She's not sick, is she?"

"Not sick in the body. More like her spirit's been crushed." She leaned toward him. "I think she misses you, Andrew."

Andrew shook his head. "I can't believe that."

"Believe whatever makes you happy. Does it make you a little bit happy to think she might miss you?"

A smile pulled at his lips. "Oh, Granny, if I believed she had one thought about missing me, I'd . . ."

Granny waited for him to finish. When he didn't, she threw up her hands in disgust. "I don't know what it is with young people. The good Lord ought to give them more sense than what they got. I remember how Simon and Anna was so at odds I didn't think they'd ever git together. I nearly wore my knees out from a-prayin' for them. Then the same thing happened with Matthew and Rani. Now I see you and Laurel just a-pinin' away for each other and you're both too stubborn to make the first move."

He shook his head. "Granny, you're wrong. You . . ."

She held up a hand to stop him. "I don't know what the good Lord has planned for you and Laurel no more than you do. But if'n I was in your shoes, I'd hate to wake up thirty or forty years from now and wonder what might have happened if I'd made that first move. Is that what you want?"

"No."

"Then do somethin' about it. Go talk to her. Git this thing settled between the two of you."

He nodded. "I'll think about it. Maybe when she gets back from Gatlinburg . . ."

"She ain't in Gatlinburg. She and Willie are stayin' here with Anna and me while their folks are gone."

He cast a wild-eyed stare around. "She's here? Where?"

"Right before you drove up she went down to the barn to check on Molly's puppies. I 'spect you'll find her there. Why don't you go down and surprise her?"

He shook his head. "I don't think . . ."

Granny leaned forward. "Thirty or forty years. What's it gonna be?"

It only took a moment for him to decide. He jammed his hat on his head and pushed to his feet. "I'm not going to wonder what might have been," he muttered. He turned and started toward the steps but whirled and kissed a startled Granny on the cheek. "Thanks, Granny."

"My pleasure. Now git on down to the barn."

He stared into her face and was humbled by what he saw. There was no anger or distrust as he had encountered with others in the Cove. He only saw love, and in that moment he knew it was the evidence of God's love for him shining in her eyes.

He leaned over her and blinked back the moisture in his eyes. "Granny, you said you prayed for Simon and Anna and also for Matthew and Rani. Do you pray for me?"

Her arm and hand shook as she reached up and patted his cheek. "Every night since the day you come into the Cove. The Lord's got great things planned for you, Andrew. All you have to do is let Him show you what they are."

"Thank you, Granny," he whispered. She lowered her arm, and her hand lay with the palm up, her fingers slightly curled, in her lap. Her arm trembled again, and he frowned. "Are you all right, Granny?"

A lopsided smile pulled at her lips. "I'm fine." He hesitated, unsure what to do. A strong wind stirred the leaves on the trees, and the smell of approaching rain filled his nostrils. "You'd better hurry if you don't want to get wet. There's a storm a-comin'."

"Do you want me to help you inside?"

She closed her eyes and shook her head. "Andrew, tonight I want you to find Psalm Twenty-three in your Bible and read it."

He nodded. "All right. Does it have special meaning to you?"

"It does. It reminds me of how beautiful the Cove is with its green fields and streams that come down from the mountains. It makes me thankful for what God has done for me and what He's going to do."

"Then I'll read it, Granny, and I'll tell you about it."

Her head gave a slight twitch. "Just tell Laurel about it. Now go find her like I told you to do. I need to rest a while."

He covered her hand with his and squeezed. "I'll see you later."

The approaching storm's first clap of thunder rumbled across the valley just as he jumped off the porch. Like a man on the most important mission of his life he strode toward the barn. His steps faltered some when he opened the gate and entered the barnyard, but his resolve urged him on. By the time he reached the barn door, great drops of rain had begun to fall. He stopped and stared into the alleyway that ran the length of the structure between the animal pens on either side. His breath hitched in his chest at what he saw.

Laurel knelt facing him about halfway down the aisle. She cuddled a puppy in her arms, and a smile curved her lips. He stood there drinking in the sight of her like a man dying of thirst. He took a step forward and she looked up. Her eyebrows lifted in surprise and she eased the puppy back to the ground beside its mother. She pushed to her feet and stepped around the dogs but didn't come closer. The braid over her shoulder swayed with her movement, and Andrew's heart beat like a drum in his chest.

"Andrew," she whispered, "what are you doing here?"

"I came to see you."

"I thought you said . . ."

"Forget what I said. I've missed you."

Her eyelashes blinked once. "I've missed you too."

He took off his hat and held it in his hands. The rain that had accumulated in the brim dripped to the ground. "I couldn't stand it any longer. I had to see you and tell you what I feel. There's a connection between us that I can't deny, Laurel. I knew it the first day I met you."

She lifted her chin, and he wasn't sure, but he thought he detected a tear in her eye. "Maybe there was, but it doesn't matter. Your father wants you to marry Lucy."

"I know. Your mother wants you to marry Jimmy. And from what I saw when he was visiting, I thought you might want that too."

"I've known Jimmy all my life. He's like an older brother. I don't want to marry him."

"And I don't want to marry Lucy."

Her lips trembled. "Have you told her that?"

"I've written to her and my father. I apologized to her if I had ever done anything to make her think I had marriage in mind. But I told you I have never so much as held her hand. The marriage was our families' idea."

"What did you tell your father?"

"I told him I wasn't going to marry Lucy, and I would appreciate him not bringing up the subject again."

Laurel tilted her head to one side. "Lucy is only part of what your father wanted. What about politics? Are you going back to Virginia to run for office?"

Andrew took another step closer. "I don't know, Laurel. I'm still trying to figure that out. Your family has other expectations for you too. They're going to move out of the Cove. Will you go with them no matter where, or do you want your own life somewhere else?"

A tear trickled down her cheek. "I don't know," she whispered.

His heart pricked at the broken sound of her voice. "There are a lot of things standing in our way, Laurel. Our families' expectations for each of us and the loyalties we owe them. But in spite of all that I've fallen in love with you."

She gasped. "Andrew, we can't . . ."

He raked his hand through his hair. "Yes, we can, Laurel," he said. "If we love each other, we can work anything out." He took a step closer. "I'm standing here holding my heart out to you. Don't think about what our parents want or the fact that I was sent here to talk your family into selling their land. Just think about me. I want you, Laurel. Now you have to decide what you want."

The sight of tears streaming down her face frightened him more than anything he'd ever experienced. He'd laid his heart out to her, and he didn't think he could bear for her to trample it under her feet. She took a deep breath.

"I want you too, Andrew," she whispered.

His body went limp with relief as he exhaled a large breath. She felt as he did. He could hardly believe it.

He didn't know who moved first, but suddenly they were running toward each other. She threw her arms around his neck just as he wrapped his arms around her and pulled her close. His lips covered hers, and she returned his kiss with an eagerness that matched his own. After a moment she pulled away and laid her cheek against his.

"I love you, Andrew," she whispered. "But I'm scared."

"I am too, but as long as we love each other, we can work anything out." He wrapped his fingers around her braid and caressed the silky tresses. "The first time I saw you I couldn't take my eyes off you. I wanted to touch your hair just to see if such a beautiful creature was real. Now we're standing here saying that we love each other. I still can't believe it."

"Neither can I."

He pulled her closer and lowered his lips to hers. She pressed her mouth to his, and waves of pleasure washed over him. When she pulled back from him, he gazed down at her. "Laurel, you are . . ." His words were drowned out by a clap of thunder that shook the barn. The rumbling had barely died down when it was replaced by a frantic scream.

"Laurel!" The high-pitched cry pierced the air, and they froze. "Laurel, come quick!"

Her face paled, and she pulled out of his arms. "That's Willie. Something's wrong."

From the sound of Willie's voice, he knew something terrible must have happened. He grabbed Laurel's hand and they bolted from the barn. The rain beat down on them as they ran into the barnyard. A drenched Willie, fear on his face, appeared at the gate. "Laurel, Nana needs you.

Come quick!" he yelled before he turned and ran back toward the house.

She glanced at Andrew, and the frightened look on her face made his heart skip a beat. Then her fingers tightened on his, and they raced to see what had happened.

Chapter 12

Willie bounded onto the front porch just as Laurel and Andrew rounded the corner of the cabin. Panting for breath, Laurel dashed up the steps with Andrew right behind and came to a stop next to her grandmother, who was bending over Granny.

Anna held Granny's limp hand and patted it. "Granny," she said, "can you hear me?"

When there was no answer, Anna, her face pale, looked up at Laurel. "I came out to check on her and found her unconscious. I don't know how long she's been this way."

Andrew eased up beside Laurel. "It can't have been too long. I talked to her right before I went down to the barn."

"How long ago was that?"

"It couldn't have been more than five minutes. The rain started just as I got to the barn door."

Her grandmother nodded. "So she hasn't been unconscious long."

Laurel grabbed her grandmother's arm. "What's the matter with her? She was fine when I left to bring you the beans."

Anna bent over Granny and raised one of her eyelids. After staring into her eye for a moment, she released it. "I'm not sure. It could be a stroke or a heart attack or something else. We need to get her inside and onto her bed." She faced Andrew. "I didn't know you were here, but I'm glad you are. Can you help me lift her?"

He shook his head and motioned for them to stand aside. "I'll pick her up and take her inside. Laurel, you hold the door. Anna, show me where you want to put her."

Laurel dashed to the door and held it open. She watched as Andrew slid his arms under Granny and lifted her from the chair as if she was weightless. Her grandmother dashed into the house ahead of Andrew.

Before he stepped through the door, he tightened his arms around Granny's still form and stared at Laurel. His Adam's apple bobbed, and his jaw trembled. "I can't believe how light she is. She's hardly more than skin and bones."

Laurel reached out and caressed the arm of the woman she'd loved all her life. "I love you, Granny," she whispered, but there was no answer.

Andrew stepped into the house, and Laurel glanced at Willie before she followed. He had backed up against the railing of the porch and looked as if he was frozen in place. Tears filled his wide eyes and he wiped at his nose with the sleeve of his shirt. "Is Granny gonna die, Laurel?"

She stretched out her hand and motioned for him to follow. "I don't know, Willie. Come on inside."

He shook his head and sank against the railing further. A tear rolled down his cheek. "I don't want Granny to die."

Laurel walked over to him and put her arm around his shoulders. "Neither do I. We all love her so much. But she would want us to be brave right now and pray for her. I need to see if I can help Nana. Are you coming inside, or would you rather stay out here?"

Willie's chin trembled, and he stared past her to the door. "I'll stay out here. Will you come back and tell me how she is?"

Laurel squeezed his shoulder and smiled. "I will. Stay right here, and I'll be back in a few minutes."

"Okay."

Andrew had laid Granny on her bed by the time Laurel arrived at the bedroom door. Her grandmother waited for Andrew to back away before she bent over the supine figure and grasped Granny's wrist with her fingers. A look of deep concentration settled on Anna's face, and Laurel knew she was silently counting the beats of Granny's pulse.

After what seemed forever, she eased Granny's arm back down to the bed and caressed the wrinkled hand before she glanced up. Tears sparkled in her eyes. "Her pulse is weak. Did she say anything to either of you about not feeling well?"

"She said she had a headache, but she dismissed it," Laurel said.

"And I noticed her arm and hands were shaking more than usual." Andrew stared at Anna. "What do you think it is?"

A worried look shadowed her eyes. "It sounds like it might be a stroke. If it is, I'm not equipped to deal with this. She needs a doctor."

Laurel glanced from her mother to Andrew. "Is there anything we can do for her?"

"There's a doctor at the CCC camp," Andrew spoke up. "I can go for him."

Nana's eyes grew large. "That's right. Do you think he would come here?"

"I'll see that he does. It shouldn't take long for me to go over there and get back."

"Then please go." Anna glanced back down at Granny, and her chest heaved with a stifled sob. "And hurry."

"I will."

With that Andrew rushed from the room. Laurel followed and watched from the front door as he dashed through the blowing rain, jumped in his car, and roared out of the yard. She stared at the taillights of the car until they disappeared from sight and then looked around for her brother. Willie, his clothes drenched, sat in one of the rockers as if he was oblivious to the rain that blew onto the porch and soaked him.

Laurel opened the door a few inches and called to him. "Willie, you don't need to stay out here. Come inside."

His head jerked around, and she almost gasped at the frightened gaze in his eyes. He sat up straight and blinked as if he had just noticed her. "How's Granny?"

"Andrew's gone for the doctor. Come on in before you catch a chill out here in this rain." His hands tightened on the arms of the chair before he reluctantly pushed to his feet and followed Laurel into the house. "Now you get some more clothes on and stay inside while I see if I can help Nana. Okay?"

He nodded and followed her through the kitchen and down the hallway to the bedroom he stayed in when at their grandmother's house. Laurel waited until he had entered the room and closed the door before she hurried back to Granny's bedroom.

Anna was in the process of cutting Granny's clothes from her body when Laurel entered the room. Laurel's heart pricked as her gaze took in the sight in front of her. Andrew had been right. Granny was no more than skin and bones. When had the vital woman she remembered from her childhood succumbed to the ravages of old age? And how could she have been so blind as to not see the changes in a woman she loved so dearly?

She blinked back tears. "Do you need any help?"

Her grandmother shook her head. "Not with this. I thought it would be easier to cut her clothes off than try to pull everything over her head." She dropped a handful of cloth onto the floor. "I do need you to go to the kitchen and bring me a pan of cold water and some cloths. Her skin is hot, and I want to try and cool her down some."

"I'll be right back." Laurel hurried from the room and returned minutes later with a pan of water.

"Thank you." Her grandmother took it from her, wrung the cloth out in the cold water, and began to gently sponge Granny's body. As her hands worked, she began to croon a hymn. Laurel recognized it as one of Granny's favorites.

She inched closer to her grandmother. "Do you think she can hear you?"

Her grandmother hand's paused in their work, and she turned to smile at Laurel. "I don't know, but I hope so." She reached down and grasped Granny's hand in hers. "Granny, give my hand a little squeeze if you can hear me."

Laurel fastened her gaze on her grandmother's hand and gasped when Granny's fingers twitched ever so slightly. "Oh, Nana, she can hear you."

Her grandmother leaned over and kissed

Granny's hand before she returned it to a resting position on the bed. She then began sponging Granny's body again. "Granny, do you remember that day in June forty-one years ago when I came to your house? I was so scared that day, but Uncle Charles told me you would take care of me for the summer. I didn't know it then, but the summer was only the beginning for us." She glanced at Laurel. "I jumped out of Uncle Charles's buggy, and Granny came rushing toward me with her arms stretched out like she'd known me all my life."

"That's the first day you saw Grandpa too, wasn't it?"

Anna smiled. "It was. He was right behind Granny. I didn't know then how much the two of them would come to mean to me. They changed my life from a strong-willed girl into a woman who let God have control of her life." She leaned forward and whispered to Granny. "Thank you for all you did for me. You helped me see what God had in store for me."

Even though she'd heard the story all her life, Laurel never tired of hearing the account of her grandmother's first summer in Cades Cove. It always reminded her that she was a result of her grandmother's decision to stay in the Cove. "But you wanted to go to New York and study nursing, didn't you?"

"I did, but God gave me the best teacher in the

world right here in this mountain valley. She taught me about helping people and loving them even when they were unlovable. And she taught me that it doesn't matter where you are if you're doing God's will in your life. Sometimes I shudder to think what would have happened to me if I'd gone to New York instead of staying here in this valley. I would have missed all the babies Granny and I delivered and having the best man in the world to love me." She smiled at Laurel. "And I would have missed having my family that I love so much."

Laurel reached down and squeezed Granny's wrinkled hand. "Granny, Mama has told me so many times how you were always there for her, especially when she and Poppa couldn't seem to get together. And you've done the same for me." She leaned closer and whispered. "Thank you for telling Andrew to come to the barn to see me today. I don't know what will happen with us, but you've made us realize that we need to at least give each other a chance."

Her grandmother's hands stilled, and she glanced up, her eyes wide. "You and Andrew? I thought you'd agreed not to see each other again."

Laurel shrugged. "We had, but we can't help the fact we have feelings for each other. We have a lot of things to work out, and I have no idea how we'll do it."

"I thought the same thing about your grandfather when I was about your age, but God showed me the way. Put your trust in Him and it will all work out."

"Maybe."

Anna chuckled and turned her attention back to Granny. "You are quite the matchmaker, Granny. You did it with Simon and me and with Rani and Matthew. Now you've taken on Laurel and Andrew. Oh, Granny, what would I ever do without you? I need you when we move out of the Cove. Don't you dare leave me now."

Tears pooled in her eyes, and she bit down on her lip as she continued to sponge Granny's body. For the next thirty minutes Laurel ran back and forth to the kitchen to bring fresh pans of water to her grandmother. She had just filled another one when she heard Willie yell from the front porch.

"Laurel, they're back. Mama and Poppa are coming down the road."

She set the pan on the kitchen table and rushed to the door. The rain had stopped, but it still dripped off the edge of the roof. Relief flooded through her at the sight of her father's truck pulling into the yard. She and Willie were down the steps and running toward the truck before her father could get out. "Poppa, I'm so glad you're back," she cried.

A startled look flashed across his face as she and Willie both threw themselves into his arms. He staggered backward at the force of their weight, but he steadied himself and clutched them in a fierce hug. "What's the matter? Has something happened?"

"It's Granny. Something's happened to Granny!" Willie wailed.

"What is it?"

Laurel jerked her head around at the sound of her mother's panic-filled voice. Willie pulled away from their father and dived into his mother's arms just as she walked around the front of the truck.

Laurel pulled away from her father and faced her mother and grandfather, who were staring at her with a stunned look. "Nana found Granny unconscious in her chair on the front porch. She thinks it may be a stroke or a heart attack. Andrew was here, and he's gone for the doctor at the CCC camp."

Her grandfather's face paled. "Where's Anna?"

"Andrew carried Granny to her bedroom. Nana's in there with her now."

She'd barely finished speaking when her mother and grandfather bolted for the house. A muffled cry of surprise drifted from the room when her grandfather burst through the door. When Laurel entered, her grandparents were standing beside Granny's bed with their arms wrapped around each other. Her mother was on her knees beside the bed with Granny's hand in hers. Willie, looking more frightened than she'd ever seen him, stared at Granny from the foot of her bed.

"Oh, Simon," Laurel heard her grandmother say, "I'm so glad you're back. I couldn't stand to go through this without you here."

"We would have been back sooner, but the rain slowed us down. Tell me what happened."

Her grandmother took a deep breath and began to relate the events of the last hour. When she finished, Rani pushed to her feet and frowned at Laurel. "What was Andrew doing here?"

Laurel's face warmed, but she didn't flinch from her mother's steady gaze. "He stopped by and talked to Granny for a while and then came to the barn where I was. Willie came and got us when Nana found Granny."

Her mother took a step toward her. "I thought you weren't going to see that boy anymore."

Her father's arm tightened around Laurel's waist. "Please, Rani. This isn't the time to discuss this."

"I agree," her grandmother said. "I don't know what we would have done if he hadn't been here. I just wish he'd get back with the doctor."

She'd no sooner uttered the words than Laurel heard a car stop at the front of the house. She pulled away from her father. "Maybe that's him now. I'll go see."

Laurel ran through the house, stopped at the front door, and breathed a sigh of relief at the sight of Andrew getting out of his car. A huge raindrop slipped off the roof and landed on Andrew's head as he climbed the steps, but he didn't appear to notice. He glanced at her father's truck sitting in the yard and then back to her. A man she had never seen stepped onto the porch right behind Andrew, and she pushed the door open for them to enter the front room of the cabin.

"Your folks are back?"

"Yes."

"I'm glad." He turned to the man behind him. "Laurel, this is Dr. Atkinson from the camp." He motioned to Laurel. "And this is Laurel Jackson, Reverend Martin's granddaughter."

The doctor nodded and smiled. "It's good to meet you, Miss Jackson. Where is the patient?"

"If you'll follow me, I'll take you, and thank you for coming."

The doctor followed her down the hall. When they walked into the room, she could almost feel the collective sighs of relief that rose from her family. The doctor strode toward the bed and stopped beside her grandfather. "Reverend Martin, I'm Dr. Atkinson. I believe we met when you came to the camp one day. I'm sorry we have to meet again under such circumstances."

Her grandfather shook the doctor's hand and smiled. "So are we, but we appreciate your coming." He stepped away from the bed. "My wife will help you with Granny, and the rest of us will get out of your way." He turned to Anna. "Let me know if you need anything."

Her eyes sparkled with tears, and she sniffed. "I'll come in there as soon as the doctor finishes his examination."

Laurel and her father led the way back to the kitchen. Her parents, brother, and grandfather continued into the front room, but Laurel hung back until Andrew caught up with her. He pulled out a chair from the kitchen table for her before he slipped into one next to her. She clasped her hands on top of the table, and he reached over and laced his fingers with hers. Tears pooled in her eyes, and she smiled. "I'm glad you're here with me."

He tightened his grip on her hand. "I'll stay with you as long as you want."

"Thank you," she whispered as a tear rolled from the corner of her eye. "I know my family's here, but I need someone just for me. Is that selfish?"

He wiped away the tear that slid down her cheek and then pulled her hand to his lips and kissed it. "Not a bit. I want to be with you."

From the other room she could hear the muffled voices of her family. It seemed strange that she didn't want to be with them at this time instead of with the man sitting beside her, but she was right where she wanted to be. She squeezed his hand, and a tingle of pleasure raced up her arm at how comforting his presence was. She closed her eyes and said a prayer for Granny, thankful that Andrew was there to share this troubling time with her.

Laurel had no idea how long they sat there, but it felt like an eternity. Then the door to Granny's bedroom opened and Anna stepped out. Her family rushed in from the other room. A forced smile pulled at Anna's lips as she walked toward them.

"What does the doctor say?" her grandfather asked before she had even arrived in the room.

She shook her head. "It's not good. He says it's a massive stroke, and he doubts if she will live. She's getting weaker by the minute." She grabbed the corner of her apron and wiped at her eyes.

Willie buried his face in their mother's side and sobbed as her father gathered them both close. Her grandfather put his arm around her grandmother, and Andrew gripped her hand tighter.

Her grandfather cleared his throat. "Does the doctor think she's near death?"

She took a deep breath. "Yes. I think all of us need to be in the room and spend whatever time she has left with her. We're the only family she's had for the last forty years, and she'd want us there." She looked down at Willie. "But you don't have to if you'd rather not."

He pulled away from his mother. "I want to be with Granny."

"Good."

Laurel followed her grandparents toward Granny's bedroom but stopped when she heard her father's voice behind her. "Andrew, aren't you coming with us?"

She turned and glanced at him. He shifted from one foot to another and shook his head. "I don't want to intrude."

Her father shook his head. "You're not intruding. From what Laurel's said, you've been a big help to our family today. I'd like for you to join us."

Laurel held out her hand. "Besides, I want you with me."

He smiled at her father, stepped forward, and grabbed Laurel's hand. "Thank you, Matthew. I'd be honored to be with all of you at this time."

Laurel clenched his hand tighter as they stepped into the bedroom. Granny lay with the quilt she'd always loved pulled up over her body. The doctor, a somber expression on his face, stood at the foot of the bed.

Anna picked up the rocker that Granny had spent many hours in, set it next to the bed, and motioned for her husband to take a seat. She reached for Granny's Bible and began flipping through the pages. A serene expression covered her face as she leaned forward and handed the Bible to her husband.

He gazed up into her eyes, and the look that passed between them made Laurel's breath hitch in her throat. They had shared more than a love for each other. Theirs had been a divine calling to minister to the people of the Cove, and Granny had been the one who had shared their journey with them all these years. Now they were about to lose her.

Laurel stifled the sob that rose in her throat as her grandparents clasped hands and covered Granny's with theirs. Her grandmother cleared her throat.

"Granny, I thought you might like for Simon to read your favorite chapter from the Bible to you. I couldn't start to count the number of times we've read this together through the years, and yet every time it blesses me more than it did the time before. I want it to give you peace now."

A sweet comfort filled Laurel at the sound of her grandmother's voice. That hypnotic tone had soothed her many times when she was a child and suffering from an illness. In her role as a midwife and nurse to the people of the Cove, Nana had seen her share of death and had perfected the lilting voice that always comforted her patients. But Laurel suspected there was a reason the timbre of her spoken words was different today. It was the love she had for Granny that made her truly sound like an angel at this moment.

Laurel closed her eyes and said a prayer of thanks for Granny's life and how she'd influenced their family. And she also thanked God for allowing her to be the granddaughter of this wonderful couple who had served the people they loved.

To Laurel they had always just been her grandparents, a man who ministered to everyone he came in contact with and a woman who'd delivered babies and treated the sick. They had served when there was no one else to do it, and they had earned the love and respect of the people of the Cove. Friends who were now gone.

For the first time the enormity of her grandparents' service to the people they loved washed over her, and she was humbled at their godly spirit. She bowed her head and prayed to be worthy of their legacy.

Andrew let his gaze drift over Granny as he stood by her bedside. It didn't seem possible that just a few hours ago they had sat on the front porch talking. Now she lay near death with nothing to be done for her.

He heard Anna speaking to Granny about Simon reading to her from the Bible, and he shifted his attention to her. Andrew bowed his head in respect and waited for Simon to begin.

"I'm going to read you Psalm Twenty-three."

Andrew's head jerked up, and he directed a wide-eyed stare to Simon. Psalm Twenty-three? That was the chapter Granny had asked him to read tonight. Now he would hear it for the first time as he stood beside her deathbed.

Simon began to read, his voice slow but sure.

The LORD is my shepherd; I shall not want.

He maketh me to lie down in green pastures: he leadeth me beside the still waters.

He restoreth my soul: he leadeth me in the paths of righteousness for his name's sake.

Yea, though I walk through the valley of the shadow of death, I will fear no evil: for thou art with me; thy rod and thy staff they comfort me.

Thou preparest a table before me in the presence of mine enemies: thou anointest my head with oil; my cup runneth over.

Surely goodness and mercy shall follow me all the days of my life: and I will dwell in the house of the LORD for ever.

Andrew couldn't take his eyes off Granny's face as Simon read to her. When he reached the part about the valley of the shadow of death, Granny's face seemed to glow. Her breathing grew shallower as Simon continued, and by the end of the passage Granny's chest barely moved.

Anna leaned past her husband and squeezed

Granny's hand. "You've always told me how God has always filled your cup with blessings even when times were bad. Now don't be afraid. You're walking out of this valley through the shadow of death into a new place, but He's right there with you. He's holding out His arms and telling you it's time to leave the Cove and live in His house forever. I love you, and I'll miss you. But I know you're going to a much better place. Just reach out for Him."

Her voice cracked on the last words, and she pressed her hand against her mouth. Simon pushed up from the chair and glanced over his shoulder at his family. "Let's join hands in a circle around Granny's bed."

Laurel pulled Andrew forward, and he responded without thinking. Matthew grasped his other hand as the family members positioned themselves around the bed. When everyone was in place, they bowed their heads, and Andrew followed their cue.

Simon's deep voice filled the room as he began to pray. "Dear God, we come to You today to thank You for the life of Your servant Matilda Lawson. She's been known only as Granny in these mountains for years, and during that time she's served You well. Each of us gathered here has been blessed because we knew her, and we thank You for bringing her into our lives. I pray that You'll give her peace now and strengthen her to face what lies ahead. And we ask You to be with each of us who must stay behind right now that we will always remember the lessons she's taught us and will serve You as she would have us do. Thank You for what she's meant to all of us. Amen."

No one spoke as they opened their eyes, then beside him Laurel began to sing. Her voice, so pure and clear, touched his soul as the others joined her in singing about God's amazing grace and how sweet it was. He didn't know the words, but as they sang, he closed his eyes and longed to know more about the love of God they sang about. When they reached the part about being blind, he wondered if that's what he'd been all his life. Was he blind to a God who loved him so much that it could change his life forever?

He glanced down at Granny on the bed and the family who stood around her singing, and he wanted what they shared. Was it possible he could find the peace in God's love they had?

The song ended, and no one spoke. They continued to stand with their hands clasped. Suddenly Granny's body twitched, and Dr. Atkinson stepped between Simon and Anna to reach her side. He pressed his stethoscope to her chest as one last breath trickled from Granny's mouth and her body grew still. Dr. Atkinson frowned as he listened intently before he pulled the eartips free and looped the tubing around the back of his neck.

"I'm sorry, Reverend Martin," he said. "She's gone."

No one said anything for a moment. A soft cry drifted up from Rani and Matthew wrapped his arms around her and Willie. Simon placed his arm around Anna's shoulders, and she sagged against him. Next to Andrew Laurel straightened her back and grasped his hand tighter. Tears ran down her face.

Dr. Atkinson placed his fingertips on Granny's eyelids and closed her eyes. Then he turned to face Simon. "Is there anyone you'd like for us to let know about this? Andrew and I can stop at any of your neighbors' homes on the way back to the camp."

He shook his head. "No, there's no need for that. All our friends are gone. In times past when there was a death in a family, word would spread quickly in the Cove, and folks would rush to the house to make sure that there was food to eat and the chores were done. Some would stay and keep an all-night vigil so that the family could sleep. Now everybody's gone. There's no one left to honor the woman who dedicated her life to serving the people she loved. It's too sad to think about."

Dr. Atkinson pulled the stethoscope from around his neck and dropped it into his medical bag. "I understand, Reverend Martin, and I'm sorry. I wish there was something more I could do."

Simon extended his hand. "You've done quite a bit for us today, and our family appreciates it. Thank you for coming."

Matthew stepped forward and nodded. "Yes, thank you, Dr. Atkinson."

"It was my pleasure." The doctor glanced at Andrew. "I suppose we should be going now."

Andrew searched his mind for some excuse that would allow him to return after taking Dr. Atkinson back. "I can come back and help with anything you need."

Simon shook his head. "Thank you, Andrew. We appreciate everything you've done today, but Matthew and I can take care of everything. Since there are so few people left in the Cove, there probably won't even be a wake. I imagine we'll have her funeral tomorrow."

"I would like to come to the funeral if that's all right."

A startled expression covered Anna's face. "Of course it's all right. Granny would want you there. You know Granny liked you since that first Sunday you came to dinner."

"I liked her too. She told me today that she had prayed for me every night since that day. That really surprised me."

Anna chuckled. "It wouldn't if you'd known her better. She prayed for everyone she came in contact with." She hesitated and stared up at him. "But I believe she had a special reason for praying for you. She told me once that you seemed sad, like you didn't know what to do with your life. She wanted you to find direction with God's help."

He tried to swallow, but it felt as if his throat had closed. "I hope I can." He sniffed and straightened his shoulders. "If you're sure there's nothing else I can do for you, I'll take Dr. Atkinson to the camp now."

"There is something you can do tomorrow to help us," Simon said.

"What is it?"

"We should probably move Granny's body to the church early in case anybody happens to hear and wants to come to the funeral. Could you come over in the morning and help Matthew and me move her?"

Andrew nodded. "Of course. I'll be here early."

Laurel stepped up beside him. "If you're ready to go, I'll see you to the front door."

Andrew and Dr. Atkinson followed her from the room into the kitchen. She stopped beside the table, extended her hand to Dr. Atkinson, and forced her lips into a weak smile. "Let me echo my family's thanks and tell you again how much we appreciate you coming, Dr. Atkinson."

"I wish I could have done something more." When the doctor released her hand, he backed away and nodded to Andrew. "I'll wait in the car for you. I know you'd like to spend a few minutes with your friend alone."

Andrew glanced down at Laurel, and his heart pricked at the tears rolling unchecked down her face. "I'll be out in a few minutes."

Neither of them said anything as Dr. Atkinson's footsteps tapped across the floor. When the door closed behind him, Andrew reached for Laurel and curled his hand around hers. She slid her fingers between his and squeezed as if he were her lifeline. He glanced over his shoulders to see if any of her family had come out of Granny's bed-room. When he didn't see anyone, he pulled her into the front room.

The minute they entered the room she fell against him, and he wrapped his arms around her. Great choking sobs wracked her body as she laid her cheek against his chest and cried out her grief. He held her with one arm around her waist and the other stroking her hair. "I'm here, Laurel," he whispered. "I'll help you through this terrible time."

The only answer was a slight nod as her shoulders continued to shake. He stood there rocking her in his arms until her sobs began to subside. When she finally pulled back, he held her at arms' length and studied her face. Even with her red eyes and wet cheeks she was still the most beautiful woman he'd ever seen. He leaned down and planted a chaste kiss on her forehead. "I hate leaving you like this, but I think your family needs some time together without anyone else around. I'll be back in the morning."

Her body jerked in a hiccup, and she nodded. "We'll be fine. Go on."

"I'll think about you every minute." He put his fingers under her chin and tilted her head up so that he could stare into her eyes. "I love you, Laurel Jackson."

"I love you too," she whispered.

He pulled her to him and lowered his mouth to her. Her lips met his, and he held her close as they kissed. After a moment he pulled away and took a deep breath. "That gives me something to hold onto until tomorrow."

He was still reeling from the contact with her as he jumped in the car and headed back to the camp. It wasn't the kiss alone that occupied his thoughts, though. He couldn't forget the love that had been shown as the family prayed and sang around Granny's bed. Nothing in his life had ever affected him as that had. He wondered what Dr. Atkinson thought, but he couldn't bring himself to ask. Someone used to facing death all the time must have learned how to cope, but this had been Andrew's first time. He didn't think he'd ever forget what he'd seen.

For some reason, though, he couldn't put into words how he felt. It had been upsetting for everyone to be sure, and yet there had been something else in that room, a feeling that had to do with the Martins' and Jacksons' faith. It was almost as if a veil of peace descended as Granny took her last breaths. He'd first noticed it when Simon read about walking through the shadow of death and had continued through the singing of the hymn about God's amazing grace.

The memory of sitting with Granny earlier on the porch and what she had asked flashed in his mind. She had asked him to read Psalm Twenty-three tonight, and that was what he intended to do. He still had the Bible Matthew had given him so he could look it up. He needed to understand what gave Laurel's family the strength they demonstrated even when bad things happened in their lives. If they found that in their faith, then he needed to understand it more because he wanted what they had. He wanted to be able to face life and deal with it the way they did.

Chapter 13

Today had to be the most beautiful day of the summer. A perfect day for saying goodbye to Granny. Anna let her gaze wander over the faces gathered around Granny's grave and then stared down at the wooden coffin resting in the hole in front of her. She was supposed to feel happy for Granny today. She, like Paul in the Bible, had fought a good fight, finished her course, and kept the faith. Her reward waited for her in heaven.

But Anna was still on earth, and she missed the woman who had been by her side for the last forty years.

She closed her eyes, inhaled the sweet mountain air Granny had loved, and lifted her face to the sun that filtered through the branches of the sugar maple tree Granny had planted next to her daughter's grave years ago. She'd often told Anna the sugar maple was Deborah's favorite tree because of its brilliant colors in the fall, and Granny had thought it appropriate that they rest side by side underneath one.

Simon opened his Bible and stepped to the edge of the grave. He began to read the description of a virtuous woman from Proverbs, and Anna let her mind drift. If there ever was a virtuous woman, Granny had been one.

The memory of seeing Granny for the first time forty years ago flashed into her mind, and she smiled. She had been such a naïve young woman when she'd come to the Cove. She thought she was ready to face the world, but thank the Lord her brother had known better and sent her to study with Granny.

That first summer had been an endless routine of caring for the sick, delivering babies, learning about the herbs used for medicinal purposes, and preserving food for the coming winter. By the time fall had arrived, Anna had come to understand life in the Cove and knew it was where God wanted her to stay. Every day since then Granny had been with her.

Anna glanced at those around the grave. Just as Simon had suspected, very few came today. Even though Ezra and Susie Nash and Thomas and Minerva Bennett had sold their farms, they hadn't moved yet and were joined by Nate Hopkins, who still hadn't given in. Names of friends drifted through her head, and she choked back a sob. Ferguson, Davis, Whitson, Long, Adams, Carter, Simmons, and of course John and Martha Martin —all gone now from the Cove and scattered like ashes in the wind. Soon their family would join them, but Granny would be staying behind.

She took a deep breath and stared across the cemetery. There were others who would be staying behind too. Uncle Charles, who had brought her to this beautiful valley, had asked to be buried here. Toward the back of the cemetery was her son Willie's grave. Not a day went by that she didn't think of that little boy and the joy he'd brought her during his short life. George Ferguson, the first baby she'd helped Granny deliver, was buried just past Willie's grave. He'd been killed a few years ago in a logging accident near Tremont.

Her gaze went to Jimmy Ferguson, George's nephew, who stood across the grave from her. He glanced at Laurel from time to time, but she didn't appear to notice. She had eyes only for

Andrew, and Jimmy didn't look too happy about that. Contrary to what Laurel said, Jimmy's feelings for her were deeper than a brother for a sister. It troubled Anna to think how he must be hurting.

Andrew seemed like a nice young man, and he'd never done anything to offend any of them. In fact, he'd bent over backward to make them comfortable even though the government increased the pressure on them to sell every day. And she had to give Andrew credit—he had been respectful enough of their love for Jimmy to tell him about Granny's death.

"And so we come today to celebrate Granny's life." Simon's words pulled her from her thoughts, and she directed her attention back to him. "Let us pray."

Everyone bowed their heads, but Anna kept her eyes open and stared straight ahead. All those she'd thought about as she stood beside the grave reemerged in her mind, and she thanked God for each of them and for what they'd meant in her life. Then she thanked God for what Granny had meant to them and all the people of the Cove she'd served so faithfully.

She prayed silently until she heard Simon say his *amen*. As her family raised their heads, she looked at each one and asked God to meet the special needs in their lives. For Rani to cope with leaving the valley she loved so dearly, for Matthew to deal with the shadow of pain that crossed his face from time to time, for Laurel to make the right choices in the bloom of first love, and for Willie—named for the little boy buried nearby—to grow into a man with character like his father and grandfather. And she prayed for those not present. Her son Stephen, who worked as a doctor in a remote African village, her grandson Charlie, who may well have been lost to them forever, her adopted son, Noah, who preached God's Word to his congregation, and her brother, Robert, who had been God's messenger to send her to the Cove.

As the mourners started to disperse, Laurel and Andrew walked around the grave and stopped next to her. Laurel hugged her and held her at arm's length. "Nana, you looked like you were a hundred miles away during the graveside service. What were you thinking about?"

Anna reached up and patted her granddaughter's cheek. "I was reminiscing about the life I've had here in the Cove and all the people who helped make it so wonderful for me. Granny was the first to welcome me, and I owe her so much."

"We all do," Laurel said.

Anna moved away from the grave as some of the men picked up their shovels and began to fill it in. "Let's go wait in the church until they're finished. Then I want to place some flowers on the grave."

Andrew touched Laurel's arm. "You go with your mother and grandmother. I'll see if I can help your father and grandfather, and then I'll come inside."

Anna motioned for Rani to join them. When she stopped beside her, Anna reached up and touched both Rani's and Laurel's cheeks. "I hope I've told both of you how much I love you. We get so busy with our everyday lives that we often forget to say it to those who mean the most to us. I'm afraid I didn't say it enough to Granny."

Rani threw her arms around her and hugged Anna. "Mama, you've always shown us how much you love us, and you showed Granny too. I'm so thankful I have you in my life. I love you so much."

Laurel kissed her on the cheek. "And I love you too, Nana. Now let's go inside and wait for them to finish with the grave."

Anna nodded and allowed them to lead her up the steps of the church. She glanced over her shoulder once more before entering and bit her lip. She felt as if a big part of her heart lay underneath the dirt that was being shoveled into the grave. After a moment she inhaled and walked into the church where Granny had first brought her over forty years ago.

Andrew hadn't expected to be invited to supper with Laurel's family after the funeral, but Anna had insisted he join them. He didn't know if

Laurel had put the idea in her head or not, but he was happy to receive the invitation. The more he was with the Martins and the Jacksons the more he realized how different their lives were from the one he'd always known. Their behavior tonight at supper had proven that to him more than ever.

He had wondered how they would react after the funeral and had come to the Martins half expecting the evening to be filled with tearful stories. Instead the conversation at supper had been cheerful as they related one incident after another of happy memories with Granny. Fits of laughter, sometimes almost uncontrollable, had punctuated each story.

One of the stories that had gotten the loudest response was Anna's account of Simon falling off the roof of Granny's house years ago when he climbed up to lay out apples to dry. Her description of Granny's skirts flopping around her legs and chickens scattering as she ran to see if he was dead or alive had all of them nearly falling out of their chairs.

There was no doubt about it. He had enjoyed the evening more than any he could ever remember. It felt so comfortable to sit with Simon and Matthew on the porch of the Martins' cabin as he was doing now. The only problem was that Jimmy Ferguson had also enjoyed the evening, and it was plain to see he had a special place in this family.

He kept reminding himself that Jimmy's ties with them went back years. There had been lots of stories about his family and Granny at supper, too. The only time the conversation had gotten serious was when Jimmy thanked Anna and Simon for saving his mother's life when she was a small child. The love that shone in his eyes for Anna when he told her he wouldn't be here today if not for her had even touched Andrew's heart.

But that didn't change the fact that Jimmy made no secret that he didn't like Andrew. Even now in the evening twilight Jimmy watched him like a hawk circling his prey. He wondered what Jimmy was planning next to keep him away from Laurel.

As if he could read Andrew's thoughts, Jimmy cleared his throat and leaned forward in his chair. "I want to thank you for backing me up with Lieutenant Gray about taking the day off for Granny's funeral and for letting me ride with you."

Andrew's eyebrows arched at the sincere tone of Jimmy's voice. "No problem, Jimmy. I was glad to do it. I knew you'd want to be here."

Jimmy nodded. "Yeah, I reckon the rest of my family would have liked to come. Of course none of them know about it yet. My pa's folks moved over to Oak Ridge when they sold out, and my ma's are with her and my pa over at Tremont." He stared into the distance for a few moments.

"Yeah, they're all gone, and I reckon I'll be leaving next week too."

Matthew swiveled in his chair to face Jimmy. "Where are you going?"

"Back to Tremont, I guess. When I signed my Oath of Enrollment for the CCC, I enrolled for six months. That time's up next week, so I've got to leave. I'll head on back home and see if Pa can get me a job in the lumber camp up there."

Simon frowned. "But I thought the camps were closing down now that the government's bought their land back."

"They're winding down, that's for sure. But Pa says they'll still be able to operate for a few more years. After that, I don't know what we'll do." He glanced from Simon to Matthew. "What are you going to do?"

Matthew settled back in his chair and stared out toward the mountains that were now barely visible in the gathering darkness. "Simon and Rani and I were on our way home from Gatlinburg when Granny had the stroke. We'd been there to sign the papers for some land we bought and to arrange with a carpenter to start building a house for us. The house ought to be ready for us to move into by spring." He glanced at Andrew. "Do you think they'll give us that much time before we have to leave?"

Andrew nodded. "I'm sure it can be arranged. I

hadn't heard you mention this. Does Laurel know about it?"

"She does. We're going to build a studio for Rani with our house right behind it. It won't be the same as living in the Cove, but at least we'll all be together."

"I hope you know I wish you the best. I know this isn't easy for you."

Before anyone could answer, the front door opened and Laurel stepped onto the front porch. A shaft of light from inside the house framed her in the doorway. Andrew jumped to his feet and pointed to his chair. "Take my seat, Laurel."

"Thanks, Andrew." She turned her attention to her father. "Poppa, Mama and Nana want you and Grandpa to come help them. They need to decide what to do with some of Granny's belongings."

Matthew pushed to his feet and sighed. "Let's go see what they're up to now, Simon."

Simon laughed and stood. Before he could take a step, Andrew spoke up. "Jimmy and I need to get back to camp soon. I enjoyed the evening. Please thank your wife for inviting me. It's always a pleasure to visit here."

Simon's gaze darted to Laurel and back to him. "We're glad to have you anytime."

Laurel waited beside the door until her father and grandfather had entered before she smiled at Andrew and walked toward him. Andrew stuck his hands in his pocket and leaned against the railing around the porch until she stopped in front of him. "So you need to get back to camp?"

"Yes. Jimmy and I need to get back before lights-out."

Jimmy's chair squeaked as he pushed to his feet. "If we're leaving soon, I'd better go tell Anna and Rani goodbye. I may not see them again before I leave for home."

A look of surprise flashed across Laurel's face. "You're going home?"

He nodded. "My time's up next week, and I'm going back to Tremont. I sure would like it if you came to visit us after I get there. Ma would like it too. What do you say?"

"I'll think about it, Jimmy, but I doubt if I can. We're going to be busy closing down the lodge. Not to mention getting ready to move. I'll let you know."

Jimmy pursed his lips and nodded. "All right."

He strode to the door, jerked it open, and entered the house. Andrew tried to hide his smile, but he didn't succeed. "Jimmy doesn't like having me around."

She stared into his eyes. "I've told you how I feel about him."

He put his arm around her waist and drew her closer. "You have, but Jimmy doesn't seem to be getting the message. I don't like the way he looks at you."

She arched an eyebrow and directed a coy look

at him. "Then you need to learn to deal with your emotions better."

His hand tightened on her waist. He put a finger under her chin and tilted her face up. "I'll try, but it's hard to do when I think about you all the time."

She smiled. "I'm glad you think about me. Can you come to our house tomorrow night?"

He shook his head. "I'm afraid not. Superintendent Eakin wants me to come to Gatlinburg. I'll probably be there for a week, but I'll come by as soon as I get back."

"We have to go to Gatlinburg next week to take some of Mama's pottery to Mr. Bryan's store. Maybe I can see you then."

"That would be great. I'll be staying at the Mountain View Hotel while I'm there. That's where the Park offices are too. While you're there, come over to the hotel. The secretary in the office will be able to tell you if I'm in town or if I'm out in the Park somewhere with the Superintendent."

"I'll do that."

He pulled her closer until their lips almost touched. "I'll think about you every minute I'm away."

"And I'll do the same."

She moved toward him, and it took his breath away that she initiated their contact. When her lips covered his, he groaned as her scent filled his nostrils. He'd never been drunk before, but the intoxicating feeling that assaulted him dulled all his senses and left him reeling in her wake.

"I love you," he whispered against her lips.

"I love you too," she echoed.

The sound of someone's throat being cleared startled him, and he abruptly released her. He turned to see Jimmy standing just outside the door. His hands were clenched at his sides, and his body shook with repressed anger. "Laurel, you're making a big mistake. This guy's not for you."

"Please, Jimmy, let's not argue." She tried to step past Andrew, but his hand on her arm stopped her.

"Look, Ferguson," Andrew said, "this has nothing to do with you. This is between Laurel and me, and I'd appreciate it if you'd let us decide if we're right for each other or not."

Jimmy directed his attention back to Laurel, and his body sagged as he exhaled. "I guess you're right. I'm sorry, Laurel. I didn't mean to cause you any trouble."

She pushed past Andrew this time and ran to Jimmy. "You're not causing me any trouble, Jimmy. We've been best friends since we were children, and I value your opinion. But I can't help how I feel."

He stared at her for a moment before he took a deep breath. "I know you can't. Take care of your folks, and don't forget I've invited you to come to Tremont."

"I won't, Jimmy."

"Then I guess that's it for now." He leaned over and kissed her on the forehead before he nodded to Andrew. "I'll wait in the car while you tell Laurel goodnight."

He hurried down the steps and climbed into Andrew's car. Laurel turned back to Andrew. "I hate hurting him."

Andrew walked over to her and put his arms around her. She leaned forward and let her head rest on his chest. "Don't worry about it. You were honest with him."

"Yes, but that doesn't make me feel any better."

He kissed the top of her head and released her. "I'll miss you while I'm gone, but I'll look forward to seeing you in Gatlinburg."

"We'll be there sometime next week."

He squeezed her hand once more before he hopped down the steps and jogged to his car. The minute he climbed in he knew it was going to be a chilly ride back to the CCC camp. Jimmy looked as if he was frozen to his seat, and he didn't move or say a single word the whole trip. When they arrived at camp, Jimmy mumbled his sullen thanks and jumped out of the car almost before it stopped. He had disappeared into his barracks by the time Andrew parked.

Andrew climbed from the car, leaned against the fender, and thought about Jimmy's reaction when he'd seen Andrew with his arms around Laurel. Given the close friendship between Laurel's and Jimmy's families, it was understandable. He tried to imagine how he would feel if Laurel preferred Jimmy to him.

Not too long ago he'd been certain he'd never marry, but that all changed the minute she said she loved him. Suddenly marriage appealed to him, especially if Laurel was his bride. Whistling a jaunty tune, he ambled to the barracks. No doubt about it. His life sure had changed since he came to Cades Cove.

Laurel walked to the window in her bedroom and stared out at the night. She'd thought she was tired when she and her family arrived home from Nana and Grandpa's, but now she felt wide awake. She pulled the brush through her hair again and smiled at the way Andrew had touched her braid yesterday when he found her at the barn. They had shared some magical moments together until Willie had found them and led them back to the house.

She held the brush close to her chest and closed her eyes as she remembered the way she'd felt when Andrew kissed her. Not too long ago she'd wondered what it would feel like to be kissed. Now she knew, and it was more thrilling than she could have imagined. Perhaps it was the fact that it was Andrew who'd delivered that first kiss and not someone else.

A sudden thought struck her, and she walked over to the table by her bed and picked up her Bible. She dropped down in the rocker next to the table and flipped through the pages until she found what she wanted. The picture she'd taken of Andrew on Gregory's Bald lay between the pages of her favorite Psalms, and she picked it up and studied it.

She remembered how he'd looked that day as he stared out over the mountain ridges that rippled across the landscape in a washboard effect. The sight had been as overwhelming to him as it was to her every time she saw it. The pensive look on his face let her know he was in deep thought. Sitting beside him and sharing the moment had been one of her favorite times with him.

A knock at the door interrupted her thoughts. "Yes?"

"Laurel," her mother called out, "your father and I would like to talk to you if you're not too tired."

She stuck the picture back into the Bible and replaced the book on the table beside the bed. "No, it's fine. Come on in."

Her mother, followed by her father, stepped into the room. The expressions on their faces caused her heartbeat to quicken. They weren't here to wish her sweet dreams. There was something more serious on their minds, and she knew there could only be one subject that they wanted to talk with her about—Andrew.

She sighed and sat down on the edge of her bed as they settled on either side of her. Neither spoke for a moment, but finally her father reached over and grasped her hand in his. "Laurel, your mother and I are concerned about you." When she didn't answer, he continued. "From the moment we returned from Gatlinburg and found that Andrew had been to see you, we've sensed a change in your relationship with him."

Laurel had known this time would come, and she'd dreaded it. Now she had to be honest with her parents. But the big question still hovered in her mind. Could she be honest with herself? She still had no idea where her relationship with Andrew was headed, but she wanted to find out.

She nodded and looked from her mother to her father. "It has changed. Andrew had told me the last time he came to church that he thought we shouldn't see each other again, but he changed his mind. He came by Nana's to ask Grandpa some questions about the Bible verses he'd been reading. He didn't know I was there until Granny told him."

"And so the two of you talked?" Her father's hand tightened on hers.

The words she wanted to say to make them

understand evaded her, and she pushed to her feet. It was impossible to talk with them sitting on either side of her. She turned and faced them. "We did, and we decided we had to know what the feelings we have for each other mean."

Her mother's forehead wrinkled in a frown. "You have feelings for each other?"

"Yes, Mama. We do. Andrew says he loves me, and I love him."

Her father shook his head and rose to face her. "Laurel, you don't know anything about this man except what you've seen since he's been in the Cove. He comes from a different world than you do."

"I know that, Poppa. That's why we're taking our time to see where our relationship goes."

A horrified expression crossed her mother's face, and she bounded to her feet. "See where it goes? That sounds like you're considering marrying this boy. You can't do that."

Laurel clenched her fists and raised her chin as she glared at her mother. "I didn't say anything about marriage. But what if I do decide he's the man I want to marry? I've always thought that decision belonged to me alone."

Her mother shook her head. "It does, darling. But you need to weigh the consequences before you decide something that important. Is Andrew going to stay in Tennessee or does he plan to return to Virginia? Do you think you could fit into

269

his family if you went to Virginia?" She reached out and grasped Laurel's hand. "All I want is for you to be happy."

Laurel glanced from her father to her mother. "All I want is someone to love me who I can love in return—just like the two of you."

"And that's what you deserve," her father said. "I want you to have what your mother and I have had. But remember this, Laurel. We had a lot of common ties. We loved this mountain valley and wanted to make a life here. And we both had a strong belief in God." He glanced at her mother and took a deep breath before he continued. "I worry because Andrew doesn't share that with you. Don't overlook that important detail in whomever you marry. All your mother and I are saying is that we want you to be careful because we want you to have the happiest life possible."

He held out his arms and Laurel stepped into his embrace. Her mother put her hand on Laurel's back and leaned over to whisper in her ear. "All we want is your happiness."

Laurel nodded. "I know, and I promise I'll pray that God will show me what to do in this situation."

Her father released her and bent down to kiss her cheek. "That's all we can ask. Now let's all go to bed. It's been a tiring day."

She kissed both her parents on their cheeks and watched as they turned to leave. When they reached the door, she called out to them. "Wait."

They turned and faced her. "What is it?" her father asked.

"I have been thinking about something all day, and I wondered . . ." Her throat closed, making it impossible to force the words to her mouth. A tear slipped from the corner of her eye.

A concerned expression flashed across her mother's face, and she was back beside Laurel before she could blink. "What is it? What are you upset about?"

"Ch-Charlie," she stuttered. "If we move to Gatlinburg, how will he find us when he comes back?"

Tears filled her mother's eyes, and she pulled Laurel close to her. "I have the same fear, darling. But he'll know to look for Mountain Laurel Pottery, and he'll find us. Try not to worry about him. Just pray for him."

"I do every night."

Her father walked back to her side and gathered her and her mother in his arms. "Your mother's right. All we can do now is pray that God will keep him safe and bring him home to us."

They stayed locked together for several minutes, each with their silent prayers ascending to the Father. Then her parents released her, kissed her again, and walked out of the bedroom. When the door closed behind them, Laurel fell back across her bed and buried her face in her pillow. Where was Charlie tonight? Did he miss them and want to come home?

"God, don't let him be too proud to come back. Help him know we love him and want him home again," she whispered.

She lay still thinking about Charlie, her feelings for Andrew, and the move that her family was being forced to endure. None of these situations could be settled tonight, and at the present time she couldn't see a solution to the problems presented by all three. After a while, she yawned and drifted into a troubled sleep.

Chapter 14

Andrew climbed out of Superintendent Eakin's car and glanced around the parking area in front of the Mountain View Hotel. For the last week he'd come back to the hotel every day expecting Laurel to be waiting, but she hadn't shown up yet. There was no sign of her today either. He'd even made a trip over to Mr. Bryan's store yesterday to ask if he knew when the Jacksons would be arriving with their crates of pottery, but the man told him they didn't follow a set schedule. They simply showed up when Mrs. Jackson had completed enough work to make the trip worthwhile.

"Is something the matter, Andrew?"

The superintendent's voice jarred him out of

his thoughts, and he glanced at the man who stared over the roof of the car at him. Andrew's face grew warm, and he shook his head. "No, sir."

"I couldn't believe how many people were in Gatlinburg today. But that's what we like, lots of visitors. In a few years these mountains will be packed with tourists, and then we'll face other problems."

"Like what, sir?"

"Oh, things like cars and trucks everywhere." The superintendent shrugged and walked around the car. Andrew fell into step with him as they trudged into the hotel. "Just think of what it's going to be like in fifty years in these mountains. We'll have gas stations and restaurants on every corner and the park will be littered with debris left by campers. Then there's the danger of some careless person not putting out his campfire. I don't even want to think about what kinds of problems that could cause."

Andrew shuddered. "I don't either. I've been afraid of fire since I was a child."

"Oh, really? Did you have a bad experience with fire?"

"I did. My clothes caught fire from a candle. I still have some scars."

"I can understand why you don't like fires. If that frightened you, just think what it would be like to see a whole forest on fire."

The thought of seeing such a sight sent a tingle

of fear down Andrew's spine. "That's something I hope I never see."

Andrew grabbed the knob on the door to the Park Headquarters Office and stepped back for Superintendent Eakin to go in first. As they entered the outer office, the secretary, Jane Cherry, looked up and smiled.

Her glasses rested on the bridge of her nose, and she peered over the top of the lens at them. "How was your morning?"

"It was interesting," Mr. Eakin responded. "We've been at the Roaring Fork Area of the park. The men from several of the camps are working on the hiking trail that's going to start there. It won't be long before hikers will be able to start out there and climb all the way to Mount Le Conte. I'm sorry we were gone so long. Are there any messages for me?"

She glanced at the closed door to his office and lowered her voice. "There's a visitor from Washington in your office. I hated to put him in there, but I didn't think I should ask him to sit out here in one of those uncomfortable chairs the department's seen fit to put in my office."

Superintendent Eakin frowned and glanced at the door. "What does he want to see me about?"

She stared past him to Andrew. "He really isn't here to see you. He came to see Andrew."

Andrew's eyebrows arched, and he took a step back. His mouth gaped open, and he cast a nervous glance at the door. Had he done something wrong that warranted a visit from one of his superiors in Washington? "Me? Why would anybody from Washington want to see me?" He hardly recognized the squeaky sound of his voice.

"Because it's your father."

"My father?" The words ricocheted off the office walls. What was his father doing here? He glanced at Superintendent Eakin. "Did you know he was coming here?"

"No. He called last week to check on how you were doing. He asked me if you'd be in Gatlinburg anytime soon, and I told him you were scheduled to be here this week. But he didn't say he was coming." The impassive expression on his face and the cool tone of his voice conveyed the same reaction Andrew had often seen from others who'd been forced to endure his father's demanding personality.

Superintendent Eakin strode to the door, pushed it open, and entered his office. "Good afternoon, Congressman Brady. Welcome to our headquarters here in the Smokies."

Andrew trailed into the room behind him and stared at his father, who gave him a fleeting glance before his lips curled into the politician's smile he'd perfected years ago. He stuck out his hand to the superintendent. "Good to see you, Ross. I hear from your superiors in Washington that you're doing a great job here. I knew you would."

Eakin shook his hand. "Thank you, Congressman. Did Jane offer you any refreshment while you waited?"

"Yes, she did, but I'm fine." He cast a disgruntled glance in Andrew's direction. "I hope you don't mind my using your office while I waited for you to return. But I need to talk with my son."

"Then by all means use my office for your conversation. I need to check on a few more things and should be gone for the next hour or so." He looked at Andrew's father. "If you're staying overnight, perhaps we can have supper together."

His father shook his head. "I doubt if I'll be here, but thanks anyway."

Superintendent Eakin turned to Andrew. "I'll see you when I return."

"Yes, sir."

The superintendent walked through the doorway into the outer office. Before he closed the door, Andrew heard him speak to the secretary. "Jane, why don't you walk with me to my car? There are some papers I'd like for you to bring back."

Andrew frowned at the statement. There were no papers in the car. Then the reason behind the words hit him. Superintendent Eakin realized the exchange between Andrew and his father was going to be heated, and he wanted to remove Jane from the office. Andrew doubled his fists at his side and took a deep breath.

His father stared at him as if he were ready to take on an opponent on the House floor in Washington. His white linen Palm Beach suit, no doubt carefully crafted by his tailor, hung loosely on his body, but it couldn't hide the anger that radiated from his rigid body. The corner of his lip curled upward in a sneer as his gaze raked Andrew from head to toe before his eyes settled on Andrew's open shirt collar.

"Why aren't you wearing a tie? And when was the last time you had your hair cut? Have you forgotten everything I taught you about keeping appearances up at all times?"

Andrew wiped his shirt sleeve across the perspiration on his forehead and sighed. "And it's good to see you too, Father. I'm afraid my unsuitable state of dress is a result of moving rocks and dirt with the CCC camp men on a work detail this morning. Which, by the way, I must say I enjoyed more than anything I've done in a long time."

His father waved his hand in dismissal. "Yes, yes, honest work and all that. I get enough of that from my colleagues in Washington. I don't need to hear it from my son too."

Andrew bit back the retort and sighed. "You're aware of the fact that this office has a phone since you talked with my boss earlier this week. I would have been happy to discuss my short-comings with you if you had called. But since you didn't, I assume there is something even more important you need to berate me about for you to take a trip all the way down here. What is it?"

His father's eyes widened for a moment before he shook his head. "There's one thing for sure, I didn't come here to listen to you be disrespectful. Please remember you're speaking with your father."

"Oh, I will. Believe me, I'm fully aware of that."

His father tilted his head to one side and regarded him with a quizzical expression for a moment before he continued. "I was very concerned when I received your letter. I thought we needed to talk about your decision in person, not over the phone."

"And what decision would that be?"

"You know very well what I'm talking about. Why have you decided you don't want to marry Lucy?"

At last the real reason had emerged for his father's hasty trip to Tennessee, and he shook his head. "I've always known I didn't want to marry Lucy. This was something you and her father dreamed up without ever asking either of us what we wanted."

"You're wrong. Lucy is very much in love with you and wants to be your wife."

"No, she doesn't. If she said that, it's only

because she knows it's what her father wants her to say."

"And you don't want to do what your father wants. Is that right?"

Andrew swallowed back his anger and took a deep breath. Arguing with his father wouldn't get him anywhere. He had to try reasoning with him. "Please, Father, try to understand how I feel. You wanted me to come here because you thought it would be good for me to have this experience listed in my background. I came because I wanted to do something to help preserve these mountains. I feel like I'm involved in something important, and I feel good about myself for the first time."

His father's features softened. "That's good. You should feel that way. Establishing this park is one of the best things that's happened in the southeastern United States in years. I'm glad you've been a part of it, but there's more for you back in Virginia. There's a campaign to begin for the state senate and there's the perfect woman for a politician's wife waiting for you."

Andrew shook his head. "I've thought long and hard on those things since I've been in Tennessee, and I know neither of those things is for me. I don't want to run for office, and I don't want to marry Lucy."

His father recoiled as if he'd struck him. "What do you mean you don't want to run for office? That's what we've always planned."

"No, Father. It's what you've planned for me ever since Winston died. He's the one who should have been a politician, not me. I'm so sorry he's not here to carry on your dream. I can't do it."

His father stared at him for a moment, and Andrew recognized what was about to take place. Every time his father found himself on the losing end of an argument he took his time to reassess what had been said and formulate a plan to turn his opponent's way of thinking into that of his own. Andrew steeled himself for what would come next.

Finally his father spoke. "If you had thought this before you left home, you would have told me. Something's changed since then. I know you like your job, but it has to be more than that." He propped his right elbow in his left palm and tapped his index finger against his lips. "I ask myself what could make a young man turn his back on everything his family has dreamed of for him, and the answer is obvious. It has to be a woman."

"How . . . how . . ." There was no use asking his father how he knew. He'd uncovered the secrets of many men in the past, and it wasn't difficult to figure out his only son.

His father laughed. "Your face tells it all. Who is she?"

"Her name is Laurel Jackson."

"A mountain girl, no doubt." His lips pursed as if the words were distasteful.

"She's the daughter and granddaughter of two of the most respected men in Cades Cove, and I'm in love with her."

His father's eyebrows arched in surprise. "Love? There's no place for the love of a woman in our lives, Andrew. We were born to serve the people. That takes all your time. There's nothing else."

A sarcastic laugh rumbled from Andrew's throat. "Oh, I know that all right. You never had time for my mother or for me after Winston's death. Well, I don't want to live that way. I want to be with a woman I love and have children with her."

"You're being ridiculous," his father hissed.

Andrew strode to the door and jerked it open. "You're the one being ridiculous. When you decide to ask me what I want out of life, we'll continue this conversation."

"Wait! Don't go!" his father called out.

He was already in the outer office when the urgent sound of his father's voice stopped him and he turned around. He stepped back into Superintendent Eakin's office and left the door open in case he needed a speedy retreat. "What do you want?"

"I don't want us to part this way. No matter what you think of me I want you to know I've only done what I thought was best for you. You have all the qualities of a good statesman, and you'll go far in politics. Don't deprive the people of your services just because you're infatuated with some little mountain girl who can never understand the world you come from."

Andrew gritted his teeth and took a step closer to his father. "I'm warning you . . ."

"Excuse me. I didn't mean to interrupt."

Andrew whirled to see Laurel standing in the doorway. He had no idea how much of their conversation she'd overheard, but her pale face and trembling chin told him she'd witnessed at least part of it.

"Laurel." Her name gushed from his mouth. "I didn't know you were here."

She stepped farther into the room. "I asked the clerk at the desk if he'd seen you, and he said you'd come through the lobby earlier with Mr. Eakin. So I came to find you. I heard your voices. I hope I didn't come at the wrong time."

He strode toward her, grabbed her hand, and pulled her across the floor with him until they stopped in front of his father. "Laurel, this is my father, Congressman Richard Brady. Father, this is Laurel Jackson, the woman I was telling you about."

His father glanced at him and then back to Laurel. The anger that had been in his eyes a few moments before disappeared and he reached out and took Laurel's hand in his. "Miss Jackson, it's so nice to meet you."

Andrew wanted to jerk Laurel away and tell her not to be deceived by his father's friendly manner. It was his public persona, and she was about to be introduced to the devious man behind the friendly façade. He tightened his grip on her hand and glanced at her.

"Are your parents at Mr. Bryan's store?"

"Yes, I walked over here to see you like I said I would." She stared at him.

"Then let me take you back to the store." He looked at his father again. "I'll see you later."

His father smiled, reached out, and took Laurel's arm. She glanced over her shoulder as her hand slipped from Andrew's and his father led her to a sofa across the room where he sat down beside her. "I want to get acquainted with this young woman who has bewitched my son."

She settled a pillow behind her back and faced him. "I don't think *bewitched* is the right word, sir. Andrew and I are friends."

"Very good friends from what he tells me." When she didn't answer, he continued. "Andrew says he's in love with you."

Her eyebrows arched. "Oh? He told you that?"

"Yes, and I think the woman whom my son loves needs to get to know his family, don't you?"

She nodded. "Of course."

Andrew stormed across the floor and stopped

in front of her. "I think it's time we left, Laurel."

She directed a cool gaze at him. "No, I'd like to hear what your father has to say."

"Evidently you are a very smart young woman, Miss Jackson. Has my son told you about how we've planned his political career for years?"

"He's told me how you've planned it. I've never been sure if he really wanted it or not."

A slight frown wrinkled his brow. "That's where we disagree, Miss Jackson. He does want a career in politics. He's just not thinking clearly at the moment. It seems he's infatuated with you. I hope you're a more sensible person than he is."

Laurel's serene expression gave no hint of what she felt. She was silent as the congressman continued.

"Andrew has a heritage of wealth. He's been raised to have whatever he wanted. You, on the other hand, have probably had a very different life living in a remote area of the mountains. I expect your family had a rough time providing the bare essentials for your family. A young man with Andrew's background and wealth can be mighty attractive for a young woman. Wouldn't you agree, Miss Jackson?"

She shook her head. "Not at all, Mr. Brady. I think you sell his abilities short if you think that's what makes him the man he is. As for my family, we are neither destitute nor ignorant. In addition to our farm in the Cove, my father owns a lodge for visitors to the Smokies, and my mother owns a pottery studio where she makes and sells her work not only in the mountains but through the distribution of a fellow potter in the New York area. We've always had what we needed, and I was able to attend school in Maryville, thanks to money from my uncle who was a doctor. I wouldn't want you to think I'm some kind of money-hungry hillbilly whose family barely scratched out a living in these hills."

Andrew suppressed a smile at the surprise on his father's face. After a moment he regained his composure. "I see that you are a smart young woman, Miss Jackson, and you understand the situation we're facing here with Andrew's refusal to come back home and get ready for his state senate race. I want that for him, and I believe it's the road he should travel. I have no idea what you think he should do, but I can tell from talking with you that family is important to you. I don't think you would want to be the cause for Andrew to turn his back on his only family."

A sad smile pulled at Laurel's mouth, and she reached out and patted his father's hand. "No, I would never do that, Mr. Brady. And I shall pray that you won't either." She pushed to her feet and faced Andrew. "Now I think it's time for me to leave."

"I'll go with you." He reached out, and she laced her fingers through his.

They had just reached the doorway when his father's voice called out. "Andrew, one more thing."

They stopped and glanced back at him. "What?" he asked.

"Lucy wanted me to remind you that her family's annual week-long trip to visit family in Asheville is coming up in September. They already have invitations to many events in the area. One of them is to a party at the Biltmore Estate. She said you'd promised to go as her escort for the week like you did last year and wanted me to check with you about when she could expect you back."

He heard Laurel's sharp intake of breath, and he frowned. "I explained all that in my letter."

His father stared at him. "What letter?"

"The one I wrote her."

"She hasn't received a letter from you."

Laurel pulled free of his grasp and bolted for the hallway. He had one last glimpse of the smirk on his father's face before he ran after her. He caught up with her just as she exited the hotel and stepped onto the sidewalk.

"Laurel, wait!"

She whirled and faced him. Sparks of anger flashed in her eyes. "What do you want?"

"I'm sorry about all that back there. That's how my father is. He's the great manipulator. He can make anybody believe anything."

She jabbed him in the chest with her finger. "Maybe his son is just like him. You made me believe you wrote Lucy."

"I did. I don't know what happened, but I wrote that letter. I wouldn't doubt that my father lied just to get this very reaction from you."

"You also made me believe you'd barely talked with her. Now I find out you spent a week at her relatives' home and you were her escort for parties. Why didn't you tell me that?"

He raked his hand through his hair. "Are you going to tell me that Jimmy has never accompanied you anywhere?"

She blinked and didn't speak for a moment. "No. We've been to parties and family dinners together."

He grabbed her by the shoulders. "That's exactly what it was like with Lucy and me. I went with her family as a friend. It was nothing else." She just stared at him, and he groaned. "Please don't let my father win. I love you, Laurel. Please believe me."

She started to speak, but Willie's voice rang out from nearby. "Laurel, come quick!"

The tone reminded him of the day Willie had called them when Granny had died. They jerked their heads around at the same time and saw Willie emerge from the footpath that connected the hotel to the settlement next door. He felt Laurel's shoulders tremble underneath his fingers.

"Willie, what is it?" she demanded as he skidded to a stop next to them.

"It's Pa. He got sick over at Mr. Bryan's store, and Mama sent me for you."

Andrew grabbed Willie by the arm. "Is he still at the store?"

Big tears rolled down Willie's face. "No. He's real sick. Mr. Bryan said it looked like a heart attack to him. He helped us load Poppa into the truck and drove us to the Health Center over there at that school. Mama wants you to come right now."

"Poppa . . ." Laurel whispered. She looked as if she was frozen with shock.

Andrew grabbed Laurel's hand and motioned for Willie to follow. "Let's go."

Willie took off at a run, sprinting at full speed down the footpath. Laurel frowned and blinked as if waking from a dream. Then she glanced from her brother to Andrew. "What if . . ."

Andrew touched her lips with his finger. "Don't even think it, Laurel. Let's go see how he is."

He pulled her forward and they ran after Willie. As they sped along the footpath, Andrew thought of Matthew Jackson and how much his family loved him. He'd dedicated his life to making theirs the best it could be, and now two of his children cried for the man they loved.

As for his own father, right now all Andrew felt for him was a burning anger that he doubted would ever go away. He envied Laurel and Willie. They had something he wanted but would never have—a father who loved them with all his heart. He hoped they got the chance to tell their father how much they loved him.

Chapter 15

Her father couldn't die. He was too young. There were too many things left undone and unsaid. She tightened her hold on Andrew's hand and marveled at the strength she gained from him when they were together.

But no one, not even Andrew, could make this moment go away. It wasn't the right time for this to be happening. Not for years to come, and not so soon after losing Granny.

"Laurel, are you all right?"

She heard Andrew's panting voice, but all she could do was nod. The memory of how totally unacceptable Andrew's father had made her feel returned, and fresh tears pooled in her eyes. Not only that, but he had accused her of being interested in his family's money. She'd never been so humiliated in her life, but she thought she'd managed to stand her ground with the man who was determined to rid Andrew's life of her.

She frowned and shook her head. This wasn't the time to be thinking about that. Her father's condition was the only thing she needed to concentrate on now. Her heart warmed at the thought that her father would never have talked to Andrew like his father had done to her today.

Laurel glanced at Andrew out of the corner of her eye. The muscle in his jaw twitched. What was he thinking? He'd stood up to his father this time. But what about the next? Defying a parent had to be the most difficult thing a person ever had to do. From her impression of Andrew's father, she knew he wouldn't give up. Over time Mr. Brady might very well break down the barriers Andrew had built. Then he might see her as his father did—a simple mountain girl who didn't have the social skills and refinement expected of women in their society. If Andrew ever looked at her the way his father had today, it would crush her.

They burst from the tree-lined path into the open field where the settlement buildings sat. She kept her eyes on Willie and followed his route until he bounded onto the porch of an L-shaped frame house. As she neared it, she could see a sign out front that identified it as the Jennie Nichol Memorial Health Center.

Willie pushed the front door open and disappeared inside. Laurel and Andrew leaped onto the porch and ran into the house. Her mother stood in the middle of a small room with her arms around Willie who clung to her. She stared at

Laurel over Willie's head as she entered the room.

"Mama, what happened?"

She glanced down at Willie and tightened her hold on him. "We were moving the crates from the truck to the store. I held the door for your father as he carried one into the store. He'd barely gotten inside when the crate dropped to the floor. I ran to him, and his hand was clutching at his chest. Then he groaned and collapsed. Thank goodness Mr. Bryan was there. He helped us get him to the truck, and he drove us over here."

Laurel glanced past her mother and for the first time saw the store owner standing at the far side of the room. She nodded in his direction. "Thank you for helping, Mr. Bryan."

He stepped forward. "I'm glad I was there. We got him out here as fast as we could. The nurses here do a good job, but we're fortunate that there's a doctor from Knoxville here for the week. He's with your father now."

Andrew touched her arm, and she turned toward him. "It's good there's a doctor here, but it may take a while for him to tell us anything." He glanced at her mother who still held on to Willie. "Mrs. Jackson, is there anything I can do for you? Get you anything or go for anyone?"

"No, thank you, Andrew. We just need to sit down and wait. And pray. We need to pray that Matthew will be all right." A muffled wail drifted up as Willie pressed closer to his mother. She reached down and tilted his face up. "I know you're upset, but you have to be brave."

Laurel sucked in her breath at the anguish on Willie's face. "B-but it's all my fault."

Her mother shook her head. "No, it's not. Why would you think that?"

"Because I was mad because he wanted me to help take the crates in. I should've taken all of them inside for him, and then he'd be okay."

Mama put her arm around his shoulders and led him to the chairs that sat around the wall of the waiting room. "It's not your fault, Willie. I thought your father wasn't feeling well this morning and asked him about it, but he assured me he was fine. Evidently he wasn't. Now I want us all to sit down and pray until the doctor comes out."

They followed her to the chairs. Laurel bowed her head and began to pray. After a few minutes she glanced up. Her mother had her eyes closed, and Willie now sat with his face buried in their mother's lap. Mr. Bryan clasped his hands between his knees and sat with his eyes closed. Only Andrew stared straight ahead. When he saw Laurel looking at him, he smiled. She smiled at him before she bowed her head and began to pray again.

She had no idea how long they sat like that, but it seemed an eternity before the closed door to the examination room opened. A lanky young man stepped through the door and pushed a stray lock of hair off his forehead before closing the door behind him.

They were all on their feet before he could reach them. "Dr. Pearson," her mother said. "How is he?"

Laurel held her breath as the doctor stopped in front of them. "Mrs. Jackson, your husband has suffered a heart attack. I have no way of knowing if there's any serious damage done or not, but anytime there's a heart attack we have to assume it is very serious."

Her mother reached out and clasped Laurel's hand. "How serious?"

"Medical science still knows very little about the heart and how to treat heart problems. However, there's a drug now that's helping some. In the medical community we call it glyceryl trinitrate, but it's really nitroglycerine."

Andrew gasped. "Nitroglycerine? Isn't that an explosive?"

The doctor nodded. "That's right, but about 1878 it was discovered that it could ease chest pain, and doctors have been using it ever since. The FDA hasn't approved it yet, but they will soon. I always carry some in my medical bag, and I administered it to your husband. He's free from pain and resting comfortably now."

"But will he recover?" Laurel asked.

"At this point I don't know. He needs to stay here for a few days so we can keep an eye on him. If he continues to be pain free, we'll let him go home. But even if that happens, his activities are going to be restricted."

Her mother swallowed and tightened her grip on Laurel's hand. "What do you mean?"

Dr. Pearson looked around the group. "He will need to cut down on heavy lifting and hard work. And he needs to stay as free from worry as he can. When I was talking with him after the pain subsided, he told me how concerned he's been over having to sell your farm and move from Cades Cove. You as his family are going to have to take a lot of responsibility off his shoulders."

Rani nodded. "We can do that. You said he'll need to stay a few days. Did you mean here at the clinic?"

"Yes. We'll keep an eye on him and monitor his progress. Maybe you and your children could stay at the hotel next door. That way you'd be close at all times."

Laurel's mother nodded. "We'll check on that later. Right now I'd like to see him."

"Of course. You can all go in now. Try not to talk about anything that will upset him, though."

"We won't." Her mother took a deep breath and glanced at her then at Willie. "I want you to be brave. Don't cry. Talk to him as if he'll be up and around in a few days."

They followed Dr. Pearson as he opened the door to the room. Laurel was about to step through the doorway when she realized Andrew wasn't behind her. She turned and stared at him. "Aren't you coming?"

He shook his head. "This is a time for your family to be together. Tell him I hope he feels better soon."

"I will." She smiled before she followed her mother and Willie into the room, but she felt the smile fading when she caught the first glimpse of her father.

He lay on a narrow bed, his eyes closed and one hand across his chest. The gray pallor of his face sent a chill up her spine, and she bit down on her tongue to keep from crying out. Her mother dropped down on her knees beside the bed and covered his hand with hers.

"Matthew, it's Rani. Can you hear me?" He didn't move, and after a minute she pulled a handkerchief from her pocket and began to dab at his forehead. "The doctor says you're going to be fine. So you just rest and get better. Laurel and Willie are here with me, and we'll take care of everything. No need for you to think of anything except getting well so we can all go home."

Laurel stared down at her father's still body, and her heart thudded. Why didn't he wake up? Or at least open one eye so he could see them. She and Willie dropped to their knees next to their mother. Laurel fought back tears as she stroked her father's hand. "We love you, Poppa."

A slight frown crossed his face, and he flinched. Her mother's head jerked up, and she shot a worried glance at Dr. Pearson. "What's the matter?"

"He's probably having some discomfort. It's not unusual."

Her father's eyes opened, and he blinked. Slowly he turned his head and looked into her mother's face. He swallowed, and a raspy whisper drifted from his mouth. "Rani?"

She covered his hand with hers. "Yes, Matthew. I'm here. So are Laurel and Willie."

His eyes clouded, and a frown pulled at his brow. "Where's Charlie?"

Her mother's body jerked at his question, and she pressed her lips together as tears flooded her eyes. Laurel put her arm around her mother's shoulders and leaned closer to her father. "Charlie's not here right now, but I am, Poppa. And so is Willie."

She nudged Willie with her elbow. He looked up at her, a scared expression on his face, and she nodded. Willie swallowed and scooted closer to the bed. "Hi, Poppa."

Her father raised his hand and motioned for Willie to move closer. He wedged himself in front of Laurel and leaned closer to his father. Laurel tightened her arm around her mother's shoulders as her father raised his hand and patted Willie on the head. "A good boy. Always been. But too young." He frowned and turned his head. "Rani?"

"Yes, Matthew. I'm here."

His gaze moved over her mother's face. "Promise me . . ."

"What? Promise you what?"

"Willie. Don't want it to be for him like it was for me. Too young to be the head of the family."

Tears began to stream down her mother's face. "You're going to be the head of this family for a long time. You'll teach Willie to be a man."

The corner of his lip curled up, and he patted Willie again. "Love you, son." He closed his eyes, then they shot open. "Laurel?"

She jumped at the sound of her name. "Yes, Poppa?" She leaned around Willie and smiled at him.

His eyes softened, and he smiled. "So beautiful. Just like your mama. Be happy, darling. Don't marry unless he loves you like I've loved your mama."

"I won't, Poppa. I'll let you help me decide who I should marry."

Dr. Pearson stepped up behind them and touched her mother's shoulder. "I think that's enough talking for now. He needs to rest. You can see him later."

Her mother nodded, leaned over, and kissed her father on the cheek. "You get some rest now. I'll be back in a little while. I love you."

He closed his eyes and nodded. "Love you, Rani. Love all of you."

Laurel waited until her mother backed away before she kissed his forehead. "I love you, Poppa. I'll be back later."

He nodded but didn't open his eyes. Willie patted his hand, turned, and ran out of the room. When Laurel and her mother entered the waiting room, Willie stood staring out the window. He didn't turn around as Andrew rose to face them.

"How is he?" Andrew asked.

"I'm not sure," her mother replied. "I'm afraid we're in for some hard times ahead." She sank down into one of the chairs. "We need to make some plans about what we're going to do."

Laurel glanced at her mother in surprise. "What do you mean? I thought we were going to stay at the hotel."

Her mother shook her head. "I'm not leaving this building as long as your father is here. But we only intended to be in Gatlinburg for the day. There are things to be done at home. The cows need to be milked and the chickens put up for the night. And we need some extra clothes for a few days."

Andrew stepped closer to her mother. "Mrs. Jackson, I'd be happy to drive out to Cades Cove and take care of everything at your home. I admit I've never milked cows, but maybe Willie could go along and show me how."

Willie's eyes lit up. "I sure could teach you, Andrew. I reckon I been milking cows since I was old enough to tote a bucket of milk."

Laurel smiled and mouthed a silent thank-you to Andrew for making her brother feel so important. Her mother, however, shook her head. "You must have other work to do here in Gatlinburg. I don't want to cause you any trouble. Besides, you and Willie wouldn't know which clothes to bring for Laurel and me."

Laurel watched the smile disappear from Willie's face at their mother's words. "Then I'll drive Willie and me home. We'll come back tomorrow."

"Land's sakes, no," her mother cried. "It's a long drive out there, and I'd be worried out of my mind with you two driving alone."

"Mama, you know I can drive. Please . . ."

Andrew held up his hand. "We could argue about this all day. So let me suggest this. I'll drive Laurel and Willie home. Willie and I will take care of the chores while Laurel gets some clothes for all of you. I'll then take them to Simon and Anna's house. I think they need to be with family tonight. And then I'll pick them up in the morning and bring them back to Gatlinburg. How's that?"

Her mother regarded him with a somber expression for a moment. "Are you sure it won't take you away from your work?"

"No, ma'am. I still have a few days' work to do

at headquarters with Superintendent Eakin, and I can be back here in the morning for that. It's no problem. And I want to help you any way I can."

A weary smile creased her mouth, and she nodded. "All right, Andrew. I appreciate you doing this for us. And I'm glad I'll be able to get word to Mama and Poppa about Matthew. They've both thought of him as a son since he was nine years old. I expect this is going to hit them mighty hard, especially after losing Granny."

He pulled his watch from his pocket and stared at it. "I need to go back to the office and let them know I'll be staying out at the CCC camp tonight, and I'll tell the hotel staff to send some supper over for you, Mrs. Jackson."

"Thank you, Andrew."

He slipped his watch back in his pocket and nodded. "Laurel, I'll take care of those things and drive back over here in about twenty minutes. I'll see you then."

He was out the door before Laurel could respond. She walked to the window and watched as he walked toward the footpath that led to the hotel. Her mother's arm circled her waist, and she turned toward her.

"The more I'm around Andrew, the more I like him."

Laurel smiled and turned back to stare after Andrew. "Did you notice how his voice sounded a lot like Poppa's when he stopped all the bickering about who should go back to the Cove? There was something about him that sounded like he was in charge of the situation."

A sob tore from her mother's throat, and she covered her face with her hands. "Oh, Laurel, what am I going to do?"

Laurel whirled and wrapped her arms around her mother. "Mama, we're going to get through this fine. Poppa will rest for a few days, and then we'll take him home. We'll be back to normal in no time."

She glanced across the room to where Willie sat, his face buried in his hands and his shoulders shaking. From the doorway Dr. Pearson gazed from one to another. After a moment he closed the door.

The click of the latch made her shiver. A battle between life and death was being waged behind that door, and she felt helpless. Her father had always been the rock of their family. He was the one who'd offered comfort for childhood injuries and the one to sit beside her bed when she'd been ill with high fevers. He'd also been the one who'd always listened when she had problems. What would she do without him?

She hugged her mother closer and stared past her to the door that stood between them and her father. All she could do was pray that God would see fit to heal her father and not let their time together end in that room.

Rani's head dipped down to her chest, and she jerked upright. She sat still for a moment to see if her quick movement had disturbed Matthew. When he didn't say anything, she reached over and straightened the quilt that covered him in an attempt to ward off the night's temperature drop.

His hand stuck out from underneath the cover and she rubbed his fingers before she pulled the quilt over him. She rose from her chair, put her hands in the small of her back, and stretched. What time could it be? It seemed like an eternity since she'd settled in the chair the clinic's nurse had brought for her.

She walked over to the window, pulled back the thin curtains, and stared out into the night. The full moon glowed like a beacon in the night sky and reminded her of evenings spent with Granny on the front porch as they tried to find the brightest star God had sent their way that night. When they found it, they would each name the blessings God had given them, and Granny would end their night with a prayer of thanks for all the blessings that came from His hand.

As a child, she'd recounted blessings such as a new dress her mother had made her or a toy her father had brought back from a trip to Gatlinburg. Later, when Matthew had returned to the Cove, it had been about God sending him into her life and the blessing of his love.

Tonight she stood alone staring at the stars. Granny was gone and her husband lay close to death. A sob caught in her throat. How could she live without him?

She tiptoed back to his bed and dropped down on her knees. The rough plank floor scraped at her shins, but she remained still. She bent over and pressed her forehead against the edge of the bed as she began to silently pray. *God, I come to You as a broken woman tonight. I have never been as afraid as I am right now. I love this man so much, and I don't want to lose him. You have brought him through so much in his life. You were with him in all the dark years following his father's death, and You kept him safe so he could return to the place and the people he loved. I want him to live so he can see Willie grow up and Laurel get married and Charlie come back home. But even as I pray for what I want, I know Matthew would tell me to pray for Your will in this matter. So, Father, be with me as I surrender my will to You. I know I can face his loss if You walk beside me. Thank You for the time we've had together. Be with our family in this trying time. Amen.*

Rani stayed on her knees long after the prayer was finished. She placed the palm of her hand on Matthew's chest and took pleasure in its rise and fall with each breath he took. As long as there was breath, there was life. Finally satisfied that he was resting comfortably, she eased to her feet, settled back into her chair, and began to nod.

Sometime later she stirred at a sound in the room. She opened her eyes and blinked into the darkness. What had awakened her? Then she heard it again. Matthew was calling her.

"Rani?"

She bolted to her feet and bent over him. "Yes, Matthew. I'm here."

A sigh of relief drifted up from the bed. "I'm glad. I thought you might be somewhere else."

She cupped his cheek with her hand and smiled. "Where would I be except at your side? That's the only place I ever want to be."

"I'm sorry I woke you up. I just wanted to see you."

"Then let me get some light in here so we can see each other better." An oil lamp and a box of matches sat on a table next to the bed. She turned her back to him so he couldn't see how her hand shook as she removed the lamp's chimney and held the struck match to the wick. When she replaced the chimney, the soft glow of the lamp lit the room. She turned back and smiled. "That's better. Now I can see you."

She pulled the chair closer and sat down. He stared at her for a moment before he spoke. "I'm sorry I gave you such a scare today. I've known for a long time I wasn't well, but I didn't want to worry you."

The memory of him wincing in pain and rubbing his chest flashed in her mind. Why had she been so blind? Maybe she could have gotten him to a doctor sooner. Then another thought struck her, and her eyes grew wide.

"Is that the reason you gave up the fight to hold onto our land and insisted we get started building the new house and studio?"

"Yes. I didn't want you to have to deal with everything alone if something happened to me."

A tear ran down her cheek, and she wiped at it. "You should have told me, Matthew. You didn't need to carry that burden alone."

He sighed. "Well, I guess my secret is out now." He reached for her hand. "I don't know if this is my time to die or not. If it is, everything is taken care of. The lawyer who handled our court case has all the papers you'll need to sell our farm. And everything's arranged about building the new house and studio. He'll also help you sell all the livestock and whatever you won't need when you move to Gatlinburg."

She reached over and placed her hand over his mouth. "Don't talk like that. You're going home with us, and I'm going to take care of you just like you have done for me for all these years. We're going to finish raising Willie, and we're going to see Laurel married, and . . ." She choked up and cleared her throat. "And we're going to be together when Charlie comes home."

He wrapped his fingers around hers and squeezed them. "I hope so, Rani. I sure hope so."

Chapter 16

It was a glorious afternoon. Or so Laurel thought. She kicked at a rock in her path as she walked to the house from the lodge that had probably seen its last guest. She clasped her Brownie camera tighter and mulled over her plans for developing and cataloguing the pictures she'd just taken. By the time she left the Cove she wanted to have pictures of everything she'd known all her life.

As she approached the house she caught sight of her father sitting in a rocker on the front porch. He stared down at the Bible in his lap. It didn't seem possible that three weeks had passed since his attack. After a week at the clinic he'd been allowed to return to the Cove, and so far he was getting better every day.

Laurel tiptoed up the steps, raised the camera, and stared through the view finder. She smiled at the image of her father. The color had come back to his cheeks, but he looked like he'd lost weight. He glanced up when he heard the camera click and scowled at her.

"Did you just take my picture?"

Laurel laughed and dropped into the chair beside him. "I did. I thought I'd see what you were up to out here on the porch by yourself. I couldn't help but take your picture."

"I figured it was about time for your mother to send somebody to check on me. If it's not her, it's either you or Willie. You're all treating me like I'm an invalid."

She laughed and patted his arm. "We're so glad to see you doing so well that we can't stay away from you."

"And you can't quit taking my picture," he growled. "Every time I look up that thing is aimed at me."

"It's because I'm so glad to have you home. It wasn't the same around here without you."

He grunted and closed the Bible. "Sweet talk will get you nowhere with me, young lady."

She set the camera down next to the chair and grinned up at him. "My, my. Aren't you grumpy today? Have you had your medicine?"

"Yes. I'm full of those vitamins Dr. Pearson gave me." He patted his shirt pocket. "And I've got my nitroglycerine right here."

"Good. Keep it close at hand in case you need it."

He smiled, leaned back in the chair, and took a deep breath. "I'm sorry I gave all of you such a scare."

"Well, everything turned out all right."

He looked at her and arched an eyebrow. "All right? I've been practically retired from working and I have to spend part of the day in bed. Not to mention all those vitamins I'm taking."

"Now, Poppa, you know Dr. Pearson said medical science still knows very little about the heart. You're lucky to be alive, so you need to follow his orders. We want you around here for a long time to come."

"I want that too, darling. One of the things I kept thinking about when I was at that clinic was that I wanted to see you get married." He frowned and glanced toward the corner of the house. "That reminds me. Where is Andrew? I heard him drive up before I came outside, but I haven't seen him."

"He's at the barn with Willie. They're doing the milking, although that's not a very big job since Mama sold all the livestock except that one cow. But Andrew keeps coming to help out."

"That boy has sure been good to help out since I've been sick." He sat in thought for a moment. "It reminds me of the time I went over to help Jimmy's grandmother Laura with the chores when Pete got hurt chopping wood. It was the beginning of a great friendship with Pete."

"I've heard you tell that story, but you were probably better at what you had to do than Andrew was at first." She swiveled in her chair to face her father. "Oh, Poppa, I wish you could have seen him that first day. He had no idea how to milk a cow. Willie had to show him. In fact Willie has really amazed me at how he's taken over the chores. You'd be so proud of him."

Her father's chin trembled. "I am proud of him. He's growing up."

"You sound like that makes you sad."

He smiled. "I know I've said he needed to grow up, but now that he is I find I'm missing the mischievous boy that he was."

Laurel laughed. "Oh, don't worry. I have a feeling that little boy is still around somewhere."

Her father nodded and gazed toward the mountains in the distance. They sat in silence for several minutes until he turned to her. "I haven't asked you how things are going with you and Andrew. Have there been any changes since I got sick?"

"No. For the last few weeks the only thing on my mind was getting you well. In fact Andrew and I have hardly talked. He's been busy every day finishing up the sale agreements with some of the last holdouts in the Cove. Then by the time he's through with the chores in the afternoon and has supper, he's ready to get back to the camp."

"I've enjoyed having him here at supper. I've really gotten to like that boy." He paused and cast a quick glance at her. "I'm still concerned that he questions whether or not he can ever turn his life over to God."

Laurel sighed. "I know. That concerns me too, as well as his relationship with his father."

"Why? Is there a problem?"

Her father listened intently as she related her

meeting with Andrew's father. When she finished, she glanced at him. He pursed his lips, propped his elbows on the arms of the chair, and tapped his tented fingers together.

"I've prayed and prayed about this, Poppa, and I don't know what to do. I don't want to be the reason for Andrew to be alienated from his father."

"It sounds to me like there was a problem before you came along. Maybe you just helped it come to the surface."

"I've thought about that, but it still worries me. The Bible says for us to honor our father and mother. I want Andrew to be able to work out his problems with his father."

"Maybe he will. Keep praying about it. That's all I know to tell you right now."

Before she could respond, Andrew and Willie walked around the corner of the house, and Willie hopped onto the front porch. "Mama says for me to take you for a walk before supper. She thinks you need some exercise."

A growl escaped her father's throat. "Oh, she does? And where does she suggest we walk to?"

"I thought we could walk down to the creek. Maybe we'd see that big fish that stays around that log in the water. How 'bout that?"

Her father smiled and pushed to his feet. "I think that's a good idea. Let's go."

Laurel watched them go before she turned back

to Andrew. "Come on up and have a seat on the porch."

"Okay." He stepped onto the porch and dropped down in the chair where her father had sat a few minutes ago. He leaned his head back and closed his eyes for a moment. "This has been a busy day."

She reached over and squeezed his arm. "We really appreciate all you've done to help out while Poppa's been sick. I know it hasn't been easy for you on top of all your responsibilities at work."

He straightened in his seat and faced her. "I wanted to talk to you about that. I talked with your mother when we brought the milk from the barn. I have to go back to Gatlinburg for a few days. I hate to leave, but the superintendent wants me there."

"Don't worry about that. We'll make do just fine. We understand you have a job to do."

He nodded and grinned. "Willie can milk that cow by himself. He's quite a boy. I think we've become close since I've been helping out here."

"I'm glad. I want you to like my family, but I worry about your relationship with your family."

His eyes darkened, and he pushed up out of his chair. He walked to the porch railing and turned to face her. "Laurel, there is no relationship with my father anymore. I thought you understood that."

She jumped up and moved closer to him. "But

that's not right, Andrew. Everybody needs family, and he's all you've got. You have to find a way to heal this rift between the two of you."

His lips straightened into a thin line, and he shook his head. "I am through living with his domineering attitude and his determination to run my life. He's not going to push me around anymore."

"But, Andrew, he's your father. You don't have to cut him out of your life. I almost lost my father, and I'm so blessed that he lived. I don't want you to live your life without your father."

"My father is very different from yours. Besides, this doesn't concern you. It's my problem."

She gasped and took a step back. "Not my problem? I thought whatever affected one of us did the other also."

He shook his head and glared at her. "Not this. My relationship with my father is my business, not yours. Don't ever mention him to me again."

She clenched her fists at her side and gritted her teeth. "Are you giving me an order?"

"If that's what it'll take to get you to leave me alone about this, then yes, I am."

Her body trembled with anger. "What makes you think you have the right to talk to me like that? Maybe the words we said to each other the day Granny died made you believe I'd obey your every command like a well-trained dog, but I assure you that's not the case."

He raked his hand through his hair. "Laurel, I didn't mean it like that. I spoke in anger."

"That's no excuse, especially if you profess to love someone. Maybe I was right to keep my distance from you when we first met. We come from two different worlds, Andrew, and we don't see things in the same way."

His cheeks turned red and his eyes narrowed. "Oh, now the truth comes out. This is not about my father after all."

She frowned. "What are you talking about?"

"It's all about me not understanding the way of life here and how all of you pray about every little detail of your life. But most importantly it's about the fact that I grew up in a more affluent environment, and the folks in the Cove don't trust outsiders. Somehow that makes everybody here suspicious of me and my motives."

"What do you mean?"

"I came here and tried to be friendly with everybody. And what did it get me? I was ordered off people's property, I had a shotgun pointed at my head, and I had the girl I love tell me we were too different to ever have a relationship. I'm sorry I didn't grow up here and have a history with you like Jimmy does, but I was too busy in Virginia grieving over my brother and mother and wondering why my father didn't love me anymore."

She held up her hands and shook her head. "You're wrong about how you were treated. If I remember correctly you were invited to Sunday dinner at my grandparents' home the Sunday you came to church and told me you were joining the CCC camp."

"I didn't tell you I was joining. I said I was staying out there, which happened to be the truth." His dark eyes bored into her. "It sounds to me like you've been thinking about my shortcomings a lot. Maybe that's why you've made a point not to be alone with me lately."

She shook her head. "That's not true, Andrew. I've been busy helping my mother with my father."

"Well, all I know is that ever since your father got sick, you've hardly had time for me. I think this is the first time we've been together without one of your family members around. What happened, Laurel? Did they convince you that Jimmy was the better choice after all?"

She frowned and shook her head. "No, they haven't said . . ."

He gritted his teeth and took a step closer. "Don't deny it. They think of me as some monster from Washington who is forcing them to give up the land they've lived on for years. I don't think they have any more intention of accepting me than my father has for you."

"That's not true. They've been nice to you since the day you came to the Cove."

"Yes, they've treated me like they would any guest who came to visit but would soon go home.

They know I'm in love with you, but they don't accept me like they do Jimmy. They never let me forget that he's practically family. They'd rather you marry Jimmy than me. Have they convinced you to give them what they want?"

Tears filled her eyes. "Andrew, please don't."

He threw up his hands in resignation. "If that's what you want, don't let me stand in your way. Why don't you do something about it? He's back at home now, and he asked you to come visit his family. Why don't you go?"

Laurel stared at Andrew and tried to see a glimpse of the man she loved in the angry man who faced her, but she saw nothing that reminded her of the Andrew she'd come to know. After a moment she took a deep breath and spoke in a soft voice. "Maybe I will. Now I think it's time for you to leave. I'll make your apologies to Mama about supper."

He blinked, but the anger on his face didn't disappear. He swallowed hard and took a step toward her, but she flinched and backed away. She wrapped her arms around her waist to still the pain that gripped her at the hurt look that flickered in his eyes. He exhaled and shook his head in resignation. "I think you're right. Evidently I've worn out my welcome around here. I think we need to take a new look at our relationship."

She pressed her lips together and inhaled. "I agree. If this is any indication of what our life may be like in the future, I don't want to go any further with you. There are too many unresolved issues in your life, Andrew. Maybe deep down you do want a life in politics and the kind of home Lucy can make for you. And perhaps you do want your father to guide your career up the political ladder. If that's what you want, then you should accept it."

"I don't want that, Laurel. You know that."

She shook her head. "I don't know that. In fact I think you're sorry you ever told me you love me because you're scared of what that means and what you have to give up in your life. But I'm afraid too. Afraid that if you choose to be with me that one day you'll come to hate me because of the life you gave up for me. I couldn't stand that."

"I would never feel that way."

"You say that now, but who knows what the future holds? You need to be sure. Decide what you want and how you can bring peace into your life. Until that time, I don't want you to come back here. Goodbye, Andrew."

She whirled and ran into the house. He reached the door just as she slammed it behind her. "Laurel," he cried. "Come back out here. I can't leave with things this way between us." His fists pounded on the door, and tears ran down her face as he continued to call her name, but she didn't give in. After several minutes his voice grew softer. "I do love you. I've never felt about anyone like I do about you, but it scares me that we may not be right for each other. I guess we both need to figure some things out. I'm going now, but I will be back. As soon as I return from Gatlinburg, we're going to settle this."

Laurel listened to his footsteps as he went down the porch steps. In a few minutes she heard his car come around the side of the house and drive off down the road. She leaned her head against the door and let the tears flow.

Never in her life had she felt like she did now. It was as if her soul had been sucked from her body and left an emptiness that filled her from head to toe. All she wanted was to curl up in her bed and cry until she fell into an exhausted sleep, but she couldn't do that. She had to put on a pleasant expression and decide what to do.

After a moment the solution came to her, and Andrew had given her the idea. She would tell her family she had decided things weren't going to work out with Andrew, and he wouldn't be returning. She was upset, of course, but knew it was for the best. Since her father was getting better and most of the livestock had been sold, it seemed a good time to get away for a few days. The Fergusons' hotel in Tremont would be the perfect place to think. The mountain scenery there was beautiful, and Jimmy could help take her mind off her problems. That should please her mother.

She wiped the tears from her eyes, took a deep breath, and headed to the kitchen where her mother was preparing supper. Her excitement at the idea of the trip grew as she approached the kitchen. She hadn't been to Tremont in quite a while, and she really would like to spend some time with Jimmy's family. The only part she hadn't figured out was who she could get to take her to Townsend to catch the train that went to Tremont.

For the last week Andrew had struggled with how he and Laurel had parted before he left for Gatlinburg. During the day he'd been able to keep busy and concentrate on his job, but the nights had been a different story. Thank goodness he'd be back in his own bed at the CCC camp tonight. He didn't think he could stand another lonely night in the Mountain View Hotel. Of course he hadn't made any friends at the camp, but at least he'd be back in the Cove close to Laurel.

As he drove along the road that led into the Cove he pondered the question that had been on his mind all week. Would Laurel want to see him again? He'd said some awful things, and his heart still pricked every time he thought of their argument. How could he have accused her of all those things? Her parents and grandparents had never been anything but good to him, and he'd accused them of only pretending to like him while working against his relationship with Laurel because they wanted her to marry Jimmy.

The truth was that deep down he was jealous. Jealous of Jimmy because they treated him like family, of Laurel because she had such wonderful parents, and of the closeness the Martins and Jacksons shared. As a boy, he'd longed for his father to put his arms around him and tell him he loved him. And it remained the same even after he was grown. He wished that just once his father would look at him the way Matthew looked at Willie.

When Matthew and Willie had left to walk to the creek the day he and Laurel argued, he'd wanted to go along. He'd wanted to see what fathers and sons were supposed to do together. Instead he'd been so jealous of Willie, his bitterness at his father had spilled over and hurt Laurel. If only he could go back and change things.

His thoughts drifted to the good times he'd had with Willie when they'd done the chores after Matthew's illness. Then there had been the family suppers that he'd enjoyed. It would be night soon, and the Jacksons would be getting ready to gather around the kitchen table for their evening meal. He wished he were there. If he was lucky, the cooks at the camp might have something left over for him to eat tonight, but he'd be alone.

Deep down in his heart he knew what made

mealtime at the Martin and Jackson homes so different. They began by offering thanks to God for their blessings. But it wasn't that they thanked God only before they ate. It was a way of life with them. That's what made their family so different from what he'd always known. They had a deep faith in God, and every decision they made was based on what Jesus taught.

That was another thing that had troubled him all week. He still couldn't figure out where they got all their faith and how they managed to hold on to it even when things were bad. He'd spent hours every night for the last week reading the Bible Matthew had given him, but he still had trouble understanding it. How could you put your faith in something you couldn't see? Laurel's family did, and he'd never known anybody as happy as they were.

He had so many questions about what he'd read in the Bible, and he needed to talk to someone. Simon seemed the logical person to help him understand the words he'd read, and his house was just ahead.

When Andrew pulled the car to a stop in front of the cabin, Simon stepped onto the front porch and waved to him. "Andrew, good to see you. Get out and come in. You're just in time for supper."

Shaking his head, Andrew got out of the car and climbed the steps to where Simon stood. "I didn't come by to eat. I wanted to talk with you."

Simon put his arm around Andrew's shoulders and laughed as he guided him into the house. "Anna always fixes enough in case somebody drops by. Granny taught her that. I think she did it because back in my single days I used to show up at her house to eat nearly every day."

The smell of baking bread mingled with the spicy aroma of cinnamon enveloped Andrew as he entered the house, and his stomach growled. He flashed a sheepish grin at Simon. "I guess I am a little hungry."

Simon laughed again and slapped him on the back. "Glad to hear it. We'll talk after we eat. I can always think better with a full stomach."

An hour later Andrew and Simon were relaxing in the rockers that faced the stone fireplace in the front room of the cabin. Andrew's belt had tightened considerably during the meal, and he considered loosening it. "That sure was a good meal. The chicken and dumplings were the best I've ever eaten."

Simon nodded and patted his stomach. "I thought so too. Anna has always fed me well."

Anna stuck her head around the door at that moment and smiled. "Do you two need anything else?"

Andrew groaned. "I'm completely stuffed, Anna. Thank you so much for asking me to supper."

"You're welcome anytime, Andrew." She glanced at Simon. "I have some catching up to do in my journal, so I'll be in the bedroom if you change your minds."

Simon rose from his chair, walked over to her, and kissed her on the cheek. "I'll be in when Andrew and I are through talking."

She smiled up at him, and the look that passed between the two of them made Andrew's pulse race. He and Laurel had looked at each other that way until a week ago, but he didn't know if they ever would again. He swallowed hard and looked down at his hands clasped between his knees.

He heard Simon return and sit down, but he didn't look up until Simon spoke. "Andrew, what's troubling you?"

The soft-spoken words held so much kindness and compassion that Andrew's throat closed and moisture pooled in his eyes. He shook his head and took a deep breath before he returned Simon's gaze. "My life is falling apart, and I don't know what to do about it."

"What's happened to cause you so much pain?"

Briefly, he told Simon about his life with his father and their confrontation in Gatlinburg. Then he related the argument that had brought about his estrangement from Laurel. "I want things to be different in my life, but I don't know what to do to change it. I've read the Bible Matthew gave me, but it's hard to believe the things I read."

Simon settled back in his chair and crossed his legs. "Like what?"

Andrew spread his upturned palms in front of him and shrugged. "Well, faith for instance. All of you talk about faith and how it guides your lives. I don't understand how you can believe in something you can't see. In fact I had a conversation with Granny about it the day she died. It was about some verses I'd read that said if you had faith you could move mountains."

Simon smiled. "I'm sure she explained it didn't mean you could literally make a mountain move to a different spot. It means you can overcome what seems impossible if you put your faith in God."

"She did, but I don't know how to put my faith in something I can't see."

Simon exhaled a long breath, uncrossed his legs, and leaned forward. "Andrew, you're not the first person to have that problem. Have you read the accounts of Jesus's birth in the Bible?"

"I have. I've read all about Him, how He preached and healed the sick and how He died."

"Then you know as Christians we believe that God sent His Son to earth to die on the cross for the sins of mankind. That means every person throughout time—you, me, everybody. If we believe in Him, then one day we'll see Him when we're called away from this earthly home. Until that time we have to live by faith here on earth."

"But what makes you have that faith?"

Simon reached for his Bible on a table beside his chair and opened it. "Let me read what the Bible says in the eleventh chapter of Hebrews. 'Now faith is the substance of things hoped for, the evidence of things not seen.' When I read that verse, I think about how many adults find it hard to have faith, but to a child it comes naturally. Children want to experience good things that they dream of, and they believe that anything is possible. Jesus often used a child as an example of how we should have faith. God wants to teach us to have that same faith, and He's given us His Word to show us how. As we read it, we hear what He wants to tell us, and He says that faith comes by hearing."

"But hearing can be interpreted differently by whoever's reading it. Seeing it is something that can't be disputed."

Simon smiled. "You can't see the wind, but you feel it. You can't see the current underneath the water in a river, but you know if you step into it, you're going to feel its power. Faith is the same way. You can't see it, but once you embrace it, you feel it. We can't come to God unless we believe and have faith that He can control our lives." He looked back down at his Bible. "Here's another verse from Hebrews. 'But without faith it is impossible to please him: for he that cometh to God must believe that he is, and that he is a rewarder of them that diligently seek him.' Do you believe that God is real, Andrew?"

Andrew stared into Simon's eyes as he debated the question. He thought of the peace that the Martins and Jacksons had in their lives. He'd come to Cades Cove expecting them to be hostile and angry because they were being forced from their homes. They'd been sad and hurt, but never disrespectful to him. They'd talked about how God would take care of them no matter where they went, and they had shown him a way of dealing with life like he'd never known.

In that moment, he knew he wanted what they had. He wanted the peace that came with turning his life over to a higher power and believing that God would give him strength and peace to face whatever he must. He swallowed and nodded. "I do believe."

Simon smiled. "Then the Bible says all you have to do is believe in Him and ask Him to forgive you of your sins. He'll come into your heart and make you a new man."

"I want that."

"Then just ask Him. He's waiting for you."

Andrew had never prayed before in his life, but somehow it seemed so easy to bow his head and say the few words that would change his life. "God, I know I've done things in the past that weren't right. I've hurt people, and I'm sorry for that. Please forgive me and make me into a new man. I believe in You, and I will live by faith from this day forward. Amen."

For a moment he didn't open his eyes but sat still and marveled at the peace that rolled through his body. It felt like he had suddenly become light as a feather and could take flight at any moment. Finally, a big smile curled his lips, and he opened his eyes to see Simon beaming.

"How do you feel?" Simon asked.

"I . . . I don't know how to describe it. I feel like a new man. It's like I want to tell everybody I know about what's happened to me." A sudden thought hit him, and his eyes grew wide. "I want my father to know. I said some horrible things to him when we last met. I need to ask his forgiveness and try to make things right between us. But what will I do if he tries to convince me this is all just some emotional experience I've had?"

"The Bible says for us to honor our father and mother. You should always respect and love him as your father, but you're a new man now. Ask God to be with you and guide you as you talk with him."

Andrew nodded. "I will. He needs to hear what God can do in his life too. I need to go to Virginia right away and talk with him." Andrew rose from his chair and began to pace back and forth in front of the fireplace. "I'll go back to Gatlinburg in the morning and tell Mr. Eakin I need a week off to go home. I won't drive. I'll go by train. Yes, that's what I'll do tomorrow, right after I stop by to see Laurel."

Simon rose from his chair and put out a hand to stop Andrew. "Laurel's not at home, Andrew. She left for Tremont earlier this week. She's gone to spend a few weeks with Josie at her hotel."

Andrew reached out and grasped the edge of the mantel to steady his shaking legs. "So she's visiting Jimmy's family?"

"She is."

Andrew sighed and rubbed his hand over his eyes. "Well, I don't have anybody to blame but myself for that. Maybe she'll be home by the time I get back from Virginia." He swallowed and met Simon's stare. "I love her, you know."

Simon nodded. "I know. Just put the situation in God's hands, Andrew. You can't change Laurel, and you can't change your father." He tapped his index finger against Andrew's chest. "The only person in this world you can change is yourself. Think about that as you face your father and Laurel."

"I will, Simon, and thank you for everything. I'll always be grateful to you. And if it means anything to you, I'd hoped in time to be a part of your family. I may have messed that up, but there will always be a special place in my heart for all of you."

Simon grasped his shoulder and squeezed. "As we do for you, Andrew."

Later, as he drove back through the Cove to the CCC camp, Andrew thought back over the events of the day. When he'd left Gatlinburg, he felt as if he'd lost everything he held dear. Now he had a renewed spirit, and he believed he could face whatever lay ahead. His father might not like the message Andrew intended to take home, but Andrew would feel better once it was delivered. He loved his father, and that wasn't going to change. They needed to find a way to have a good relationship in the future even though Andrew had no intention of letting his father dominate his life any longer.

Laurel was another matter entirely. A future with her might have ended with the words he spoke to her a week ago. He would always regret that, but he'd survive if she rejected him. Simon had been right about having faith. No matter how things worked out with Laurel, he knew God would take care of him. That was what having faith was all about.

Chapter 17

The mountain air chilled Laurel, and she pulled her shawl tighter around her shoulders. She'd been in Tremont for over a week, and every night she'd sat out on the front porch of the Tremont Hotel and watched the moonlight reflect on the waters of the Middle Prong of Little River that ran through the town. The hotel, situated across the river from the main part of town, was connected to it by a footbridge.

Her mother had explained to her before she came that the small town had been established to serve as the base of operations for Little River Lumber Company's logging camps that stretched up the mountainside. At the height of the logging in this area it had boasted a post office, a general store, a community center that served as a church, a movie theater, a school, and of course the hotel Jimmy's mother, Josie, managed. Soon all of it would be gone. By the end of the year Little River would abandon all their logging operations in this area. Josie hadn't mentioned what her family would do when the hotel closed, and Laurel hadn't asked.

The front door of the hotel opened, and Jimmy's mother and grandmother stepped onto the front porch. They walked over to where Laurel sat and eased down into two chairs on either side of her.

Josie Ferguson smoothed the hair on the sides of her head back into the bun at the nape of her neck and sighed. "We got all the dishes washed and the bread for tomorrow rising. I thought we'd spend some time out here with you before we go to bed."

"I'm glad you came out. I still think I should have helped with the dishes."

Pearl, Jimmy's grandmother, waved her hand in

dismissal and shook her head. "There ain't no reason for you to do that. You're our comp'ny, and we just want you to have a good time."

"Oh, I'm having a wonderful time. I just wish that Jimmy could be here, though."

His mother nodded. "I do too. When he came back home from the CCC camp, he took the first job that opened up with the lumber company. He and his pa are helping close down the operation up at Thunderhead and move it over to Spruce Flats. They're staying at one of the shanty houses further up the mountain, but they'll be home this weekend."

Laurel swiveled in her chair and faced Josie. "There's something I don't understand. Little River's land was bought up by the government for the park years ago. Why has it taken so long for them to get out?"

Josie sighed and shook her head. "You sound just like your mama. She let me have an earful the last time I visited in the Cove, but I explained it to her. When Mr. Townsend, the man who owns Little River, sold his mountain tracts to the government back in 1926, he asked them to allow him to gradually stop his logging operation. They gave him fifteen years to completely shut down. That was a blessing to folks like us who worked for the company. It gave us some time to make plans about what we'd do next."

"Will Ted and Jimmy work over at Spruce

Flats until Little River turns the land over to the government?"

Josie sighed and shook her head. "I don't think so. With Tremont closing down there won't be any need for a hotel, so we'll leave too."

"Do you know where you'll go after the hotel closes?"

Josie nodded. "Ted and me have been saving for a long time. We have a little money, and we're gonna buy us a little place over at Oak Ridge close to Ted's folks. Ma and Pa are coming with us. We heard there's gonna be some factories opening up there soon. Ted thinks it'll be a good place for him and Jimmy to get jobs. That's what we're planning."

Laurel frowned. "The plans for where we'll go are all made. By next spring we'll be living in Gatlinburg at the new house."

Josie reached over and grasped Laurel's hand. "But just think how wonderful it will be for your mother to have a new studio. It will be better for your pa too. He won't have that farm to keep up anymore."

"I know, but we'll miss the Cove."

Pearl nodded and pushed to her feet. "There ain't a day goes by I don't miss the Cove and the way it used to be. But it ain't the same anymore. Neighbors are gone. Cabins are torn down. When your family leaves, that'll be the end of our ties there." She grunted in disgust. "But I don't need to start a-thinkin' about that tonight. I better get to bed."

Laurel grabbed her hand as Pearl walked past her toward the front door. "No matter where any of us live, we'll always be friends."

Pearl smiled and glanced over at Josie. "Maybe better than that. I was kinda hoping you might be family someday."

Laurel's face grew warm. She released Pearl's hand and wrapped her fingers around the arms of the chair. Neither she nor Josie said anything until Pearl had entered the hotel. "Don't mind Mama," Josie said. "She set her mind a long time ago that her grandson and Anna's granddaughter would marry someday. But I have to admit that I did too."

"I know. You and Mama have never made a secret that you'd like to see Jimmy and me get married. What none of you seem to understand is that Jimmy and I are good friends. We don't love each other like married folks should."

Josie stared at her for a moment before she nodded. "You're right. Married folks should love each other like your ma and pa do."

Laurel nodded. "And like you and Ted do. I don't feel that way about Jimmy. I would only end up hurting him if I married him when I don't love him."

Josie's chin trembled. She took a deep breath and straightened in her chair. "You're right. When a wife doesn't love her husband, it only ends up hurting both of them. I don't want that for Jimmy. I want him to have a wife who loves him with all her heart."

"He'll find the right person. He's such a good man. You've raised him well, Josie."

"And what about you? Have you found the right person in that young man from Virginia? Jimmy's told me about him."

Laurel clasped her hands together in her lap. "I don't know how to answer that. There are a lot of things standing in our way right now. I thought I might be able to see things more clearly if I got away from home and had some time away from my family to think."

Josie reached over and squeezed Laurel's arm. "All I want is for you and Jimmy to both be happy. I hope you can decide what that's going to be for you. I'm sure your folks have told you to pray about it, and I'll pray too." She stretched and yawned. "Now I think I'll get ready for bed, too. Are you ready to come inside?"

"Not just yet. I think I'll sit out here for a while."

"All right. See you in the morning."

Laurel watched Josie enter the hotel, and then she leaned back in the chair and closed her eyes. She wondered what Andrew was doing tonight. Had he helped Willie with the chores since she'd been gone, or had he stayed away as she told him to?

A tear rolled down her cheek, but she didn't wipe it away. She stood up, walked to the porch railing, and stared up at the stars. She'd been honest when she told Josie there were too many things standing in the way of happiness for her and Andrew. In her heart, though, she knew the real problem. The love they shared would never bring them happiness until they had a foundation to build their relationship on. She wanted what her parents had, and that was a marriage built on their shared belief in God.

Until Andrew accepted the need for God in his life, he would never understand how important that was to her. And until then there was no hope they would ever be able to overcome the other differences between them.

The taxi pulled up in front of the stately white mansion that Andrew's great-grandfather had built almost a hundred years ago. Thankfully it had survived the Civil War and in time had been passed to his father. Another one of his father's plans for Andrew's life was for him and his family to inhabit the house one day, but Andrew had very little interest in living there again.

He paid the driver, climbed from the cab, and stared at the wide steps that led to a porch with six white columns across the front of the house. He'd lived here all his life until he left for college, and yet he felt like an arriving guest. He would much rather be in Cades Cove tonight with the Jacksons and the Martins. But he had come home on a mission, and the sooner he got on with it the better off he'd be.

Taking a deep breath, he climbed the steps. He hesitated before opening the door. Should he knock? No, that would be ridiculous. He turned the knob and stepped through the door into the large hallway entry of the house.

As usual, everything looked neat and in its place. He couldn't conceive of its being otherwise. Household staff members knew their jobs depended on keeping his father happy, and they worked hard every day to do so.

The stairway with the winding bannister he'd slid down as a boy stood halfway down the entry, and he stared up to the landing at the top of the stairs. From the entry he could see the closed door of his father's second floor office to the right of the top step. He shook his head and sighed.

He took a step toward the stairs, but before he reached them Mrs. Oliver, the housekeeper, appeared from the direction of the kitchen. She gasped in surprise when she saw him and then smiled. "Mr. Andrew, welcome home. Your father didn't tell us you were coming."

He smiled at the woman who'd been a fixture in their house ever since his mother's death. "I didn't tell him, Mrs. Oliver. I thought I would surprise him." He glanced up the stairs. "I see his office door is closed. Is he in there?"

"Yes, sir. He went in right after dinner."

"Then I'll go up and see him."

She nodded. "Would you like something to eat? I'll tell the cook to fix you a tray, and I'll be glad to bring it to your room."

He shook his head. "No, thanks. I had something to eat on the train."

She reached out to take his suitcase. "Then I'll put your bag in your old room."

"Not yet," he said. "I have some things to say to my father first. After I get through, he may not want me to stay here tonight." He set the bag down. "I'll come back downstairs and get it whatever way our conversation turns out."

Her eyebrows pulled down across her nose, and she shook her head. "I know there have been some problems between you and your father, but he's really a good man. He's done a lot for the people in this district, and he loves you."

"He has a strange way of showing it."

Mrs. Oliver clasped her hands in front of her and took a step closer to him. "No matter how you feel about him, you need to remember he's your father and you need to honor him."

Andrew's eyes grew wide. "Someone else told me that not long ago." He tilted his head to one side and let his gaze drift over Mrs. Oliver's face. "Are you a Christian?"

She squared her shoulders and nodded. "Yes, sir."

"When did that happen?"

"About the time you went away to college. I can't believe I lived all those years without having God in my life. He's given me strength and the great peace to face every day no matter what happens."

Andrew shook his head in amazement. "This is great news. I've come home to tell my father that I've become a Christian and that I've decided to stay in Tennessee instead of returning to Virginia to run for office."

Her eyes lit up, and she reached out and squeezed his hand. "Oh, Mr. Andrew, that's wonderful. I'll pray for you while you're talking with your father."

"Thank you, Mrs. Oliver. That's very comforting." He glanced up the stairs and sighed. "Well, I guess there's no time like the present to get this over with."

He mounted the first step and trudged up to the landing. He paused outside the door and knocked. From inside he heard his father's muffled voice. "Come in." Andrew pushed the door open and walked into the room. His father didn't look up from the papers spread across his desk. "Yes, what is it, Mrs. Oliver?"

Andrew closed the door and took a deep breath. "It's not Mrs. Oliver, Father."

The pen dropped from his father's hand and

his body stiffened. He looked up with a startled expression on his face. "Andrew? What are you doing here?"

"I came to talk with you."

A slow smile curled his lips and the congressman stood up from his chair. "So you finally decided to see things my way. It's good to have you home."

He started to walk around the desk, but Andrew held up his hand to stop him. "Please don't get the wrong idea about why I'm here. I felt like we needed to do something to repair the damage done by our meeting in Gatlinburg, and I asked Mr. Eakin for a week's leave. I don't know if I'll need that long or not, but I wanted to see you."

A small frown furrowed his father's forehead, and he motioned for Andrew to sit down. "This sounds serious."

"No, I feel like I need to stand when I tell you this."

A hint of anger clouded his father's eyes. "Tell me what? Don't waste my time; just get on with it."

"All right. I came to tell you that there's been a big change in my life since I last saw you. I've accepted Christ into my life, and I'm trying to right some of the wrongs I did in the past. I want to ask you to forgive me for the angry words I spoke to you in Gatlinburg."

"You've become a Christian?" The words were nearly a whisper.

"I have, and I've never been happier. But as I said, I want to make amends for some of the things I've said and done. I felt like I needed to start with you."

A big smile flashed across his father's face. "Well, you know I never have put much stock in that religion stuff, but if it makes you happy, I'm all for it."

Andrew breathed a sigh of relief. "Thank you, Father. I was afraid you might have some objections."

"Why should I object? You just apologized and said you want to make amends. I'm pleased that you have. So when will you return home to begin your campaign?"

Andrew's mouth dropped open, and he stared at his father. "What campaign?"

His father shrugged. "I figured if you were making amends that meant you were finally going to marry Lucy and get on with your political career."

"No, no. You misunderstood me. I came here to let you know that I love you, and I honor you as my father. But that doesn't mean I'm going to let you run my life. I've turned that job over to God, and I expect His plans for me are going to be better than anything either of us could ever dream up. I only want to know that you understand and will support my decision."

Andrew had seen his father angry many times,

but he'd never witnessed anything like the fury that crossed his face. "Support your decision to ruin your life? I wouldn't do that in a million years." He raised his fist in the air and began to pace back and forth across the room. It reminded Andrew of watching him once on the House floor. Suddenly he stopped and glared at Andrew. "It's that girl, isn't it?"

"Laurel doesn't even know I'm here. In fact, I haven't had a chance to tell her about having become a Christian."

"But she influenced you in this. She made you turn your back on the only family you have. I could tell the minute I saw her she was nothing more than a little . . ."

"Stop it!" Andrew yelled. "I won't let you talk about her like that. She's the kindest person I know, and she wants me to have a relationship with you."

His father closed his eyes for a moment and took a deep breath. "I'm afraid I have no desire to welcome her into our family. If you really love me and want to honor me as you say, then you'll forget all this foolishness about defying me and get on with the plans we've had for years."

Andrew had known it would be difficult talking with his father, but he'd known it was the right thing to do. Now all he could do was turn the situation over to God.

"I will always love you, and I will always honor

you as my father. But I must do what I think is right for me. I don't know where I'll work or even whom I'll marry at this point, but I know Lucy and politics have no place in my future. I hope someday you can accept my decision. Now I think I'd better go."

His father raised his trembling index finger and pointed it at Andrew. "If you walk out of this house now, don't you ever bother coming back."

Andrew's heart felt as if a knife had just sliced through it and left him mortally wounded. "Father, think about what you're saying. We're all that's left of our family. We need each other."

"I don't need you if you're going to leave me. I made it fine after your brother and mother left, and I'll do the same when you're gone."

Andrew shook his head. "You didn't make it fine after their deaths, Father, and neither did I. I needed you to put your arms around me and tell me you were here for me even if Mother and Winston were gone, but in your grief you tried to remake me into Winston. I'm not my brother. He would have loved politics because he was so much like you. I'm sorry, but I can't be him for you."

"You're right. You're not like him at all. He didn't have a choice in leaving; you do. Don't make a mistake and walk out that door. I warn you I won't welcome you back through it."

"I'm sorry to hear that. I want you to know that wherever I live, I will always welcome you to my home. Goodbye, Father."

He opened the door, stepped into the hall, and closed the door behind him. At the top of the stairs he glanced again at his father's office, but after a moment descended the stairs and stopped beside Mrs. Oliver.

"How did it go?" she asked.

Andrew shook his head. "Not very well. He ordered me to leave and never come back."

A tear rolled down her cheek. "Oh, Mr. Andrew, I'm so sorry."

"So am I, Mrs. Oliver." He glanced toward his father's office again. "Take care of him for me."

"I will. You can count on me."

"Thank you. Would you mind if I wrote to you? I'd like for someone to know where I am in case Father ever needs anything."

She reached out and clasped his hand between both of hers. "Of course you can, and I'll write to you and let you know how he's doing. But most of all, Andrew, I'll pray for you and your father. God can heal this situation."

"I know He can."

He leaned over and kissed her on the cheek before he reached down and picked up his suitcase. Then, without looking back, he walked to the front door, opened it, and stepped into the Virginia night.

As he trudged along the road that led into town, he looked up at the stars and swallowed back the hurt that had settled in his throat like a huge weight. "God, please be with my father. Help him to know You love him, and that I always will. Help him come to see we need to be in each other's lives. Watch over Laurel tonight and keep her safe until I see her again. Thank You for walking with me and letting me know I'm not alone. I don't have any idea where You're going to take me, but I'm ready to go. And I'm sure looking forward to finding out what You have planned for me."

The pain in his throat eased some, and he strode along the road toward the lights of town in the distance. He'd find a hotel room for the night. Then he'd board the first train headed on the long journey back to the Smokies. At the moment, there was no place he'd rather be.

A cuckoo clock struck eleven o'clock just as Laurel strolled into Tremont's general store. She smiled at the sound of the bird's call drifting through the store and glanced around at the well-stocked shelves. It almost looked like a smaller version of Mr. Bryan's store in Gatlinburg. There were canned goods on the shelves, candy in jars, and bolts of cloth on tables at the back of the store.

A mirror hung on the wall to her left, and she

gasped when she caught sight of her reflection. Her hair looked like it hadn't been combed this morning. Her face grew warm when she realized the young man behind the store counter was staring at her. Quickly she reached up and smoothed her stray locks into place.

"The wind is really bad this morning. I've been in Tremont for nearly two weeks, but I haven't seen it blow like that."

The store clerk smiled. "You never can tell about the winds in this part of the mountains, but today it seems worse than usual. You said you'd been here awhile. Are you visiting, or have you moved here?"

"I'm visiting the Fergusons over at the hotel. Our families have been friends for years. I live over at Cades Cove for the time being."

"Yeah," he grunted. "We're all living on borrowed time in these mountains. I expect Tremont will be a ghost town before long." He inhaled. "But nothing we can do about that. What can I help you with today?"

She pointed to the fabric on tables at the back of the store. "I want to look at the material back there."

"Help yourself. If you need me to cut you a piece, I'll be glad to do it."

Stopping to look at items from time to time, she ambled to the back of the store. She'd just reached the first display of fabric when the clerk appeared at her side. He wiped his hands down his white apron that stretched nearly to the floor and stuck a pencil behind his ear. "Anything special you're looking for?"

She shook her head. "Not really. Mrs. Ferguson's mother told me she'd make me a dress. I'm not sure what I want."

He picked up a bolt of seersucker and put it on another table. "There's not enough material left on that one to make a dress. What kind of dress is it? Sunday? Party? Housedress?"

"Um, maybe a Sunday dress."

He pulled a bolt out from the bottom of the stack and held it up. "How about this? Silk is still a favorite of a lot of women."

Tiny white geometric designs covered the pink silk material. Laurel tilted her head and studied it for a moment before she shook her head. "Maybe something in a solid color."

He pulled an emerald green piece from the bottom and laid it in front of her. "What about this?"

She rubbed her fingers over the soft fabric. "This is more like it. I think I'll take . . ."

"Jim!"

She jumped in alarm at the sound of a man's voice at the front of the store. The clerk jerked his head around. "What?"

"Better come out here. I think we got some big trouble headed our way."

The clerk dropped the fabric onto the table, and Laurel followed him as they ran from the store. A large crowd of people surged down the road in the direction of the community center. Laurel glanced over her shoulder at the hotel and caught sight of Josie hurrying across the footbridge toward her. When Josie reached her, Laurel fell into step beside her.

"What's wrong? Why is everybody going to the community center?"

"There's a fire up the mountain."

Fear gripped Laurel, and she stopped in her tracks. "A fire? Is it where Ted and Jimmy are working?"

Josie shook her head. "I don't know. That's what I want to find out."

Together they ran into the community center and looked around for a place to sit. Nearly all the chairs were already taken and people were standing around the walls. They pushed their way through the crowd standing in the center aisle and inched to the front row, where they found two seats and dropped down into them.

Two men stood in deep conversation at the front of the room a few feet from Laurel. She strained to hear what they were saying but was only able to catch a few words which made little sense. After a few minutes, the older of the two stepped to the center of the room and faced the crowd. The room grew immediately silent.

"May I have your attention, please," he said. "Thank you for coming. I think most of you know me. I'm Bill Mercer and this is Jeb Smith. We represent Mr. Townsend here at Tremont. We brought you together this morning to tell you about a situation we have. We don't know what caused it, but we've got fire above us in the mountains. With the wind gusts we've had, it's been impossible so far to get it under control. The Park Service has men up there, and our employees are working with them, but this wind is presenting a problem. We wanted to let you know just in case the wind shifts, and the fire comes this way."

A man beside Laurel jumped up. "What do we need to do?"

"The Park Service is sending some men from the Cades Cove CCC camp to help out. They should be arriving on a train from Townsend in about an hour. If you work for Little River, you need to board the train and ride up the mountain. If your families want to leave Tremont, they should be ready to get on when it makes the return trip to Townsend. If you want to stay, I'd suggest you get all the buckets, pots, and pans you can find. You may need them to water down your property. Are there any more questions?"

Josie stood up. "How far up did the fire start?"

"Right above the Thunderhead operation."

Josie's face turned white. "What about the men working up there?"

He looked around at the man beside him, and they exchanged quick glances. "They're fighting the fire right now."

Josie sank down in her chair and grabbed Laurel's hand. "Ted and Jimmy," she whispered.

Laurel's stomach roiled at the look of terror in Josie's face. "Don't worry," she whispered. "They can take care of themselves."

Mr. Mercer pursed his lips and glanced around the room. "If there are no more questions, I'll let you go make preparations for whatever you need to do." The people in the crowd started to rise to their feet, but Mr. Mercer held up his hand. "Oh, one more thing for those of you who'll be boarding the train to ride up to the fire. That's the last trip it'll make up the mountain until the fire's out. You'll have to walk back. Now the meeting's dismissed."

All around them people stood and rushed for the back door. Laurel looked over at Josie. Her face had grown pale and fear flickered in her eyes. Laurel touched her arm. "Josie, shouldn't we get back to the hotel and gather up buckets like Mr. Mercer said?"

She blinked and turned to face Laurel. "Laurel?" she whispered. A frown flashed across her face as if she'd forgotten she wasn't alone.

"Yes, Josie. I'm here. We need to go now."

She nodded. "Ma and Pa. They need to get ready and leave on that train when it comes back." Her gaze settled on Laurel's face. "And you do too. You must go home."

Laurel shook her head. "I can't leave you. I want to be here when Ted and Jimmy come back. Besides, you need me to help you if the fire gets too close to the hotel."

"No. You can't stay." She jumped to her feet and pulled Laurel up with her. "Your mother is sick with worry because of Charlie leaving and your pa being sick. I'm not going to let anything happen to her daughter if I can help it. Now let's go get your clothes packed."

Laurel knew it would do no good to argue with Josie. As badly as she hated to leave Josie behind, she would do as she asked. As they ran from the community center toward the hotel, Laurel glanced up at the sky, and her heart pounded at what she saw. In the distance a trail of smoke drifted up toward the sun. It was impossible to tell how far away it was, but she prayed that the deadly sparks would soon be extinguished before the wind blew them down the mountain onto those in the base camp.

Andrew hadn't slept much on the return trip from Virginia, but just minutes ago the conductor had announced Townsend as the next stop. That's where he'd left his car, so it wouldn't be long before he was back in his room at the CCC camp in Cades Cove.

As tired as he was, he couldn't ignore the excitement he felt at being back in Tennessee. In the short time since he'd been here, it had come to be home. Nothing would make him happier than to stay in the mountains for the rest of his life, but he would go wherever God's plans led him. He couldn't help hoping, though, that those plans included Laurel.

He could hardly wait to see her. First he'd go to the camp and clean up some. Then he intended to drive straight to her house and tell her what had happened to him in the days since they'd seen each other. Maybe her grandfather had already told her about his visit, but he hoped not. He wanted to tell her that story himself.

The train slowed in preparation for the stop at the station. He gathered his belongings and waited for the train to come to a stop. When it did, he climbed down the steps onto the station platform and looked around in surprise at the men gathered there. Even without the blue denim work suits and caps they wore, he would have recognized them anywhere. These were the men from the Cades Cove CCC camp.

Before he could recover from his surprise, Lieutenant Gray emerged from the group and held up his hand for silence. The group stilled immediately. "As soon as this train leaves for

Maryville, ours will arrive. Be ready to board when it gets here."

There was a mumbled acknowledgment from the group before they resumed their conversations. Andrew hurried across the platform toward Lieutenant Gray.

The lieutenant saw him coming. "Brady," he called out. "So you got back from Virginia?"

"I did." Andrew cast a bewildered glance over the assembled men. "What's going on?"

"There's a fire on the mountain up near Thunderhead. We've been called to go help out."

Andrew's heart thudded at the news. "A fire? How bad is it?"

Lieutenant Gray shrugged. "Any fire's bad here on these slopes, but they're trying to keep it from reaching Tremont."

At the mention of the name Tremont, Andrew's heart constricted. Laurel. Was she still there? No, she should be home by now. He was sure she was.

He realized Lieutenant Gray had said something, but he hadn't heard him. Andrew blinked and shook his head. "What?"

"I asked if you want to come along and help out. You know, since you work for the Park Service, you may want to experience a fire for yourself."

Andrew shuddered at the thought. Experience a fire? He'd done that when he was a child, and it had left a memory that still haunted his dreams. He opened his mouth to decline, but his eyes grew wide as he heard the words he spoke. "I'd like to go with you. Let me go put this suitcase in my car that's parked beside the station. I'll be back in a minute."

Andrew ran to his car, unlocked it, and shoved the suitcase in the backseat. He was about to relock the car when he froze at the small voice niggling in the back of his mind. *You really don't want to do this,* it said. *Get in your car. Go to Cades Cove to see Laurel. You can tell Lieutenant Gray later you changed your mind.*

A whistle blew, signaling the departure of the train for Maryville. Andrew stood, unsure what to do. Should he board the next train to Tremont, or should he hop in his car and drive to Cades Cove?

Then he remembered the day he had asked Granny if faith could give him power to face things that seemed impossible. He recalled how she'd smiled as she answered him just hours before her death. "If you put your trust in God and believe in Him, He'll give you the power and strength to face whatever comes your way, Andrew."

He looked up into the sky and breathed a prayer of thanks for the lessons Granny was still teaching even after her death. Then he locked the car and ran toward the platform so he could be ready to board the train when it arrived.

Chapter 18

It had only been thirty minutes since they'd seen the first evidence of fire on the mountain but already clouds of smoke were pouring into the sky. Laurel blinked back tears and grasped Josie's hand as they stood on the porch of the hotel and stared at the darkening sky. Somewhere out there Jimmy and his father were engaged in fighting the inferno that appeared to be spreading.

The front door of the hotel opened and Josie's parents stepped onto the porch. Josie's gaze swept them. "Where's your suitcase?"

Mr. Davis shook his hand. "Got no reason to pack. We ain't going nowhere 'til you and Ted and Jimmy come along with us."

She shook her head. "I don't want you in danger. Please go to Townsend. I'll come as soon as they're back."

Mrs. Davis put her arm around her daughter's shoulders and hugged her. "This is our place, Josie. You're all we got left in this here world, and we ain't a-leavin' unless you come with us."

Josie's face crumpled and her body shook with sobs. "Oh, Mama," she wailed. "What if something happens to Ted or Jimmy? I don't think I could live without them."

Her mother grabbed her by the shoulders and

shook her. "Now let's have none of that talk. There are a lot of men out there fighting this fire, and they got family worryin' 'bout them too. We just got to pray that God's gonna bring all of them back safely."

Josie's wild-eyed stare reminded Laurel of an animal that couldn't escape the trap it was caught in. "But Mama, I've heard all these stories about what happens to men when they're fighting a fire. It's not just the flames that kill them; it's the heat in the air. They breathe it in, and it melts their lungs before the fire reaches them." More tears flowed down her face. "I don't want that to happen to Ted or Jimmy."

Mrs. Davis frowned and shook Josie harder. "Get control of yourself, Josie. The guests who're leavin' on the train could come out here any minute. We don't need to go upsettin' them. And you need to start thinkin' about trying to save this place if the fire comes this way." Her features softened, and Mrs. Davis pulled Josie into another hug. "Besides, your pa and I are gonna be right here with you until Ted and Jimmy come home."

Josie hugged her mother, then pulled free and wiped at her eyes. "Thank you, Mama and Poppa. I'm glad you're here." She sniffed and glanced at Laurel. "Now you need to head down to the depot. Do you want me to walk with you?"

Laurel shook her head. "There's no need for that. It's just down the road, and I'll be fine by myself. I'd rather you stay here and get things ready in case the fire shifts this way." She stepped closer to Josie and hugged her. "Your mother's right. Ted and Jimmy are going to be fine. We just have to believe that."

Josie smiled through her tears and kissed her on the cheek. "Tell your mama I love her, and I'll write to her as soon as this is all over."

"I will." Laurel hugged the Davises, picked up her suitcase, and tramped down the steps. As she stepped onto the footbridge, she glanced over her shoulder and waved to the three who stood watching her depart. "Goodbye."

"Take care," Josie called as all three waved.

A train whistle echoed through the valley. That had to be the train with the men from the Cades Cove camp on board. She might recognize some of them who had attended Sunday services at their church. Laurel increased her speed so that she might arrive at the train stop before the train did.

As she approached the small building that served as a depot, she saw a large group of men milling about. The ones who would board the train for their trip up to the fire, no doubt. A smaller group of women and children, holding boxes and suitcases, stood to the side of the building. They had to be the ones who would climb aboard with her when the train returned.

She walked to the front of the building that faced the tracks and watched the train slide to a stop a few feet away from her. The first train car appeared to be empty. She walked alongside the next and peered at the windows in an attempt to see a familiar face, but she didn't recognize any of the men sitting by the windows.

Satisfied she knew nobody from the Cades Cove CCC camp, she turned to walk back to the front of the train. The engineer hung out the window of his locomotive and yelled to Mr. Mercer, who stood next to the train. He hollered something in return and then signaled the loggers from the base camp to board. The group surged forward and jostled each other as they waited in line to climb the steps to the vacant car.

Laurel had almost reached the small depot when she heard a voice calling from the other direction. "Laurel, wait!" She jerked to a halt at the familiar voice. Andrew? It couldn't be. Then she heard it again. "Laurel!"

She gasped, dropped her suitcase, and whirled to see Andrew running toward her. Her heart pounded like striking an anvil at the sight of him. His eyes sparkled, and his face radiated joy like she'd never seen before. Her mouth dropped open as he skidded to a halt in front of her. "Andrew?" she gasped.

"I couldn't believe it when I looked through the train window and saw you walking by." He grabbed her by the shoulders and stared at her as if he was memorizing every detail of her face.

"What are you doing still here? You should be in Cades Cove."

She opened her mouth to reply, but no sound came out. She swallowed and tried again. "I've been with the Fergusons, but I'm leaving on the train back to Townsend."

His hands on her shoulders relaxed, and he breathed a sigh of relief. "Simon told me you were here, but I hoped you'd already left. You need to get as far away from here as you can. They say this fire is destroying everything in its path."

She licked her dry lips and frowned. "What are *you* doing here?"

He nodded toward the train. "I'm with the men from the Cades Cove camp. I saw them at the station in Townsend when my train arrived from Virginia, and I came up here with them."

"Virginia?" She squinted her eyes and shook her head. "What were you doing there?"

His eyes danced with excitement, and he threw back his head and laughed. Not only did he look happy, but his laughter sounded like that of a man at peace with the world. Something had happened to Andrew since the last time she saw him. "Oh, Laurel. I have so much to tell you. I was so upset after our argument that I went to see your grandfather. While I was there, I turned my life over to God, and I've never been happier. The first thing I wanted to do was talk to my father and try to make things right with him. So I went to Virginia, and I was headed back to Cades Cove to tell you how my life's changed when I ran into these fellows."

The train whistle blew, and Laurel glanced over her shoulder. The men no longer stood beside the train. "Andrew, the men are on board. They're ready to go. You need to get back on the train."

He gripped her shoulders again and shook his head. "Not until I tell you I'm sorry for the way I acted and the things I said to you the last time we were together. I was angry. I was jealous. I was all the things I've never wanted to be. And I took it out on you. But that's all changed. I'm a different person now. God did that for me. I promise you I'll never act that way again. I love you, Laurel, and I want us to have a life together. One like your parents have."

Her throat constricted, and her eyes filled with tears. "Andrew . . ."

He pulled her to him and pressed his lips to hers in a demanding kiss that told her he had missed her as much as she had him. The train engine lurched forward, and the cars hooked to it rattled as they began to move. He pulled her close and nuzzled her ear. "I love you, Laurel, and we belong together. I need you so much. Put me out of my misery. Tell me you'll marry me."

She wrapped her arms around his neck and pulled his face down to hers. "I love you, Andrew. Yes, I'll marry you."

She pressed her lips to his once more and then pulled away. She caught a glimpse of one of the train cars as it rolled past. "They're leaving. Get on board."

He backed away, never taking his eyes off her. "Wait for me at your parents' house. I'll come as soon as this fire is under control." He turned and ran toward the train as it picked up speed. She held her breath and closed her eyes as he leaped for the steps of the last car. When she opened them, he stood on the bottom step, clutching the handrail. "I love you," he yelled as the train moved up the mountain.

"I love you too," she cried.

She waved until the train disappeared from view, and then she picked up her suitcase and walked back to the front of the depot. Andrew's words still echoed in her mind. He had turned his life over to God, he loved her, and he wanted to marry her.

In the span of a few minutes her entire life had changed. The man she'd seen today wasn't the same person she'd first met. That man had seemed unsure of himself and fearful of what the future held for him. Today Andrew had the appearance of a man who'd suddenly been pardoned from a death sentence. He was happy, excited, and on his way to confront the inferno blazing up the mountain.

At that moment a sudden gust of wind swept through the town and sent debris flying in its path.

Trees swayed as if they might bend to the ground, and Laurel stiffened. The smell of smoke drifted from the direction of the fire. She closed her eyes and said a prayer for the safety of Andrew and the men on their way up the mountain and for those already there.

A sudden thought sent shivers up her spine, and her eyes popped open. The fire. Andrew was on his way to fight fire, the one thing he feared most in the world. Her body began to shake, and she thought of Josie's words about how the hot air could suck the life out of a firefighter. A bench sat at the edge of the platform next to the small depot. She stumbled toward it and dropped down on it.

She clutched her hands in her lap and beat them against her knees. Now she understood why Josie had refused to leave when she knew Ted and Jimmy were in danger. She wanted to keep watch for the return of those she loved. And so did she.

Andrew faced great danger, and there was no way she would go back to Cades Cove and wait for what might be days until she knew if he was all right. She would be here in Tremont to meet him when he came back down that mountain.

Taking a deep breath, she picked up her suitcase and began to walk back to the hotel.

The day grew darker as the train chugged up the mountain. Smoke swirled through the air swept on by the increasing gusts of wind. Andrew stared out the window and wondered how much further they could go before the engineer would have to stop. Already they could smell the acrid stench of the fire, and several men in the train car had begun to cough.

The train jerked to a halt, but nobody moved for a moment. Since leaving Tremont, they had climbed higher into the mountains, and Andrew stared out the window at the steep incline beside the train that led on toward the summit. He shook his head in sorrow not at what the fire had done, because it hadn't reached this spot yet, but for what man had done. The total desolation of a mountainside stripped of its forest spread out to the left and right as far as he could see. All that remained of the trees that had once covered the landscape were the dried-out trunks that had been left behind and debris from the ones that had been shipped out long ago.

He gritted his teeth at the giant swath man had cut through the Smokies, and he recalled telling Superintendent Eakin he wanted to help preserve these mountains so they could be enjoyed by people for generations. As he stared at what the lumber company had done and smelled the smoke that threatened to destroy even more, that resolve grew stronger. It was as if God had suddenly opened his eyes to where his future lay. He knew he would never be able to live anywhere but in these hills.

"Shaconage," he whispered.

The man sitting next to him turned to him and frowned. "What did you say?"

Andrew pointed to the mountain. "The Cherokee called this the place of the blue smoke because of the haze on the mountaintops."

"Well, it ain't very blue today, is it?"

Andrew shook his head. "Maybe we can help make it that way again."

Lieutenant Gray stepped through the door at the front of their car at that moment and everyone sat up straighter in their seats. His mouth was set in a grim line as he let his gaze drift over the men sitting before him. Nobody moved.

He spread his feet in a wide stance and cleared his throat. "Okay, men, listen up. The engineer's afraid the fire may keep him from getting to the next spur, so he's going to turn the train around at this one. Before we get out, there are some last-minute instructions. Make sure the canteen you were issued before we left Townsend is securely attached to your belt. Sometimes that metal hook on the back of the cover can be tricky to get on. If you've had problems with it, let someone help you. It's very important that you have water when you face the heat from the fire. When you exit the train, there will be some Little River employees beside the train. They've been asked by the Park Service people to head up the digging of a fire line on this mountain. They'll divide us into squads and take us to the spots where we'll be working. Listen to what they have to say. There are other firefighters spread out all across this section of the mountain range, but we probably won't come into contact with them. When you get off the train, you'll be given either a Pulaski or a shovel."

"What's a Pulaski, sir?" The question came from someone toward the front of the car.

"It's a tool with an axe on one end and a grubbing hook on the other. The Park Service uses it as standard equipment now in fighting fires. Any more questions?"

A man at the front raised his hand. "Sir, do you know how long we'll be up here?"

Lieutenant Gray shook his head. "I have no idea. They're bringing in men from three more of the CCC camps in the park area, and I understand volunteers are coming in from surrounding towns. We're going to be spread out on this mountain, so you probably won't see me. Again, listen to the men who work up here. They'll let you know when replacements have arrived. Anything else?" When no one spoke, Lieutenant Gray took a deep breath. "All right. Let's get to work."

The men rose silently, formed a single line down the aisle, and filed to the front. Andrew stood and checked the canteen that dangled from his belt before he stepped forward. When he exited the train, he grabbed the Pulaski a man handed to him and glanced up at the sky. The sun was now completely hidden behind the dark clouds of smoke in the air.

A group of men, Little River employees no doubt, stood beside the train and waited for the men to climb down. Andrew glanced over his shoulder and saw that a group waited at each car. He turned his attention back to the men who would lead his squad and the man who appeared to be their leader. If his soot-streaked face and ash-stained clothes were any indication, he'd been on the mountain for quite a while. He unfolded a map he held and laid it on the ground. Andrew inched closer to hear what was being said.

Just as he reached the group, one of the men who had his back to him turned, and Andrew stared in unbelief into the face of Jimmy Ferguson. The surprised look on Jimmy's face was probably a reflection of his own. Jimmy's mouth dropped open and his eyes grew wide. "Brady!" he said. "What are you doing up here?"

Andrew glanced up at the smoke-filled sky and then to the Pulaski he held. He suddenly felt ill-equipped to tangle with a wildfire. He shrugged. "I came to help dig a fire line."

Jimmy stared at him a moment before he smiled and nodded. "Thanks. We need all the help we can get."

"Laurel didn't tell me you were up here. I guess I should have known you'd go to work with Little River when you came back home."

Jimmy's eyes grew wide. "Laurel? Where did you see her?"

"She was at the depot in Tremont. She's going back to Townsend when the train gets back."

Jimmy breathed a sigh of relief. "Good. Did you see my mother and grandparents?"

Andrew shook his head. "No, she was alone."

Jimmy closed his eyes and ran his fingers over his face. "Oh, no. Me and Pa were hoping they would go to Townsend. If this fire turns, it'll go right down to the base camp."

Andrew's heart dropped to the pit of his stomach. He hoped that didn't happen before Laurel got on the train. "Then we need to make sure that doesn't happen." He glanced over at the group of Little River employees who appeared focused on the map their leader had spread on the ground. "Who's in charge of our detail?"

Jimmy pointed to the man who knelt in the middle of the group. "My pa. He's the one assigning the locations right now."

As if on cue, Jimmy's father stood and studied the group. "We're going to lead you men up to a spot on the mountain where we're going to dig a fire line. When we get up there, we'll spread out to work. I'm in charge of this squad, so I'll be the lookout. I'll be monitoring your work as well as trying to keep you safe. If you're ready, let's go."

Mr. Ferguson glanced at his son before he

turned and started up the mountain. Everyone fell into step and followed as they climbed higher. As the path grew steeper, the air thickened with smoke and Andrew tried to stifle the cough that choked his throat. They climbed steadily for what seemed an eternity before Mr. Ferguson veered to the left and led the group toward the back side of the mountain.

For the first time Andrew caught sight of the fire. He swallowed back the fear that rose in his throat but couldn't take his eyes off the flames that rose from the forest at the far side of the adjacent ridge. The man in front of him glanced over his shoulder. "That's a right scary sight, ain't it?"

Andrew nodded. "It is."

"You think it might get this far?"

"I don't know."

A stick crunched under Andrew's foot, and he glanced down at the dried remnants of the logging operation that littered the ground. The ground around them was a tinderbox just waiting for a spark. He stared up the mountain and a second thought struck him. The logging operation had stopped about halfway up, and giant trees covered the upper half all the way to the peak.

A sinking feeling washed over him, and he stubbed his foot on the exposed root of a tree that had once stood in that spot. He glanced down at the dried ground under his feet and then up the mountain to the tree branches bending in the wind. The truth hit him like a punch in the stomach. If the fire spread this far, it could ignite on either side of them and leave them trapped between two deadly forces.

He hardly had time to process the thought before Mr. Ferguson held up his hand for them to stop. He pointed to a rock outcropping to the right and moved his arm in a straight line to his left. "That rock is our anchor point. We're gonna start digging there and cut that line all the way across here. For you not used to a Pulaski, don't raise it over your head to swing down. That just wastes energy, and it's dangerous. Bend slightly at the waist and use chopping motions. We need a line about twelve inches wide all the way across with the dirt taken all the way down to the mineral soil." He cast a worried glance at the fire that appeared to have moved closer since Andrew first spotted it. "If we can get this line dug and if the wind don't get stronger, we may be able to make this fire burn out. Any questions?"

When no one said anything, he nodded. "Then let's get to work."

The men spread out across the area Mr. Ferguson had indicated. Andrew took up a place on the line and nodded to the man beside him and then to Jimmy, the next man down. Jimmy jerked his head in the man's direction. "Hey, Brady. This is Glenn Carter. He works for Little River, but he grew up in the Cove. His folks sold out and moved a few months back."

Andrew stuck out his hand. "Glad to meet you, Carter."

He nodded and shook Andrew's hand. "You too."

Without further conversation they set to work. For a while the sound of picks and shovels striking ground echoed across the mountainside. Andrew glanced up from his work from time to time to watch as the fire crept closer. It had now reached the trees in the middle of the neighboring ridge and appeared to be spreading unchecked closer to their location.

After about an hour of digging, Mr. Ferguson signaled for everybody to take a short break. Andrew, Glenn, and Jimmy walked about ten yards uphill from their work position and dropped to the ground. They each pulled their canteens from their belts and took a drink before anyone spoke.

Jimmy held his canteen and motioned toward the fire. Its tongues were licking at the sky. "It looks like it's playing leapfrog the way it jumps from one tree to the next. I've never seen any-thing like it."

Just then swirls of dust and debris kicked up all around them as a huge gust of wind ripped across the mountain. Andrew closed his eyes and ducked his head as dirt peppered his face. "It's this wind," he yelled. "If this keeps up, that fire's gonna be on top of us."

A loud explosion split the air, and Andrew jumped to his feet and stared in the direction of the sound. He stood wide-eyed and unable to move as the whole mountainside facing them lit up like a fireworks display. Huge sparks propelled by the wind rocketed across the sky and spewed a trail of fire in every direction. Within seconds the whole area fanned into one huge inferno.

Jimmy and Glenn hopped to their feet, and the three watched in spellbound horror as deadly flames whizzed through the air and landed in the tree-stripped area they had climbed to reach this elevation. As the missiles hit the dry debris left by the loggers, the sparks ignited and raced across the ground.

Mr. Ferguson and the work detail were already running toward the spreading flames. His voice could be heard yelling at the men. "Hurry! Shovel dirt on this fire!"

Jimmy rushed down the mountainside with Andrew right behind him. As he ran, Andrew glanced over his shoulder and spotted Glenn Carter sprawled face-down not far from where they'd sat minutes ago. He skidded to a stop and ran back to Glenn. The man was clawing at the ground in an effort to push himself into a sitting position.

Andrew sucked in a breath at the sight of

Glenn's leg. Halfway between the knee and ankle the lower half of Glenn's shin jutted outward at a forty-five degree angle from the upper half. His foot lay wedged underneath the loop of a tree root that protruded from the ground. Andrew dropped down beside him. "What happened?"

Pain contorted Glenn's face, and he groaned. "I snagged my foot on a tree root. I think my leg's broken."

"I'll cut you free." Within seconds Andrew had cut the tree root away. Andrew glanced over his shoulder at the spreading fire behind him and then back to Glenn. "Your leg's broken all right. Don't move. It'll only make the pain worse. I'll go help put out the fire, but I'll be back for you."

Glenn's face turned pale, and he raised his head enough to dart a glance at the men below them frantically shoveling dirt. "Okay."

Andrew whirled and ran to join the men in what appeared to be a futile effort. He chopped at the earth with his Pulaski and scooped the loose dirt onto flames that seemed to be spreading faster than they could contain it. A sudden wind rushed across the ridge and fanned the flames higher.

From where he worked further down the mountain Mr. Ferguson stopped, cupped his hands around his mouth, and yelled. "Men, this fire's about to get out of our control. We need to get out of here before we're trapped."

More projectiles of fire sailed through the air

and landed inches away from Andrew. Searing pain shot through his body as his shirt sleeve blazed. He dropped to the ground and rolled until the flames died. Strong hands grabbed him and pulled him to his feet. He stared up into the face of Jimmy Ferguson.

"We gotta get outta here, Brady. The wind's blowing the fire this way," Jimmy yelled.

The fire now crackled and blazed all across the lower part of the mountain. Smoke billowed up all around them as the wind transported new missiles of fire that crashed to the ground.

Andrew pointed up the ridge and yelled to be heard over the hissing flames. "Carter's up there with a broken leg. I'll get him and be right behind you."

Jimmy shot a terrified glance up the mountain and took a step in that direction. "I'll help."

He gave Jimmy a shove. "No! Get out of here!"

Andrew turned and scampered up the mountain to Glenn. Terror lined his face. "We're gonna be trapped!" he cried.

"Not if I can help it!" Andrew yelled. "Now I'm going to get you up, but this is going to hurt."

Andrew knelt with his back to Glenn, grabbed his arm with one hand and his good leg with the other, and draped him across his back. Then, with all the strength he could muster he pushed to his feet. With Glenn's full weight on his back, Andrew started down the incline.

His gaze swept across the area they'd been digging earlier. The fire had jumped the line and now swept across everything in its path. One opening still remained in the wall of fire that climbed toward him, and in that small window Andrew saw Jimmy still beating at the flames. He glanced up and saw Andrew. "Come on!" he yelled. "I'm keeping this open for you."

At that moment a violent wind swept across the mountain. It was as if fire rained from the heavens. Behind him trees that had been left by the logging company exploded in flames. Andrew could barely make out Jimmy's image as he beat at the fire bombs that landed all around him.

Then, with a great roaring sound, a wall of fire rose in front of Andrew, cutting off his escape route. He thought he heard Jimmy's agonized voice calling his name on the other side, but he couldn't be sure.

He slid to a stop and stared into the approaching wall of fire that now raced up the mountain toward him. He looked over his shoulder and swallowed the fear rising in his throat as the trees toward the peak exploded like Roman candles.

Glenn moaned, and Andrew darted a glance at him. He appeared to have passed out. It was just as well. There was no need for him to know that the fire was about to cover this entire mountain, and they stood in the middle of the inferno with no escape route.

Chapter 19

Andrew stood transfixed as he stared at the blazing trees on the mountain peak being devoured by the red and orange flames that reached toward the sky. It was as if the swaying branches beckoned for all to join them in the spine-chilling dance of death they promised.

Andrew tore his gaze away from the sight and glanced to his right and left. The fire had now cut off both escape routes. A quick look over his shoulder told him the flames below were almost upon them.

He closed his eyes for a moment and shook his head. His life couldn't end like this. Not on a mountaintop with his remains devoured by fire. He didn't want to leave Laurel that way.

But what could he do? There was nowhere to go. Should he drop Glenn to the ground and sit beside him until the flames overtook them?

Fear gripped him like he'd never known. Then he remembered Granny's words about being able to face whatever came his way. He tilted his head back and stared up into the smoke-filled sky. "God, be with us. Help me know what to do."

The fear he'd felt moments ago vanished, and peace rolled through his body. Suddenly the words he'd read from the Bible on his return trip from Virginia flashed in his head. *I will lift up mine eyes unto the hills, from whence cometh my help. My help cometh from the LORD, which made heaven and earth.*

He hadn't memorized those words when he read them, but they rang in his mind as clearly as if he'd known them all his life. But why was he remembering them now?

A gust of wind blew across the mountain, and for a moment the smoke lifted. To the right of the peak Andrew saw trees that weren't burning. Maybe if he could reach that spot he'd have an escape down the back side of the mountain.

He tightened his grip on Glenn, summoned every ounce of strength he had, and stumbled toward the summit. The smoke descended again and blocked his view, but he knew the direction to go. As he climbed, he kept a wary eye on the fire that approached from behind.

The added burden of Glenn's weight sucked the breath from him and left him panting. When he felt he couldn't take another step, the words would flash in his head again, and he would continue his ascent.

He had no idea how long he climbed, but he knew his body was nearing the breaking point. Suddenly more explosions shattered the air as the wind carried blazing shards of fire to the remaining trees at the top of the peak. The sky lit up, and Andrew's heart sank.

His legs collapsed beneath him, and he sank to the ground in defeat. Smoke swirled around him, and his lungs burned. This was the end. There was no way out of the fire that was quickly closing in on them. He closed his eyes for a moment and thought of Laurel. "God," he prayed, "help Laurel to have a good life."

It was if a voice in his head responded. *I will lift up mine eyes unto the hills, from whence cometh my help.*

Confused, he opened his eyes and glanced around at the spot where he had fallen. Less than three feet away a rock formation with a round hole in the center jutted out from the side of the mountain. He shook his head in disbelief. A cave? Probably used by the black bears who inhabited this area, but there would be no bears in there today. Any of them who'd returned after the logging company abandoned this mountain would have fled the approaching fire.

Before he had time to question his decision, he grabbed the unconscious Glenn and dragged him to the opening. He had no idea how far back into the mountain the cave went, but it was worth a try. He wiggled through the hole with room to spare, reached back for Glenn, and pulled him inside.

When they were both safely in, he ran his hands down the side of the rocks. The cave appeared to run straight back into the mountain. He scooted along the ground and pulled Glenn with him until the tunnel widened, and he sensed they had entered a large area.

Smoke from the fire outside blew into the cave, and Andrew covered his mouth as a new thought hit him. They could still die from the smoke. Working quickly, he turned Glenn on his stomach and positioned him with his face pressed down into the cave floor. Then he lay down beside him and did the same. His body ached from exertion. All he wanted was to go to sleep, but if he did, he might not wake up again.

As the smoke swirled through the cave he fought the urge to give in to sleep. Just as he thought he could stay awake no longer, more words from the Psalm he'd read flashed in his mind. *He that keepeth thee will not slumber.*

The words calmed him and his breathing slowed. There was nothing more he could do to keep himself and Glenn safe. All he could do at this point was trust God for whatever might come. He smiled, closed his eyes, and sank into a deep sleep.

Although the sky was still dark with smoke from the fire, the sun had managed to poke a few rays through from time to time during the afternoon. But now it was setting in the west. Soon darkness would cover the mountains and bring with it the fear that the fire would turn toward Tremont during the night. Laurel let her gaze drift over the pots, pans, and every container they had been able to find scattered across the hotel's front yard. If the fire came, they would be used to bring water from the river. But for now, all they could do was wait.

The firefighters had begun to trickle into Tremont about fifteen minutes ago. Laurel and Josie had watched the returning men from their spot on the hotel's front porch. So far there was no sign of Ted, Jimmy, or Andrew.

Laurel put her hand on Josie's arm. "Do you want me to go check on those pots you left on the stove? I'd hate for your supper to burn."

Josie shook her head. "It's all right. Mama's in there. She can take care of it." She turned to Laurel. "Why don't they come? Some of the men they work with have already made it down. Why not Ted and Jimmy?"

Or Andrew, Laurel thought, but she swallowed back her fear and slipped her arm around Josie's waist. "They'll be here soon. That man who came by a few minutes ago said all the men had to leave the mountain. I'm sure he would have said something if anyone had been injured."

"I suppose you're right," Josie murmured, "but I'm so scared."

Laurel didn't say anything, but she couldn't help wondering about Josie's state of mind ever since they'd first found out about the fire. According to a conversation Laurel had overheard between her parents several years ago, Josie wasn't happy in her marriage and was considering moving back to Cades Cove to live with her parents. When she'd asked her mother about it later, she said some people never had the happiness that comes from loving a man the way she did Laurel's father.

In the end, though, Josie's parents had sold their farm and moved to Tremont to live with their daughter. Maybe that had helped keep the Fergusons' marriage together. Whatever had happened, she was happy for Jimmy. She knew how much he loved both his parents.

At that moment another group of men appeared down the road. They were covered in soot and ash from their heads to their feet, and Laurel couldn't distinguish one's features from another. Their shoulders drooped, and they shuffled along as if each step would be their last.

Josie squinted at the men for a moment before she gasped and ran down the steps with Laurel right behind. As she ran, Josie stretched out her arms. She didn't take her eyes off the approaching men.

Ted Ferguson, his eyes wide and his mouth open, stopped in his tracks as Josie hurled herself at him and threw her arms around him. "Ted! Ted!" she cried. "I was so afraid something had happened to you."

Laurel stopped a few feet away from them and smiled at the surprised look that flashed across

Ted's face for a moment before his arms closed around Josie and pulled her close. "It's okay, honey," he said. "I'm all right."

She pulled back and studied him a moment before she ran her fingers over his soot-streaked face. "Are you sure? You're not burned anywhere?"

He shook his head. "No. Really I'm fine."

She put her arms around his neck and pulled him close again. "I was so afraid you'd die in that fire and I'd never get to tell you."

He patted his wife's back and smiled. "Tell me what?"

"How much I love you." Her voice cracked on the last words.

Ted's hand stilled on his wife's back and he tightened his grip. His Adam's apple bobbed up and down as he swallowed. After a moment he cleared his throat and spoke in a soft voice. "I've always loved you, Josie," he whispered.

As if speechless, Jimmy stared at his parents in disbelief and glanced at Laurel before he turned back to his mother. "What about me? Were you worried for me too?"

She laughed and pulled away from Ted and reached for Jimmy. "Of course I was." She kissed him on the cheek, then stepped between them and looped her arms through theirs. "I've never been so relieved in all my life to have my men home safely."

Ted smiled down at his wife. "Well, if I'm going

to get a reception like this every time I go fight a fire, I may just sign up for that kind of work full-time."

"You'll do nothing of the sort," Josie said. "I'm keeping you both close to home where I can keep an eye on you."

Laurel glanced down the road and then back to Jimmy. "Did you see Andrew while you were up there? He went up on the train with the CCC camp boys from the Cove."

Jimmy's face clouded, and he shot a pleading look to his father. Ted slipped his arm from Josie's, stepped in front of Laurel, and reached for her hand. "Laurel, Andrew was on the mountain with us. When the fire overtook us, he ran back up the ridge to get Glenn Carter, who'd fallen and gotten hurt. He was bringing him back down when a wall of fire cut him off."

A violent tremor started at the top of her head and radiated through her body. "No!" she screamed. "It's not true."

She stumbled backward, looking at Jimmy as if pleading for him to say it wasn't true. The young man's eyes sparkled with moisture. "I stayed and tried to beat a path through the fire for them, Laurel, but it didn't do no good. That fire was just vicious, and the wind just spread it everywhere. I caught one glimpse of Andrew with Glenn on his back right before the escape hole through the flames closed."

She gasped for breath and shook her head. "He was caught behind the fire?"

Jimmy nodded. "I tried to get to him, but there wasn't anything I could do."

She backed away and shook her head. "But he's not dead, Jimmy. I know he's not."

Jimmy glanced at his father again, and he inched closer to her. "Laurel, I know it's hard, but you have to face facts. That fire just exploded all around us. Even the trees at the top of the mountain were blazing when I looked back. There's no way he could have gotten out."

Wild-eyed, she darted quick glances from Ted to Jimmy. "But he shouldn't even have been up there. He's been scared of fire ever since he was a child. Why didn't he run down the mountain with the rest of you?"

"Because he wouldn't leave Glenn behind," Jimmy said. "I told him I'd go help, and he shoved me back and told me to get out of there while I could. He saved my life, Laurel."

A roar like the sound of a wounded animal tore from her throat. "He's not dead," she wailed. She reached out, clutched the front of Jimmy's shirt, and shook him. Soot rose from his shirt and covered her face and hands.

He clasped her hands in his, and she looked into his eyes. The sorrow she saw there pierced her heart, and she gave another long wail as she sank to her knees. Ted and Jimmy reached down and lifted her to her feet. Tears ran down her face as she allowed them to lead her back to the hotel.

When they reached the hotel, Josie and her mother helped her into the bedroom where she'd slept since arriving. They pulled her shoes off and settled her on the bed, but she said nothing.

Josie leaned over her and squeezed her hand. "Maybe Andrew made it out of the fire, Laurel. You rest for a while, and we'll keep watch for him."

Still she said nothing. She rolled onto her side away from Josie and closed her eyes. All she wanted was to remember how Andrew had looked when he'd waved to her from the train's steps. At that moment he'd been young, in love, and happy. How could things change so much in such a short amount of time?

Tears leaked from her closed eyes and her body shook with great wracking sobs. All she wanted was to awaken from this horrible dream. But she wasn't asleep, and there was no dismissing the horrible truth. Andrew was gone from her life, and she had no idea how she could face the future without him.

Laurel awoke sometime later and sat up in bed. She realized she was still wearing the clothes she'd had on when Josie and Mrs. Davis had helped her to bed. She stared through the window at the darkness beyond and listened for sounds in the house, but she heard nothing. What time was it? At that moment, the grandfather clock in the entry hall struck two o'clock.

She threw her legs over the side, pulled a quilt around her shoulders, and tiptoed through the hotel to the front porch. When she stepped outside, she found that she wasn't alone. Ted Ferguson sat on the top porch step. He stared toward the orange glow that lit the sky in the distance.

He looked over his shoulder and smiled when he heard the door open. "Laurel, what are you doing out of bed?"

She walked over and sat down beside him on the step. "I woke up and wondered what was going on. I thought I'd come outside."

He pointed to the sky. "The fire's still burning, but it's traveling away from us. I don't think we have anything to worry about now. I sent everybody else on to bed and told them I'd watch for a while just to make sure."

Fresh tears pooled in her eyes, and she blinked them back. Instead of giving in to her grief, she turned to Ted and smiled. "Josie was so worried about you and Jimmy. I've never seen her act like that before. She kept saying she didn't know how she'd live if anything happened to you."

Ted shrugged and shook his head. "It was probably Jimmy she was so concerned about. She sure does love that boy."

"She loves you too, Ted. Don't ever doubt that. You were the one she ran to first."

Ted cocked his head to one side and smiled. "Come to think of it, I was." He appeared lost in thought for a moment before he chuckled. "I guess I've loved Josie ever since the day your grandma saved her life."

Laurel laughed. "I've heard that story all my life, but I never get tired of it."

Ted nodded. "I was about five or six years old, and Josie was just a toddler. All the folks in the Cove had come to build Cecil and Pearl a barn after theirs had burned. Pearl missed Josie, and Miss Anna asked me and my sister to look for her. I'll never forget how scared I was when I found her floatin' face-down in the pond. Simon waded right in and pulled her out, and Miss Anna worked on her and breathed in her mouth."

"That story's been told a lot in the Cove all these years."

Ted smiled. "Yeah, Miss Anna saved Josie for me. Of course I didn't know it at the time, but I guess the good Lord already had it planned for us to marry one day."

The tears she'd tried to suppress gushed from Laurel's eyes. "I saw Andrew when the train stopped here."

"You did?"

"Yes, he asked me to marry him, and I said I

would." She moaned and buried her face in her hands.

Ted reached over and patted her on the shoulder. "Laurel, you know our families have been so close through the years that I think of you as the daughter I never had. I'm sorry you're hurtin' right now. But I want you to know that boy is a hero in my book. He didn't have to go back for Glenn, but he chose to do it. When things cool off on that mountain, I aim to go back up there and search for his remains. I promise you I'll bring him back to have a decent funeral."

She leaned over and squeezed Ted's arm. "Thank you. I appreciate that. Now why don't you go on inside? I'll bet Josie would like that. I'll stay out here and keep watch for the rest of the night. You deserve some rest after what you've been through today."

"I think I'll take you up on that offer." He pushed to his feet and smiled down at her. "And who knows? That boy may walk out of those mountains yet."

"That's what I'm praying for, Ted." She stared at the orange glow in the distance. "That's what I'm praying for."

Andrew awoke with a start. He lay still in the darkness and listened for any sound, but he heard nothing. No hissing fire or blowing wind. Only silence. Hesitantly, he placed his hand on

Glenn's back. He breathed a sigh of relief at the steady rise of his body.

Andrew pushed to his knees and crawled down the tunnel toward the entrance. With the absence of the crackling and hissing he'd heard before, he guessed the fire had passed them by. Now a new fear filled him. What if debris from the fire blocked the cave's entrance? There could be charred trees or even a rockslide that had been triggered by the fire. Not to mention layers of ash and dust that might have sealed them in this tomb.

As he crawled closer to the entrance, a few beams of light danced on the cave walls. And then there it was, just as it had appeared when he first saw it. Nothing blocked it.

He crawled out of the cave, pushed to his feet, and stared in wonder at the landscape around him. Burned-out tree trunks from the summit above littered the side of the ridge in crisscross patterns. Huge boulders lay scattered about and ashes covered the ground.

Andrew turned in a complete circle and surveyed the damage the fire had inflicted on the mountain. Desolation lay everywhere except at the mouth of the cave. The words from the last verses of the Psalm flashed in his mind as he stared at the cave. *The LORD shall preserve thee from all evil: he shall preserve thy soul. The LORD shall preserve thy going out and thy coming in from this time forth, and even for evermore.*

He sank to his knees in the ashes of what had once been a great forest, raising his hands and face toward heaven. "Thank You, Lord, for providing a safe place for us in the fire and for saving our lives. I promise You from this day forward my goal in life will be to serve You and show Your love to every man I meet. Now I ask You to give me strength to get Glenn down this mountain. I'm weak this morning, but I know You'll be helping me with each step I take. Amen."

He kept his face turned up to the sun for a few minutes. Its rays penetrated every pore and sent a warm rush through his veins. It was good to be alive. He smiled, pushed to his feet, and crawled back in the cave to get Glenn. He had a long walk ahead of him, and carrying Glenn wasn't going to be easy. But he could do it. He had a promise that he would never walk by himself again. God would be there guiding each step.

Laurel had kept her vigil since the wee hours of the morning. Josie hadn't insisted she join the family for breakfast and the noon meal and had even brought them to her. Now with mid-afternoon approaching, she'd grown restless. She stood up from her chair and paced back and forth for a few minutes.

The front door opened, and Jimmy stepped onto the porch. "How're you making it?"

She stopped pacing and went to stand by the porch railing. "I'm fine. I keep hoping that I'll catch sight of Andrew coming into town, but so far it hasn't happened."

Jimmy stuck his hands in his pockets and rocked back on his heels. "Laurel, I wish I could give you some encouragement, but I don't think that's going to happen. You didn't see that fire. It would have taken a miracle for anybody to survive it."

"But that's exactly what I'm hoping for, Jimmy. A miracle."

Jimmy shook his head and rubbed the back of his neck. "I know, but it ain't likely that happened."

Tears pricked her eyes again, and she blinked. "I can't give up, Jimmy. I love him. He asked me to marry him when he got off the train yesterday, and I said yes."

A big breath gushed from Jimmy's mouth. "I guess that don't come as no surprise to me. I saw how you two looked at each other when I was visiting your folks. I didn't want to believe it. Maybe I still had some notion that someday you and me would get together. Our folks have always wanted it that way."

"Yes they have, but we both know we have never been more than friends. You're going to find somebody you love, and I'm going to be happy for you." She smiled. "I'll try to like her better than you did Andrew."

Jimmy grinned. "Well, I have to say I saw a different side to him up on that mountain. I never would have figured him to put himself in danger for a fellow he didn't even know. I'm sorry I didn't try to see his good side earlier."

Laurel smiled. "That's okay. I knew it was there. He just had to find it for himself." As she said the last word, she realized that's what Andrew had found when he visited her grandfather. When he'd turned his life over to God, he'd discovered the man just waiting to be awakened by God's love. And now she had to accept the fact that he was gone. She burst into tears. "Oh, Jimmy, why did he find it so late?"

Jimmy put his arms around her, and she buried her face in his chest as she sobbed out her grief. She didn't know how long they stood that way, but she suddenly felt his arms tighten. He gave a low whistle and said, "Well, would you look at that? I wouldn't have believed it in a million years."

She pulled back from him and stared up into his face, but he gazed over her head into the distance. A smile curled his lips. He placed his hands on her shoulders and turned her to face in the other direction. At first she didn't know what she was looking for. Then she saw him.

Andrew stumbled along the road that led into Tremont, and he had a man's body draped over his back. "Andrew!" she screamed as she raced down the front steps and across the footbridge to the road.

Behind her, she could hear Jimmy's voice. "Pa! Come quick! Andrew's back."

She ran as fast as her legs would carry her. Andrew staggered and dropped to his knees in the road right before she got to him, but he didn't let go of the man on his back. Ted and Jimmy got to him just as she did and took hold of Glenn, but Andrew frowned and tightened his grip.

"No," he rasped. "Have to get him to a doctor."

Ted pried Andrew's hands loose. "It's okay, son. We've got him now."

Together they lifted Glenn, who moaned aloud. Laurel dropped to her knees in front of Andrew and cupped his face in her hands. She could hardly make out his features from the tears streaming down her face. "Andrew, can you hear me? It's Laurel."

He frowned and swayed. "Laurel? I've got to get back to Laurel."

"I'm here, Andrew. Don't you see me?"

A violent fit of coughing attacked him, and his body shook uncontrollably with spasms. When they passed, he leaned over and spit phlegm onto the ground. Laurel's eyes grew large at the flecks of soot it contained. She cast a terrified glance at Ted. "What's wrong with him?"

"I don't know. We need to get him and Glenn both over to the doctor's place."

Several men ran up about then. "Need any help?" one of them asked.

Ted pointed to Andrew. "These fellows just made it down the mountain from fighting the fire. We need to get them over to the doctor's office."

They nodded, reached down, and lifted Andrew to his feet. Then they positioned themselves on either side and supported his weight as they followed Jimmy and Ted, who carried Glenn. Laurel ran ahead of them to alert the doctor that two injured men were being brought in.

When she reached the building that served as the camp infirmary, she pushed the door open and ran into the waiting room. "Doctor, we need help!"

The doctor appeared in the doorway of an adjacent room. "What's wrong?"

"They're bringing in two of the injured fire-fighters."

"Tell them to bring them on in here when they arrive." He whirled and disappeared back into what she assumed was the examination room.

Before she could answer, Jimmy and Ted staggered through the door. She pointed toward the exam room. "In here."

As they disappeared inside, the men who supported Andrew entered the building. She bit her tongue to keep from crying out at his appearance. Red welts ran up his arm where his shirt had burned away, and his red lips stood out in contrast to his pale face. He mumbled something, but she couldn't make out what he said.

She watched through the open door as they laid Andrew on one bed and Glenn on another. When they had them settled, Ted pointed first to Andrew and then to Glenn. "Doc, this is Andrew Brady. He works with the Park Service. And this is Glenn Carter. He's one of the Little River workers. They were trapped by the fire up on the mountain. We thought they were dead, but Brady just now stumbled into town carrying Carter on his back." He shook his head in amazement. "The last time we saw them they were trapped behind a wall of fire. I don't know how they survived, and I sure don't know how Brady carried Carter all the way back to town on his back."

The doctor nodded. "Sounds like they've had a mighty rough time. Now if you men will wait outside, I'll let you know how they are after I complete my examination."

The men turned and rejoined her in the waiting room just as the front door flew open. A woman in a nurse's uniform rushed inside and headed toward the examination room. "I'm sorry, sir," she said, "I was at the general store when I heard we have patients. What's the problem?"

The door closed before the doctor could answer, and Laurel was left to pace the floor. Jimmy stepped in front of her and blocked her path. "Do you want Mama to come stay with you until the doctor can tell you something?"

She shook her head. "No, you stay with me."

He nodded. "I'll stay for as long as you need me."

Laurel glanced around and realized the men who'd helped them had already left. She directed her gaze at Ted. "Why don't you go on too?"

"I need to stay and find out about Glenn."

"I'll stay for you, Pa," Jimmy said. "I'll find out what the doctor says."

Ted nodded. "I'll go tell Mr. Mercer that Glenn's here and then go back to the hotel."

Laurel watched Ted leave before she walked to one of the chairs along the wall and dropped down. She clasped her hands in her lap and squeezed them together. The memory of how happy she'd been when Andrew appeared on the road returned. That joy had soon turned to fear when she realized he didn't even recognize her. She cast a nervous glance at the closed door.

Andrew was going to be all right, she told herself. He had to be. After all, he'd survived a fire when no one said it was possible. God wouldn't let him come through that experience only to let him die now that he was safe. Surely God wouldn't do that.

She bowed her head. "Please, God. Let him live," she prayed.

The first thing she saw when she opened her

eyes was a clock on the opposite wall. She stared at it as it ticked off the minutes. With each movement of the clock's minute hand, she added a new plea for the life of the man she loved.

Chapter 20

For the past hour Laurel had divided her time between pacing across the waiting room floor and sitting in her chair with her gaze riveted on the wall clock. The minutes ticked by slower than she could believe. Why hadn't the doctor come out and told her something about Andrew's condition?

Almost as if she'd conjured him up, the door popped open and the doctor stepped into the room. She and Jimmy were on their feet instantly. She balled her hands into fists and clenched them at her sides as he walked toward them.

He smiled as he stopped in front of her. His gray hair and wire-rimmed glasses combined with the kind expression in his eyes reminded Laurel of Uncle Charles, who'd been a mountain doctor and traveled these hills for years. She held her breath and waited for him to speak.

"I didn't get a chance to introduce myself when you came in. I'm Dr. Caldwell. Which one of the patients are you with?"

She swallowed hard and took a deep breath.

"I'm Laurel Jackson. I'm with Andrew Brady. I'm his fiancée." The word felt strange on her tongue, but it also felt so right because it bound her to Andrew in a special way.

Beside her Jimmy spoke up. "I'm here for Andrew too, but Glenn works with me. I need to let the Little River people know how he is."

The doctor nodded. "Does he have any family in this camp?"

Jimmy shook his head. "No, sir. His family lives at Townsend."

"I see. Well, I'm sure you realized in addition to exhaustion and some smoke inhalation he has a broken leg. I've got a temporary splint on it, but he needs a hospital. As bad as the break is, I'd recommend sending him on to Knoxville. Tell Mr. Mercer we need either a car or truck to transport him."

Jimmy nodded. "I will. And what about Andrew?"

The doctor turned to Laurel. "That's a mighty brave young man you've got there, Miss Jackson. He's got a bad burn on his arm, and we've got that taken care of for the present time. But it's the other thing I'm worried about."

Her heart skipped a beat, and she sucked in her breath. "What other thing?"

"He's suffering from smoke inhalation too. I'm sure you noticed he was disoriented and coughing and how his lips were a bright red. These are all signs of smoke inhalation. I'm afraid his is much worse than the other young man's."

Her legs trembled, and she reached for Jimmy's arm to steady herself. "How much worse?"

The doctor pursed his lips and stared into her eyes. "I wish I could tell you. Right now it's a wait and see game. He's coughing up a lot of the phlegm that's settled in his lungs, and that's good. One of the dangers, though, is that the airways will start to swell and he won't be able to breathe or to cough up the phlegm."

Her eyes grew wider. "Is there anything you can do?"

"I'll watch him closely for the next twenty-four hours. If I see that his throat is closing up, I can run an endotracheal tube down to keep the passageway open. That's quite uncomfortable for the patient, so I hope I don't have to do that."

She nodded. "I see. So in the meantime we just wait."

"That's right. My nurse will sit with him tonight and will let me know if his condition changes."

"Can I stay too?"

He regarded her with a smile and shook his head. "You need your sleep so you can help him recuperate. Go back to the hotel and come back in the morning. If he's better then, you can sit with him all day. You might even be able to take him back to the hotel tomorrow."

Laurel looked at the closed door and then at

the doctor. "Can I at least see him before I go?"

"Yes, for a few minutes, but he may not be awake."

"That's all right. I just need to see that he's alive. I'd almost given up hope he'd make it back."

The doctor smiled, and his eyes crinkled at the corners. "I understand. Come with me."

As she started to follow him, Jimmy touched her arm and stopped her. "I'll go make arrangements for Glenn to be transported, but I'll come back and check on you."

She nodded and walked behind the doctor into the small exam room. Andrew and Glenn lay on beds at opposite ends of the room. She rushed to Andrew and stared down at him.

The soot had been washed away, but his red lips reminded her of the seriousness of his condition. A lightweight quilt covered him, and his bandaged right arm lay on top of it. She dropped to her knees beside the bed and wrapped her hand around his fingers. "Andrew," she whispered. "It's Laurel. You're safe now, and you're here with me."

The doctor leaned down and whispered. "I've given him a light sedative. He probably can't hear you."

She scooted closer to the bed, bent over, and kissed him on the cheek. He stirred in his sleep, and his mouth twitched in a slight smile. "That's all right. He knows I'm here."

"Help!"

Andrew bolted to a sitting position. Frantically, he turned his head from side to side and looked for the person who had called for help, but he couldn't see anything in the dark cave. A hand touched his arm, and he recoiled.

"Mr. Brady, you're safe."

He scooted up in the bed until his back touched the headboard. He pulled the covers up to his chest and cast a terrified glance at the figure leaning over him. "Who are you?"

"My name is Millie Prescott, Mr. Brady. I'm a nurse at the infirmary in Tremont. You've been brought here because you were injured in a fire."

He frowned and tried to focus on the kind voice in the darkness. Why couldn't he see? He blinked his eyes and then rubbed his hands across them. "Who screamed for help?"

"You did, Mr. Brady. You cried out in your sleep."

"In my sleep?"

"Yes." A cool hand touched his forehead. "I'm here to help you."

He blinked again and tried to concentrate on his surroundings. Now he saw that he wasn't in total darkness at all. A small lamp sat on a table a few feet away and it gave out a warm glow. Objects about the area began to come into focus, and he realized he was in a room. The voice belonged to a woman who was dressed in white. What had she said? He was in an infirmary?

"I'm not in the cave?"

She put her hand on his shoulder and urged him to lie back down. "Is that where you were? We wondered how you survived the fire. But you're safe now. You need to rest so you'll feel better."

Her kind words made him want to obey, and he slid back down in the bed. His head had just touched the pillow when a new thought crossed his mind, and he sat up again. "Laurel? Is she here?"

The nurse shook her head. "Not right now. She's been here, but she went back to the hotel to sleep. And that's what you need to do too. She'll be back in the morning, and I promise I'll wake you when she gets here."

He closed his eyes and settled his head on the pillow once more. A cough shook his body and sent pain racing through him. As the spasm subsided, he swallowed and winced. He didn't remember any childhood sore throat hurting like the one he had now. And his arm burned. The memory of his shirt on fire flashed in his mind, and he groaned.

The nurse's face appeared above him again. "Are you in pain, Mr. Brady?"

"Yes," he whispered. "My throat and arm hurt."

"You have quite a nasty burn on your arm, and

the sore throat is because you inhaled so much smoke. I'll get something to make you feel better." Her footsteps tapped on the floor as she walked away from the bed, but she returned minutes later. A cool swab rubbed his arm, and then he felt a prick. "This will help with the pain. Relax and go to sleep. You're safe now."

He heard the words, but he couldn't get the memories out of his mind—trees exploding and shooting fire bombs off like rockets, a wall of fire that stretched as far as he could see, a cave in the side of the mountain, and the desolation of a great forest.

"I will lift up mine eyes unto the hills, from whence cometh my help," he whispered.

"What did you say?"

He wanted to speak the words to her, but his thoughts were becoming fuzzy. *The medicine must be taking effect,* he thought. He welcomed the drowsiness that was overtaking him. There was no fire pursuing him now. He was safe, and he could rest.

Laurel had been sure she wouldn't be able to sleep last night, but she'd been wrong. Probably her sleepless night before and the relief at Andrew's safety had been the reasons for her drifting off the moment her head touched the pillow and not awakening until well after sun-up this morning. Now as she approached the infirmary, she could hardly contain her eagerness to see Andrew and tell him the fire that had almost taken his life was slowly being brought under control.

As soon as she stepped through the door into the waiting room, she spotted the nurse she'd seen yesterday. She sat at a desk in the corner of the room and looked up when Laurel entered. Her tired smile and the dark circles under her eyes told Laurel the woman hadn't gotten much sleep last night.

"Good morning, Laurel. You must be here to see Mr. Brady."

Surprised that the woman knew her name, she gave a slight nod. "Yes, I am."

"I saw you yesterday when you were here. My name is Millie. I've been taking care of Mr. Brady. When I was feeding him his breakfast, I could hardly get him to eat for talking about you. I'm glad to meet you."

A wave of relief rippled through her body. "If he's eating, he must be better. That's good news. May I see him?"

The nurse shook her head. "Not right now. Dr. Caldwell and a man from the Park Service are in there with him."

Laurel's eyebrows arched. "A man from the Park Service? What does he want?"

"I suppose to talk about the fire." She glanced at her watch and frowned. "I've been here all night and was about to leave when you came in. I'm sure the doctor will let you go in when they've finished talking."

"All right. Thank you for taking good care of Andrew."

"You're very welcome. It was a pleasure."

Laurel walked over and eased into a chair after Millie left the infirmary. The room had a hushed atmosphere, and she could almost hear herself breathe. She wondered what could be going on behind that closed door. She wished they would hurry. She wanted to see Andrew and assure herself that he really was alive.

It frightened her to think how quickly life could change. A few days ago she thought her relationship with Andrew had come to an end. The next thing she knew she stood beside a train accepting his proposal. Then the fire, and now his return. But he was alive, and that was the important thing.

The door to the exam room opened, and the doctor and a man she'd come to know well since he'd been in the mountains stepped into the room. His smile made her heart leap into her throat. She jumped up from her chair and stared at the man who'd spent many hours at their home talking to her father about buying their farm. "Superintendent Eakin, what are you doing here?"

He smiled and walked toward her. "Miss Jackson, it's nice to see you again. I've been in the area ever since the fire began, but I didn't know until this morning that Andrew had been injured fighting the fire. I thought he was still in Virginia. I came as quickly as I could."

"That was nice of you. I'm sure Andrew was glad to see you."

He pointed toward the door to the room. "That's a brave young man in there. I'm proud to have him on my team. His dedication to his job has impressed me from the start, and this act of heroism has confirmed my confidence in him. I wanted to let him know and tell him how thankful we are that he survived what was a horrible experience."

"I don't know all the details yet, but I'm eager to find out how he escaped."

Superintendent Eakin chuckled. "It's quite a story. Yes, quite a story." He turned to the doctor and shook his hand. "Thank you for taking care of Andrew. Have you heard from the young man he carried out of the fire?"

The doctor shook his head. "Not this morning. They transported him to a hospital in Knoxville last night. I hope to hear something today."

"Well, let us know how he's doing." He turned back to Laurel. "And you take care of that boy in there. He's a good man."

Laurel's heart raced at the respect for Andrew she saw in his boss's face. "I will, sir." He nodded to the doctor and strode out the door. Laurel watched as he closed the door behind him before she turned back to the doctor. "Now tell me how he really is today."

"I'm happy to say he's better this morning. He's lucid. In fact he remembers everything that happened on the mountain. He told the whole story to Mr. Eakin and me, and he knows he's in the infirmary at Tremont. There's no swelling in his throat or nasal passages, and he's not coughing as much as he was. In fact he wanted two things when he woke up—some breakfast, and to see you." He leaned over and winked at her. "He didn't necessarily ask for them in that order. I think you were his first choice, but he got the food instead."

She breathed a sigh of relief. "Oh, doctor, that's good news. When can I take him home?"

"Where is home?"

"Cades Cove. I want to take him to my parents' house so he can recuperate."

He thought for a moment before he answered. "I want to observe him for a day or two. There's really not any treatment for smoke inhalation except to replenish the body with oxygen, so he needs to rest and let nature take its course. So I'd say you might be able to leave the day after tomorrow if he continues to improve."

She glanced past him at the closed door. "When can I see him?"

"Right now." He smiled, opened the door, and led her into the room. "Mr. Brady, you've got another visitor, and I expect you're more than ready for this one."

Laurel stopped just inside the door and let her gaze travel over Andrew. He sat propped up in bed with two pillows behind his back. Soot no longer covered his clean-shaven face and his dark hair was combed neatly in place. His lips weren't as red as yesterday, a good sign she was sure. He smiled and held out his hand.

"Laurel."

She dashed across the floor to his bedside and fell on her knees beside him. She grasped his hand in both of hers and looked into his eyes. There was so much she wanted to say to him—to tell him how much she loved him, how thankful she was he was alive, how she had prayed for him—but her voice had deserted her. Huge tears began to roll down her face, and she closed her eyes and pressed her forehead against their clasped hands. He reached over with his injured arm, and his fingers caressed her braid. "Don't cry," he whispered. "It's all right now."

Her body shook with sobs for several minutes before she finally remembered the doctor. Had he witnessed her breakdown? She straightened and glanced over her shoulder, but he had left and closed the door behind him. "Oh, Andrew, I've never been so frightened in my life."

"Neither have I. But then I realized God was with me. He took care of Glenn and me, Laurel. It was like His voice spoke in my head and told me what to do."

Her eyebrows arched. "What do you mean?"

He motioned to a chair across the room. "Drag that chair over here and sit down beside the bed. I want to tell you everything that happened after I got on the train and left you at the station."

For the next few minutes she listened to the story of his experience on the mountain. When he told of facing the wall of fire, her heart raced at the thought of how scared he must have been facing the danger he'd feared since childhood. Tears pooled in her eyes when he told of the Scripture popping into his mind and finding the cave. She couldn't start to imagine the torment he and Glenn had endured as they lay on the floor of that dark cavern and wondered if they had climbed into their final resting place. But it was his words about how he struggled with exhaustion every step of the way back to the base camp as he tried to get them to safety that wrenched her heart.

He reached for her hand and wrapped his fingers around it. "I couldn't have done any of it if God hadn't been walking with me. He brought me back to you."

"And now we're here together."

He scooted over in the bed and motioned for her to sit beside him. She got up and settled on the edge of the bed. He pulled her hand to his lips and kissed each of her fingers. "Do you remember what you promised beside the train?"

She smiled. "Yes. I said I'd marry you."

He nodded. "You did, and I'm holding you to that promise. I told you I went to see my father, but it didn't go well. I told him I'd accepted Christ and that I wasn't going to come home and enter politics."

Her eyes grew wide. "What did he say?"

"He ordered me to leave and not come back." She started to speak, but he held up his hand to stop her. "It's all right, Laurel. He'll come around in time. When I asked you to marry me, I had no idea what I would do to support us. I knew the job I had with the Park Service was about to come to a close because nearly all the Cades Cove land is bought. And when I came to work for Superintendent Eakin, he wasn't too happy about having me as an employee. He felt like he'd been forced to take me. Naturally, I expected him to ask them to terminate my job."

"Andrew, please don't worry about this now. We have plenty of time to figure out what we're going to do."

He shook his head. "No, I won't get married until I'm settled in a job that will support us."

She swallowed. "What do you want to do? Go back to Virginia and look for a job?"

He shook his head and smiled. "I don't have to. When Superintendent Eakin was here, he offered me a new job."

Her pulse raced, and her eyes grew wide. "Here? In the mountains?"

He nodded. "How would you like to be married to the Assistant Chief Park Ranger?"

"Really?" she cried. "Where will we live?"

He put his arm around her waist and scooted her closer to him. "In Gatlinburg." His eyes danced with excitement. "I didn't know how I would ever be able to leave here, and now I won't have to. We'll be in Gatlinburg with your folks. What do you think about that?"

"Oh, Andrew," she squealed, "it's too good to be true! When do you start the new job?"

"He wants me to take over right away. He's contacting the office in Washington, and I'll start as soon as I'm recovered." A look of dismay crossed his face, and he frowned. "We're talking about getting married, and I haven't even asked your father yet. What if he doesn't agree? He may not want me for a son-in-law."

Laurel threw back her head and laughed. "Don't be silly. Of course he'll agree. All he's ever wanted is for me to be happy. And I am."

"Well, if you think so, then when do you want to get married?"

She thought for a moment. "My folks will be moving to the new house in Gatlinburg in the spring. With Poppa sick I really need to be home so I can help Mama get ready to move. If we get married then, we can all move at the same time. How does that sound to you?"

He exhaled a long breath. "That sounds wonderful to me."

She threw her arms around his neck and hugged him. "A spring wedding at the church in the Cove. It's what I've always wanted."

He wrapped his arms around her. "Then it's settled. That is, if your father agrees. I still don't know how he's going to feel about this."

She laughed. "Don't worry. He's liked you since the day you came to the Cove." A sudden thought made her pull back and stare at him. "But what about your father, Andrew? How do you think he'll take this news?"

Sorrow flickered in his eyes, and he shook his head. "I don't know. I'll write and tell him. He probably won't answer, but I'll write him every week. And when it's time for the wedding, I'll invite him. I want to keep in contact with him, but it's up to him if he wants to do the same."

She cupped his chin with her hand. "I'll pray he does."

He slipped his hand to the back of her head and drew her down until their lips almost touched. "The day I saw you on the street in Gatlinburg I would never have believed how much you would change my life. I'll always be indebted to your family for showing me what it means to be a member of a family who loves each other and who depends on God to lead them. I want to be a husband and father like Simon and Matthew. I promise you I'll try, Laurel, and I'll always love you."

"I'll always love you too, Andrew."

He pressed his lips to hers, and she said a silent prayer thanking God for sending this man into her life and prayed she would be worthy of his love.

Chapter 21

June 1, 1936

Andrew didn't think he'd ever seen a more beautiful day. The mountain peaks might be shrouded in their hazy fog, but the spring sunshine found its way to the valley below. He'd waited months for this day, and it had finally arrived. Soon he would exit the room where he waited and walk to the front of the church with Simon. Together they would watch Laurel enter on the arm of her father and join him for her grandfather to speak the words that would bind them together for the rest of their lives.

The door to the room opened, and he glanced around to see Jimmy Ferguson entering. He grinned and closed the door behind him. "I didn't mean to be gone so long, but I got to talking to some of the folks coming in. Finally I had to tell them I was neglecting my duties as best man and needed to see how you were holding up. I'm glad to see you didn't lose your nerve and run off while I've been gone."

Andrew ran his finger between his neck and shirt collar and frowned. "I didn't expect to be this nervous. How long is it now until we start?"

Jimmy laughed and slapped him on the back. "You got a few more minutes of single life left."

Andrew grinned and nodded at the man who had become his best friend over the last eight months. "Jimmy, I want to thank you for standing up with me today. There isn't anybody I'd rather have beside me when I marry Laurel."

Jimmy's smile dissolved into a somber expression. "And I want to thank you for asking me and for gettin' me a job with the Park Service. I'm glad I could stay in Gatlinburg when my folks moved to Oak Ridge."

Andrew shook his head. "No need to thank me. You earned that job by helping with the fire at Thunderhead."

Jimmy stared at him for a moment and then chuckled. "Who would've thought we'd end up friends? We sure got off on the wrong foot when we first met. I'm sorry about that. I guess it took a fire to show me your good qualities. I've always been protective of Laurel, and I know you're going to make her a good husband."

"Thanks, Jimmy. I'm sure if I mess up you'll be right there to tell me."

He laughed. "You got that right, buddy."

The door opened again and Simon walked into the room. He glanced from Andrew to Jimmy and smiled. "It's almost time. Are you ready?"

Perspiration trickled from Andrew's forehead, and he wiped at it. "How many people are out there?"

Simon shook his head. "Not many, I'm afraid. Jimmy's folks are here, and some of the men from the Park Service." He grinned at Jimmy. "And there's a pretty redheaded young woman from Gatlinburg. Am I going to be performing another wedding soon?"

Jimmy's face turned crimson and he glanced down at his feet. "You never can tell."

Andrew hesitated before he asked the question that had been rolling around in his head all day. "Is my father here?"

Sorrow flickered in Simon's eyes, and he placed his hand on Andrew's shoulder. "I'm sorry, but he's not." Then a smile pulled at his lips. "But Nate Hopkins walked in right before I came in here."

Andrew pushed the hope that his father would come from his mind and smiled at the memory of the first time he encountered Nate. "Did he bring his shotgun with him?"

Simon laughed. "No. I was over at his place a

few days ago, and he told me he'd come to think a lot of you. That's why he finally signed the papers to sell his farm. He's leaving for Maryville next week."

Andrew turned back to the window and stared at the mountains once more. He'd come to this valley a year ago to do a job. The boy he'd been then had come with the expectation that he could work wonders where others had failed. He would be the one who would convince the stubborn mountain people to accept the fact that their lives were about to change. Instead he was the one whose life had changed.

Soon there would be no one living in this remote valley. Nature would reclaim land that had once been rich farmland, and names of those who had resided here would be forgotten in time. But he knew as long as he lived he would always be thankful to God for bringing him to a place where he had learned what it meant to live and love in the security of God's love.

Laurel stepped from her father's truck and glanced around at the vehicles parked in the churchyard. She recognized Ted and Josie's truck and the car her grandfather had finally broken down and bought two months ago, but there were several she'd never seen before. They probably belonged to some of Andrew's friends from Gatlinburg.

Her father came around the truck, glanced

down at the bouquet of mountain laurel blooms she held, and smiled at her. "Are you ready, darling? I imagine that boy's waiting to see if you're really going to show up."

She laughed and gave him a playful punch on the arm. "Oh, Poppa, I'm so glad Mama and Willie came with Grandpa and Nana today. I enjoyed my last few minutes as a single woman just being with you."

Moisture flooded his eyes, and he sniffed. "I'm glad too. I can't believe my little girl's getting married. But I really like Andrew. He's a good man, and he's going to make you a good husband."

"He is." She looked around the yard and sighed. "I had hoped Andrew's father would come today. Andrew's written him every week since the fire, but he hasn't heard from him. He invited him to the wedding. I've been praying he'd come, but it doesn't look like he's here."

Her father took her hand in his big, work-roughened one and smiled. "Keep praying. Maybe he'll come around."

"Maybe so." She took a deep breath and slipped her hand through the crook of her father's arm. "I'm ready if you are."

They were about to mount the steps to the porch when the sound of an approaching automobile caught their attention. Superintendent Eakin drove his car to a stop a few feet away from them and stopped. He climbed out and smiled. "I was afraid I was going to be late. I had something come up and didn't get away as soon as I expected."

Laurel shook her head. "No, you're just in time. Go on in."

The passenger door of the car opened, and Laurel glanced at the man who got out and stared at her over the roof of the car. "Do you mind if I come to your wedding, Laurel?"

Her mouth dropped open and she tightened her grip on her bouquet. "Mr. Brady?" she gasped. "Is it really you?"

He walked around the car and stopped in front of her. "I know the last time we met I said some unkind things to you. I hope someday you'll be able to forgive me. Andrew's letters have made me do a lot of soul searching, and I realize I don't want to lose the only son I have left. I asked Ross if I could come with him because I want to be here today. But I'll understand if you'd rather I not attend."

Her eyes grew wide. "Of course I want you here. I've prayed for weeks that you would come."

He cleared his throat and frowned. "Why would you want me here after the way I talked to you?"

She reached out and took his hand. "Because I love Andrew, and I want us to be a family. I hope you can come to accept me not only as Andrew's wife, but as your daughter."

He stared at her for a moment before he leaned over and kissed her on the cheek. "I don't think that's going to be hard to do." He straightened and stuck out his hand to her father. "I assume you're Mr. Jackson, Laurel's father. I'm pleased to make your acquaintance."

Her father shook his hand. "We're glad you're here. Go on in and take a seat. I know Andrew is going to be happy to see you."

As Mr. Brady and Superintendent Eakin disappeared into the church, Laurel turned to her father and smiled. "I can't wait to see Andrew's face. Let's go."

Her father leaned over and kissed her cheek. "Be happy, darling. I love you."

"I love you too, Poppa."

They climbed the steps to the church she'd attended all her life and stopped at the door. After today there would be no more services in this place. This door would no longer welcome those who wanted to worship. But the spirit of love and selflessness the church had demonstrated in their lives would illuminate her for as long as she lived. She closed her eyes and said a prayer of thanks to God for allowing her to be a child of the Cove. Then she walked in the church toward the man who waited at the front for her to join him.

The wedding was over, the guests had left, and Laurel was alone with her husband in the church. He took her hand and pulled her over to the pew where he'd sat with her the first Sunday he'd come to the Cove. He put his arm around her shoulders and pulled her close. She snuggled against him and rested her head on his shoulder.

"Are you happy, Mrs. Brady?"

She sighed with contentment. "Ecstatic, Mr. Brady. I'm still excited because your father came. I know you're going to have the relationship with him you've always wanted."

"It's all because of you," he whispered in her ear. "All I am is because of you."

She smiled and snuggled closer. "God has been good to us, Andrew."

"He has, and I believe He's going to bless us even more."

They sat beside each other without speaking for a few minutes before he pulled out his watch and looked at it. "We need to be going. The trucks left with your parents' and grandparents' furniture and belongings this morning. I'm sure they're ready to go to Gatlinburg."

She pushed to her feet. "And for us to get to our house. I can hardly wait."

He wrapped his hand around hers and they walked from the church together. As they came down the steps, her grandfather motioned for them to follow him. "We're going to Granny's grave before we leave."

Together they walked to the cemetery and joined

the rest of the family beside Granny's grave. Laurel surveyed her family, all present except one. At least they'd received a letter from Charlie. He was living in Florida, working on a fishing boat. Her father doubted he'd stay there long. Charlie was too much like Grandpa Jackson, he said. She wondered if they'd ever see him again.

She directed her attention back to her grandfather when he cleared his throat and spoke. "It's time for us to say goodbye to Cades Cove, the place we've lived and worked for years, but we can't go without paying homage to the woman we loved. Let's pray." They bowed their heads as Simon began to speak. "Oh, God, You know how our hearts are breaking today as we leave our homes and begin life in a new community. But we can't leave this place without thanking You for the privilege of living in this beautiful valley and for putting the influence of Granny Lawson in our lives. We pray the lessons she taught us will not be forgotten but will pass to the new generations that will come from our family. Thank You for her life, Lord, because we realize without her prayers, we wouldn't be standing here as a family today. Help us to always be worthy of the prayers she prayed for each of us. Amen."

No one spoke for a moment, and then Anna looked across Granny's grave to Laurel. "I don't want the story of this valley forgotten, Laurel. I want you to tell it."

Laurel's eyes grew wide as she stared at her grandmother. "Me? How can I tell the story?"

She glanced down at the grave once more. "Since the day I arrived at Granny's house over forty years ago I've kept a journal about life in the Cove. The first one contained all the things I was learning from Granny. Then I began to write about our lives and our family. You have a gift for photography, and you've created a visual history of the Cove. I'm giving you my journals and I want you to put our story in a book. We can't let our way of life here be forgotten. You have to record it for future generations."

Laurel glanced at Andrew, and he smiled and squeezed her hand. "You can do it, Laurel."

She turned back to her grandmother. "I will, Nana. I'll put it all down on paper so people will remember us and know how we lived." She glanced at her new husband. "But Andrew has some news he's been waiting to share with you."

They turned to stare at him, and he smiled. "The Park Service has decided they made a mistake in wanting the Cove to return to a wild state. They're going to reconstruct some of the cabins that were torn down and preserve the ones left, as well as the churches. Generations to come will understand how the folks in Cades Cove lived in days gone by."

"That's good news indeed," Simon said. "I think we can leave happier knowing a symbol remains

of those who called this valley home for generations."

Silently, they filed by and placed their hands on
Granny's tombstone before they trudged to the
vehicles parked at the front of the church.
Matthew, who looked as if he was about to burst
into tears, took one last look at the church before
he got into the truck. Her mother grabbed Willie's
hand and they got in beside him.

Andrew held their car door open for Laurel, but
she stopped and glanced back at her grandparents as, hand in hand, they climbed the steps to
the church once more. She moved back to the
bottom of the steps so she could see what they
were about to do.

They stopped at the door, and each placed their
free palm against the wood and bowed their
heads. After a moment she heard her grandfather speak. "Anna, before we married you told
me God wanted to give us one heart to serve the
people in the Cove, and we've done that for over
forty years. Now they're all gone, but my prayer
is that our ministry will have touched their lives
and they'll pass it on to others."

Her grandmother smiled, leaned over, and
kissed his cheek. "Simon, we've done what God
asked us to do here, but our ministry's not over.
There are people outside this valley who don't
know the peace God can give them. Now we
have to serve Him somewhere else."

He smiled at her. "We promised Him as long as we're together that's what we'd do."

They turned, and Laurel almost gasped at the happiness that radiated on their faces. She backed away as they walked down the steps. With their heads held high, they got into their car and her grandfather drove away from the church. Her parents' truck followed.

"Are you ready to leave, Laurel?"

She smiled at her husband and nodded. It was time for a new life in a new place. She climbed in the car, and Andrew drove away to join the little caravan that headed to new beginnings.

About the Author

Sandra Robbins and her husband live in the small college town in Tennessee where she grew up. They count their four children and five grandchildren as the greatest blessings in their lives. Her published books include stories in historical romance and romantic suspense. When not writing or spending time with her family, Sandra enjoys reading, collecting flow blue china, and playing the piano.

To learn more about books by Sandra Robbins or to read sample chapters, log on to:

www.harvesthousepublishers.com

Center Point Large Print
600 Brooks Road / PO Box 1
Thorndike ME 04986-0001 USA

(207) 568-3717

US & Canada:
1 800 929-9108
www.centerpointlargeprint.com